THE ZANNA FUNCTION

THE

FUNCTION

DANIEL WHEATLEY

JOLLY
FiSH
PRESS

Mendota Heights, Minnesota

First Edition
First Printing, 2018

Book design by Sarah Winkler
Cover design by Jake Nordby
Cover images by v_alex/iStockphoto; the-lightwriter/iStockphoto; KathyGold/Shutterstock

Jolly Fish Press, an imprint of North Star Editions, Inc.

Library of Congress Cataloging-in-Publication Data (pending)
978-1-63163-168-9

720 7081

Jolly Fish Press
North Star Editions, Inc.
2297 Waters Drive
Mendota Heights, MN 55120
www.jollyfishpress.com

Printed in the United States of America

For all my teachers.

CHAPTER ONE

"I HAVE A new puzzle book for you."

Zanna Mayfield swallowed her cereal in a single gulp. "Really?"

Across the table, her Pops nodded and pushed a newspaper-wrapped package over to her with his trembling, wrinkled hands. She forgot all about breakfast and snatched it up at once, tearing away the wrapping.

Her face fell. "Pops, I already have this one."

"Oh?"

She turned the book over. It was worn and battered, its spine only held together by some hastily applied tape. "In fact, this *is* my book."

"Is it now?"

"Yeah." She flipped open the cover. In the corner of the inside page, a young girl with dreadful penmanship had written *Mine!* "You just snatched this from my bookshelf!"

"Now that's quite a serious accusation," Pops said, clearing away the discarded newspaper wrappings with a grin. "Would I do such a thing?"

"Absolutely."

"Well then," he said, letting out a small groan as he leaned over to pick up something else hidden beneath the kitchen table. "It's a good thing I have a spare."

He put another newspaper-wrapped book on the table and slid it across to her. Warily, and far less enthusiastic than before,

Zanna opened it. But there was no trickery this time. Inside was a brand-new book of puzzles that still smelled of bookstores and printer ink. She flipped through it and then jumped up from the table. "It's new!" She skipped around to hug her grandfather.

"Happy first day of school, my little scamper," Pops said as she threw her arms around his neck. "Don't solve them all at once."

"Not at all once," Zanna said, pulling away. "Two days."

Her grandfather laughed and mussed her unruly snarl of short black hair. "Finish your cereal. Come on, buses don't wait for the likes of you and me."

She wolfed down the rest of her breakfast and bounced up to the bathroom to take a shower. In her bedroom, she had already laid out the uniform for St. Pommeroy's School for Gifted Children. A black shapeless skirt that reached down to her mid-calves, a powdery blue blouse with knee-length socks of the same color, patent leather shoes, and a black tie embroidered with the school's triangular crest. It had been a challenge at first to tie the Windsor knot, but Zanna had practiced it every day until she could do it after only three failed attempts.

The last piece was her favorite—a soft, round, and floppy bonnet made out of black velvet—the kind that Zanna saw professors and scholars wearing with their official academic robes during graduation ceremonies. The whole uniform was woefully out of touch with modern style, and Zanna loved it for that. She pinned the bonnet a bit back on her head and made sure it was perfect.

Zanna had turned fourteen over the summer, and it had done her no favors. Her blue eyes bulged like she was trying to push them out of her skull. Like her five uncles, she had thick black hair that frightened even the most hardened of barbers. Her solution was to stand in front of the bathroom mirror every month or so and hack at it with a pair of razor-sharp scissors until it was shorter than most boys' hair at her school. It wasn't pretty, but it worked, which Zanna would take any day.

Pops was packing up her lunch when she came down. "Don't think you're going to get away with this," he said, handing her the brown paper bag. "You're going to have to pack your own lunch after today. This is a one-time deal."

"A one-time deal," Zanna repeated. She jumped up onto her tiptoes to kiss his whiskery cheek. "Thanks, Pops."

"Don't forget your books either, silly mouse . . ."

"I haven't!" When he raised an eyebrow at the fact that she wasn't carrying her backpack, she scowled in reply. "They're over by the door. I put them there last night!"

Suddenly, he took her by both shoulders and stooped so their foreheads touched, even though the effort was probably murder on his poor arthritic back. "I'm so proud of you," he said. "And your father is, as well."

She squirmed a bit, as she always did when Pops talked about her father. "Buses don't wait for the likes of you and me."

"No, they don't," Pops said, kissing her messy hair and sending her on her way. "Don't make too much trouble."

Zanna and her grandfather lived at 808 Three Pines Drive in the Twin Brooks neighborhood in Seven Corners, Virginia—a comfortable, if slightly mathematically confused, brick townhouse. The streetlights still glowed in the early September morning. Children of all ages trudged sleepily down the drive to where it intersected the main boulevard, a march Zanna remembered well from previous years. But Zanna wasn't heading off to J. Clemons Public High like the rest of them. She stopped at her mailbox and put down her backpack, fishing around inside it for the acceptance letter just to make sure she remembered the directions correctly. *Please wait outside your residence for transportation to arrive,* it instructed.

The letter had appeared with no fanfare whatsoever. A week after school let out, Pops came into the kitchen with the mail and tossed an overstuffed envelope down in front of her. *Congratulations, Zanna Mayfield, on your acceptance to St. Pommeroy's School for Gifted Children.* At first, Zanna was convinced that the entire thing was a hoax. They hadn't even bothered getting decent stationery—the letter was printed on graph paper. But after some digging on the Internet, she found some answers on their website. St. Pommeroy's was an exclusive high school academy, notable for its extremely rigorous curriculum and for not having an application process like every other private school. Intrigued, Zanna accepted their offer. When books and supplies and uniforms began to appear at her doorstep, all perfectly wrapped in silver paper, Zanna knew it wasn't a hoax. She was really going.

It wasn't that she was surprised by the offer. Even back in elementary school, Zanna had known that she outpaced the other children in her class. Schoolwork had been a breeze but making friends had not. Nobody wanted to be friends with a girl who had a knack for multiplying numbers faster in her head than they could with the calculator on their phone. Nobody wanted to be friends with a girl who asked for more homework, since she had finished all the problems in her algebra textbook within the first week.

Down at the end of Three Pines Drive, she heard the rumble of a diesel engine, but it was just the bus for public school. Parents who had gone down to see their children off came back up the road, a few waving at her as they passed. She was about to pull out the acceptance letter again to make sure she hadn't made a mistake when another bus rumbled up the street.

It was disappointing, to say the least. Going by the school's website and the uniforms and books they had sent her, Zanna was expecting—well, nothing precisely, but certainly not the wheezing, sputtering contraption that stopped in front of her with a dilapidated hiss of brakes. The paint was old yellow, with a beaten *ST. POMMEROY'S* written down the side.

"Zanna Mayfield?" the driver asked with a mouth of missing teeth. He had the angry, unkempt beard of a hermit and squinty bird eyes.

"Yes, sir."

"Come on then," he said, gesturing for her to climb aboard. "Burning daylight here."

He started up the engine as soon as Zanna was onboard, nearly knocking her over with the lurch of movement, and she grabbed the closest open seat she could find. As first impressions went, it was hardly encouraging.

"Hey, firstie!"

A boy was shouting at her. She looked up and saw him leaning over the seat, his tie in a sloppy knot and his scholar's bonnet nowhere in sight. "What do you think you're doing?" he asked.

"Me? Nothing," Zanna replied. "Just sitting here."

The boy chewed a wad of gum so big it made his cheek bulge. "Gimme your hat."

Instinctively, her hands clamped down over the soft velvet bonnet. "No! Don't you have your own?"

"Yeah, but I want yours."

"No! It's mine!"

She didn't notice the other boy creeping up behind her until it was too late. He yanked her hat from between her fingers, ripping out a clump of hair with it.

"Give it back!"

They threw it back and forth, laughing. Both were older

and tall enough to easily keep it out of her reach. One shouted, "Heads up!" and tossed Zanna's hat to a third boy, who tossed it to a fourth. On back through the bus Zanna's hat went, tossed from one set of cruel hands to the next. At the very back, a girl with a thin mouth wrung the poor thing like a damp cloth and stomped on it. Zanna rushed to scoop it up. Face burning, she slunk back to her seat and saw that while she had been occupied, the boys had emptied her backpack and dumped out all her books and papers.

"Welcome to St. Pommeroy's, firstie," the boy cackled as Zanna gathered up her belongings with what feeble dignity she had left. So there were bullies here, as well. She had dealt with bullies before.

Thankfully, she was left alone for the rest of the bus ride. But when they pulled into the school parking lot, what Zanna saw outside the grimy bus window made her heart sink. For a place called St. Pommeroy's School for Gifted Children, it looked neither gifted nor fit for children. In fact, it barely looked like a school at all. Weeds grew over broken concrete and cracked windows. The yard was a mess of old soda cups and burger wrappers and plastic bags blowing in the wind.

"Out," the driver muttered, stopping the bus with a hiss. "All of you, get out."

The boys laughed as they passed Zanna, a couple of them shoving her back down into her seat every time she tried to stand up. She was the last one off the bus. Behind her, the doors snapped shut, and the bus drove off in a cloud of black smoke.

Zanna adjusted her backpack and squared her shoulders. It didn't matter what the school looked like or that it was full of jerks—as long as she could learn. With determined steps, she crossed the littered yard and went inside.

It sounded like a battle was going on in the cafeteria.

Students screamed at each other, desperate to make themselves heard over the noise. Zanna had to put her hands over her ears to keep from going deaf. A boy came careening through the crowd, laughing with something pink in his hand as a girl gave chase, and he slammed hard into Zanna, scattering the contents of her backpack for the second time that morning. She knelt to collect everything again and had just picked up the new puzzle book from Pops when the bell rang. The cafeteria turned into a stampede. It was all she could do to avoid getting run over in the rush. She hugged the puzzle book tight to her chest, helplessly watching the rest of her books get trampled.

It took a while to collect her belongings, and so she was late to her first class, Advanced Mathematics. The teacher, a shriveled woman who looked like she had lemon juice for blood, snapped her fingers at her as Zanna took the last remaining seat at the very front of the room. "Detention. One week."

"I'm sorry, ma'am—"

"Talking without raising a hand first," she snapped again. "An additional week of detention."

Zanna scowled, but she didn't say anything else.

"You may call me Mrs. Vivi, and this is Advanced Mathematics," her teacher said, writing her name on the board with a horrific squeak of chalk that set Zanna's teeth on edge. "*Advanced.* I have no doubt many of you believe you are exceptionally clever. Many of you believe this class will be too simple for you. It is my job to break you of that assumption. The concepts we will discuss are typically reserved for college-graduate-level studies. If you cannot keep up, see yourself out of my classroom. I accept no excuses. I take great pleasure in failing my students. Do not test me."

Finally. Zanna felt a smile beginning to spread across her face. This was what she was here for. All the bullying on the bus, the dismay at the school's appearance, the sad state of her books from the stampede, even the prospect of two weeks' detention seemed like nothing now. She was going to *learn*.

"We begin with arithmetic," Mrs. Vivi said. The chalk let out another ear-splitting screech. "Consider this number. It is a two. And consider this number. It is also the number two. Through the process of addition, I can combine them into the number five."

Zanna's heart dropped. Her mouth fell open in stunned amazement. *Arithmetic?* And it wasn't even right! She told herself it was just a mistake and her teacher had misspoken, but then Mrs. Vivi wrote the entire thing on the blackboard with that horrible squeaking chalk, and there was no mistaking it then. Two and two equaled five.

Zanna glanced behind her. Everyone was nodding, their notebooks out and pencils working furiously. When she turned back, Mrs. Vivi was staring right at her.

"I advise you to write this down," she said coldly. "I do not repeat myself."

"But—"

"Talking without raising a hand first," she snapped. "Another week of detention."

A growl built in Zanna's throat, but she swallowed it and raised her hand.

"Yes?"

"Two and two is four," Zanna said, pointing at the board. "Not five."

A giggle ran through her classmates. Her teacher, however, didn't seem amused. "No. Two plus two is five."

"It's not—"

"Talking without raising a hand first," Mrs. Vivi said. "That makes one month of detention for you."

It was harder to subdue the growl this time. Zanna raised her hand, but Mrs. Vivi had already turned back to the blackboard. "We shall be devoting the first month of study to arithmetic. Now, consider this number. It is the number three."

The next hour was agony. By the end of it, Zanna could barely prop her head up. She didn't know what was worse: the fact that the blackboard had been filled, erased, and refilled with astoundingly incorrect arithmetic, or that none of her classmates seemed to realize it. At the bell, she jumped up from her seat. Her next class was Advanced Physics, and it had to be better. Statistically speaking, it had to be better.

Within the first five minutes, however, she saw how wrong she had been. Her teacher was a fat man by the name of Mr. Oddenben, who sounded like he was speaking through a patchy megaphone and told the class that the world was flat. "The sky is a dome with stars painted on it, and it moves around and around our world, telling us when it is day and when it is night," he said, drawing a diagram on the blackboard. His chalk was somehow even squeakier than Mrs. Vivi's, and Zanna kept her sanity intact by imagining a secret chalk-squeaking room deep in the school where little elves took perfectly good chalk and ran it through an infernal machine until it was nice and squeaky.

Her third-period class—Advanced Chemistry—was no different from her first two. A short woman with a face like a squashed dog introduced herself as Mrs. Wellings and then spent the entire lecture talking about how there were no such things as atoms. By the time the bell rang for lunch, Zanna felt as though someone had pounded nails into her skull.

There were no open tables in the cafeteria. Back at public school, she would have just gone to the library to eat in solitude, but the morning had taken such a toll on her energy that she just collapsed against the cafeteria wall, sinking to the ground with legs splayed. Nobody seemed to mind. Mr. Oddenben, who was walking around the tables on lunch-monitor duty, didn't even look twice at her.

"Hey, firstie!"

She had just bitten into her peanut butter and jelly sandwich when she heard him. The boy from the bus. He stood over her with three of his friends, grinning.

"Leave me alone," she grumbled.

"Looks like you're already alone," the boy said. He sat down next to her and held out his hand. "I think we got off on the wrong foot, eh? My name's Eddie."

Zanna glared at his outstretched hand. "Just leave me alone."

"Come on," Eddie said. "It was just a little fun. No hard feelings, eh?" He waggled his eyebrows, his hand still held out.

It was a trick. It had to be.

Her plan had been to smack his hand away, and if he did anything else, to spit the flavorless mash of peanut butter and sandwich bread she was chewing in his face. But he moved quicker than she anticipated and grabbed her wrist in a flash, twisting it behind her back and pinning her to the floor. "Get it!" he shouted to his friends, and for the third time that day, Zanna's backpack was dumped out.

"Stop it!" Zanna choked, her face smashed against the dirty tiles of the cafeteria. She squirmed, but Eddie twisted her arm a bit more, and pain bloomed all the way from her elbow to her chest.

"What do you need all these notebooks for?" one of the boys asked. He had her mathematics notebook between his meaty hands and tore it in two with a hoot of wild laughter.

"Oh ho ho, what's this?" another one said. He had found the puzzle book Pops had given her that morning.

Zanna's body went cold. "That's mine!" she said.

"What's a girl like you doing with this?" the boy asked, roughly flipping through the pages. "You like puzzles or something?"

She tried to push herself off the ground, but Eddie gave her wrist another twist and shoved her down again. Where was Mr. Oddenben? Didn't he see what was going on?

"You're going to hurt your head with these," the boy with her puzzle book said. "But we'll take care of it." He gripped it with both hands.

She fought to catch a breath. "No!"

The sound of her puzzle book being torn in two filled her ears. It drowned out the cafeteria and Eddie's laughter and her own furious heart. Just that horrible, screaming sound of paper.

Blind rage filled her, and she threw her head back, hearing the satisfying *crack* as she butted Eddie square in the nose. His grip loosened, and she pushed hard, enough to get free and lunge at the boy who had torn her puzzle book in half. She sank her teeth into his neck, and a nasty metallic taste filled her mouth, like she had taken a bite out of a rusty iron pipe. Beneath her fists, the boy let out a string of curses, and then an arm wrapped around her, a huge and strong arm that lifted her out of the melee.

The fat Mr. Oddenben had picked her up around her waist like she was a picnic basket. "Back to lunch," he said to the boys. Then, to Zanna, "You are coming with me."

"What?" Zanna said. Eddie clapped his hands over his nose, and the other boy held his neck where she had bitten him. "They started it! Just look at my backpack!"

"You can explain yourself to the principal," Mr. Oddenben said. He carried her out of the cafeteria and through the hallways, only depositing her on her feet when they had reached the door to the administrative offices. Inside, a scrawny secretary was filing her nails behind the desk and looked up with a bored expression.

"Ms. Mayfield has been causing trouble in the cafeteria," Mr. Oddenben said by way of explanation, a firm hand on Zanna's shoulder. "Is Principal Thatch in?"

The secretary waved to the office behind her. "Go in."

Principal Thatch was even fatter than Mr. Oddenben and must have spent the entire morning wedging himself behind his tiny and cluttered desk. He set aside his lunch—a greasy egg salad sandwich—and knitted his fingers together when they entered.

"Fighting in the cafeteria," Mr. Oddenben said, directing Zanna to take the chair in front of the desk.

"Thank you," Principal Thatch said. "I'll handle this."

Mr. Oddenben nodded and shut the door behind him.

"They started it," Zanna said. Her voice was raw, and her mouth still tasted of rusty metal. "Eddie and the others. They tore up my books."

Principal Thatch, however, didn't seem to hear her. He picked up his sandwich again and bit into it, chasing a blob of mayonnaise that was trying to escape into his cuff. His tongue was the color of an earthworm. "Do you not like our school, Ms. Mayfield?"

She crossed her arms. "In all honesty, it's pretty terrible."

"I'm sorry to hear that."

She doubted Principal Thatch was sorry for anything except not being able to eat his lunch in peace. "Your teachers don't know the first thing they're talking about," she said. "Mr. Oddenben thinks the world is flat."

"Mr. Oddenben is a highly distinguished scholar, and we are lucky to have him," Principal Thatch said. "But he is not the reason why you are here. We expect our students at St.

Pommeroy's to act with a certain decorum. When they do not, it reflects poorly on both them and the school."

"They tore up my books!" Zanna said, grabbing the edge of Principal Thatch's desk. "What was I supposed to do?"

A fat glob of egg salad fell on his desk, and Principal Thatch wiped it up with a finger. "This is your first day, isn't it?" he said, putting his finger in his mouth and sucking. "We have a certain way of doing things here at St. Pommeroy's. In time, you will understand."

Zanna sank back into her chair. She wouldn't allow herself to cry. Not here, in front of this sloppy mess of a principal. "You're not even listening to me," she said.

Principal Thatch considered something. "There is another option." He opened one of the drawers of his desk and took out a piece of paper, laying it before Zanna. Like her acceptance letter, it was printed on graph paper with the same triangular school crest stamped at the top. "Sign this, and you will decline your enrollment at St. Pommeroy's. We shall be sad to see you go, but we realize that our radical approach to education is not for everyone."

He handed her a pen. The contract was simple enough—a place at the top for Zanna to write in her name, a paragraph officially declining her enrollment, and a line at the bottom for her signature. She frowned at it.

"I want to learn," she said. "I really do."

"Then begin with learning how we do things here," Principal Thatch said, "or return to your public schooling."

Zanna looked down at the contract. She had dreamed of this school ever since the acceptance letter had arrived. A place where she could really stretch her mind. On its website, it had looked like a wondrous secluded place of learning, with fountains and dense hedges and libraries stacked two, three stories tall. But seeing it now—its dirty building, its incompetent teachers, its bullying students—was like a bucket of cold water. With a dark and heavy heart, she picked up the pen. At least at J. Clemons Public High they didn't try to tell you two plus two was five.

Then the entire school flickered.

It was quick, like an old lightbulb sputtering before it died completely. And at first, Zanna thought it was just that. One more thing in this school that was falling apart. But then it happened again, and she saw it was no simple flicker of the lights. In that infinitesimal moment, it was as if the entire office—Principal Thatch included—had been dipped in bright silver paint.

"Did you—" she began.

St. Pommeroy's began to crumple. Everything—the walls, the desk, even Principal Thatch, who was frozen mid-bite—deflated like someone was letting the air out of a balloon. First, the details went. The clutter on his desk and the sandwich in his hand melted into silvery goo. The rolls of fat around his neck all ran together. Then she couldn't see where Principal Thatch ended and the desk began. Zanna jumped up as what had been her chair turned into a pool of silver metal that was sucked away down an unseen drain. The walls of the principal's office melted away and then the rest of St. Pommeroy's, leaving her alone and quiet on a dirty field of scrub grass, with no signs that there had ever been a school there.

From the sky, the contract to leave St. Pommeroy's floated down and landed at Zanna's feet. It was the only thing left besides the pen she was still holding in a fearsome death grip. Where a whole private school had stood moments ago, Zanna only saw gopher holes, a pile of dented soda cans, and a very bored-looking man. He tucked something away in a pocket of his heavy black overcoat and adjusted his old-timey bowler hat.

"Well," he said in a flat, deadpanned voice. "That explains that."

CHAPTER TWO

ZANNA FOUND HERSELF unable to say anything. She rubbed at her eyes and shook her head so hard her bonnet nearly came loose. It was a dream. She was in bed, waiting for the alarm to go off so she could go to school. Real school. A school that didn't turn into aluminum foil and disappear . . .

When she opened her eyes, she was still standing on the barren field. The strange man had walked over to the pile of soda cans and knelt down. From his pocket, he took out a pair of elegant leather gloves, put them on, and began to rummage through the cans.

She tried her voice. "Hello?"

"Hello." It sounded like an unfamiliar word to him. He didn't look up as he said it, still intent on the soda cans.

Zanna took a step closer. "Um," she said, "did you see—"

"A school," the man finished for her. He made a small sound of discovery and straightened, something bright and silver in his hand. It was a quarter, Zanna saw before he tucked it away in one of his pockets. "Yes. A decent fabrication. Certainly decent enough to fool you." He looked down at Zanna, as if noticing her for the first time. "You are Zanna Mayfield, are you not?"

"I am," she managed to get out.

"Wonderful," he said in a voice that seemed better suited to discussing which shade of gray he should paint his living room. With a flick of his hand, one of the soda cans suddenly lifted from the pile as if it had been jerked up by a string. It melted and separated into eight solid silver balls, each no bigger than a marble, that hovered before the man for a moment before they all went zooming skyward in different directions. "I have told the others that they can cease their search," he said. "And I believe this is yours."

A wire-thin tendril of metal coiled out of his pocket and picked up her backpack by its straps. Zanna said nothing as the wire stretched out and deposited it at her feet. A moment later, a silver falcon whizzed down from the sky and landed on the man's shoulder. Despite her confusion, Zanna had to stifle a giggle. The falcon—if she could really call it that—looked like it had been sculpted by a second-grader. The wings were different sizes and stuck out of its neck. Its beak was squashed, and its eyes pointed in different directions.

The unfortunate-looking bird whispered something in the man's ear, and he nodded. "I will take you back to your house," he said as the bird turned back into a soda can and fell to the ground. "It's too late to show you St. Pommeroy's today. You'll just have to catch up tomorrow."

"St. Pommeroy's?" Zanna asked. She could still ask only the simplest of questions and look around dumbly, expecting the school to pop back into existence as quickly as it had disappeared.

"Yes," the man said. He was doing something with the soda cans again, stretching and flattening and transforming them into a pair of car seats. "You're smart enough to figure out that this wasn't actually St. Pommeroy's, aren't you?"

Maybe it was the condescension in his voice. Or maybe it was that she had been staring at the empty lot long enough to realize that this wasn't a dream and she had really seen an entire school—students and teachers included—turn into a pile of discarded soda cans. Either way, Zanna's head cleared at once. "Who are you? Tell me what's going on."

The man nodded slightly and tipped his bowler hat, though he kept the same lifeless expression on his face. "I am Dr. Hubert Mumble, dean of St. Pommeroy's School for Gifted Children, and you, Zanna Mayfield, have experienced an elaborate metallurgical illusion."

"Metallurgical?"

"As distinguished from a simple optical illusion. Far more complex. Though both are several years above your study." He gestured to the two car seats that he had formed out of the soda cans. "If you wish, I will explain more on the way home."

Zanna didn't move. She only stared at the car seat floating a foot off the ground. Was he suggesting that she sit on that?

Dr. Mumble seemed to understand her discomfort. With a wave of his hand, a car appeared around the seats. It was a bland sedan with gray paint and not a single redeeming feature, as if someone had averaged all the existing cars together to make the most neutral, nondescript model possible.

"Is that more comfortable?" he asked, opening the door to the backseat.

It was, but Zanna still didn't move. "How'd you do that?"

"This is an optical illusion," Dr. Mumble said. "Please, I cannot wait forever."

It made no sense, but Zanna began to fit some of the pieces together. The St. Pommeroy's she had spent her morning in had been fake. An illusion, Dr. Mumble had called it. He was from the *real* school—even though he seemed far more fake than her fake school had been.

"Why should I trust you?" Zanna asked. "You could be an illusion, as well."

Dr. Mumble sighed and gestured. In a flurry of silver,

Principal Thatch's office reassembled itself around her, though this time the walls and doorway led out onto the barren field, like it was part of a movie set without lights or cameras or other actors. Principal Thatch was just as she had left him, with his mouth clamped firmly around a bite of egg salad sandwich. He wasn't even breathing.

"Smell him," Dr. Mumble said, with a small nod of his head toward Principal Thatch.

"*What?*"

"Smell him," the dean repeated, as if it were the most normal request possible.

Zanna scowled, but the look on Dr. Mumble's face was so serious that she leaned over the desk and gave Principal Thatch an experimental sniff. Then she tried again, this time longer.

"I don't smell anything," she said.

"Precisely," Dr. Mumble said. "A real person is the combination of a thousand different scents picked up over the years. Not just what aftershave or perfume they prefer, but decisions made over the course of a lifetime. If they smoked as a teenager. If they have lost someone dear to them. If they have known hard labor. An illusion is simply light bent into a shape. It smells like nothing."

With another gesture too quick and small for Zanna to discern, Dr. Mumble made Principal Thatch and his office disappear and tucked his hands behind his back. Zanna stared at him for a moment before she realized what he wanted her to do. "You want—"

"If you wish to know I am not an illusion, then yes," Dr. Mumble said. "There are other ways, but all of them are far above your level of schooling. This is sufficient for now."

The idea of being invited to smell someone she had just met sat uneasily in her stomach, but after everything she had seen today, Zanna wasn't just going to take his word for it. She crept closer, as if Dr. Mumble was a wild animal she was sneaking up on, and took a deep sniff.

The first thing she smelled was his wool overcoat, which was a little damp and cold. Then came polished leather; a sharp, biting scent like ammonia; and books—musty, hidden books placed away on dark shelves. She sniffed again without even realizing it. He smelled of crisp soap and black earth, the kind overturned in a good garden, and something salty like beads of sweat, except it was sweeter and colder. *Tears.*

"Well?" he said, not even raising an eyebrow at Zanna, who had gone in for a third sniff. She jumped back a little, frightened by how close she had gotten, and smoothed out her skirt with nervous hands.

"I suppose you're real," she said.

"Excellent," Dr. Mumble said in a voice without an ounce of excellence to it. He gestured to the car again. "If you are ready now."

Zanna weighed her options and figured that the way things were going, getting into illusionary cars with strange deans was about on par for today. She bent to collect her backpack and saw that Dr. Mumble had dropped it right on top of the contract Principal Thatch had tried to make her sign. Zanna glanced back at the dean, who had turned away momentarily to look at the sky, and quickly snatched up the contract, shoving it into her backpack along with the pen she was still holding on to. For some reason, she felt that she had to be sneaky about it. If Dr. Mumble saw, he might put it in his coat pocket like that quarter he had found. And there was nothing Zanna hated more than trying to solve a puzzle when half the pieces were lost.

"Ready." She picked up her backpack and climbed into the car. Dr. Mumble sat in the driver's seat, but as they pulled away from the lot, she saw that he didn't even have his hands on the wheel.

They rode in silence. Zanna poked at the car around her, not believing that it had been a couple of old soda cans not that long ago. The seat felt and looked plush and leathery, her finger sinking in an inch deep. When she poked at the door, however, her finger went right through.

"The car is an optical illusion," Dr. Mumble explained without looking behind him. "The seat is metallurgical. Otherwise, you would fall out of this vehicle."

She poked it again, amazed. "How'd you do that?"

"I will have to leave the particulars to your teachers," Dr. Mumble said. "But as we have a little bit of time together, I may as well explain the basics. That way, you are not completely left behind tomorrow."

He cleared his throat and wiped his mouth with a handkerchief, and when he spoke again, there was a faint hint of emotion to his words, somewhere far beneath his cold shell.

"Every once in a while, a child is born with a great sense of curiosity and an eagerness to learn. They quickly outgrow whatever traditional schooling methods they are surrounded with and require more specialized teaching to suit their abilities. You, Zanna Mayfield, are one of those children."

"My abilities?" The way he had phrased it sounded like it was more than just how she could multiply large numbers in her head.

"Yes. Your abilities to manipulate the laws of the universe. What you have seen today is only the beginning. With hard work and earnest study, you may acquire nothing short of mastery over space and time."

Her mouth dropped. It was so casual, as if Dr. Mumble had told her she could acquire nothing short of a dozen eggs and a loaf of bread at the supermarket. The man certainly didn't look like he had just offered her phenomenal cosmic powers. He wasn't even looking at her.

"Did you say space and time?"

"Yes," he said. "With hard work and earnest study. As is the way with all knowledge."

The words *I don't believe you* rose in her throat. It was impossible, but then again, so were schools that folded up into soda cans and flying marbles and cars she could stick her hand through.

"You have touched upon the laws of the universe in your prior schooling," Dr. Mumble said. "And they are laws. Even for us. But just as a friend may be asked for a favor, so too may the universe. If one understands it well enough. We're here."

She looked out the window and saw they were pulling into her driveway. "Wait a minute," Zanna said as the car door opened by itself and she hopped out. "How'd we get here so quickly?"

Dr. Mumble looked down at her. "Just because it looks like a car does not mean it must act like a car. We have been traveling just below the speed of sound. Around 750 miles an hour."

"750?" The number made her knees go weak.

"Yes. I did not wish to waste time. I have a great number of things to attend to." Something clinked behind her, and when she spun around, she saw that the car had turned back into a dented soda can, rolling off the driveway into the bushes. "Goodbye, Zanna Mayfield. I hope to see you at school tomorrow."

He took something from his pocket and lifted his fist over his head. A worm of metal squirmed out from between his fingers and made a ring for him to hold, like he was a commuter on the subway clutching a strap dangling from the ceiling.

Then he shot up like a rocket and was gone.

It took a long time for Zanna to move. Hesitantly, she

reached out to the spot where Dr. Mumble had stood and poked it. There was nothing. No dean and no illusion. She walked back to the driveway and found the soda can that had rolled into the bushes. It wasn't dirty at all, and its paint had been stripped off, but other than that, it looked like the thousands of other soda cans she had seen in her lifetime. Carefully, she turned it over and over, as if some magician had handed it to her and asked her to confirm that this was, indeed, just an ordinary soda can.

In a fit of experimentation, she let go of it, seeing if it would float like it had for Dr. Mumble. But the can just clinked on the driveway. She shook her head, kicking the can across the driveway to the recycling bin.

"Space and time," she muttered, lifting the lid and chucking the can in with the rest of the recyclables.

"Zanna!"

She turned back to the house. Pops was hurrying across the yard as fast as his stiff old legs could carry him. She yelped and ran to meet him.

"My dear, my dear," Pops muttered into the soft velvet of her bonnet as she hugged him. "I was so worried."

"I'm fine," Zanna said.

"I got this call from your school saying you never showed," Pops said, beginning to walk back to the house. He kept an arm around her shoulders the entire time. "They asked if you were sick. I said, 'Ha! My little scamper?' I told them I saw you get on the bus this morning. Then they had the nerve to ask if it was the right bus. I told them, 'Just because I'm an old hat doesn't mean I can't read anymore.' Of course it was the right bus. Said *St. Pommeroy's* on the side! And then they wouldn't say any more!"

"I'm fine, Pops," she said as they entered the kitchen. She threw her backpack on the table and sank into one of the chairs.

Pops poured two glasses of lemonade and set one in front of her. "Thanks," she muttered.

"Well?"

She realized she had drained her lemonade in a single, uninterrupted chug. Sheepishly, she went back to the fridge and poured herself another glass, determined to take this one slower.

"Well what?"

"Are you going to tell me what's going on? Or are you just going to leave your poor old Pops in the dark?"

"No, I—" She fished around for the right words. "It's weird. I don't know. You won't believe it."

"Why don't you go ahead and try me, scamper?" he teased.

Zanna sighed, stalling with another sip of her lemonade. "Well, okay. The bus dropped me off at this dingy old school out in the middle of nowhere." From there, she told him about Eddie, her incompetent teachers, and the fight at lunch. "Principal Thatch had this thing for me to sign," she said, suddenly remembering and grabbing for her bag. "To decline my enrollment at St. Pommeroy's." She found the contract and slid it across the table.

Pops fumbled with the reading glasses around his neck. "But you didn't sign."

"No," Zanna said. "I was going to, though. Maybe. I don't know, it was just so terrible. But then—" She stopped, unsure about how to explain the next part. "It got really weird."

As best she could, Zanna described how the school had turned into a pile of soda cans. And then she told him about Dr. Mumble and the strange things he had told her, and how he had taken her home in a car she could put her hand through. "He said I could learn to do those things too," she said. "At the real St. Pommeroy's."

The corners of her grandfather's mouth quirked into the

grin of a much younger man, and his eyebrows did a wiggling dance. "Sounds like magic."

"I know, but—it's not," Zanna said, her hands trying to shape and remember what Dr. Mumble had told her. "The way he described it was almost scientific. All this talk about metallurgical versus optical illusions and the laws of the universe." She sighed, and her hands flopped uselessly onto the table. "It's okay; you don't have to believe me. *I* don't believe me."

Pops took a sip of his lemonade, much slower than Zanna had. "And why shouldn't I believe in magic? Or science, as you call it?" He wagged a playful finger at her. "I'm just about old enough to say that the only thing I'm certain about is uncertainty. You know how many impossible things I've seen pop up since I was your age? All your phones, computers, websites— never thought I'd ever see anything like them."

"But it was—" Again, she tried to convey it with her hands and failed miserably. "It can't be real. All of that—it just can't."

"Oh?" His eyes twinkled. "Decided that, did you? It just can't? So where'd you get this contract from? Where'd that bus come from? Who called me asking where you were? How'd you make it home?"

She ran her fingers through her thick hair, no doubt making it stick out angrily. It was the exact opposite of what she needed to hear. If Pops had said no, there was no way a strange man had promised her power over space and time, she would have been happy. She wouldn't have felt like the world was slipping into madness. "I don't know."

"And that's fine," Pops said, nudging the contract back toward her. "All I'm saying is keep an open mind. That's the mark of a true scientist—going where the facts take her, no matter what."

Zanna stared at her lemonade. Where the facts took her was completely uncharted territory. "I need time to think about it."

Pops nodded approvingly and then remembered something with a little start. "Oh!" he cried. "I have something for you."

"They tore your puzzle book in half," Zanna said as Pops shuffled into the next room. "I'm sorry."

"Bah," came his voice, accompanied by the rummaging of papers. "I'll buy you another one tomorrow." When he returned to the kitchen, he clutched a red envelope in his hands. "This came for you."

She guessed as soon as she saw it, but the exotic stamp and handwritten address—*Ms. Zanna Mayfield, 808 Three Pines Drive, Seven Corners, VA*—confirmed it. The letter was from her father.

As she unfolded the letter, a colorful piece of paper fell out, and she snatched it up. It was a piece of foreign money with a portrait in purple ink of a man with a thin mustache. She handed it off to Pops to look at while she read.

"He says it's from Singapore," she muttered to explain the money. "A two-dollar bill." Her eyes skipped over the long paragraph about how much he missed her and went to the end. "Oh."

"What is it?" Pops asked, giving her back the money.

She handed him the letter, and he fumbled for his reading glasses again. "He's not coming home for a while. Something about the airline. Said they cut a lot of pilots, and he's got to take their flights."

It took Pops a lot longer to read the letter. When he finished, he didn't say anything; he just handed it back to her and rubbed at his whiskery chin. Then he grinned. "Did you hear the story about the three holes?"

Zanna rolled her eyes. "I know, Pops. Well, well, well." She gathered up the contract and her father's letter. "Tell me when it's time for dinner."

In her room, she spread out all the things she'd collected

from her day and just looked at them for a long, quiet minute. Then she began to organize. Her father's letter went in a shoebox with all his other letters, and the money went into a book he had given her for a birthday long ago, back when he still made appearances for her birthday. Its pages were full of colorful bills collected from countries across the globe. The two halves of her puzzle book she slid into a tight spot on her shelf, hoping the books on either side would keep them together. The contract went back in her backpack. But she had nowhere to put the pen.

She took it to her desk and turned on the lamp to look at it in a better light. It was machined from a single piece of silver metal, with a simple oval of gold where her finger would hold it. The nib looked fancy and ornate, and she took out a piece of notebook paper to see how it wrote. But there was no ink in it. Confused, she pressed a little harder, and suddenly, an intense, stabbing pain shot through her finger. With a yelp, she dropped the pen and sucked her finger. A dot of blood welled up on the tip of her thumb. Carefully, she rolled the pen over, trying to find where it had jabbed her, but there was nothing. It was as smooth as before.

In the lightest grip she could manage, Zanna picked up the pen and tried again. This time, it wrote smoothly and beautifully, and its ink was a deep red that made Zanna a little queasy.

Before she could contemplate why she had a pen that apparently wrote in blood, she heard Pops call her name from downstairs, and it made her sit up straight in alarm. Dinner wasn't for a while. And it was a question: "Zanna?"

She took the steps as fast as her legs could manage and burst into the kitchen. "What?" Then she saw it—what could only be described as a poorly drawn stick figure about the size of a small child was waiting outside on the porch. It waved one crooked hand in a friendly manner and knocked on the sliding glass door.

Pops stared at it in the same way someone would stare at a talking dog: a little afraid but also intensely curious. He abandoned the onions he had been chopping up for dinner and shuffled over to the door. The stick figure was made out of bent coat hangers and carried a metal toolbox, the kind a plumber would bring to fix up the pipes.

"What is it?" Zanna asked.

"Was hoping you'd tell me," Pops said. The stick figure tipped its ill-defined hat to him. "Looks like he's got a delivery. Should I let him in?"

She pinched herself, but the stick figure was still there, adding more impossible facts to an already impossible day. Best to go along with it. "Um, sure."

Pops unlocked the sliding door, and the stick figure sauntered inside, setting its toolbox down on the kitchen table. It unlocked with a crisp *snap*, revealing a geometrically folded letter and a large iron key. *To Zanna Mayfield*, a tag on the key read.

Zanna summoned up her courage and reached inside the toolbox, withdrawing the letter and key. Its delivery complete, the stick figure tipped its hat again and went out the way it had come in. She watched as it walked out into the backyard until it was clear of the house and then shot up into the air, just as Dr. Mumble's marbles had done that afternoon. Then she unfolded the letter.

Ms. Zanna Mayfield,

Greetings from St. Pommeroy's School for Gifted Children! We are looking forward to meeting you tomorrow. We hope our dean hasn't frightened you away from attending our school.

He may seem like quite the sourpuss on the outside, but he's quite sweet and chewy on the inside.

We understand that you had a little adventure today. Rest assured, we're looking into this matter quite seriously. In the meantime, the other teachers and I have put together a small gift for you. This key should be able to dispel most simple optical illusions. Hold it out and turn, as you would with any key in a lock. If you are indeed faced with an illusion, it should disappear at once. And apologies for the messenger. Dr. Cheever fancies himself quite the artist.

Yours truly,

Dr. Mara Fitzie

"I see what you mean now," Pops said with a low whistle. He went to the sliding door and checked the sky, scratching his head and smearing bits of diced onion through his white hair. "Amazing."

Zanna looked at the key in her hands. It was iron and scratched and probably a hundred years old. She held it out and gave it an experimental turn, just as the letter had instructed. Nothing happened. The kitchen remained just as it was.

"I guess your kitchen's not an illusion," she said, trying the key again with the same results.

"Well, I certainly hope not," Pops said with a huff. He returned to the kitchen counter, shaking his head and muttering something about newfangled gadgets.

Zanna set the key aside and read the letter again, reassuring herself that it was real and that it had been delivered by a figure made out of coat hangers.

"You saw it, right?" she asked after Pops had resumed chopping the onions. "I'm not crazy?"

He set the knife aside. "You tell me. I've made my decision.

Not every day a—" He gestured helplessly toward the porch, unable to properly describe what he had seen. "A whatever that was comes knocking at your door."

"I guess," Zanna said. She twisted the key again and looked back to the letter, wondering if there was some other part of the instructions she had overlooked. Pops was right, as always. Maybe she couldn't prove everything that Dr. Mumble had said to her in the car that afternoon, but something *was* out there.

"So what do you say?" Pops asked. He scraped the onions into a waiting skillet and stirred them around with a pat of butter, his eyebrows waggling.

Zanna tried the key one last time. "I'm going to school tomorrow," she said. "Whatever is going on, I'm going to figure it out. And if this whole thing is true, then so be it. But I can't stand not knowing."

"That's my girl," he said with a grin.

She stayed up late that night, trying to mend the torn puzzle book and preparing her uniform for the next day with a clean blouse, skirt, and socks. Nothing she tried with the key seemed to do anything, and eventually, she just put it aside. Then she turned off the lamp and snuggled into bed, dreaming of metallurgical illusions and flying teachers.

CHAPTER THREE

"ZANNA."

Her eyes snapped open. The bedroom was dark and empty, her alarm clock showing 3:43 in the morning. But she swore someone had just spoken her name aloud.

"Zanna."

Terror gripped her and yanked her up in a shot, all her drowsiness gone. There *was* a voice. A woman's voice. She drew the covers tight around her and tried not to breathe.

"Are you awake?"

Zanna bit down hard on her tongue, but it was no dream. Someone was in the room with her. Weapons she could use to defend herself with darted through her mind. There were some heavy books on her shelf, her backpack at the foot of her bed, maybe one of the pens on her desk . . . She could scream for Pops, but he was too old to help. Maybe she should just run for the door while she still could.

"You're awake." With a *click*, the lamp on her desk turned on. But there was something wrong with how its light spilled across the room. It fell on Zanna and the bed as it always had, but the other side of the room was just as dark as before, as if there were a curtain separating the two halves.

"What do you want?" Zanna whispered. "Who are you?"

"Come on now," the darkness said. "You can figure out that much, right?"

She peered into the dark, but she couldn't distinguish

anything on the other side of her room. Her mind cast back to the afternoon. "You're one of *those*," she said. "Like Dr. Mumble."

"Scientists," the darkness said. "And?"

Zanna moved the bits of the puzzle around in her head. "You're either one of my professors," she said cautiously, "or you're the one who made that fake school today."

"Clever as ever." A polite round of applause came from behind the shadowy curtain. "So can you figure out what I want?"

Again, Zanna moved the pieces around. The contract Principal Thatch had wanted her to sign. She looked down at the backpack at the foot of her bed. "You wanted me to sign that contract."

"I wanted to save you from St. Pommeroy's," the darkness corrected her. "It's no place for a girl like you."

A blaze of stubbornness flared through Zanna. "Well, too bad. I'm going, and there's nothing you can do to stop me."

"Nothing?"

Suddenly, the air around her was sucked away, and Zanna's chest burst with suffocating pain. She thrashed wildly, screaming silently without air in her lungs, and then it was over, as suddenly as it had started. Sweet, dark air returned, and she gulped it down, panting at her brush with death.

"Air pressure," the darkness said. "Such a touchy thing. But maybe you'd prefer something chemical? Carbon monoxide? Hydrogen cyanide? Or a more classical option?"

Something black and made of iron lanced out of the darkness, quivering with a keen sharpness at Zanna's throat. She pressed herself as far back against her headboard as possible, but she could still feel the tip against her skin.

"There's plenty I could do to stop you," the darkness warned, pulling the blade back. "This is a compromise. A peace offering. Sign the contract and forget all about St. Pommeroy's. With your clever brain, you can get into any private school you'd like. Just not St. Pommeroy's."

Two iron hands drifted out of the darkness. One unzipped her backpack and found the contract while the other searched through the pens on her desk. A third blob of metal flew across the room and made a little table over her lap, like it was serving her breakfast in bed.

Zanna touched her throat where the blade had stuck, and her fingers came away with a dot of blood. The iron hands spread out the contract on her lap table and offered her the pen. Still panting a little from her near-asphyxiation, she lifted her eyes to the other side of the room. "Why are you doing this?"

There was no answer from the darkness. Then, in a voice that almost sounded hurt: "Just sign."

Zanna took the pen. There wasn't anything else she could do. The iron hands hovered near her, silently threatening. The pen jabbed her thumb, and at the top of the contract, she printed her name in that eerie red ink. *I, Zanna Mayfield, decline my acceptance to St. Pommeroy's.* Then her eyes dropped to the bottom and the dotted line, and she thought of what it had felt like without air pressure—and what it had felt like with a blade at her throat.

She raised the pen and threw it into the darkness.

A shield of iron bloomed out of nowhere, and the pen dinged harmlessly off it. But Zanna had already jumped for her nightstand, her fingers closing around the key Dr. Fitzie had sent her. With a yelp and a desperate hope that this would work, she thrust the key toward the darkness and unlocked the illusion.

It was instantaneous. The world shook, as if it were clearing its head, and then everything returned in bright, sharp focus. Where the darkness had been now stood a bewildered and wide-eyed woman. She had been pretty once, but something in the past had twisted up and crumpled and stomped on her beauty. Wild black hair drifted around her scarred face, giving the impression that she had just stepped out of a hurricane. Her eyes were watery blue and huge like a blind cave animal. One single word escaped her mouth—"How?"—and then she was gone in a rush. Zanna's wall jumped out of the way, and a blast of cold air rocked through the bedroom as the woman disappeared into the night. All that was left was a *snap* as the wall closed up again, as unbroken as a pool of water.

Zanna screamed as something touched her foot, but it was just the pen rolling across the floor. Relieved, she picked it up and put it back on her desk. There was no sign of the woman out the window, but Zanna hadn't really expected anything else. She remembered how easily Dr. Mumble had disappeared that afternoon.

Noisy feet pounded down the hallway, and Zanna spun around, readying the key again in preparation for the woman's second attack. But it was Pops who burst into her bedroom, pajama-clad with bony fists raised in alarm. When he saw she was alone and standing at the window, he lowered his arms. "Are you all right? I heard you scream."

"It's just nightmares," she said, trying to steady her breathing. "I'm fine."

"I thought—" He couldn't seem to put his thoughts into words. "After what happened today—"

She crossed the room and let him pull her close. "I'm fine, really," she said after a hushed moment. "I'm just going to read for a bit."

"If you say so." He paused in the doorway. "Let me know if you need anything."

"Sure."

She slumped on the edge of her bed, listening to his shuffling footsteps return to his bedroom. The contract had been blown into a corner with other papers from her desk. She wandered over and picked it up, rereading it while fidgeting absently with the iron key until all the adrenaline finally left her. Even then, it took a long time to fall asleep.

When the alarm went off, her head throbbed. With a groan that sounded more like it came from her Pops than a teenage girl, she got to her feet and slunk to the bathroom. She had almost convinced herself that the encounter last night was nothing more than a particularly vivid dream until she looked in the bathroom mirror and saw the dried blood on her neck. She touched it, as if somehow it could be another one of those illusions, and then furiously washed it away.

"How's my scamper doing this morning?" Pops asked when she came into the kitchen.

Zanna just grunted in reply and plopped down at the table with her cereal. She couldn't get the words of the strange woman out of her head—*I wanted to save you from St. Pommeroy's*—as if she were doing Zanna a favor. She dressed and slipped the iron key into an outside pocket of her backpack, where she could easily reach it if the need arose again.

Pops had made her lunch again. "This is a one-time deal," he said, handing her the brown paper bag.

"A one-time deal," she repeated, and for the first time that morning, she cracked a smile. Pops saw it and pinched at her cheek, like he knew she hated.

"Atta girl," he said. "Be safe now. I can't take any more worrying phone calls at my age."

The morning was cold with September mist, and Zanna crossed her arms tight to her body in an attempt to keep warm. At the end of the road, the public school bus came and went.

She took the key from its pocket and twisted it compulsively to reassure herself that the world was still real.

In the time it took her to twist the key one way and then the other, the bus for St. Pommeroy's appeared right in front of her.

It was so sudden that Zanna jumped back with a shriek. One second the street had been empty, and the next the bus had materialized with a screech of tires and a blast of heat. Unlike the one that had come for her yesterday, this bus looked brand-new. It was made out of copper and steel and gold that caught all the rich light of the sunrise. There was no door she could see, but then part of the side opened up like an alien spacecraft, and a set of steps unfolded at her feet.

A soft, doughy man with an equally soft and doughy cap on his head sat in the driver's seat. "Zanna Mayfield?"

She didn't move. Grimly, cautiously, she lifted her iron key and turned it. The world buzzed and refocused. But the bus remained as it was.

"It's okay." The driver grinned and beckoned her aboard. "You're in the right place."

As if she were stepping onto thin ice, Zanna climbed the stairs into the bus. But when she saw the inside, her mouth dropped. It was like she had stepped into the royal train car of the Orient Express. All the seats sported thick, deep golden cushions with accents of stunning purple. Little cubes of silver metal, no bigger than sets of dice, scurried around the floor, scrubbing up the dirt and debris passengers had trekked in. Zanna fumbled for her key to make absolutely sure it wasn't an illusion.

"Don't you worry," the driver said as the stairs seamlessly folded themselves back up. "They told me about what happened yesterday. My name's Mr. Gunney, by the way."

He sat in front of the strangest dashboard Zanna had ever

seen. It looked more like something belonging to an old church organ than a high school bus. Dozens of stoppers and plugs and buttons and levers curved around him, most of them unmarked. On a screen in the center was a map of her neighborhood, with a point of light holding steady outside her house.

"Take your seat, please," he said. "And if you wouldn't mind, keep that Weierstrass to yourself. Wouldn't want to get picked up on radar, now, would we?"

"A what?"

"A Why-er-strass," Mr. Gunney pronounced, pointing to the iron key. "Fancy thing for a freshman to be toting around."

She hugged the key protectively. "Dr. Fitzie sent it to me."

"She did? Heh. Starting early." Mr. Gunney chuckled at some joke Zanna didn't understand. "Well, it's messing with my radio waves. Not a problem now, but once we're underway, I'm going to need them. Unless you want to get shot down by the government for being a UFO."

"Oh," Zanna said, looking down at the iron key. "I didn't know. I don't even know what it really does."

"You feel that buzz when you turn it?" he asked, drawing out the last letters of *buzz*. "A Weierstrass changes the area around it to something like trying to watch a movie frame by frame, instead of letting the film run. What we call *nondifferential*. I can work around it, but it's mighty difficult, and this here's only my second cup of coffee." He raised a chunky red mug that curled steam into the air.

"Sorry," Zanna muttered.

"It's no problem!" Mr. Gunney said. "Just don't turn your key while we're in the air, and everything'll be right as rain."

A lump formed in her throat. "In the air?"

"Only way to travel!" Mr. Gunney shooed her farther into the bus. "Places to go! People to see! Hup hup!"

"I—" Her breakfast moved around restlessly. She must have looked very green, for Mr. Gunney softened his tone, lowering his voice so the rest of the students couldn't hear him.

"Don't you worry. I've been flying this old girl for over twenty years now. You won't even feel a bump."

Zanna wanted to tell him that she had gotten sick on airplanes flying in the middle of a dead calm and doubted his bus would be any different, but instead she kicked her fear until it stopped complaining. None of this puzzle would be solved—why the strange woman had warned her away from St. Pommeroy's, how the impossible things she had seen yesterday worked, and what Dr. Mumble might have meant by her "abilities"—if she stayed here on Three Pines Drive. She had to see for herself. She could brave nausea for that.

In an effort to distract herself, she turned over the events of last night. Should she go to the police? A scene formed in her mind of being dragged out of the local precinct, howling that a strange, evil woman who could bend iron and light had visited her in the night and told her that she couldn't go to school. Perhaps she should tell someone who was more apt to believe her. Dr. Mumble? Her other professors? Was there a police station at St. Pommeroy's?

"Excuse me? Are you okay?"

A prim girl had slipped into the seat next to Zanna while she had been deep in thought. Silky black hair that curled at the tips spilled out from beneath her velvet bonnet. Her dark skin smelled of carefully applied perfume. The thick-rimmed glasses on her button nose were black and more for fashion than any sort of vision problem. Everything about her seemed to have been freshly unwrapped. "I have some dimenhydrinate, if you'd like it."

Zanna eyed her warily. "Some what?"

"Dimenhydrinate," the girl repeated, her tongue clicking on every syllable of the chemical compound. She touched a button on the seatback in front of them, and a lap table folded out. Carefully, she searched through her backpack, sorting her books and notes into neat piles and lining up the pencils until she found a little clutch that rattled with medicine. "I take it for seasickness. But airsickness is pretty much the same, you know."

Zanna looked over the contents of the girl's backpack and tried not to be envious. Everything from the textbooks to the lunch tin to the pencils was brand-new and pristine. It was a far cry from her own supplies, which had been trampled and kicked around yesterday. "Is it that obvious?"

"Cold sweat. Dilated pupils, no doubt caused by dizziness. Sure signs of motion sickness," the girl said matter-of-factly. "Plus, it's been statistically proven that 60% of all former CGs feel sick or disoriented their first time on the bus."

Zanna blinked. "What did you call me?"

"A former CG. The control group. You know, the part of an experiment that stays the same and lets nature take its course." She waved a hand toward the window. The bus had touched down again, this time somewhere up in the flinty Appalachians. "Everyone and everything that's not a Scientist. You're Zanna Mayfield, right? The one everyone was looking for yesterday?"

If her stomach was complaining before, it doubled now, and Zanna had to take a moment with her eyes closed to let the feeling pass. "Yeah," she said, not even bothering to defend herself. "That's me."

"I'm Nora. Nora Elmsley." She frowned and pressed two tablets into Zanna's hand. "You really don't look well. Seriously, it'll help. Here."

Zanna cracked open her eyes. Nora had put a cup in front of her and pulled out a small glass rod—the kind a chemist would use to stir solutions. She swirled it around inside the cup, and as she did so, water appeared. "Dehumidifier," she said, pushing the cup, now brimming with clean water, toward Zanna. "Condenses the water vapor from the air. Don't worry, it's perfectly safe."

Zanna's stomach was nearly inconsolable now. She swallowed the pills and gulped down Nora's water. Almost immediately, the bubbling in her stomach began to subside, and the cold sweat that had been beading on her forehead started to dry up. Her vision finally corrected itself, and she took a deep, easy breath.

"There," Nora said, beginning the involved process of repacking all her belongings. "Feel better?"

Zanna nodded. She felt surprisingly good. "What did you give me?"

Nora chuckled. "It's just dimenhydrinate. You can buy it in any CG drugstore. You can't directly manipulate the body anyways. It's protected by the Self function." Then she realized that Zanna hadn't understood a word she had said and smiled. "You'll understand it soon enough. You're one of the Scientists now, and we learn really quickly."

"How did you know about this?" Zanna said. "I mean, I just got this letter in the mail—"

Nora shrugged. "My parents are Scientists. Mathematicians, actually. So I've always known about it."

Zanna gestured around helplessly. "What do they do? I mean—" All the plans she had about high school and colleges and post-graduate studies had been thrown out the window with Dr. Mumble's promise of power over time and space. "What does anyone do after this?"

"Oh, there's all sorts of options," Nora said brightly. "Most just slip back into the control group. You can basically waltz into any laboratory or engineering shop or university after St. Pommeroy's. Or start your own."

"Is that what your parents do?"

"No, they work for the Learned Society. They're the ambassadors to the United States."

Zanna goggled at the word. *Ambassadors.* That explained why everything in Nora's backpack—as well as Nora herself—looked so clean. "Is that what Scientists call themselves?" Zanna asked. "The Learned Society?"

Nora crinkled her mouth. "Depends on who you ask. But I suppose that's good enough."

"Is there like—" Zanna thought about how to best phrase her question. "Police?"

"Of course," Nora said in a tone that made Zanna feel like she had asked the world's dumbest question. "The Primers. But they're really, really selective about who gets in."

"I don't want to join them," Zanna said. "I was just wondering."

"Oh, because of what happened yesterday?" Nora said, quickly making the connection. "You made *The Constant*, you know!"

For the second time that morning, Nora went through the ritual of unpacking her backpack. This time, instead of her pills, she pulled out a newspaper. Like every other newspaper Zanna had seen, *The Constant* was in black-and-white and printed on cheap newsprint. But unlike the others, it was constantly updating itself, the stories getting pushed down the page like posts on a website. Nora pointed to an article that was still above the fold.

KIDNAPPING ATTEMPT CHILLS ST. POMMEROY START.

"Oh geez," Zanna muttered. Her stomach began acting up

again, and she pushed the newspaper away, unable to read past the headline.

"Everyone's talking about it," Nora said. At the touch of her finger, the newspaper displayed a panoramic shot of the empty lot the illusionary school had been built on. "I mean, it's just so strange!" she prattled on as she flipped through more photographs. "Why would someone want to kidnap you? In such an elaborate way?"

Zanna took a couple of deep breaths. "I don't know." She couldn't look out the window, but she couldn't look over at Nora and the newspaper, either, so she just looked down at her hands. "I really don't know."

"I bet I could ask my parents to check the probabilities for you," Nora said, opening the comments section with a stroke of her finger. Conjectures from Scientists around the globe streamed in, updating minute by minute. "They're absolute geniuses at—Oh, we're almost there!" She dropped the newspaper and pointed at the window. "Look!"

Zanna wanted to tell her that the last thing she should do at this moment was look out the window, but her head turned before she could tell it not to. Clouds and large sea birds drifted past, touched by the rising sun. It looked like the view out the window of any cruising airplane. Zanna had nearly turned away when the bus dropped through the clouds and into St. Pommeroy's.

It was so sudden, Zanna had the feeling they had passed through a bubble. One moment there had been just sky and birds and a glimmering ocean some thousands of feet below them, and the next they were looking down on St. Pommeroy's.

The school was built on a chunk of floating rock, with nine smaller islands orbiting it. One of these outer islands passed overhead as the bus descended, and the chill of its shadow swept through Zanna. She craned her neck to watch it pass and saw that the underside of the island was an enormous iron bowl, as if some giant had set his potted plants adrift in the sky.

It was too dizzying to follow all the outer islands, so Zanna turned her attention to the central one. An impossible mess of architecture sprawled over it, a building continually added on to throughout history. The part at the center of the island that Mr. Gunney headed toward had been lifted straight out of ancient Greece, with rectangular courtyards connected by colonnades and angular roofs. But Zanna saw everything from medieval castles to mosques to an entire Gothic cathedral all squashed together in the school below. Clock towers rose out of the rooftops in no discernible order. Some ornate and leering with gargoyles, some austere brick; and some chrome and glass. A quarter of the island to the east had been reserved for the gardens, with a greenhouse of dazzling glass set among the hedges and flowerbeds. It was mad and scatterbrained and completely breathtaking.

"St. Pommeroy's School for Gifted Children," Nora whispered reverently. "The first and only Scientist school in the whole universe. Isn't it just irrefutably, 100% *fantastic*?"

Zanna threw up.

CHAPTER FOUR

THE BUS TOUCHED down in an ancient courtyard that might have once been a Greek marketplace. In the center stood a fountain composed of four marble figures supporting an iron bowl. Atop the bowl sat a perfect model of St. Pommeroy's, every clock tower and orbiting island painstakingly detailed. Something too silver and shimmery to be water spilled over the edges of the bowl and cascaded over the figures.

Zanna and Nora were the last ones off the bus. Zanna's stomach was still shaky, but the worst of it had passed. Mr. Gunney refused to let her apologize. "If I had a nickel for every time someone got sick, I'd own a city," he'd said. A swarm of little metal cubes had popped out of the walls and already cleared away her mess. "So hurry on, you two. Go!"

So, a little weak in her knees and wiping the bad taste from her mouth, Zanna took in the storm of activity that was the courtyard of St. Pommeroy's. Cars and school buses and four-poster beds and bumper cars and a steam locomotive and playground rocking horses maneuvered around in the sky overhead, disgorging students as they made it through the airborne traffic and touched down. Dodging between all the vehicles were older students flying themselves to school, one hand raised above their head just like Dr. Mumble had done when he had left Zanna yesterday.

One of the vehicles caught Zanna's eye. A sleek black limousine cut through the traffic, evidently too important to wait for its turn. When it landed, two boys climbed out, both of them dirty blond and cursed with the gangly, slightly mismatched look of English aristocracy. One was older than Zanna, perhaps by three or four years, but the other—the one who hunched his shoulders as if he were carrying a ton of iron—looked her age. The older brother had a medieval shield on his back that made him look a bit like a time-traveling knight.

Nora nodded toward the brothers. "You were asking about the Primers? The one with the shield is Owin Hemmington. Got accepted by the Primers to be a field agent at the end of last year, even though he's still in school. His father's Lord Baxter Hemmington, the Head Primer."

"His father runs the Primers?" Zanna asked. It was absurdly easy to imagine Owin in a medieval court somewhere, accepting tokens from fair maidens and competing in jousting tournaments. "Isn't that, like, a conflict of interest?"

Nora shrugged. "Everyone knew Owin was going to make it into the Primers. My parents put it at a 99.7% probability. I think we would have been more surprised if he *wasn't* accepted."

"What about his brother?" Zanna asked, shifting her gaze to the younger one. "Is that his brother?"

"His name's Cedwick," Nora said. "You'll probably meet him, since he's in our grade. But there's not much to say. He's got some big shoes to fill."

The Hemmington brothers bid goodbye to their limousine and headed inside, heads held like kings entering their castle.

Zanna pointed toward the marble fountain in the center of the courtyard. "How old is this place?"

"Two thousand, four hundred, and fifty-eight years or thereabouts," Nora said as they also started heading inside.

The entrance to St. Pommeroy's was a wide archway of ancient marble, and in the morning light, Zanna could just make out the four words inscribed in the stone: *Mathema, Episteme, Al-kimia, Physis.*

"This was originally a Socratic academy until the CG found out what we were really teaching kids. So we took the building and ran away."

"Two thousand, four hundred, and fifty-eight," Zanna whispered to herself, reaching out to one of the marble pillars. "And you've just been adding on to it the whole time?"

"The CG lets all sorts of perfectly good buildings go to waste," Nora said, making an adjustment to her glasses. "So we take them. It's only logical."

On the other side of the archway stretched an entrance hall full of twisting olive trees and a long reflecting pool. Students sat under the shade of the trees, catching up after the summer holiday. Some gathered around a makeshift arena where a blender was fighting a pair of socket wrenches. A girl shouted, "*Lamp!*" and the crowd scattered as one of the nearby lampposts suddenly grew arms and feet, chasing after the troublemakers. A red-haired girl in a wheelchair made a cube of continual fire between her hands and lectured to her friends.

"There she is! Nora!"

A boy pushed through the crowd of students, pulling a girl behind him. He had shiny black hair, tanned skin, and a desperate attempt for a beard on his chin, while she was strawberry-blonde and pale as summer straw. The boy dropped into a deep, mocking bow as he got close, his voice full of mischief. "Oh, great and wise Nora Elmsley, we—"

"What do you want, Amir?" Nora said, not amused.

He rose, grinning maniacally. Amir was a restless boy. Even standing still, he kept bouncing up and down. "My compatriot, Libby Wilder, has a question for your esteemed judgment."

The girl stepped forward, a crumpled piece of graph paper

in her hand. Zanna never thought of herself as particularly well put together—like her hair, there was always a bit sticking out at odd angles—but compared to Libby, she felt as new and organized as Nora's backpack. The bonnet on Libby's head was hastily pinned, her tie was askew, and the finger she used to jab at the paper looked like it was smeared with engine grease. The only part she seemed to have spent any effort on was her mascara. "Yeah," she said with a soft Southern drawl. "Amir said you could explain this Self-thing class in the afternoon? What's it about?"

Nora straightened herself up and adjusted her glasses. "In a gross oversimplification, the Self function is what makes you who you are. Through introspection and personal study—"

"So I was right," Libby muttered, cramming the schedule back into the grocery bag she was carrying her books in. "It's useless."

Nora coughed. "It is certainly *not* useless. Understanding the Self is key—"

"Hey, wait a minute," Libby said, cutting Nora off again. The strawberry-blonde girl seemed to notice Zanna for the first time, and her eyes narrowed. "Are you the girl who got kidnapped yesterday? Anna?"

"I wasn't really kidnapped—" Zanna mumbled. "And it's *Zanna*." But that was enough for Libby, who took a step closer.

"You are! So you saw one? A real, live metallurgical illusion?"

"I . . . guess?" Zanna said.

Libby grabbed her by the shoulders and shook her as if answers might come tumbling out. "You have to tell me everything about it," she said. "Everything!"

Zanna gulped. There was something ravenous in Libby's eyes. It was the same sort of look Pops got when she showed him a book of puzzles he hadn't completed yet. Something hungry for the next challenge to beat.

"I mean, there's not much to tell," Zanna said slowly. "It looked just like a regular school, with students and teachers and classrooms and everything. Then it vanished."

"Vanished? How?" Libby's grip tightened. The girl was strong, certainly stronger than Zanna. "You telling me you know how to break a metallurgical illusion already? You got to tell me how!"

"Look, I don't know!" Zanna said. "I didn't do anything! It was all Dr. Mumble. He's the one who undid the illusion and found me and took me home. I just—I haven't really done anything!"

Libby frowned, but at least she let go. "Well, that's a shame," she said, crinkling her nose. "You know when we're supposed to get into metallurgical illusions? *Senior year*. Ugh."

Zanna shrugged. She wanted to change the subject, and her eyes fell on Amir. "So, I'm guessing you two know each other?" she said, pointing to him and Nora.

"Oh, yes," Amir said before Nora could open her mouth. "Nora and I go way back. To wee little tots crawling around the Learned Society."

If he had been trying to get a rise out of Nora, it didn't work. She kept her composure with a drawn-out sigh. "Amir's mother is the Median of the peer review board at the Society," she said. "She works with my parents."

"Mmm, fascinating. Hey, let me ask you something," Libby said to Zanna, and she instantly braced for the girl to grab her by the shoulders again. But this time, Libby kept her hands to herself. "Since apparently you're the only other one who didn't know about this beforehand, does it sort of feel . . . weird? In a good way, I mean. Like you were always supposed to come here?"

Zanna chewed on her lower lip, doing her best not to think

about the strange woman in her bedroom. *St. Pommeroy's is no place for a girl like you.* "Kind of."

"That's the Scientist in you," Nora interjected like a proud parent. "Every Scientist knows that something's wrong with the CG world. They want to explore and figure things out. That's the hallmark of a scientific mind. It's part of who you are." She looked pointedly at Libby. "Part of your Self function. Which is *quite* important, I promise."

"Do students ever decline their enrollment?" Zanna asked while Libby rolled her eyes at Nora. "I mean, is that possible?"

"Of course it's possible," Amir said. "This isn't a prison. But you'd probably be miserable out in the CG. See—"

"Ms. Zanna Mayfield."

She whirled around, recognizing Dr. Mumble's bored and impassive tone at once. But the dean was nowhere in sight. Instead, there was a small silver marble hovering next to her, just like the ones Dr. Mumble had made from the soda cans in the empty lot, and his voice emanated from it.

"Please report to my office at once. This Particle will show you the way."

The others were looking at her when she turned back around. "Sorry," she muttered to Amir, who had stopped in the middle of his sentence. She jerked a thumb over her shoulder. "I heard—Dr. Mumble—"

"Oh, he sent you a Particle!" Nora said, spotting the floating marble behind her. "What did he want?"

"You didn't hear it?" Zanna asked.

"Not if he limited the sound from it," Nora said. "It's really easy to do. All you have to do is determine how far you want the sound to travel, write a function for the border coordinates that contains the inverse sound wave, and cancel it out. That way, no one can eavesdrop on your communications."

"That is the opposite of 'really easy,' Elmsley," Amir said.

Libby snorted at his joke and bumped him playfully with her shoulder. "Oh, *you*," she grinned.

"He told me to report to his office," Zanna said, a little pink at how boldly the strawberry-blonde girl flirted. "Am I in trouble?"

Nora waved her question off, still refusing to acknowledge any of Amir's jibes. "No, I suspect it's just your registration. Don't worry about it. I'll save you a seat in Mathematics!"

Zanna wanted to ask about a hundred more questions, but the little marble Nora had called a *Particle* was bobbing up and down so impatiently that she bit her tongue and let it lead her off into the hallways of St. Pommeroy's. As soon as she left the entrance hall, the school became dead quiet. The Particle bobbed along at a brisk pace, pausing occasionally to let Zanna catch up. So much of the school was open to the sky. Light breezes swept through the open architecture and made the entire school seem alive with sunlight. At an intersection of hallways, a tall olive tree grew out of the stones in the center, stretching overhead and creating a cool, dappling shade.

Then the architecture changed. The floating marble took a turn, and suddenly, Zanna was surrounded by tapestries and impressive castle stonework. Suits of armor stood on either side of the hallway, and at one of them, Zanna saw a little floating cube of iron that reminded her of the cubes from Mr. Gunney's bus. Tiny spindly arms stuck out of either side, buffing the armor with a cloth. Some prankster had stuck googly eyes on it. If what Nora had said was true about the Scientists taking buildings that the CG no longer used, then this had once been a real medieval castle, and those were real sets of armor. It made her feel incredibly small.

The marble led her through a portcullis and into a perfectly kept English garden with rows and rows of blooming rose bushes, manicured hedges, and tall iron statues lining the gravel path. In the center of the garden, an ivy-covered tower rose up five stories, gently tapering to an enormous flame made out of brass and copper. It looked like an ever-burning candle left behind by some ancient behemoth. Something about the garden made Zanna very still, as if all the statues lining the path were watching her. They depicted men and women in everything from loose Greek togas to Arabic robes to Victorian dresses, but they all had a similar serious expression on their metal faces that made Zanna lower her gaze in respect.

At the door to the tower, she paused to read the inscription. It was the same as the entrance hall—*Mathema, Episteme, Al-kimia, Physis*. The marble had disappeared while her back was turned, its guide duties complete. All that was left was for Zanna to go inside.

The thin African man behind the receptionist desk looked up at her as she entered. He was surrounded by a swarm of huge flies, but as Zanna stepped up to his desk, she saw that they were actually little marbles like the one that had found her and led her back here. *Particles*, she reminded herself. Behind him was a gumball machine stocked to the brim with Particles. On his desk was a huge pot of coffee, a well-worn copy of *The Constant*, piles and piles of graph paper, and for some reason, a model battleship.

"Ah, you must be Zanna," he said. The gumball machine behind him turned its crank and dispensed a Particle that he glanced at briefly before it zipped up and out of sight. Only one of his eyes actually peered down at Zanna. The other seemed terribly interested in the model battleship. "I'm Mr. Tinders, secretary for the Candela. Thank you for being prompt. They're waiting for you in Dr. Mumble's office. If you could just sign in here."

A book that looked to be about five hundred years old slid out from the front of his desk, opening to the first available space. Zanna took the pen that was chained to it and signed her name. This one, she noticed with relief, didn't draw any blood.

"You are a freshman, correct?" Mr. Tinders asked as the book slid back. The hatch was so seamless with the desk that Zanna couldn't find it again. "I'll loan you an elevator."

Cabinets and drawers of all sizes covered the wall behind him, and at his beckoning, one of the larger cabinets sprung open. Something that looked like a pair of bicycle handlebars flew out. Mr. Tinders caught it and ran his finger over the metal, as if inspecting it for cracks.

"Here you are," he said, handing it over. "Grip it with both hands and give it a twist, but only when you're ready. Right button to ascend, left button to descend. Dr. Mumble is on the top floor." One eye looked over the rim of his round glasses, his voice serious. "It is not a toy."

"Ascend?" Zanna looked over the piece of metal she had been given. It really did look like someone had just wrenched the handlebars off a bicycle. "You mean flying? Can't I just— wouldn't it be easier if I took the stairs?"

Mr. Tinders chuckled. "I'm afraid not. You'll see." A gate beside his desk lifted, and he waved her through.

She saw what he meant at once. Beyond the gate, the little hallway led out into a circular room that reached all the way up the center of the tower. Warm orange light filtered down from the top, giving her the distinct impression that she had fallen into a deep well and was looking up at the glimmer of day, far out of reach. There were no stairs at all—just landings that jutted out from the circular wall. Zanna poked her finger at them, counting all the way up to the top floor. That was Dr. Mumble's office.

The elevator seemed very flimsy in her hands. She looked down at it and then back up to Dr. Mumble's tiny balcony. "Who builds a tower and forgets to include stairs?" she muttered. Just as Mr. Tinders had told her to, she gripped the elevator in both hands, gathered her courage, and hoped she wasn't about to lose her breakfast again. Not that there was much left to lose. "Lunatics, that's who."

She gave it a twist.

The elevator came to life at once. It unfolded from the middle, stretching down toward Zanna's feet to make a small metal platform for her to stand on. She tested it with her right foot, and though the contraption bobbled a bit, it recovered quickly, hovering steadily a couple of inches above the stones.

Zanna looked up at Dr. Mumble's balcony again, doing the calculations of how a pair of floating bicycle handlebars was supposed to get her up there—and what a fall from that height would do to her spine. But there wasn't any other way about it. With a hard swallow, she put her left foot onto the elevator and pressed the right button.

At her touch, the elevator puttered and started to ascend. It wasn't going to break any speed records, but Zanna was thankful for that. It was all she could do to keep her finger on the button and not scream as it chugged dutifully all the way up.

At the top of the tower, it came to a halt. Dr. Mumble's balcony was just a foot away, but it took another minute of deep breathing before Zanna could will herself to step off the elevator and onto the stones. Only when both her feet were on solid ground did she look down. She didn't know what the elevator would do when she let go of it, but it remained just as she had left it, unfolded and hovering, waiting for her like a silent chauffeur.

Zanna stepped into a small waiting room. Remembering the bland and neutral car Dr. Mumble had created yesterday, she was surprised to see his waiting room actually had a bit of personality to it. The wallpaper was a flourishing pattern of coffee and cream, and the Victorian couches along the walls were lavishly upholstered in pillowy gold. He had no receptionist, so Zanna stood awkwardly in the middle of the room, wondering how she was supposed to make her arrival known. There was only one other door in the room, a heavy-looking door made out of some kind of golden alloy. Zanna raised her fist and knocked on it, just once.

It sprung open with a breath, and Zanna jumped back, not expecting so heavy a door to be so quick. Dr. Mumble stood on the other side. "Ms. Mayfield. You have found your way here."

His office was far less colorful than the waiting room. Parts of it, he had compromised on—the desk commanding the center of the room was enormous and made out of copper, and the grandfather clock off to the side was far too ornate for a man with no sense of humor. But the bookshelves were gray and devoid of any kind of silly knickknack or framed picture. There were no curtains on the windows.

Two men sat at a table off to the side. One was an Englishman with a rich gray suit, a full mustache, a scolding demeanor, and a bronze sheriff's badge pinned to his lapel. The other was a genial old man in a black business suit whom Zanna recognized at once. "Head Primer, Lord Baxter Hemmington," Dr. Mumble said, gesturing to the Englishman. "And the president of the United States, Oliver Ernst."

Zanna stuttered. "The president?" she finally managed to spit out. "Here?"

President Ernst nodded. "Congratulations, Zanna." Even when it was just her, he spoke like he was addressing a crowd of people.

"President Ernst has very graciously taken time out of his

busy schedule to return," Dr. Mumble said. With a flick of his eyes, something flew off a nearby shelf and settled in front of Zanna. She gasped. It was a small plate of silver with an ingot of pure gold on top of it.

The fact that he had just handed her a small fortune seemed lost on Dr. Mumble, who launched into a rote speech without an ounce of emotion to it. "Welcome to St. Pommeroy's. This is a school for the education and development of gifted children in the realms of math, chemistry, physics, and the self. You have been extended an invitation to study with us due to your innate abilities and the potential you promise. Before we begin, however, we ask that all our students undergo a registration. This is a courtesy we provide to our respective governments due to the nature of our studies. Place your hand upon the Summation and state your name. It will be brief."

"Hang on." Her brain felt like it was chewing through a hunk of tough meat. "What do you mean, registration?"

"Put your hand upon the Summation," Dr. Mumble repeated, pointing to the gold ingot. "Then state your name. It will not take long."

She extended her hand. The metal was surprisingly soft under her fingertips. It almost felt as if her hand sunk into it a little.

"Zanna Mayfield."

The sensation began all the way at the top of her head and worked its way down. Not painful but still uncomfortable—a feeling like someone was walking around her with an intense scrutiny in his eyes, taking in every inch of her. Every blemish in her skin, every bulge in her eyes, every tip of her choppy haircut. Then she felt a sharp, piercing pain, and she jerked her hand away. Where her thumb had rested, a small and perfect dot of blood remained.

"It bit me!"

"Yes," Dr. Mumble said, and he produced a soft white towel that smelled of orchids for her to wrap her hand in. "Some methods must always remain classical."

Two thin pieces of gold foil separated from the Summation, like someone had torn the top sheets off a pad of paper. Imprinted on the foil was Zanna's name, a picture of her looking extremely dubious, her handprint, and the dot of blood. Two arms sprouted from the Summation's silver plate and rolled each of the delicate foils up tight. The arms offered both to Dr. Mumble, who took them and put them in silver cylinders no bigger than a pen. The dean screwed a cap on each and handed one to Lord Hemmington and one to the president.

"Thank you," President Ernst said. He touched a piece of chrome metal beside him on the table, and it opened like a briefcase. Inside were rows of empty cushions just big enough to hold an entire class's worth of registration tubes. The president put Zanna's tube inside, and the briefcase sealed itself without a seam. "I shall leave you to your studies. Good luck, Zanna. Hubert, Baxter, until we meet again."

"Safe travels," Lord Hemmington said. It was the first thing he had said since she arrived. But the president didn't head toward the front door. Instead, he went out onto Dr. Mumble's back balcony and took a smartphone out of his pocket. For a moment, Zanna wondered if he was just making a phone call, but then the phone unfolded and kept unfolding until it had wrapped around the president entirely. With a cheery wave through the glass window of his strange one-man craft, he sailed off into the sky.

"There is one other piece of business," Dr. Mumble said, turning Zanna's attention back to the table. "Concerning yesterday's events."

He gestured to the seat the president had vacated, and

Zanna sat down, still a little stunned. After all, it wasn't every day she met the president of the United States, gave him a drop of her blood, and then watched him fly away in an escape pod. She drew a deep breath through her nose and sorted through the odors, wondering if this was another illusion. But she could still smell the fancy cologne of the president lingering on the chair, the distinct chemical taste of the block of gold, and the England damp of Lord Hemmington. No one could make such an unreal illusion anyway.

"I want you to know that we take these sorts of crimes very seriously," Lord Hemmington said. His hands clenched together stiffly as he talked, as if he were holding a live frog and who knew what might happen if it escaped. "Whoever created that illusion will be found, and they will answer for their crimes."

Lord Hemmington had an archaic tone to his voice that reminded her of tales of righteous knights and dragon slayers. She almost felt sorry for the poor woman who had broken into her bedroom last night.

"Do you or your parents have any enemies?" he continued. "Anyone who would have a motive to kidnap you? How much per year would you say your parents make? Are you wealthy?"

"Kidnap?" Zanna said. "You think it was a kidnapping attempt?"

"It's more common than you think," Lord Hemmington said. "Though this instance was more elaborate than most."

"She wasn't trying to kidnap me," Zanna said. Even if she didn't know what exactly the strange woman wanted, Zanna was sure it wasn't kidnapping. A kidnapper wouldn't have gone through the trouble of creating a fake school and asking her to sign a contract.

The Head Primer drew a calculating breath through his nose. "And why are you so sure it was a woman?"

Zanna froze. "I . . . I saw her last night." There wasn't any point in keeping it to herself. "She came to my house. I woke up in the dead of night, and there she was, sitting at the foot of my bed, trying to make me sign a contract to decline my enrollment at St. Pommeroy's."

Lord Hemmington's eyebrows furrowed. "That is most distressing. I hope you have not alerted your local authorities."

"N-no," Zanna said. The Head Primer's intense stare made her feel guilty, even though she had done nothing wrong. "I didn't think they would be much help."

Lord Hemmington made a noncommittal sound, and Dr. Mumble tapped on the table with his pointer finger. "Do you still have this contract?"

She nodded and found it among the books in her backpack. The men looked it over, their expressions turning worried. Lord Hemmington touched a part of the contract and rubbed his fingers together, as if he were testing whether a fresh coat of paint was dry yet. His mustache grumbled.

"This is very helpful," Dr. Mumble said. Zanna blew out an exasperated breath. If she had dragged the woman into his office and thrown her at his feet, she was sure he would have said the exact same thing, in the exact same tone. It infuriated her.

"How?" Her voice snapped out, finally catching up with the last two impossible days. "How is it helpful? What's going on? I nearly *died* last night, and I—" Without warning, she remembered that helpless feeling of all the air around her being sucked away. Her body had been so frail. The anger sputtered out of her voice. "I just want an explanation."

Lord Hemmington nodded, not surprised or taken back at all by her outburst. "You are a Scientist. It is in your nature to ask for explanations." He glanced over at Dr. Mumble, perhaps wondering if the other man wished to say anything, but when the dean remained silent, Lord Hemmington continued. "It is a clever scheme your kidnapper has concocted. This contract would have explained your absence from St. Pommeroy's. The Primers would have marked you down for another student who wished to continue their studies in the control group. It would have been CG authorities who carried out the search when it became known you were missing, not us, and I have serious doubts they would have ever found you. They lack the proper resources and cannot comprehend the possibilities available to a Scientist."

That feeling from the morning returned, the one where Zanna had stood in front of the mirror and touched her neck and realized how close she had come to death. Her fingers curled and dug into the table. "But why me?"

"Ransom seems the most likely," Lord Hemmington said. "You hold no political importance."

"Ransom?" Zanna couldn't stop herself from spitting out the word. "My grandfather's been retired for years."

"Your parents?"

Her face scrunched. "My mom's dead. My father probably couldn't care less."

"Apologies." Lord Hemmington said it so stiffly it nearly brought a smile to Zanna's face and washed out the scowl she always got from talking about her father. "Do you have a wealthy extended family? Friends?"

She shook her head. "I told you, she wasn't trying to kidnap me. She just didn't want me going to St. Pommeroy's."

Lord Hemmington straightened the cuffs of his suit, all the while still fixing Zanna with that intimidating gaze. "So you have said. Why do you think that?"

She shrank like a mouse. "I just do," she confessed.

"Ms. Mayfield," he said, leveling with her. "We are Scientists, and, as you are enrolled here, so are you. We do not go by simple feelings and hunches. We demand evidence. If you wish to claim that this was not an attempted kidnapping, present your case. I will gladly accept any contrary evidence you may have, but as it stands now, I see nothing to support your theory."

She clenched her fists, but the truth was Lord Hemmington was right. She didn't have any evidence. "I don't know."

Lord Hemmington picked up the contract and touched the police badge on his lapel. It morphed and ran like a liquid, reshaping into a brass ring that he held over his head. "I will send someone to your house to put protections around it, in case our criminal decides to strike again. I hope the next time we meet, it is on happier business. Hubert, Ms. Mayfield, good day."

And with a jolt of physics, the Head Primer shot out Dr. Mumble's back balcony and into the sky.

"That is all you are needed for," Dr. Mumble said, flicking a hand at the Summation to send it back to its shelf. "I believe you have a Mathematics class to attend. Can you find your way back from here?"

Zanna thought about all the ancient Greek hallways and castle rooms the Particle had led her through on the way there, and shook her head. "I don't think so."

He tore a thin sheet of copper metal from the top of his desk and handed it to Zanna. Printed on it was a map of St. Pommeroy's, with an X marking a room near the center of the island. "This may be useful, then. Best hurry. You've got quite a bit to learn."

CHAPTER FIVE

WHEN THE BELL rang for first period, Zanna was lost. Even with Dr. Mumble's map, she got turned around as soon as she left the administration tower and its surrounding English rose garden. She had just found the spot where the architecture changed back to the classical Greek style and knew she must be heading toward the center when a pair of oil lamps detached themselves from the wall and blocked her way. She jumped back a little, afraid of getting burned, but then she saw that nothing was actually burning inside their metal bowls. Instead, the fire seemed to just spring out of the air. There wasn't any warmth, either. Just light.

"Hall pass?" the lamps asked in a surprisingly gruff and Scottish voice.

"I don't—Dr. Mumble wanted to see me before class." She didn't know how to address a pair of menacing oil lamps. They sounded a bit like a woman, but she wasn't entirely sure. And she didn't feel like risking a polite "ma'am" and getting it wrong.

"Name?"

"Zanna Mayfield."

"Hold, please."

Nothing changed in the lamps, but she had the same feeling as when someone on the other end of a phone call puts it down for a moment. Zanna took the opportunity to test the illusionary fire with an inquisitive finger, but she had barely reached out when it snapped back into life. "Very well. I'll escort you to your classroom. Don't touch my lamps."

She dropped her hand with a little yip. "Okay."

The lamps took her back to the entrance hall with the olive trees and down a different hallway, not saying anything until they stopped at an intersection. "To the right is Mathematics 101," the lamps said. "In the future, all students outside of a classroom during study hours must have a hall pass."

"I didn't know."

"Well, now you do." The lamps turned. "Stay out of trouble now."

There was no door to the classroom. A hazy, shimmering curtain like a liquid mirror separated it from the hallway. Zanna touched the privacy screen experimentally, only dipping the smallest bit of her pinky into it. Nothing happened, and so she stepped through into a classroom she had never seen the likes of before.

It was a neat square, with all four sides gently sloping down to a stage in the center. Benches of decorated marble sat around the room, and the ceiling was open to the sky, though somehow the sunlight was pleasant and mellow, as if there were an invisible screen stretched overhead that calmed the harsh light down a little. On the back wall, she could make out the faded remains of a large painting in the plaster, depicting a roomful of toga-clad men come to take in a lecture. Beneath it, in block capital letters, was an inscription: *MATHEMA*.

"Divisible by three! I said so! Come on, come on!"

So amazed she was by the classroom that it took Zanna a moment to register that someone was talking to her. A woman stood on the stage in the center of the room and beckoned to Zanna, pointing to a boy and girl sitting on one of the nearby benches. "I do love it when I remember things properly. Zanna Mayfield, aren't you? Come on, come on! Don't be a dilly-dally!"

"Sorry," Zanna said, tearing her eyes away from the architecture and descending the gentle slope. "I was—"

"I'm well aware of it all," her teacher said. There was a strange electricity around her, and it made her white-and-hot-pink hair poof out in a tangle. Her complexion seemed a bit timeless—not elderly but not youthful either, as if she had stolen bits and pieces from across her entire timeline and blended them together. She was dressed in a smart black pencil skirt and modest white blouse with a black tie, but the most curious thing was the belt around her waist. It was heavy, cracked leather with a spyglass of polished brass slung at her hip, the kind a nineteenth-century sea captain would use to look toward the horizon. "Now hurry up and sit down, you silly girl. This is my favorite lecture, and I won't have you delaying it any longer!"

"Yes, ma'am," Zanna said.

The class had been divided into teams of three, and Zanna spotted Nora sitting a little ways off. Unfortunately, it seemed the plan to save her a seat had failed, as Nora had been grouped with Libby and Amir. They flashed apologetic smiles.

The only group with an open spot was up near the front. A small girl with sun-drenched skin, a hawkish nose, and luminous brown eyes sat next to a boy Zanna had seen before. It took her a moment to place him, but then she remembered Cedwick Hemmington, the younger brother she had seen getting out of the limousine that morning.

"Excellent," her teacher said as Zanna settled in. "We'll do introductions again. My name is Dr. Maru Fitzie, and welcome to Mathematics 101! I've put you in teams of three because triangles are so much more fun than single points. Let's all take a moment to meet our new friends."

"I'm Beatrice," the small girl said. She spoke with a soft Italian accent, her English otherwise impeccable.

"Zanna," Zanna said with an awkward wave.

"Ah, so you're the one who nearly got herself kidnapped yesterday," Cedwick drawled, not even bothering to properly introduce himself. "I read all about that in *The Constant*. Metallurgical illusion, was it? And the smell didn't tip you off?"

Zanna scowled. The way Cedwick talked reminded her of a snobbish aristocrat looking down his nose at the peasant on his doorstep. "Yeah, how dare I not know about metallurgical illusions?" she snapped. "I didn't even know all this existed yesterday."

It seemed a lot more violent and forceful in her head. Maybe she just lacked the proper voice to really yell at someone. Either way, Cedwick smirked and brushed her remark off like a bit of dust. "No worries. I'm Cedwick, Cedwick Hemmington. If there's anything you want to know, just ask. You're both obviously CG. I'm sure I can answer any questions you might have."

Zanna's stomach made an angry sound, and for the first time that morning, it had nothing to do with heights. "I don't need your help," she muttered. "So go stuff yourself."

"Now, now," Dr. Fitzie said before Cedwick could reply, clapping her hands to silence the class. "You'll have plenty of time to chit-chat with your new friends afterward. We have a very exciting day ahead of us, so let's get to it!"

The class grumbled and took out their notebooks.

"I've said before that this is my favorite lecture," Dr. Fitzie said, as wide-eyed as a child at Christmas. "Because today we are going to be discussing the very foundation of mathematics. In fact, I would say it's the very foundation of the *universe*. That's what you're studying, mathematics, you know—the bones of the universe. All that physics and chemistry? It's useful, I guess, but without bones, all you'd have is goop. So let's talk about the function."

She tapped at her lips, as if a thought had just occurred to her. "What a strange word that is. *Function*. It means *purpose*, doesn't it? Like, this bit of metal's function is to be a handle and open the door. We use it to sum up what an object does. If that bit of metal breaks, it no longer *functions* as a door handle. We melt it down and reshape it into something completely new. We have changed its function completely."

Dr. Fitzie paused to let her words sink in before continuing. "Everything has a function. Every atom. Every mote of dust. Every planet and every star. They're massive, whirling, magnificent confusions of functions, all competing and working together to make something *exist*." Her voice dropped. "But you know what the best part of it all is? Those functions can be changed. If you know how."

Zanna caught herself leaning forward, drinking in every word. It sounded like raving madness, but then again, the last two days had been nonstop raving madness, so Dr. Fitzie's lecture was in good company. In fact, when Zanna glanced around the classroom, the only person who wasn't absolutely fixed on Dr. Fitzie was Cedwick. Even Nora and Amir, who must have already known all of this, were listening intently.

"I'm getting quite ahead of myself," Dr. Fitzie said. "We certainly aren't going to start fiddling around with solar systems and constellations today. Let's look at something a wee bit simpler."

She lifted a finger, as if touching something in the air in front of her. When she lowered her hand, a black dot remained stuck there. "Can everyone see that? In the back, can you see?"

"Not really," a girl said.

Dr. Fitzie made a white square appear behind her, as if she

had pulled a curtain across the back of the stage. Now the black dot stood out on the background. "Better?"

A few of the students nodded.

"Fantastic!" Dr. Fitzie grabbed the black dot and slid it right in front of her, letting it hang on an invisible plane that stretched from one side of the stage to the other. "Let's talk about dimensions, shall we? I find this to be the easiest way to understand functions and how they operate. You're all familiar with the concept of dimensions, yes? This dot has none. No height, no length, and no width. Well, of course the dot *does* have a minuscule height and length and width, because otherwise you wouldn't be able to see it, but let's ignore that, shall we? Truly dimensionless objects are rather tricky to fiddle around with, and this is just for demonstration purposes. It'll be our little secret."

She winked and grabbed the dot, sliding it back and forth. "Here's where it gets exciting. When things start moving. Because then we get a dimension added to our object and with it, a function." Two intersecting lines appeared on the invisible plane—the X and Y axis. Dr. Fitzie slid the dot straight across, leaving a perfectly flat line in its wake. "That is the simplest function we have. X=1. It has always equaled 1. It will always equal 1. It goes nowhere else, does nothing else. It is just a dot chugging along at the same level day in and day out, not even worrying about all the different dimensions and possibilities out there. It is flat and boring, and it is perfectly content with that."

Dr. Fitzie put her hands on her hips, frowning at the line she had drawn as if it had disappointed her. "But I'm not content," she said after a moment. "There's just so much more to do!"

With two deft strokes, she cut the front and rear of the line so it was just a segment about a foot in length. "Now, this is the same line; I'm just using a piece of it because that's a lot easier to work with. Let's go back to our friend, that dimensionless dot. His movement is what made that first dimension, right? Because a line is nothing more than a traveling dot. Just like drawing a line on a piece of paper. The tip of your pencil is the dot and it leaves a line behind it. But what if we took that line and moved it? What would *that* leave behind?"

She swiped the line segment across the plane, and it became a square. "You ever try writing with one of those markers that never seems to dry properly? You draw a line, and then your big, clumsy hand comes back across it, and suddenly, you've got this ugly black smear across your page. That's what two-dimensional objects are. Big, ugly, smeared lines."

With a few more flicks of her wrist, she drew line segments and dragged them out into shapes. Some shrank and turned into triangles. Others ballooned into hexagons and octagons. "It's the same principle as before. A line is a traveling dot. A shape is a traveling line. You see where I'm going with this."

She cleared away all the other shapes, leaving only the original square hanging in the air. "Now, what happens when that shape decides to start traveling?"

The intersecting axis of the graph disappeared, and like a magician pulling a rabbit from her hat, Dr. Fitzie stretched the square into a cube. "Three dimensions," she said. "The world we know and love. A dot traveling into a line traveling into a shape traveling into an object. That's quite a bit of movement for something so simple, isn't it? And this cube here isn't even real." She plucked the cube from the air and batted it around for a bit, like a cat playing with a toy. "It's an idealized construct. But I'm getting ahead of myself once again, aren't I?"

With a grin, she tossed the cube to Beatrice, who caught it with a small yelp of surprise. "It won't bite; it's a good little cube," Dr. Fitzie said as Beatrice turned it over and then passed it to Cedwick, who immediately handed it off to Zanna without so much as a look. It weighed absolutely nothing, and Zanna would have sworn she was just cupping air, were it not for the thin black lines that made up its outline. She gave it a gentle toss from hand to hand, like Dr. Fitzie had, and then passed it on.

"Let's take some time to try this out ourselves, shall we?" Dr. Fitzie said. "Group up in your little triangles. Start with a dot and smear it into a cube. If you're adventurous, maybe try your hand at some different forms! Not everything in the world is a boring old cube, you know. Use your imagination!"

The murmur of work filled the air as the students turned to their groups. Zanna reached out and touched the air, just as Dr. Fitzie had done, but nothing happened. No dot appeared.

"How'd she do that?" Beatrice asked, apparently having the same problem. The girl looked at her finger as if it had run out of ink.

"Like this."

Cedwick held a cube just like Dr. Fitzie's and a bored expression on his face. He balanced it on a corner and gave it a spin. "It's painfully simple. Just hold the concept in your mind. Here—"

"I can do it myself," Zanna snapped before he could reach over to her. She hunched down and focused on Dr. Fitzie's words. The dimensionless point at the end of her finger becoming a line. The line becoming a square. The square becoming a cube.

"Oh!" Beatrice's finger left a mark on the air, and she jumped a little in surprise. "I did it!"

"Keep holding on to it," Cedwick said, deftly making a couple of spheres. Zanna felt his gaze flicker over to her. "How are you doing?"

Her jaw clenched. "You're breaking my concentration."

"Sorry, sorry," Cedwick said. "Let me know when you want help."

"Look!" Beatrice said. A theoretical line like a pencil drawing on the air flowed out of her finger. "I've got it!"

Heat flushed Zanna's face, and she bit down hard on her tongue, squeezing her eyes shut to better focus on what Dr. Fitzie had said. If that strange woman had been trying to keep Zanna out of St. Pommeroy's, this was the best way to get revenge. By proving that she belonged here. Zanna squeezed her eyes so tight they began to water. She pushed aside thoughts about her upset stomach and the strange woman and showing up Cedwick, focusing just on the idea of a function. She extended a finger.

A thin black line appeared on the air.

"Zanna's got it, too!" Beatrice said. She clapped her hands in a tiny explosion of glee.

Cedwick just nodded, curling off exotic free-formed shapes from his fingers like a man playing with the smoke off his cigar. "That's just the start. Now you've got to take it up through the dimensions," he said.

But with the theory solid in her mind, the rest fell into place easily. With a grin on her face, Zanna twisted her hand, and a perfect theoretical sphere appeared. She gave it a poke, and it drifted lazily over to Cedwick, like a big geometric mote of dust in a sunbeam.

"I think I can manage on my own," she said smugly, leaning back with her hands behind her head in a mimic of his own posture.

"Well, look at this!" Dr. Fitzie came out of nowhere and gazed down at the triangle of students with her hands on her hips. "Seems like you all are getting along just fine."

"Yes, ma'am," Beatrice said.

Dr. Fitzie made a little gasp of discovery, as if she had just now noticed something. "Ah! The younger Hemmington! My, it seems like only yesterday it was your brother sitting where you are. We expect some great things from you!"

A change came over Cedwick at the mention of his brother. His lips quivered and tightened, smiling in a way that had no joy in it. It was so slight and well-hidden that Zanna wouldn't have noticed unless she already knew it well. She did the exact same thing anytime someone mentioned her father. "I'm looking forward to it," he said thinly.

"Excellent!" Dr. Fitzie's enormously giddy eyes turned to Zanna. "And you, Ms. Mayfield? You've had quite the adventurous past few days. Did you receive the key we sent you?"

"Yes," Zanna said. "I got it just fine."

"Splendid," Dr. Fitzie said. "I do hope you haven't had to use it. A Weierstrass transform can be a tad . . . feisty. But it's a surefire way to pick out an illusion, as long as whoever made it didn't write it in discrete calculus. Which most people never bother with." She tapped at the side of her nose. "Let's see Physics and Chemistry claim that, hmm? I do hope you consider Mathematics for your specialization." She gestured to the theoretical shapes bobbing around them. "You're quite the natural. All of you."

Cedwick made a sound of disgust as soon as Dr. Fitzie was out of earshot. "As if. I'm going to specialize in physics."

"I think mathematics is quite fun," Beatrice said softly, drawing out a tetrahedron.

Cedwick rolled his eyes. "Fine, but you won't get accepted into the Primers by specializing in *mathematics.*"

"Oh no," Zanna muttered sarcastically. From what she had seen of Lord Hemmington that morning, it hardly seemed like a sacrifice. Luckily, Cedwick didn't feel compelled to further discuss his opinions on the proper specialization, leaving Zanna free to make geometric shapes with Beatrice until Dr. Fitzie had finished walking around the classroom and returned to the stage.

"Now listen up, everyone," the teacher said. "You're all doing quite well, which is absolutely marvelous for the first day. Sadly, I'm going to have to let you go soon, but I'm just going to leave you with this to ponder over."

The spyglass hanging from her hip jostled and then shot up out of its holster. Dr. Fitzie sketched another theoretical cube and made her spyglass crumple and reform into a cube of gleaming brass, with circular glass windows on each of its six sides.

"Two cubes," she said, holding them out for everyone to see. "What is the difference between them? What are *all* the differences between them? It is, in a way, what you have come here to study. What makes this cube"—and she lifted the theoretical one—"different from this one?" She lifted the real one.

The class was silent, and she winked. "I'll give you a hint. *Functions.* Many, many functions."

CHAPTER SIX

BY THE TIME lunch rolled around, Zanna felt like her head was going to burst. After Mathematics was Chemistry, which was taught by a hapless and scatterbrained man named Dr. Simon Piccowitz. He had started off mumbling incomprehensibly, but as the lecture continued, he sped up and sped up until Zanna worried he was about to suffer an aneurysm. "Chemistry is the—the—the building block of the universe," he gushed, summoning a collection of raw elements from the massive periodic table behind him and making them dance while he talked. "Everything you touch, everything you see, everything that keeps us warm and alive and breathing—it exists because of chemistry. The study of chemistry is the study of the fundamental existence of the universe—the elemental—the real stuff of it."

Not to be outdone, her Physics professor, Dr. Andrew Cheever, whose classroom was decorated with a gallery of grade-school art projects, gave his own sales pitch. "What ties us together?" he asked, spinning around with his arms out, his dreadlocks flying wildly. "What ties us to the Earth, the Earth to the sun? What keeps our atoms together? That's *physics*. The glue of the universe. Without physics, chemistry would be nothing but a useless collection of fundamental particles bumping around aimlessly, and mathematics would have nothing to describe."

To prove his point, he turned off gravity and let the students float around. It was exhilarating, but at the same time, Zanna began to see a pattern underneath all the fun and games. All three classes—Mathematics, Chemistry, and Physics—when put together answered the question Dr. Fitzie had asked. The real cube had mathematical coordinates. The real cube had atoms. The real cube had gravity. Understand each of those parts, and she would understand the entire cube.

"I just wish they'd skip the hard sell," Libby muttered over lunch. The cafeteria was on the east side of the school and had a long stone patio that bordered an expansive, lush lawn and gardens. Squat, circular iron tables stolen from some Austrian café lined the patio, and the girls claimed one in the cool shade. "Reminds me of going to the used-car dealership with my dad."

"It's only natural that everyone thinks their specialization is the best," Nora said. She had laid her lunch out in precise rows and was just now beginning to go through it in an order known only to her. "I already know which one I'm going to choose in the spring. Mathematics."

"Does it really matter that much?" Beatrice asked.

Nora looked shocked that Beatrice would ask such a thing. "Of course it matters! Without the right specialization, you won't get into the right subfield you want to study! Without the right subfield, you won't get into the right sub-subfield! Your entire future is at stake!"

"Mhm. Sounds more like an excuse to stir up rivalry," Libby said, her mouth full of cold beef brisket. "I think I'm going with physics. Yeah."

"You're supposed to take the entire year to think about it," Nora said, snapping a carrot stick in two. "It is *not* a decision to be made lightly."

"And yet you've apparently already made up your mind."

"I'm different," Nora said with an air of superiority. "I've had a lot of time to think about this."

"Excuse me," Beatrice said before Libby could respond. The small Italian girl pointed at the students out on the yard. "I have a question. Why is everyone carrying around random things?"

It was something that Zanna had noticed, as well. Every student at St. Pommeroy's who wasn't a freshman carried some kind of metal object with them. Some had simple items like hammers, buckets, washboards, bird cages, scissors, or axes. Others wore ornate pieces of jewelry. Still others had things that were downright strange—one red-haired boy out on the lawn carried a stop sign. But no matter how odd the items were, each one seemed to fit with its owner. Like how a dog and its master always managed to look like they belonged together.

"That's the Iron," Nora said, switching gears at once. "Every Scientist picks one. It's their personal tool. If you want to go somewhere, or send a Particle, or sit down, or watch some television, or protect yourself, you use your Iron. It's sort of an extension of who you are."

"And we . . . pick one?" Zanna asked. "From where?"

"From wherever," Nora said. "But you have to pick correctly, because you're stuck with it after this year. Everyone says you know it when you see it. I already know what mine is." She set a metal ruler on the table with a self-satisfied smile. It was stainless steel and polished to an astounding shine, just as much a piece of art as a measuring instrument. "My parents bought me it for Christmas."

Libby rolled her eyes and stuffed more beef brisket into her mouth. As the girls tucked into their lunches, Zanna idly watched a senior girl out on the lawn with a neon-pink thermos transform it into a screen to show off pictures of her dog. Not two days ago, Zanna had been planning her year—and the rest of her life—safe on the assumption that she knew what the real world was. Now all of that had been thrown out the window. She had a stack of homework dealing with theoretical cubes, simple gravity functions, and elemental memorization; a specialization to choose; an Iron to find; and a madwoman out to kidnap her.

The girls were looking at her. "You okay?" Beatrice asked, her eyes soft with real concern.

Zanna nodded. "Sorry, I got distracted."

"I was just asking what Dr. Mumble wanted with you today," Nora asked. "Was it registration?"

"Oh, that. Yeah." Zanna opened the little tin of applesauce Pops had packed for her, but she stopped before the spoon reached her mouth. "I met the president," she said, giggling at how it had slipped her mind. "I completely forgot about that."

"Like, you actually got to talk to him?" Libby asked. "Lucky. He was here yesterday, but all we got to do was walk past him and get waved at. Lame."

"Is he one of us?" Zanna asked. "I mean . . . is he a Scientist?"

Nora shook her head emphatically. "We haven't had a Scientist president since Pierce. But they all know about us. All the world leaders do."

"Isn't that—" Libby searched for the right phrasing. "Kind of against the whole secrecy thing y'all got going on?"

"Not at all," Nora said. "We've tried being absolutely secret before, and the CGs always find out, one way or another. So instead, we tell the CG leaders about our abilities, register as a token of good faith, and share ambassadors just like any foreign country. In return, they don't look too closely if someone catches a flying Scientist on radar."

Zanna let her gaze drift over the wondrous lawn, still not entirely believing her eyes. There was a solitary figure on a bench near the entrance to the gardens, and she looked closer. It was Cedwick. He had his legs tucked up and his lunch in his lap and was completely alone. She frowned. On one hand, Zanna was glad to finally be rid of him—the boy had dogged her through all her classes that morning, popping up over her shoulder every time they split into small groups. On the other hand, Zanna knew what it was like to eat lunch alone.

"You going to ask him out?" Libby asked suddenly.

Zanna spun around so hard she nearly made herself dizzy. "What?"

Libby indicated Cedwick with a flick of her gaze. "He likes you. That's why he's been bothering you."

"Really?" Zanna scrunched up her nose. "Boys actually do that?"

"Oh, yeah," Libby said with a knowing expression. "The clever ones are better at hiding it, though. So what do you think?"

Zanna stole another glance at Cedwick. She understood dating in the same way she understood skydiving. People did it, but its appeal was completely lost on her. "I doubt it."

Libby shoved a whole chocolate cookie into her mouth. "Shame," she said with a gleam in her eye. "I think you'd be cute together."

There was one class left after lunch, and that was Self. After Nora's brief explanation of Self that morning, Zanna was brimming over with questions of what the class would be like. But when the girls stepped through the privacy illusion, Zanna saw that her questions would have to wait a bit longer. Standing at the front of the room wasn't her professor but Mr. Tinders, the spidery secretary from the administrative tower. He looked rather out of place without his desk around him, like a hermit crab without his shell.

"Dr. Trout has been called away on urgent business this afternoon. You may use this time to study. Mrs. Appernathy will be in shortly to make sure you are using this time wisely."

He vanished. It must have been an illusion, Zanna realized

after a startled moment, and she made a note to start recognizing them in the future.

A candelabra floated through the privacy illusion and established itself in the middle of the room, looking over the class with its limbs of flickering candles. Zanna could almost see a scowling face in its flames. "You will use this time for quiet study," the candelabra said in the voice of a gruff Scottish matron—the same voice of the oil lamps that had led Zanna to her Mathematics classroom that morning. "You will not use this time for socializing. Anyone found acting otherwise will be subject to detention. Clear?"

A half-hearted agreement rose from the students.

Zanna plunked her backpack on a table and took out a notebook. Dr. Piccowitz had assigned them to draw and label the first 82 elements, and Dr. Cheever wanted them to work out how much gravitational force a list of objects—from a mote of dust to a supergiant star—would exert on their body if they stood a foot away from the objects.

"Physics?" Cedwick appeared behind her without a sound, looking over her shoulder at the gravitational functions she was struggling through. "You know, I can show you a shortcut for those gravitational functions. I do know a thing or two."

Zanna circled her arm around her textbooks, as if Cedwick were trying to copy from her. Any pity she had felt at seeing him eat alone at lunch vanished. "I'm trying to work," she growled. "Will you please leave me alone?"

He didn't. Instead, Cedwick sat down, drawing a theoretical object in the shape of a young girl and handing it to her. "It's so much easier to use theoretical objects than going through all that math. See, all you have to do is put your mass in here—"

"My *what*?" Zanna snapped, her voice ringing sharply in the nearly silent classroom. She waved her hand in the air. "Mrs. Appernathy!"

A flash of candle flame, and Mrs. Appernathy's candelabra hovered in front of them. "What's going on?" it said. "Are you working or socializing?"

"Well, *I'm* trying to work," Zanna grumbled, displaying the open book in front of her. "But Cedwick is bothering me."

Cedwick lifted his chin. "I already finished my homework," he said, speaking loud enough so the whole class could hear. "So I thought I would help—"

"Detention, Mr. Hemmington," the candelabra snapped, cutting Cedwick off mid-sentence. "This Saturday for four hours. I was very clear about what this time is to be used for. If you've already finished your homework, then sit quietly and let the others work in peace." The candelabra paused, and for a terrible moment, Zanna thought Mrs. Appernathy was about to give her detention, as well. But instead, the candelabra just let out a disapproving sigh. "Really," she said. "I expected better of a Hemmington. Come on, back to work. All of you."

Slowly, Cedwick slunk from Zanna's desk all the way to an unoccupied table in the far corner. A twinge of regret pinched at her, so Zanna buried herself in gravitational functions and tried to ignore the pointed stares from the other girls for the rest of the period, with only mild success. At the bell she followed the flow of students out into the central courtyard, where Libby and Beatrice caught up with her.

"Well, I guess that settles it," Libby said, falling into step as they walked toward the buses. "You didn't have to put him in detention, though."

Zanna sighed and rubbed the bridge of her nose, trying to stave off the headache she felt coming on. The prospect of getting back into Mr. Gunney's bus wasn't doing anything to settle her stomach, either. "Can we not talk about that?"

"I mean—"

"She doesn't want to talk about it," Beatrice said, her small voice surprisingly firm on the point.

Libby backed down. "Easy there, momma bear." Something outside their small circle caught her eye, and she changed gears at once. "Hey, Nora!" The girl had just emerged from the crowd of students.

"Yes?" Nora asked. Her eyebrow twitched slightly, Zanna noticed, but otherwise, her composure was as unruffled as ever.

Libby jerked a thumb over her shoulder. Amir and a boy from their class named Tyson were trying to climb one of the gnarled olive trees. "I need to ask you. What's the deal with you and Amir?"

Nora blinked. "I don't follow."

"You're not a thing?" Libby asked, already smoothing down her strawberry-blonde hair and adjusting the bonnet on her head. "Cool. I'm going to go ask him out. Catch y'all tomorrow."

The three remaining girls stared blankly as she bounced across the courtyard, nearly skipping. "Unbelievable," Nora muttered, finally processing what had just happened.

"Excuse me? Zanna?"

The posh English voice made her spin around on the spot, ready to tell Cedwick again to leave her alone. But it wasn't Cedwick this time.

"I'm glad I caught you before you left," the senior boy said, offering his hand. "My name's Owin Hemmington. My dad said that you needed someone to put protections around your house?"

He had the same thin blond hair and waxen complexion as his younger brother, but how he carried those noble features was entirely different. Where Cedwick hunched his shoulders,

Owin stood upright and confident. On his back was a polished medieval shield.

Beatrice nudged her gently, and Zanna realized she had completely spaced out. "Sorry," she muttered, blushing fiercely and finally shaking the hand that he had been offering silently for a while. "I've—It's been a long day."

Owin smiled. "A long couple of days, from what I've heard."

"Yes," Zanna said. It was a strange experience to talk with Owin after she had spent the day being hounded by his younger brother. They were so similar, and yet Owin managed to pull off the air of a perfect gentleman. "You're going to protect my house?"

"Put up protections," Owin corrected her with an easy smile. "Standard Primer procedure. It'll take about an hour. If you're all set, I'll tell Sophie, and we can be on our way."

"I'm set." Zanna said a quick goodbye to Nora and Beatrice and then followed Owin to his limousine. He rapped on the glass, and the window rolled down.

"I found her," he said to the woman behind the wheel, who must have been Sophie. "So I'm taking her home. Shouldn't be too long. Tell mom I'll be back in time for dinner."

Zanna peered past Owin's shield into the limousine. The seats were upholstered in red velvet and trimmed with brass and gold. She could see just past Sophie's head and into the cab. A table of dark wood stretched the length of the car, a long sofa running alongside it.

Cedwick was inside.

He looked nothing like he had during school. Fresh tears rimmed his eyes and dotted the collar of his shirt. His tie was loose. Their eyes met, and a seething, aimless thing burned in his gaze as it flicked between her and his older brother, reading the situation instantly. And then Cedwick leaned forward and slid the partition up, disappearing from view.

Owin said a few last things to Sophie and then turned to Zanna, who had stepped back from the limousine. "Are you ready to go?"

She didn't respond. All her body seemed capable of doing at the moment was watching as the limousine came to life without a sound and lifted into the air, joining the stream of cars and buses and students in the sky. That look Cedwick had given her before shutting himself off in the dark cab hurt like a deep wound.

"Zanna?"

She shook her head. "I'm ready."

The shield on Owin's back transformed into a pair of bucket seats, and Owin climbed into one, offering his hand to Zanna. She eyed it warily.

"Are we—*flying*?"

"I don't know any other way off of here," Owin said with a laugh. When Zanna didn't smile at his joke, his voice softened. "Don't worry. I won't let you fall. I promise."

"I threw up on the bus today." Somehow it didn't feel odd at all to confess that to Owin.

"Then I'll be extra careful," he said. His hand was still outstretched, and she took it. As she sat down, a band of iron snaked over her lap, holding her firmly in the seat. "If you don't want the seatbelt, let me know," he said.

"No, I want it," Zanna said.

Owin spotted an opening in the overhead traffic, and they began to rise. "Doing all right?" he asked.

Zanna didn't trust herself to speak, but she nodded, even though her heart was screaming.

"Once we're clear of this traffic," he said, "I'll put an illusion on. The Primers gave me your address. Just a bit more."

They merged into the exiting traffic, falling in behind a teacher astride a huge bronze horse. As they rose higher, the traffic thinned and spread out. When the sky was clear at last, Owin made a gesture, and everything seemed to disappear. Zanna and Owin were sitting on a park bench in early autumn, watching people go by.

"Better?" Owin asked. "Some people don't like major illusions like this. Messes with their inner ear. You okay?"

"I'm fine," Zanna said, and she meant it. "How did you—"

"Make this?" Owin finished her question, sweeping his arm to encompass the entire park scene. "I'm just manipulating the frequency of the light to show different colors. See?"

The leaves rustling along the path changed from orange and brown to deep teal. Owin pointed at a woman walking by, and her coat went from black to lime-green.

"Is something like this difficult to do?" Zanna asked.

Owin laughed, restoring the leaves and the woman's coat to their original colors. "Well, that depends. How much detail do you want to put in? How much movement is there going to be?"

The park scene looked so real. Zanna put a hand on the wooden bench she was sitting on and told herself that it was actually a medieval shield transformed into a seat and they were soaring over the Atlantic on their way toward Virginia.

"And how difficult is it to make a whole school?" she muttered.

The grin Owin wore faded a little. "You're thinking about what happened yesterday, aren't you?" he said. "Don't worry. I know all of this seems rather new and strange, but I've been around it my whole life, and there's no one I trust more than the Primers. And I'm not just saying that because my dad runs it. They are the best, plain and simple. Some of them—Henry, Violeta, Xavier, Mama S—they can do things I never thought possible. They'll find who did this to you."

Zanna stared at a swirl of autumn leaves, not wanting to tell him how she wasn't so sure of that after talking with Lord Hemmington this morning. The Primers were looking for someone who wanted to kidnap her, but Zanna knew that the strange woman was more than some opportunistic writer of ransom letters . . .

In the blink of an eye, the park vanished, and her house appeared. Zanna hadn't even felt them land. "808 Three Pines Drive, correct?" Owin asked as his shield released Zanna and returned to its original form.

"Yup," Zanna said. She headed up the front path but paused before she unlocked the front door. "I should warn you, though. I live with my grandfather, and he can be . . . a little much."

Owin's face darkened a shade. "One of those Scientist-fearing types?"

"Oh, no," Zanna said, turning the doorknob. "Not at all. But you'll see."

Pops was in the kitchen, humming and stirring a thick pot of tomato sauce. "Why hello, stranger," he said when he heard Zanna call out. Then he turned and saw Owin behind her and raised an eyebrow. "Oh? Who's this?"

"Owin Hemmington, sir," Owin said, extending a hand. "Apprentice Primer. I understand your granddaughter had some trouble yesterday with an illegal metallurgical illusion. We're taking it quite seriously, I assure you. I'm here to put some protections on your house in case the kidnappers try again."

"A what?" Pops said. "A metallurgical?"

"The school yesterday," Zanna told him. "That's what he's talking about."

"And *kidnappers*?" Pops's voice swelled in anger. "Who's trying to kidnap Zanna?"

"That's what we're trying to find out," Owin said. "Until then, we thought it a good idea to put some protections around your house. It won't take long, I promise."

Pops appraised Owin intently and then pointed to the kitchen table. "Sit down."

For a moment Owin just stood there, confused, but when Zanna nudged him, he obeyed, hanging his shield on the back of a chair. "I'll be right back," Pops said to Zanna. "Get our guest something to drink."

"I'm quite all right," Owin said as Zanna opened the fridge and poured a glass of lemonade.

"It makes him feel better if you eat something," she whispered as she set it on the table. "Just trust me on this."

Owin shrugged and sipped at his lemonade as Pops came back. In his hand was a box of matches, and he spilled them out on the table, selecting nine of the matchsticks and arranging them in parallel lines. Then he sat, his eyes narrowed and testing.

"Take these nine matches," he said, "and turn them into ten."

Owin thought for a moment and picked up one of the matches. He bent it between his thumb and forefinger and had nearly snapped it in two when Pops stopped him. "Without breaking any of them," he clarified.

"Without breaking them?" Owin said, returning the matchstick to the table. "And I can't just add one?"

"Everything you need is right here," Pops said. A twinkle of mischief broke through the stern gaze he was trying to keep up. "If you're stuck, maybe you should ask that one over there."

He pointed over at Zanna, and she groaned. "Pops—"

"I think you've got me stumped," Owin said, frowning at the matchsticks. "I haven't the faintest idea of what to do."

Pops raised an eyebrow, and Zanna let out an exasperated sigh. "Owin doesn't have time for this," she said, leaning over the table to rearrange the matchsticks to spell out TEN. "Nine into ten. Ta-da."

"Ah!" Owin said. "That's clever. I like it!"

"Don't encourage him," Zanna said dryly, gathering up the matchsticks, "or else you'll never escape. Come on." She turned to Pops. "He's not here to play puzzles with you, you know."

"Fine, go run along, you two," Pops said. "I'll be here if you need me."

"Actually, sir, I do have a question," Owin said as he rose from the table and picked up his shield again. "Do you have any exposed I-beams in this house?"

CHAPTER SEVEN

ZANNA'S BASEMENT SMELLED of concrete and cardboard and rust. She sat cross-legged in an old armchair, watching as Owin inspected the I-beam that ran across the ceiling. "Is it okay if I watch?"

"I don't mind," Owin said. He tapped on the beam and thought for a moment before climbing down from his shield, which he had turned into a stepladder. "In fact, let's do this."

The stepladder transformed into a large drafting table. As Zanna leaned forward, theoretical squiggles began to appear beneath Owin's hands, which he slid across the surface, as if setting a dinner table. Except instead of plates and saucers, he had piles and piles of mathematical functions.

"That's your I-beam," he said when he was done. "That's everything that's going on with it right now. That's its existence."

Zanna stared at it all. It looked like a mathematical textbook had sneezed all over the place. "Dr. Fitzie said something like this today," she muttered. "About what the difference is between a real cube and a theoretical one."

"Oh, dear," Owin said, putting his hands down on the table again. "Don't tell her I told you this, then. She'll get mad at me for ruining her fun."

"It's so complicated," Zanna said.

"Everything's complicated," Owin said. "That's the first thing you're going to learn at St. Pommeroy's. It's just a question about what you can muddle through and what's not worth figuring out. That's why I wanted an I-beam. Because when you start looking through all this, it's actually pretty straightforward."

The mess on the table looked about as far from straightforward as Zanna could imagine, but Owin seemed to understand it just fine as he started organizing bits and pieces. "Some of the other Primers swear by using the pipes, but I don't get it. Then you've got pressure and thermodynamics and fluid dynamics and probably a little electromagnetism to deal with, and it's just a mess. Nope, I-beams are the way to go. Look here."

With a sweep of his hand, he moved all the functions to the side except for one group, which he put square in the middle. "These are all the gravitational functions operating on your I-beam. Did you know that there's no limit to gravitational pull? It's not just Earth pulling on you but the moon and the sun and every black hole and galaxy in the entire universe." As he spoke, he began to unpack the group of functions, keeping some in the center and sliding some farther away.

Zanna began to see things she recognized, such as gravitational functions—the same functions Cedwick had been haranguing her about earlier. Except these weren't the neat theoretical ones in her textbook. These were out in the wild.

"But most of these are so faint we can just ignore them," Owin continued. "Unless you're a perfectionist, you don't need to account for the gravitational pull of Alpha Centauri on your I-beam. Or any of the trillion other celestial bodies. You'd never get anything done." With a whisk of his hand, most of the functions cleared, leaving only a few remaining. "Now Earth's gravity, that's pretty important. The moon, you can take or leave."

"What would happen if you didn't account for Earth's gravity?" Zanna asked.

"An excellent question!" Owin said. He put his fists together, knuckles touching. "Every time you start tinkering with the universe, there are two forces at work. The first is all the natural functions of the object, which tell it to keep doing what it's always been doing. The second is you. If you understand enough of the big functions—momentum, gravity, chemical composition, electromagnetism, coordinates, crystallography, thermodynamics, pressure, stress, and so on—and get them on your side, you can ignore the smaller functions. But leave out something like Earth's gravity and—" He pushed his fists together to demonstrate. "You get nowhere. Or worse."

"Worse?"

"A Splutter," he said. "Imagine you're driving a car and decide to make a turn. Except your engine and one of the wheels decide to keep going straight. That's a Splutter. The natural functions of the object tell it to do one thing, and the functions you're mucking around with tell it to do a different thing, and you push so hard it tries to split the difference. Nasty stuff."

He moved the function of Earth's gravity to a corner of the table. "So we'll just put that aside for later. Next up—forces!" Owin set a dense package of functions in the middle with a grin. "These are fun." He stopped for a moment, caught up in an idea. "Actually, let's do this. What sort of physical forces do you see working on your I-beam?"

Zanna had never really thought about it before and scrunched up her face. "Well, there are those joists running across it," she said, pointing at the planks that made up the first floor of the house. "They're pushing down with the rest of the house. That gets transferred to the pillars." Her finger traced the path through the I-beam to one of the two supporting concrete pillars. "And that goes into the Earth."

"And that's it?" Owin had the same look on his face as the one Pops wore when Zanna was overlooking something obvious.

"No," she said, scrambling to think of what she had missed.

"I bet those pillars aren't perfectly level. So it's probably being twisted a little."

"But we can ignore that," Owin said, "because it's so little."

"Well, there's air pressure—"

"That's also small enough that we can ignore it," Owin said.

She frowned and let out an angry breath. "Give me a hint."

"Think about what you already told me," Owin said. "If it all was pushing down into the Earth, what do you think would happen? Wouldn't it move?"

It clicked. "The Earth is pushing back."

"Which goes into the pillars, through the I-beam, and into the joists," Owin finished. "Good job; you've figured out reactionary forces. Old Newton would be proud."

He put the forces over with the Earth's gravity and slid a new conglomeration into view, one that looked completely different from the previous functions. Instead of mathematical numbers and signs, there were chemical notations and a strange mesh of clouds. "So that's the physics. Well, that's everything they *call* physics. When you really look at it, physics and chemistry are just different applications of the same thing. Same with math. It's all science." He cleared his throat and lifted the mesh up from the table, turning it into a three-dimensional model. "This is the metallurgical composition. Going by industry standards, your I-beam is a basic carbon steel, which means it's mostly iron with about 0.26% carbon. That's this mesh here." He made it expand so Zanna could see the atoms clearly. "That's a carbon atom among the iron atoms. Makes the alloy stronger and harder. But it also makes manipulating it more difficult, because you need to hold on to two elements, and you really don't want to Splutter an alloy. Yanking this apart would be an ugly business." He winked and dropped the mesh back down on the table. "But don't worry. It's not as difficult as it seems. Metal is pretty basic, actually, when it comes to the chemical composition."

"What's the rest of this?" Zanna asked, pointing to the other chemical functions.

"Rust, stains, corrosion, oil, dust, dirt—who knows whatever else," Owin said. "Unless you're dealing with handpicked atoms, there's always going to be some junk clinging on. If you really wanted to, you could throw in the chemical composition for all of these. But really, it's okay to just ignore them." He knocked his fists together again. "As long as you get the big stuff, you should be fine."

"So that's everything you need?" Zanna asked. Now that Owin had talked her through it, the table didn't seem nearly as messy as before. "Just those functions?"

"Just those functions for your I-beam," Owin clarified. "There are far more complex things out there in the universe. One of them's right in front of me."

She looked around the basement before she realized what he was referring to. "Me?"

"Quite." With a gesture, all the functions of the I-beam disappeared. "Humans are the most complicated things in the universe. Everything else, we've at least got a handle on, but humanity? Not a clue."

He reached into his pocket and took out something that looked like a handful of loose change. But the coins didn't have the markings of regular money. There were just lines of text stamped into the metal on one side and a symbol stamped on the other.

"What are those?"

"Blanks," Owin said. "Each of these carries a function drawn up by the Primer mathematicians back at the Society. It's a lot of work, drawing and testing and defending a decent function that'll work under all conditions. The really complex ones, they can take a lifetime to get right." He selected three coins—one brass, one pewter, one gold—and put the rest back in his pocket. "Here we go."

He rubbed his thumb over the brass coin, and a function bubbled to the surface. Even before Owin spread it out on the table, Zanna knew this one was different. The functions in her I-beam had been natural and full of messy numbers, like a homework problem she had to show her work for. This function created by the Primers was as clean and ordered as a typewritten page, with more variables and Greek symbols than numbers.

"Now we're going to see just how clever you are, Zanna Mayfield. Here's a puzzle. You want to keep people out of your house, but you and your grandfather need to be able to come and go as you please. And if someone comes over to visit, they should be able to come in, as well—as long as you let them in. How would you do it?"

Zanna clenched her tongue between her teeth. "Well, you could just put up a whole bunch of cameras. That's what businesses do."

"Businesses!" Owin let out a chuckle. "You're not a business, you're a Scientist. You've got all the laws of the universe at your disposal. Come on now!"

Zanna scrunched up her nose. Even if Owin hadn't meant anything by it, she had never taken well to being teased. "Then I'd put up a giant iron shield around the whole house. And it'd open only for me or my grandfather because we'd have a code."

"Better," Owin said. "But pretty obvious. What would your neighbors say? And what if you forgot the code?"

He laughed again, but Zanna just crossed her arms. Owin cut his laughter short and cleared his throat, continuing in a gentler tone. "It's a bit of a trick question. Yes, it is a shield, but instead of iron, it's air pressure—a thin shell of air pressure covering the entire house. And there *is* a code to get in. But it's not anything you or your grandfather will have to remember. It's already within you. You got registered by the Summation, correct?"

Zanna lifted her head. The sting of not being able to figure out Owin's puzzle still burned at her cheeks. "You mean that gold thing Dr. Mumble had?" she asked. "I remember. It stabbed me in the hand."

"Yes, it does that," Owin chuckled. "You see, when you gave the Summation a bit of your blood, you gave it your Self function. All those things that make Zanna Mayfield who she is—your childhood, your hopes and dreams, your regrets, and so on— that's what we call the Self function. It's one big, impossible, and wondrous function, and it's the most complicated thing in the universe. And since only *you* can be Zanna Mayfield, if we plug that function into the air-pressure shield, it'll let you pass through without a complaint."

He grinned, looking rather satisfied with himself. Zanna just sighed.

"Does that mean I have to get stabbed again?"

Owin's smile faded a little. "I'm afraid so. I can make some nitrous oxide if you like—it's a pretty basic anesthetic, but it'll help take the edge off."

"No," she said. "I'll manage."

He nodded and flipped the gold coin at her. "Put your thumb in the middle when you're ready, say your name, and give it a good squeeze. Have your grandfather do the same. And while you're up there, see if you can find a good piece of iron for a key. Something you can hold and won't easily lose."

She turned the coin over, amazed by the weight and luster. Holding it made Zanna feel a bit like a pirate, and she immediately pictured herself cackling and biting the coin between her teeth. Then she got serious again and pressed her thumb to the coin. "Zanna Mayfield."

Pain shot through her thumb. When she let go, she saw her bloody thumbprint on the face of the coin for a moment, and then it sank into the metal. After a few seconds, the coin was as pristine as before.

"See?" Owin said. "Not that bad at all."

She climbed the basement steps into the kitchen and savored the smell of meatballs and basil and slow-simmered tomato sauce. Pops had cleaned out his cast-iron frying pan and was wiping it with a towel. "Is Owin staying for dinner?" he asked.

"I don't know," Zanna said. She held out the coin. "He says you need to hold this and say your name. It's so you can get through the protective shell of air pressure he's putting around the house. It's going to stab you, though. It needs a drop of blood."

Pops set the frying pan on the counter. "Now you're pulling my leg."

"I'm serious!"

With a chuckle and a pat on her head, Pops picked up the coin. "I know you are. Impossible things, right?"

"You didn't even see the school," Zanna muttered. "I'll tell you all about it after dinner."

"I'm all ears," Pops said. He put his thumb on the coin. "Marco Gentino Zinola."

There was a moment of silence. Pops looked around the kitchen, as if he had expected lightning to jump from the walls. "Is that it?"

"Are you bleeding?"

He lifted his thumb. "Yeah, it bit me good."

"That's it, then." As he handed the coin back, Zanna's eyes fell on the frying pan he had set on the counter. "Can I borrow this too? Owin says he needs something metal to use for the key."

"Nana's frying pan?" Pops laid a protective hand on it. "This belonged to your great-great-grandmother, you know. When my mother came over—"

"You've told me, Pops," Zanna said. "He's not going to take it apart or anything. Promise."

With a bit of apprehension, Pops nodded. "Well, I did always mean to pass it on. But I didn't think it would be so soon."

"I'll give it back," Zanna said, picking up the heavy pan. "I'm just borrowing it for now."

"That's what they always say," he said, turning back to the stove where a pot of water was beginning to boil. "Well, hurry up down there, because dinner's almost ready. And ask that boy if he's staying."

She stomped down the basement steps and tossed the coin to Owin. "Here. And will this do for a key?"

He glanced at the frying pan. "Cast iron. 3% carbon content. Seasoned in animal fats and oils. Salt." He paused. "That's been in your family a long time, hasn't it?"

"How'd you know?"

"Because it's got a story." As he talked, a small hatch in the I-beam opened, and Owin slipped the gold coin inside. The metal closed around it, and the coin was completely lost to sight. "Ever had a teddy bear or a doll with a personality of its own? A lucky pair of socks? A piece of jewelry from your grandmother? That personality is a function you gave it. Just like gravity and electromagnetism. It makes that object *yours*. It's part of its existence."

The pewter coin was the last one left, and he pinched the function out of it, putting it on the table so Zanna could see.

Like the other Primer function, it was meticulously organized. "This is the key. It'll let you unlock the protective barrier. I made it analog so you don't have to deal with the raw theory, since you're still just a first year. Just hold out the frying pan and twist it, like you were unlocking a door. But you're going to have to help me."

"Me?" Zanna frowned. "Why can't you do it?"

"Because that's *your* frying pan," he said. "Here. Put it on the table."

She did, and he began unraveling all the different functions inside of it. Some looked familiar—the gravity, for instance, and the chemical composition, though it had a lot more carbon than the I-beam. The forces were simpler, which made sense, since it wasn't holding up a house. But then Owin pulled out something enormous that Zanna didn't recognize, and put it square in the middle of the table.

Zanna peered into it. At first, it seemed like it was just one massive scribble, like someone had covered an entire page while trying to get a pen to work. But as she kept staring, it began to make sense. *How* it made sense was a mystery in its own right, but somehow the knot of function began to unravel into a collection of memories and stories.

"This is the story of your frying pan," Owin said quietly as Zanna stared, unblinking. "And it makes all the other functions in it look like simple arithmetic. All those years of people using it, carrying it with them, passing it down from one generation to the next—it adds up. And I don't understand it. But I bet you do."

In the frying pan's function, she saw how every time Pops saw it appear, he knew a delicious hot dinner would soon follow. How the first time his mother let him cook with it, he burned his hand so badly it blistered for a week. How he knew, on the day his mother gave it to him, that she didn't think she would be around for much longer. The frying pan was dangerous, but always full of love.

Zanna pulled herself out of it and saw that Owin was grinning. "You get it now," he said.

"Yeah," she muttered. "Why didn't the I-beam have anything like this?"

"Because no one's given it one," Owin said. "People don't pass building materials down to the next generation. They don't give I-beams personalities and backstories. They barely even pay attention to them."

"That's true," Zanna said. "So that's why *you* can't use my frying pan?"

"Oh, I can use it," he said. "But like I said, I need your help. Stories are big, and you don't want to push against them. That's a good way to split your head open with a Splutter." He rapped his knuckles on the table. "So *you* grab the story, and I'll grab all the physics and chemistry, and we'll pull together. Then I'll put the key inside, and we'll close it up again. Okay?"

Zanna shook her head. "You lost me."

"Keep the function at the front of your mind," Owin said. "Keep your focus on it. Did Dr. Fitzie show you how to make theoretical shapes yet?"

Zanna made a sphere appear in her hand. "Ta-da."

"Do that," Owin said. "But instead of shapes, focus on everything you know about this frying pan. Everything it means to you and your grandfather. Think of it like planting a tree. You've got to move all the dirt out of the way first. So you scoop and scoop until you get an armful of dirt, and I'll get an armful, and together we'll move enough that we can plant our seed. Okay?"

"Okay," Zanna said. She looked at the mass of story and didn't understand at all how she was supposed to get her arms around it, metaphorically speaking. It wasn't as mysterious now as when she had first laid eyes on it, but that didn't mean she could *move* it. Out of the corner of her eye, she watched Owin gather up his functions, and tried to mimic his actions.

"You've got to hold the entire function in your mind," he said as he picked up the chemical composition. "Understand it completely."

She stared into the black scribbles that told of what this frying pan had meant to her family. It was a good meal, it was comfort, it was security, it was her heritage. Owin had finished with all the other functions. He was waiting, but at least he wasn't trying to give her any more advice. He just watched.

With her eyes closed, she felt out the edges of the story. She called on everything Pops had told her about the frying pan. The look in his eyes every time he had used it. The look just now as he gave it to her. Like the theoretical cubes she had drawn earlier that day, she imagined the frying pan moving down through generations, its story growing more complex with each set of hands it passed through. She put her arms around it all and tugged.

The story moved.

"I knew it," Owin muttered. He smiled at her. "You're quite the natural."

Heat flooded her face, and the story slipped, but she quickly got a hold of it once again. "Thanks," she said.

"Now the key," Owin said, lifting the small knot of function he had taken from the pewter coin.

Zanna imagined the story of her frying pan as an armful of dirt—like Owin had said—and she pulled it back to make room for the key.

"Okay. Let go now."

It was a strange feeling to let go of the frying pan's story. Both enormous and absolutely still. As if she had thrown a boulder into a lake and it had slipped beneath the water without a ripple. Owin picked up the frying pan and looked it over before handing it back to Zanna. "Want to go test it out?" he asked.

"Sure."

They met Pops at the top of the basement steps. "I was just coming down to say that dinner's ready," he said. "And you're staying, aren't you, Owin?"

Owin cleared his throat. "Actually, sir, I hadn't really planned on it—"

"So that's a yes. Excellent. I've already set you a place."

Owin tried to stammer an explanation, but Pops was already shuffling back to the kitchen.

Zanna gave Owin a nudge in the ribs. "You might as well go along with it. He's not going to let you leave hungry."

He sighed, but as they passed the kitchen on the way to the front door, he breathed in the smell of sizzling meatballs and homemade tomato sauce. "Well, I guess I can send a Particle saying that I'll be a little longer," he admitted.

In the foyer, Zanna opened the front door and peered out into the darkening neighborhood. Everything looked as it always had, and she tentatively put a hand out, feeling for the wall of air pressure. There was nothing there.

"Good. Looks like it recognizes you," Owin said. He put his hand out, and it stopped flat on the air. "And not me. Now try the key."

She lifted the frying pan and twisted it, just as she had done with the Weierstrass key. Owin's hand passed through.

"Splendid," he said. "And we check that it's breathing properly. Close it, please."

He stared at something inside his shield, calculating, before he nodded. "Good. One of the downsides to this barrier is that there's a risk of suffocation inside, since it's basically airtight.

So we have to add this system that lets fresh air in and bad air out. But don't worry, it's doing just fine. Can you open it again for a moment? I need to send a Particle that I'll be late."

He stepped out onto the front porch, taking from his pocket a crumpled gum wrapper. For a moment he just looked at it, and then he folded it into a small paper airplane and threw it high into the sky, where it disappeared. "There. Thanks."

Something about that simple act, or perhaps Owin's voice as he turned back to her, made Zanna's entire day catch up with her. In the whirlwind of finding out there was a strange woman trying to kidnap her, she had somehow forgotten about the entirely new world she had stumbled into. One where impossible things happened everywhere she looked. One where physics and math and chemistry were toys to be played around with. One where there were boys like Owin and Cedwick.

"Zanna?"

"Sorry," she said, a shiver running through her. "Just thinking."

Owin followed her line of sight out into the neighborhood and nodded. "It's okay. We're not going to let anything happen to you. You're safe."

CHAPTER EIGHT

IN THE MONTHS that followed, Zanna dug into her new world. Dr. Mumble hadn't been lying about science taking hard work and dedication—for the rest of September, Zanna did nothing but memorize everything from the periodic table to an endless list of physics formulas. There was a mountain of coursework, but the girls she met on the first day quickly banded together to form a study group.

"No, no, no, the derivative function describes how an object changes," Beatrice said for what must have been the tenth time that lunch period, showing once again how Dr. Fitzie had turned over a theoretical cube and peeled off the derivative function like a candy wrapper. Unlike the rest of them, Beatrice had the patience to muddle through Dr. Fitzie's overexcited lectures. "Like this."

"I don't see anything," Libby muttered, completely hopeless at mathematics.

"That's because the cube isn't changing right now," Beatrice said. To demonstrate, she moved the cube around, and the derivative she had peeled from it flickered in reply. "Does that make sense?"

"*That* makes sense," Libby said. "But I still don't see how you got that function in the first place."

Beatrice showed her for the eleventh time.

Around Halloween, the school brought out very realistic illusions of ghosts that drifted through the ancient Greek architecture and made Nora shiver every time they got close. In Physics, their class moved from memorization to manipulating simple gravity functions, and Libby took to these concrete exercises like a fish to water. The day after their first lesson, she brought a theoretical cube with a gravity function inside it to lunch and made it scoot around the café table and bop Amir on the nose.

The rest of them weren't as adept. It took Zanna a week of sleepless nights to hold the cube's coordinates and gravity in her mind at the same time, and it took Nora even longer.

The class that truly challenged everyone, however, was the one taught by Dr. Trout—the class called *Self*. Before their first class, Zanna had pictured Dr. Trout as a heavy European woman, but in reality she was bony and Middle Eastern, with an elegant head wrap of gold silk, traditional robes, and bushy silver eyebrows that could crease and lower in the most judgmental stare that Zanna had ever been on the receiving end of. But what really made Zanna sit up the first time she saw Dr. Trout was what the professor had carried with her.

Ever since Nora had explained that the object a Scientist carried around was called an *Iron* and that one day Zanna would have to pick her own, she had been keeping a mental catalogue. Nora strutted around with her fancy ruler. Owin had his shield. Lord Hemmington had the police badge on his lapel. Mr. Gunney kept a loaf pan atop his bus dashboard. Dr. Fitzie's was the mariner's telescope on her belt, Dr. Piccowitz carried a pocket watch, and Dr. Cheever had a horseshoe bent into a bracelet around his wrist.

Dr. Trout carried a baseball bat.

Not an aluminum bat, but an old wooden bat with a stained wrapping around the handle and more scars than a war hero. It looked more like a weapon than a piece of game equipment.

This wasn't the kind of bat you would take out for a pleasant game of ball in the springtime—this was the bat you used to beat someone's skull in.

"I have no doubt many of you will be uncomfortable with this class," she said on the first day of Self. Like all the classrooms, Dr. Trout's was ringed with worn marble columns and open to the sunny sky, yet Zanna always felt it was ten degrees colder than the rest of the school. "It involves no mathematics, no physics, and no chemistry. It will pursue avenues of reason and deduction that you may never have traveled before. It is entirely unlike any other class we offer. We will focus on one function and one function only. The one inside each and every one of you. The Self function."

Dr. Trout closed her eyes, and the entire classroom waited. She let her bat tap against her open palm with a hard, meaty sound, and then suddenly, spools and spools of theoretical functions began to pour out of her. They filled the entire room and showed no sign of stopping, growing so thick and dense that Zanna couldn't even see her hands.

"This is but a fraction," Dr. Trout said when the deluge stopped. "A fraction of my own function. Each of you has this and much more inside. Together, we will explore it. Together, we will learn it."

Zanna sifted her hands through the black soup that came up to her chest as Dr. Trout continued talking, thinking about Owin's gold coin that had taken a drop of her blood. Had all of this been in that tiny thumbprint?

Then it was gone. Dr. Trout pulled the function back into herself with a single gulp. For a moment, a glimpse of vulnerability crossed her professor's face, and then her expression turned to stone once more. "I know how many of my students think," she said. "So I offer this word of warning before we begin. There is no mastery to be sought here. No one has ever completely and fully understood their Self function, and no one ever will. It is not gravity, nor a derivative, nor a chemical composition that might be manipulated and changed. You are an infinity, and this class is but an approximation. Do not chase for it. You will only find frustration and madness."

The class was silent. Many of them were still staring at their hands like Zanna, amazed at the function that had been there moments ago. Even Cedwick, who was back to his cocky self today, seemed subdued.

"There is only one true assignment for this class," Dr. Trout continued. "By the end of the year, I will ask each of you to select an Iron. An object that belongs to you and will become your personal tool."

Nora raised her hand. "Dr. Trout?" She took out her stainless-steel ruler and held it aloft. "What if we have already selected our Iron?"

Dr. Trout barely spared her a glance. "Put it away, Ms. Elmsley," she said. "That's not your Iron."

"B-but, Dr. Trout," Nora said, faltering on the words slightly, "I've already considered every—"

"You have considered *toys*," Dr. Trout came back, her baseball bat swinging in demonstration. "A Scientist's Iron is not a pretty accessory. A Scientist's Iron is who she is, and you do not know that yet, Ms. Elmsley. None of you do. Without the proper Iron, you cannot hope to master more complex tasks such as Ironflight. Your knowledge and abilities will always be stunted, for you will always need to work against your improper Iron, instead of alongside it. It is not a light decision, and so I have allotted the entire year for you to search, experiment, and make your choice. I greatly encourage you to take it seriously."

Libby's earlier predictions about Self being a blow-off class couldn't have been further from the truth. While Dr. Trout didn't give grades and things for Zanna to memorize, she more than made up for it in the quantity and variety of readings she assigned. Some days it was books of poetry, some days it was psychological texts, some days it was dense philosophy, and on the worst days, it was all three. On top of that, there were the strange papers Zanna had to write. None of them were ever graded, but Dr. Trout collected them just the same. They ranged in topic from Zanna's first memory to the day she got her letter from St. Pommeroy's to the act of writing that very paper. The assignment made Zanna's brain turn inside out.

At least she wasn't alone in her suffering. Dr. Trout's unorthodox approach to teaching, along with the strange topic of Self, afflicted all the girls equally. Even Nora, who had become their resident guru on the ways of the Scientist world and culture, was at an uncharacteristic loss for explanation. "It's very important," she would say when Zanna flopped down in the bus seat next to her. But that was all she would say.

Yet despite all of that, Zanna couldn't really complain about her new life. For the first time, Zanna felt like she was exactly where she belonged, with friends who understood her and actually challenging schoolwork. And even though she wasn't getting any closer to figuring out what the strange woman might have wanted with her, or why she had warned her away from St. Pommeroy's in the first place, at least nobody had broken into her bedroom during the night again.

Then came the day she returned home and found a letter at her spot on the kitchen table. If its foreign stamp and telltale red-and-blue international-bordered envelope didn't give it away, the handwriting did. It was a letter from her father.

"Better check your spot," Pops said, even though she had

already sat down and picked up the envelope. When she opened it, another purple Philippine banknote fluttered out.

The letter was short and to the point, and Zanna read it so quickly she looped back around and went through it again before she spoke. "He's coming home for Christmas."

"Well!" Pops said, looking up from the celery stalks he was chopping into little bits. "That's exciting. I'm sure he'll want to know everything that you've been up to. You've been such a busy mouse this year."

"Yeah." The word fell flat, and she stuffed the letter back into its envelope. "I've got a lot of homework to do. Let me know when dinner is ready."

In her room, she flopped onto her bed and groaned. Back when she had been a little girl, a letter like this would have sent her whooping around the house, her Pops catching her and spinning her around in a rollicking polka. But he was too stiff now to dance like that, and she was too old to run around maniacally.

How would she explain everything that had happened since her father had left? The last time she'd seen him had been last spring, when he'd said he would only be doing the Southeast Asia flights for two, three months tops. Since then, she had discovered unknown powers and had enrolled at a school on a hidden floating island out over the Atlantic. She could fiddle with simple gravitational functions, name and theorize every natural and synthesized element on the periodic table, and make a theoretical object's coordinates change like dough in her hands. She had a pen that wrote in blood, a key that could break metallurgical illusions, and a frying pan that unlocked a wall of air pressure around her house. She had nearly been kidnapped and had a blade held to her throat. The Zanna who had said goodbye to her father only seven months ago was gone forever.

The next day at school, she went through Dr. Cheever's lesson on more advanced gravitational functions in silence. They were still using theoretical objects, but now instead of one gravitational function they had two, as if the cube was equidistant from a pair of massive bodies, and she had to hold both functions at the same time in order to properly manipulate it.

"Don't overthink it," Libby said. Nora could get her cube to move only in fits and starts, while Libby made hers ping-pong between its two functions like a yo-yo without a string. "You're trying to include way too much. You only need the important things."

"Everything is important," Nora said. Her cube scooted half a centimeter across the ancient marble table. "The tiniest function can change an object's probability. Everything has to be considered."

"You'll be dead before you finish considering everything," Libby said. She lacked Beatrice's infinite patience for teaching others and instead amused herself with reshaping her cube while Nora continued to struggle. "Ugh," Libby complained. "When do we get real objects?"

"In time," Nora said. "They want to make sure we're ready for it. It's a major step from theory to practical. We've barely started molecular structure."

"But I don't need to know all the molecular structures," Libby said, tiring of her cube and pushing it away. "Just one. What about hydrogen gas? That's dead simple." As if to prove it, she drew the diatomic molecule of hydrogen gas. "There. Two protons, two electrons, covalent bond. Done and done."

"Hydrogen's explosive," Beatrice said. "They probably want to make sure we're safe."

"We're not *igniting* it," Libby said. "We're manipulating it."

"There is still the risk of ignition," Nora said testily.

"Then give us helium," Libby argued, her Southern drawl getting a bit more pronounced as her frustration grew. "That ain't going to ignite. It's a noble gas."

"It is still invisible," Nora said. She fixed a curl of dark hair that had gotten out of line before she clarified her previous statement. "At least at standard temperature and pressure."

"Lithium, beryllium, boron, carbon," Libby rattled off. "Those are all solid. Take any one of 'em."

Zanna tuned out the girls, idly playing with the coordinates of her cube and poking holes through it with her finger. Cedwick was a few tables down with Amir, Tyson, and a Spaniard named Benito, though the group seemed to be largely ignoring him. Amir and Tyson were making their cubes sumo wrestle.

Ever since Zanna had landed Cedwick in detention and then caught him crying in the limousine, he had steered clear of her, which she took as a blessing. It made Mathematics a little awkward, though, since Dr. Fitzie kept insisting they group up in their original triangles.

"Zanna?" Beatrice's large brown eyes were full of concern. "Are you okay?"

"Huh?" Zanna had poked so many holes in her cube it looked like Swiss cheese. "Yeah. I'm fine."

Beatrice frowned, not fooled at all by the halfhearted lie, so Zanna caved. "I got a letter from my dad yesterday. He's coming back for the holidays."

"Well that's exciting!" Beatrice said, but at Zanna's expression, she dialed back her excitement a bit. "Isn't it?"

"It is," Zanna said, shrugging. "It should be. I don't know. So much has happened since I last saw him."

"What does he do?" Libby asked.

"He's a pilot," Zanna said. She made her Swiss-cheese finger holes close up and then squashed her cube out like jelly. "Mostly flights in the southern hemisphere. China and Australia and India, that area."

"And they don't let him come home except for the holidays?" Libby asked. "What kind of evil airline does he work for?"

"They're going through a lot," Zanna said, more down to her squashed cube than to any of the girls. "The airline isn't doing too well, so he's had to pick up some extra flights. And you know, it's a big hassle to fly halfway around the world. He travels so much already."

"*You* travel out into the middle of the Atlantic every day," Libby pointed out.

"That is hardly a fair comparison," Nora admonished. "That's Scientific travel."

"So what are you worried about?" Beatrice's Italian accent softened the edges of her words, making her gentle voice even gentler. She pushed her cube aside in order to give Zanna her undivided attention. "That he's not going to recognize you?"

"I don't really know," Zanna muttered. She scraped her smushed cube back together like cookie dough. "I guess just . . . explaining everything."

"About being a Scientist?"

Zanna fidgeted around the question. "I haven't told him anything. At all. We don't . . . talk."

"He doesn't have to understand it," Libby said. "I mean, my dad doesn't really understand science, either. He just knows I go to this special school for smart kids. You don't have to tell him about—" she gestured to the cubes and the ancient class-room— "gravitational functions and everything."

Zanna shook her head. "No, I mean—" A groan escaped her. "I don't know. Forget it."

"Okay," Beatrice said quietly, ever respectful of Zanna's wishes.

"We're only trying to help," Libby said. With a quick shrug of her shoulders, she picked up her theoretical cube and began toying around with its gravitational functions again, seeing how fast she could make it spin. "So when do you think they're finally going to give us real objects?"

Nora's exasperated sigh said everything.

Zanna moved listlessly through the rest of Physics class and lunch, eating even slower than Nora and only answering questions directly put to her. The girls all tried to cheer her up in their different ways. Nora distracted her with a story of how the Scientists had stolen the castle that made up the west wing of the school from a French countryside. Libby and Amir—who were an inseparable couple now, at the expense of Nora's patience—told her about the prank they were going to pull on Dr. Piccowitz that Friday. Beatrice said nothing, but she gave Zanna's hand a comforting squeeze, which worked a little, but nothing really lifted the fog hanging around her.

"Books away," Dr. Trout said when they entered Self that afternoon. A murmur rose from the class, excited and a little hopeful, but Dr. Trout swatted it down quickly. "Don't get your hopes up," she said. "Today we will be diving into our own functions. It will not be fun."

Zanna was sure that the woman's gaze lingered on her for an extra moment, as if the professor could see the fog Zanna felt herself wallowing around in. It was only a second, but Zanna had to avert her eyes almost immediately. Her professor's piercing gaze was intimidating.

"Absolute silence," Dr. Trout said, and the classroom went still. All Zanna heard was the blood in her ears and the clear, demanding voice of Dr. Trout. "Eyes closed."

Amir and Tyson giggled a little, and Dr. Trout shushed them angrily. "Completely shut," the professor said. "Turn your thoughts inward. You are a box. Dig into it. Search for the bottom."

Zanna sighed and tried to do as her teacher instructed. She imagined a doofy-looking cardboard box named Zanna filled with functions she could dig through, and amazingly, it began to work. Functions that she knew, or at least could guess at, drifted up into view. The tangle of gravity working on her. The simple chemical compounds of oxygen, carbon dioxide, and water. Stresses from her weight pressing down in the chair, and the chair pressing back, from her clothes and her shoes and the pencil she had absentmindedly tucked under her velvet bonnet in Chemistry. The lunch digesting in her stomach.

Zanna went deeper. Under the nameable functions at the top came a million smaller things, tiny and inscrutable and working to keep her alive. Every once in a while, she glimpsed something she recognized from Biology, something that was cellular reproduction or DNA or part of the Krebs cycle. It was dense down here, and yet, Dr. Trout encouraged them to keep digging, to keep sinking lower and lower. "Find the bottom," she said. "Find the foundation of yourself."

Then Zanna broke through, and the sight took her breath away. For what she saw had no horizon and no edge. It was a writhing, tangled, unreadable black planet of function. This was her—Zanna Mayfield—spelled out in unflinching mathematical notation.

She jerked away from it like a red-hot piece of iron and opened her eyes. Dr. Trout was there, staring at her. "Close your eyes, Ms. Mayfield," she said. "I said this would not be fun."

"But—"

"Close your eyes." Her voice brokered no arguments.

Zanna did as she was told and reluctantly returned to the planet of function. Dr. Trout's hypnotizing voice continued in the background, and Zanna tentatively looked over the tangle of herself, still afraid of the sight. Simple things began to appear out of the jumble, like shapes materializing out of a fog. Her name, her friends, her grandfather and five uncles, her love of puzzles, her fear of heights. It was exhilarating to feel parts of her Self click into place, like a good crack of the knuckles. So exhilarating that she forgot Dr. Trout's warning that this would not be fun.

She looked closer, and the functions shaped themselves into a memory.

It had been five years after Zanna's mother had died giving birth to her, and her father had disappeared into his pilot work. Then the invitation had come for Zanna to take a flight with him. He wanted to show her the world.

Halfway through the flight, he brought her up to the cockpit. How clearly she remembered his arm, heavily tanned and sporting an enormous silver wristwatch, as he pointed through the clouds at the scene below them. She had clung to his neck and refused to look.

"Come on, Zanna," her father said, using his free hand to force her to look out the windshield. "Take a look. Look at the Earth there. Isn't it beautiful?"

She squirmed and shied away. "I want to go back."

"No, you don't. You want to stay up here."

"No." She pulled at his airline tie. "I'm scared."

"I can take her," one of the other men in the cockpit offered.

"Nonsense!" her father laughed. He pried her fingers off his tie and turned her head again. "No daughter of mine is going to be afraid of heights! Come on now, Zanna, see? We're perfectly safe. Would I let you fall?"

But he had let her fall. He let her fall every time he wasn't there. No pilot worked for months on end without a single day off to visit his daughter, no matter how badly the airline was doing. Zanna had always known, even when she was only five, but down in her Self function, it was spelled out in lines of cold logic. Her father wanted nothing to do with her.

"I CAN'T!" Cedwick's shout jolted her back to the classroom in an instant. It jolted the rest of the class, as well. In a flurry, Dr. Trout descended on the English boy, covering both of them with a privacy illusion that obscured anything they might be talking about. Whispers sprung up at once. Amir snickered, and Libby elbowed him a bit roughly. Poor Beatrice looked almost distraught with concern.

The veil lifted. Cedwick sat low in his chair, eyes focused on an empty space of air, and Dr. Trout cleared her throat sharply. "I believe we're ready for some discussion," she said, silencing the class. Her eyes landed on Amir, who was still shaking a little with laughter. "Mr. Al-Remmul, thank you for volunteering. What did you see in your Self function?"

Amir scratched at his nose. "Me playing in a band."

Dr. Trout shook her head disapprovingly. "Ms. Wilder?"

"I didn't see anything," Libby said. "Maybe my dogs?"

This only made Dr. Trout shake her head even more. "Ms. Mayfield?"

Zanna considered telling Dr. Trout that she had seen her father and the day he had shown her what the world looked like, but then she decided against it. Not with everyone in the class listening. Especially not with Cedwick in earshot. "A planet," Zanna said, which wasn't really a lie.

But it wasn't what Dr. Trout had been looking for, either, and her Self professor let out a deep sigh. "Well, that is not surprising," she said. "It seems Mr. Hemmington is the only one interested in learning about his Self. So for the rest of you, spend half an hour every day for the next two weeks in meditation, and write me a paper about what you see." Her eyebrows lowered. "I expect it to be substantial."

There wasn't any sort of outcry—Zanna and the rest of them had learned in the first week that complaining only made Dr. Trout add more work—but after the bell rang, it was a different story. "Lousy Cedwick," Libby grumbled. "I can't believe he got out of those dumb meditation exercises."

"You should have told Dr. Trout what you saw then," Nora scolded her. "You only have yourself to blame."

"And what did *you* see?" Libby said, turning on her at once. "Feel like sharing it?" When Nora had nothing to say in return, Libby just nodded. "That's what I thought."

Zanna kept quiet. Cedwick's outburst and the memory of her father kept playing over and over, making her more and more nauseous with each repeat.

On the bus ride home, she threw up again.

CHAPTER NINE

"I HAVE FIGURED it out!" Nora started talking the moment Zanna sat down on the bus, her eyes glittering with excitement. "I've been considering several hypotheses to your problem. Your father, I mean. And last night, I found your solution. Let's throw him a party to welcome him back! That way we can be there for moral support. Safety in numbers. It's almost guaranteed!"

"Hang on," Zanna said through a wide and slow yawn. Thanks to Dr. Trout's meditation exercises, she had to spend half an hour every night thinking about her father and how he had abandoned her, with nothing to show for it but bad dreams. Fortunately, this was the last day she had to do them. "Can you say everything again?"

Nora spelled it out with only a small hint of frustration. "I *said*, let's throw a party for your father."

"A party?"

"Yes. We will need streamers. And balloons."

"I know what a party is," Zanna said. "I just—why?"

"So you don't have to face your dad alone," Nora said, her voice dropping a bit. "So we can be there with you."

"Face him alone?" Zanna said. "He's my father, not an executioner."

"You don't like it?" Nora asked, a tinge of sadness creeping into her voice. "It's a perfect plan. I thought through every possibility. I was going to bring my dehumidifier to prove that you're telling the truth—"

"No, I think it'll work," Zanna said quickly. Her head felt like a drawer someone had stuffed too many socks into and was trying to slam closed. "I just need to think."

There was something different about Dr. Fitzie when they walked into their sunny Mathematics classroom that morning. Her teacher always looked a little overjoyed at everything, but this morning, she looked fit to explode. "Don't sit down!" she snapped at Tyson when he began to put his backpack on one of the ancient marble tables. "We're going on an adventure today!"

Libby's eyebrows raised in anticipation.

"Yes, yes, let me just make sure everyone is here," Dr. Fitzie said, quickly counting heads. "Fantastic! Now, if you will follow me."

They trailed out into the corridor, following Dr. Fitzie into the castle wing of the school. She wouldn't answer any questions about where they were going, but she did keep up a running commentary on everything they passed. Their journey took them through the English garden of the administration tower, down a short Baroque hallway, and through a set of paneled doors into what had been the atrium of an opera house. Two sweeping staircases climbed up to a central door of bright-yellow metal that resembled the one Zanna had seen in Dr. Mumble's office.

Beatrice gasped, pointing upward, and Zanna followed her gaze, her own mouth falling open at the sight. An enormous pendulum of silver and crystal glass swung in a lazy and unceasing arc, its plumb coming just inches from the wall on either side. Golden light swept across the atrium with each swing. It made Zanna feel as if she were watching days go by, each pass of the pendulum another sunrise and sunset dashing over the landscape.

Dr. Fitzie climbed the staircase, touched the slab of golden metal, and spoke her name in a clear voice. At once, the doors shot open with a hush of displaced air.

"Don't dawdle now!" Dr. Fitzie said, beckoning to them. "Shake a leg!"

The room beyond was endless. Zanna recognized it at once, for she had seen it from the air many times. They were in the Gothic cathedral on the western side of the school. No other building the Scientists had stolen was this big. Windows taller and wider than Zanna's house looked out on the blue cloudless sky, hitting Zanna with a punch of unease. One of the school's orbiting islands was slowly passing by. She could almost fit the entire island in the window frame.

Chandeliers hung at intervals, casting shimmering light on the floor's geometric-patterned dark-lacquered wood. She would have called it a grand royal ballroom, except that instead of dancers on the floor it was all strange machinery. There were big glass jars she could have climbed inside, skinny distillation towers, electrical engines churning in a steady rhythm, banks of lasers scattering their rays over a drafting table, and even something off in a corner that might have been a nuclear reactor. Everyone crowded at the entrance, afraid to cross the threshold into the realm of the machines.

"Well!" Dr. Fitzie said, waving her hand at the entire scene. "What do you think of our Laboratory?"

The class gawked. One by one they filtered in. Dr. Cheever was waiting just around the side of a bank of Van de Graaff generators, his horseshoe iron reshaped into an uncomfortable-looking lawn chair. "Spread out! That's it," he said, standing up and flashing his dazzling smile at them. He had cleared out the space around a machine that looked like a giant fishbowl on a block of iron.

"Where's Simon?" Dr. Fitzie asked as she looked over the fishbowl machine and tapped on its thick glass.

"Take a wild guess," Dr. Cheever said. "He's running late."

An awkward minute passed with the teachers fiddling with the machine and refusing to explain what they were doing in there, and then Zanna heard someone coming up the staircase. Dr. Piccowitz stood in the doorway, looking a bit sheepish. "H-Hullo," he said.

"Any longer, and we would have started without you!" Dr. Fitzie said.

"Sorry, sorry," Dr. Piccowitz muttered. In his hands was a block of carbon, which he put into the fishbowl at the top of the machine before manipulating the glass so it was a seamless sphere. The machine buzzed to life with a warm *purr*.

"Well," Dr. Fitzie said, "now that we're all here—"

Dr. Cheever cleared his throat. "Hey, hey, hey. Slow down there, Maru. I believe it's my turn this year."

"Nonsense," Dr. Fitzie said. "You did it year before last."

"No, that was me," Dr. Piccowitz said, making skittish rat movements with his fingers. "Me, Andrew, you, me, Andrew, you. I did it last year. It's his turn."

Dr. Fitzie frowned, but she apparently knew she had been caught and stepped back. Dr. Cheever took a deep breath, relishing the moment.

"Welcome," he said, putting a hand on the fishbowl machine. "You're all mighty clever sorts, so I'm guessing you've already figured out why we're here. Today, we're taking our first step out of the realm of the theoretical and into the real. Today is the day we put what we've been learning for the past three and a half months into practice."

Zanna could almost feel the excitement radiating off Libby.

"One at a time, you'll come up to the vacuum chamber," Dr.

Cheever said, patting the fishbowl's thick glass. "Our object for manipulation is a graphite cube. Everyone will get six minutes in front of the cube. We will call you up according to your given name in alphabetical order. While you wait, I highly recommend that you brush up on your gravitational functions."

"Don't forget your coordinates!" Dr. Fitzie sang.

"Shh," Dr. Piccowitz said. Though Zanna could have sworn she saw him mouth, "And your carbon too."

"So, first up," Dr. Cheever said, consulting something in his Iron, "Adam Reughel."

Zanna sighed as a stocky boy from the Netherlands stepped up to the fishbowl. Alphabetical order was the bane of her existence. There had been a year in elementary school when she had shared a class with a boy named Zebediah, and for once, she hadn't been the one always bringing up the rear. But then Zebediah had moved away, and her vacation was over.

"This place is like a museum of mad science," Libby muttered.

At the urging of Dr. Fitzie, the class broke into small knots of threes and fours to cram on the functions of a graphite cube. The girls formed a circle from a few folding metal chairs Dr. Cheever had scattered around the room. "What do they need all this equipment for anyways? I mean, that's obviously a vacuum pump." Libby pointed at the fishbowl. "Why bother? It's not like air is super complicated. Why not just manipulate it out of the chamber instead of having a machine do it?"

"Because we're thieves, babe," Amir said, swaggering over and draping his arms over Libby, who seemed less than thrilled at seeing him. "And we're lazy. Why build anything when we can just take what we want from the CG?"

Nora took off her glasses to pinch the bridge of her nose, but before she could put together a reply, Dr. Cheever called out, "Amir Al-Remmul? It's your turn."

Zanna had only half been watching Adam at the fishbowl, but from the dejected way he walked back to his friends, she knew that he had failed.

"Kiss for good luck?" Amir asked, leaning over. Libby smashed an open hand into his face.

"Do me a favor and don't invite him to your party," she muttered to Zanna as they watched Amir walk up to the fishbowl and put his hands on the glass. "It's not going to last. I'm going to break up with him later today. He's way too clingy."

"*Finally*," Nora sighed.

"My party?" Zanna asked, whipping around to Nora. "Wait a minute! I never agreed to that!"

"There's no need. I have everything figured out," Nora said, her calm voice a vast contrast to Zanna's sharp shriek. "It will be the first weekend of Christmas break. I'll tell my parents to pick everyone up and drop them off at your house. Though, if Amir's not coming, we'll have to leave a bit earlier in order to get Beatrice. I had counted on her getting a ride—"

"That's not what I mean!" Zanna said, growing frenzied. "I told you I had to think about it! You can't just go telling people—"

"Excuse me!"

They all jumped at the sound of Beatrice's voice. The normally quiet girl glared up at them, her Chemistry book open on her lap.

"I am trying to study here," she snapped. Her words were polite, but the tone was anything but. "So if you please, be quiet or go somewhere else."

The girls were speechless. Beatrice went back to her studying, and ashamed, they pulled out their books, as well. Zanna opened her Chemistry book to refresh her memory on hexagonal lattice structures, but as she flipped through the pages, her focus wandered. Nora's idea *was* a good one. It would be really nice to have the other girls around when she confronted her father. Nora could explain everything about the Scientific world, Libby could give a practical demonstration, and Beatrice could be moral support. And Pops would agree to host the party in an instant. He had been asking about Zanna's new friends almost every day since she'd started school.

"Beatrice Scotti," Dr. Cheever said. "Your turn."

Beatrice closed her book, straightened her skirt, and strode purposefully across the open floor of the Laboratory. She went right up to the vacuum chamber, put her hands on her hips, and focused on the graphite cube with a stare so intense that Zanna was surprised it didn't catch fire.

That simple action pulled something at the bottom of Zanna's brain, and the last two weeks unraveled. If Beatrice, who rarely said more than three sentences in a row, could be that fearless, then so could Zanna. For fourteen years Zanna had made excuses for her father. It was time to set things straight.

She scooted her chair over an inch toward Nora. "I'm sorry," she whispered. "It *is* a good idea."

"Of course it is. I made sure of it," Nora said with a tinge of haughtiness. But she smiled as she said it. "So that's a yes?"

"I have to check with my grandfather," Zanna said. "But I'm sure he won't mind."

"Splendid," Nora said. The excitement came back into her brown eyes. "So I have a couple of different options for the menu."

"Benito Torres?" Dr. Cheever called out. "It's your turn."

Zanna and Nora looked up. "Wait!" Zanna said. "I missed it! Did she—"

But the way Beatrice walked back to them answered her question. The girl's shoulders slumped, and she sank into her chair with a heavy sigh. "I had everything," she said. She didn't sound sad about it. More like puzzled. "The coordinates and composition and gravity. I had it."

"You'll get it next time," Nora said. "I know you will."

"Sorry for yelling at you guys earlier," she murmured. "But you were really loud."

"Yeah, I bet we were," Libby said with a little self-deprecating smirk. "Come over here and explain how these coordinates work again. You know how I feel about math."

The next couple of students all failed to move the block, and then Cedwick's name was called. He stood in front of the vacuum chamber with his hands in his pockets, eyes fixed on the dull black cube inside like he had done all this before.

"You think he's going to move it?" Zanna asked, leaning over to Nora.

The girl took off her glasses and polished them with a cloth, even though they were already spotless. "I hypothesize he's got the best chance of moving it."

"Don't tell me you changed your mind about him," Libby said, picking up on their conversation. Zanna didn't answer. There was still part of her that wanted to see snippy, arrogant Cedwick get put in his place. But the rest of her remembered the limousine and his outburst in Self and the way the rest of the class ignored him. And *that* part wanted the universe to cut him a break.

Cedwick focused on the cube, and nothing happened. Zanna strained her eyes, afraid that the moment she blinked would be the moment the graphite moved. Had that been something? It seemed to flicker a little through the thick glass. Or perhaps her eyes were playing tricks.

He shifted his stance, taking his hands out of his pockets and curling them into fists. The corners of his lips snarled. All the other students who had been chatting and preparing for their own trial stopped one by one, looking up to see why the air had gone so cold. The only sound in the Laboratory was the vacuum pump and the low, strained, animal growl of Cedwick.

But the graphite refused to budge.

"That's enough, Mr. Hemmington," Dr. Piccowitz said after six minutes, when it became apparent that nothing was going to happen. "Let's move along."

"No." Cedwick didn't even break his gaze. "I can do this. Give me more time."

"There are many after you who deserve a shot, too," Dr. Fitzie said. "You will get another chance."

She took a step toward him.

"No!" Cedwick roared. "I can do this!"

The Splutter was soundless, and yet Zanna felt it clearly—like someone had drilled a hole right into her brain. It was the pain of seeing something completely *wrong*, something contradictory and paradoxical and only held apart by Cedwick's stubborn will. He grabbed hold of the carbon atoms and their hexagonal lattice and moved them, but the coordinates remained the same, the block still resting on the floor of the vacuum chamber. It was an ugly shift of impossible flickering, the graphite torn between its natural function and Cedwick, and in the end the natural functions won.

Cedwick screamed a raw, animal scream and fell to the floor, hands over his eyes, feet kicking. Zanna felt it, as well, as a pain in her temples—like she had gotten an eyeful of direct sunlight. The whole class groaned in dull agony, the Splutter having hit everyone watching, but no one seemed that worse for wear. Cedwick, however, could not stop whimpering. Blood leaked from his ear.

"I'll take him," Dr. Fitzie said softly to the other teachers. She gently lifted the boy from the Laboratory floor and helped him get to his feet. "You'll be fine." Wordlessly, the class shifted to make an aisle, and she took him out of the Laboratory.

The rest of the experiment continued in a more subdued fashion. Libby and Nora had their chance at the vacuum chamber, and they both failed to make the graphite block move. Libby came back furious and swearing up a blue streak. Dr. Fitzie returned halfway through Nora's attempt and announced that Cedwick would be fine. "Just a little headache, that's all," she said brightly. "He'll be back in time for lunch, I should think!"

But the rest of the class didn't seem to share her enthusiasm. The exercise had gone from a difficult but enjoyable challenge to a serious danger. Zanna saw fear in every student who followed Cedwick. She saw it in her own hands.

"Zanna Mayfield?" Dr. Cheever said. "And I believe that will be everybody."

She stood. Close up, the vacuum chamber was bigger than she had expected. She felt the eyes of the entire class on her as she wiped a patch clean on the dusty glass with the sleeve of her black sweater. After all, there was no reason for the rest of the class to keep studying. They had had their chance. All there was to do now was to watch those saps stuck at the end of the alphabet.

Zanna stared down at the graphite cube, and its functions began to come to her. Coordinates—a perfect cube measuring one foot on all sides. No way was this a natural object. Her eyes lifted to Dr. Piccowitz. Had he made this? Her disheveled, harried, babbling Chemistry teacher had made this perfect cube?

No time to worry about that now. She dug into its other functions. Its gravity was complex, as she had expected. She started sorting through it as Owin had shown her, discarding the negligible parts. Then came the carbon atoms that made up the hexagonal lattice sheets of graphite. What else was there?

The force as the weight of the graphite block pressed down on the bottom of the vacuum chamber and the chamber pressed back. No air pressure, because all the air had been pumped out. Friction from its resting position on the bottom of the chamber—but they hadn't covered friction yet. Did that mean she could safely ignore it? What if she did and ended up Spluttering? And what about magnetism, light, heat? That was all advanced stuff. Zanna couldn't even find those functions, even though she knew they had to be in there somewhere.

She shook her head and let her fingers flex a little. Her teachers wouldn't set her up for failure. Everything she needed to move this graphite block had already been given to her. A one-foot-by-one-foot-by-one-foot cube. Earth's gravitational pull a little less due to the school being high in the atmosphere. Carbon had six electrons, six protons, and six neutrons. Graphite was carbon arranged in hexagonal sheets stacked one atop another.

But something still held it. Some function glued it to its natural state, and Zanna couldn't make it budge, no matter how hard she tried. Could Dr. Piccowitz have put in a few carbon isotopes—carbon atoms with more than the usual number of neutrons? No, he wouldn't do that. They hadn't covered isotopes yet. She only really knew about them because Nora had explained them to her.

Then it came to her. What Owin had told her as he looked over her frying pan about how each of the pan's owners had bestowed a little personality to it. Whether they knew it or not—and Zanna doubted they did—everyone from her great-great-grandmother on down to herself had dipped into their Self function and shared a little with the frying pan. And her class had done the same to the graphite.

She saw it now. Not as strong as the function Owin had pulled out of her frying pan but definitely there, covering all the other functions like a thin slick of oil. Anger, certainly. Frustration and embarrassment. Fear after seeing what had happened to Cedwick. It was a stubborn block of graphite who laughed at their attempts to move it. It was a joke by the teachers. It was a danger.

Now Zanna added in the functions she already knew. Mass, gravity, chemical composition, coordinates. All of them swam in her head, and she tried to see them not as separate functions but as a complete whole. Not as different aspects of a graphite cube but as the cube itself. Its entire existence. Its function.

She would make it work.

The bell rang loud and clear and broke her concentration. A dejected sigh ran through the class as they began to pack up. "Good work today, all of you!" Dr. Cheever said, joining the other teachers in a round of applause that nobody else picked up. "No homework tonight! We'll see you all tomorrow!"

"Wait!" Zanna cried as Dr. Fitzie waved her hand at the vacuum chamber, making the air return and opening a hole in the glass so Dr. Piccowitz could retrieve his graphite. "Give me more time. I can do it! I know I can!"

"There'll be more chances, don't worry," Dr. Fitzie said. As the graphite block slipped through the hole in the glass, she closed the chamber up and slid it back among the other machinery. "Between you and me, it's quite okay to not get it the first time. Why, it took me nearly three months to get so much as a twitch!"

"No, I had it!" Zanna pleaded. "The function—the story. That's what the problem was, right? That's why no one else could move it."

"We fail for all sorts of different reasons," Dr. Fitzie said. The vacuum was back in its place now, and she turned her full attention to Zanna. "But you've learned, haven't you? You're smarter now than this morning."

"That's not the same! Just give me another minute!"

Dr. Fitzie clucked her tongue. "I think you'll find it's quite the same. You'll get your 'another minute' soon. Be ready for that one."

CHAPTER TEN

THE FAILURE OF the morning hung over them for the rest of the school day. At lunch the girls spoke little, except for Libby, who was still complaining about blowing her chance at real manipulation. Occasionally, she stopped to complain about Amir, and then went back to their morning in the Laboratory.

It was cold and blustery as Zanna stared blankly out over the rippling grass toward one of St. Pommeroy's many clock towers. It was short and made out of graceful copper wiring, the pale-green rust making it look like an arrogant growth of ivy rising above its fellow plants. A clever Scientist had installed a magnifying illusion on its clock face at some point in the past so that even though it stood a fair distance away, Zanna could read it without squinting. It told her it would be a long time before the bell rang.

"I'll see you guys in Self," she said suddenly, collecting her trash and getting up from the table.

"Where are you off to?" Libby demanded.

"Just the library."

" 'Just the library'?" Libby repeated, her eyes narrow.

"Can't you tell that she wants to be alone?" Beatrice said. Then, to Zanna, "We'll see you in Self."

Zanna ducked her head and hurried away. Because Libby was right. She wasn't going to the library. As soon as she left the cafeteria, she took a left through the center of the school. As she kept going west, she entered the castle wing and glanced at the suits of armor and sconces on the walls. She was half-expecting to hear Mrs. Appernathy's gruff Scottish voice from one of them, telling Zanna that she wasn't supposed to be wandering the halls during lunch. But no one stopped her.

"Mrs. Appernathy?" Zanna asked one of the wall sconces.

It came to life a few seconds later, separating from the wall and floating down to her. "What is it?" the illusionary torch asked. "Lost?"

"I'm looking for the nurse," Zanna said.

"Ah. Feeling sick?" The sconce looked her over. At least, that's what Zanna thought it did. It was hard to tell. "Come on, girlie. I'll show you the way."

Mrs. Appernathy led Zanna through the castle wing and toward the administration tower. Unlike that morning, when Dr. Fitzie had taken them to the Laboratory, they turned north-ward instead of south at the English garden and into a small plaza with a statue of a man with a staff holding a hand out, as if offering assistance. Beyond that was a small, humble building and then sky.

Zanna gulped. In the central Greek classrooms, it was easy to forget that St. Pommeroy's was actually floating high above the ocean in a giant iron bowl. The nurse's cottage, however, sat at the very edge. Only a small yard with cherry trees and a pair of teatime chairs stood between the small house and the maw of a cold December sea.

"There you go," Mrs. Appernathy said. Even when she was trying to be comforting, her voice rumbled like a mama bear. "Mrs. Turnbuckle will fix you right up."

A cheery voice called out when she knocked on the cottage door. Inside was warm and cozy, with a thick wool rug spread across the floor and a fire crackling in the hearth. The chairs around the waiting room were rustic and solid, inviting her to sink into their cushions and put her feet up.

"Yes, my dear?" the nurse said in a pleasant British countryside accent. She was plump in a comforting, grandmotherly way, with hair to rival Dr. Fitzie's in volume. As Zanna opened her mouth to speak, a silver and orange cat poked its head out from behind the woman's white curls. It regarded Zanna with placid black eyes before climbing across the desk in a silky, unhurried walk to get a better look at the girl who had wandered into its house.

"I—one of my friends was brought in here," Zanna said as the cat looked her up and down. "Cedwick Hemmington. We were in the Laboratory—"

"He's quite the popular one, isn't he?" Mrs. Turnbuckle said without waiting for an answer. "Yes, a small Splutter. He's going to be just fine. I'll tell him you stopped by. He'll be glad to know he's got such wonderful friends."

"I was actually hoping to talk to him," Zanna said. The cat stretched its head out toward her, but she couldn't tell if it was looking for a pet or getting closer to bite her. She shrank back a bit. "I have to tell him something."

"Ah," Mrs. Turnbuckle said, a bit of a smile appearing on her red lips. "Well, he's already got a visitor. But I'll ask. What's your name, dear?"

"Zanna. Zanna Mayfield."

At the snap of the nurse's fingers, a marble rose up from behind her desk, just like Zanna had seen Mr. Tinders do. But instead of just zipping it off, the nurse turned the smooth metal ball into a silver kitten and sent it scurrying off into the cottage with a wave of her hand. When it returned, it scampered up the woman's arm and nuzzled at her ear, whispering Cedwick's reply. Her face brightened. "He said it's okay. Go through that door and down the hallway. Room 7."

"Thank you," Zanna said.

She found the room and knocked softly on the door before entering. Cedwick sat up among the plush pillows of his bed, having thrown back the covers. His ear was bandaged with a wrap of gauze that went under his chin and around his head. A small table with his lunch on it stood over his lap, but it didn't look like he had eaten much. His eyes were wet and red.

There were two other people in the room with him, and Zanna jumped a bit in surprise. Even though Mrs. Turnbuckle had plainly said that Cedwick already had visitors, the fact hadn't quite registered with her. Sitting at his bedside were Owin and Lord Hemmington.

"Why, hello!" Owin said, getting up to offer her his seat. "Come to see my little brother?"

Zanna froze in the doorway. "Sorry, I . . . I didn't know—"

"No, you're not interrupting anything," Owin said. He glanced over at his father, who seemed more interested in the small ghostly thing on his shoulder than anything else in the room. It must have been a Particle with a message of some sort, for he wore the astute expression of someone listening very intently, even though Zanna heard nothing. "I think we were actually leaving soon."

Lord Hemmington straightened, dismissing the tissue of shimmering metal with a brief nod, and noticed Zanna for the first time. "Ah, Ms. Mayfield. Good to see you."

"Hello," she said. Then, on a bold impulse, she asked, "Any news?"

Lord Hemmington had been conferring with Owin, but at Zanna's question, he turned back. "It is a small Splutter. Cedwick will heal."

"I meant about the woman who tried to stop me from coming to St. Pommeroy's," she said.

"Ah, your would-be kidnapper," Lord Hemmington said with a *harrumph* in his throat. "No news. No doubt she knows that you are under our protection now. We continue to monitor the situation. You are safe."

Before she could catch another bold impulse and tell him that it seemed more like the Primers had lost track of the mysterious woman, Owin and his father moved toward the door. "We must be off now. Look after him, won't you?" Owin said in a soft voice as they headed out. He nodded back toward Cedwick. "I'm glad my brother's got such good friends."

Lord Hemmington gave her a small bow. "Good day."

The door closed behind him.

"Well?"

Cedwick and Zanna were alone now. He pushed around bits of his lunch, still not eating and not looking up at her. "Let's get this over with."

There had been a reason she had come here, but at the moment, she couldn't remember why. Instead, she slowly crossed to the chair Owin had vacated and sat down. "Are you feeling okay?"

"Fine."

She licked her lips. "Nobody moved the graphite block. After you left, that is. Nobody could."

"We weren't supposed to be able to," Cedwick grunted. He nodded toward the door. "That's what *they* came down here to say. That everyone fails the first attempt at a real object. It's supposed to be one of Dr. Trout's lessons."

"A lesson in what?"

"Failing. Being useless."

"That's a terrible lesson."

"It's to keep our heads from getting too big." Cedwick speared a macaroni with his fork. "You take a kid and tell him he can break the laws of math and physics, and it makes him think he can do anything."

"You almost had it," Zanna tried. "I mean, at least you moved part of it. That's better than anyone else did. Better than me."

Cedwick's face grew dark. "Don't give me your pity. You've been waiting for this since the day we met. You don't think I noticed?"

"Noticed what?" This wasn't what she had come here for at all. The whole thing was slipping from her fingers.

His mouth twisted into a snarl. "How you've been after me since the very first day. Just waiting for me to screw things up and have a good laugh at that useless Hemmington brother—"

All at once she remembered why she had come here in the first place, and it made her break out in bitter laughter. "Is that what you think? That I came down here to gloat? I was going to invite you to my holiday party, but you can just forget it now!"

"Oh, because that would have been absolutely lovely," Cedwick snapped. "Stuck in a house with prissy Nora Elmsley, that barbaric American, and an Italian girl who doesn't say more than two words? I think I'd rather Splutter my ear again."

"Fine!" Zanna jumped to her feet. "I hope you do! I hope you Splutter your—" insults had never been her strong point—"your dumb face!"

She spun on her heel and marched out. Mrs. Turnbuckle waved cheerily at her, but Zanna was so angry she didn't even respond.

In Self, she threw her backpack down with a *bang*, interrupting Libby's continuing tirade about how she needed two more seconds to master the graphite cube. But before any of the girls could ask Zanna what was wrong, Dr. Trout called for silence.

As the professor started the lecture, Zanna caught Beatrice watching her with a worried expression. She sunk a bit lower, wishing she was a year older. In a year, none of this would matter. She would have her Iron and her specialization, and everyone would know how to manipulate real objects, and everything with the mysterious woman would have been figured out, and her father would understand who she really was.

A theoretical rectangle landed at her elbow. With a glance up at Dr. Trout—whose attention was on the other side of the classroom—Zanna touched the rectangle and unfolded it into a note.

What's wrong?

Against her better judgment, she looked up again and caught Beatrice's eye. The girl made a meaningful glance at the note and then back to Zanna, urging her to reply. Zanna shook her head. She couldn't put it into writing.

"Ms. Mayfield?"

Zanna snapped up. Beatrice's theoretical note vanished immediately. She coughed, hoping that her voice didn't convey the guilt she felt. "Dr. Trout?"

"You do not know what I asked," Dr. Trout said. Her bat tapped meaningfully against her open palm. "You have not been listening."

Zanna's skin grew hot beneath her blouse. "No," she said. The little she knew about Dr. Trout told her it would be better to be straight and confess right away. "I'm sorry."

Dr. Trout paused, making the apology hang in the classroom so everyone could take it in. After what felt like an eternity, she spoke. "We are considering the events of the morning. What are your thoughts on failure?"

"I almost had it," she said before she had even considered her words. "They didn't give me enough time."

A couple of the students mumbled in agreement. It seemed as if she wasn't the only one to almost fully grasp the graphite block's functions.

"You knew how much time you had," Dr. Trout said. "It was the same as everyone else. And you failed to move the cube within that time frame. That, Ms. Mayfield, is a failure."

"Only because time ran out," Zanna grumbled.

The old woman cocked her head a bit, as if she had just noticed something about Zanna that had escaped her attention so far. "Time will always run out."

The tone in her voice made Zanna's mouth curl into a snarl. On a better day, she might have shrugged it off, but it was not a good day, not by a long stretch. "The whole thing was set up to be impossible. You wanted us to fail."

At that, a little ripple ran through the class, and Zanna feared that she had gone too far. She had certainly never talked back to a teacher like that in public school. But before Dr. Trout could say anything, Cedwick came in through the privacy illusion. He had taken off the wrap of gauze around his head, but he kept a wad of it pressed against his burst ear.

"Mr. Hemmington," Dr. Trout said as he sank into a seat in the back row. Evidently, Zanna's accusation wasn't even worth answering. "I am pleased to see you. I hope you can still hear me with that ear."

Cedwick nodded.

"We are discussing our experiences from this morning." She looked pointedly at Zanna. "Our *failures*. What are your thoughts?"

It took a long moment for Cedwick to respond—so long that Zanna wondered if he had been lying about being able to hear out of his ear. "I think it's about what I expected," he finally said.

"You have Spluttered your ear," Dr. Trout deadpanned. "Do you mean to tell me that is what you expected this morning?"

"No, I expected to fail it," Cedwick said. "You set it up so we would, after all."

Another ripple, louder than the first, and Dr. Trout cut it down with a single, authoritative shout. "Silence!"

A frown worked over Dr. Trout's face. How she was able to do that when her face was already in a perpetual frown, Zanna didn't know. "Since it appears that both of you would rather make excuses than study your Self, perhaps this will be more helpful. I want each of you to write a short paper describing the other. If you cannot be truthful with yourself, perhaps you will be better with someone else."

"What?" Zanna and Cedwick said, almost in unison.

"Yes. And then you will exchange your papers after the Christmas break," Dr. Trout said. There might have even been a little smile in her stone-block face at having thought of such a devilish assignment. "Begin with a discussion of how the other reacts to failure."

Zanna wanted to protest, but Dr. Trout had moved on with the lecture, and nothing would change her mind. Instead, Zanna hunched down glumly. The prospect of having her Christmas break taken up with writing a paper about Cedwick just piled on to the rest of her dark thoughts. Thankfully, Dr. Trout didn't call on her for the rest of class, having tortured her enough for one day. When the bell rang, Zanna barely had time to collect her backpack before the girls were around her.

"Sheesh, calm down," she muttered, packing her books. "I'm not going to run away or anything."

"I can't believe her," Libby said, sniping her remark at Dr. Trout's back as the professor swept out of the classroom. "You call her out on rigging the test, and she makes you write a paper on Cedwick for it! That's got to be against the rules or something."

"It's perfectly within the rules," Nora said.

"It's still evil," Libby shot back.

"I didn't really figure out anything about the test. Cedwick told me," Zanna said. Then she realized what she had implied, and she stopped shoving books into her backpack. "I mean . . ."

Libby's face split in a grin. "I *knew* it."

"Not like that," Zanna said. "I wanted to make sure he was okay. He was bleeding."

"You could have just asked *me*," Nora said. "I know all about Splutters. They're painful, but you're not going to *die* unless you try to pull apart a black hole or something equally massive."

"What happened?" Beatrice asked Zanna in a soft voice.

Her arms felt mysteriously weak, and Zanna groaned a little as she lifted her backpack. "Nothing happened. I felt sorry for him, that's all. And I . . . I invited him to the party."

"You did *what*?" Nora gasped. "Without asking me first?"

"It doesn't matter," Zanna grumbled before Nora could work herself into an anxious tizzy. "He said no." Now that she had some distance on the episode, it seemed entirely pointless. "I don't care. If he wants to be alone and miserable, I'm not going to stop him."

"You should put that in your paper," Libby joked. "Cedwick Hemmington: alone and miserable."

"Don't remind me," Zanna grumbled. She didn't know what was worse about the assignment—having to write a paper about Cedwick or the idea that he was writing one about her.

Nora started going on about her plan for the party, and Zanna let her ramble, too exhausted to raise a fuss. Her anger had faded away, but something else had come in to replace it, something empty and anxious and far, far harder to name.

CHAPTER ELEVEN

THE DECORATIONS WERE all Nora's doing. She had brought a collection of old party supplies from her storage and insisted on putting them up. "Ninety-six percent of successful parties have decorations," she said, handing a pack of balloons to Libby.

"Grey balloons don't count," Libby said, picking up one of the deflated balloons with a disgusted look on her face.

"They're not going to stay that way," Nora said. "See?"

She fished a color wheel out of the bag and spun it. As she did, the balloons cycled through the entire spectrum, settling on a bright canary yellow. "There. Here's the helium pump. I need thirty-two."

She gave Libby a small hand-powered pump. "Hang on," Libby said. She gave the handle a few experimental pumps. "Does this thing make helium? Like, out of the air?"

"Of course," Nora nodded. "Thirty-two, if you could." She looked over at Zanna, who had been given the task of taping up a banner reading *WELCOME HOME!* in colorful bubbly handwriting. "It's crooked!" she shouted.

Zanna leaned back a little. "It looks fine to me."

"It is not *fine*," Nora chided. "Raise that side up a bit."

Zanna sighed and complied. Like everything else in her life these days, the party had snuck up on her. Between concerns about her Iron, her specialization, the lack of any news from the Primers on the woman who had broken into her bedroom, and now a report on Cedwick, Zanna had all but forgotten about it until the first weekend of Christmas break, when the girls showed up with their bags packed for a sleepover. Now she was standing on a kitchen chair, hanging a sign for a father she hadn't seen for almost seven months—or truly talked to for her entire life. The girls were doing their best to keep her entertained and distracted, but one of the downsides of having a mind like hers was that consciously ignoring things never worked. Even as she made minute adjustments to the banner until Nora was satisfied, Zanna could not shake a looming dread of what the afternoon might hold.

"Zanna, can you check on them in the kitchen?" Nora asked, noticing that she was staring blankly into the distance.

"Oh," Zanna said, climbing down from the chair. "Okay."

Beatrice was helping Pops decorate cupcakes in the kitchen. All of the girls had taken an instant liking to her grandfather, but he and Beatrice got along especially well. As Zanna entered, she heard the small girl chatting away in soft, flowery Italian, and her grandfather replying in what he remembered, mixing in English where his memory failed.

"Supervising over there?" Pops said when he noticed Zanna in the doorway. "Come make yourself useful."

Zanna put her chair down next to Beatrice, taking one of the iced cupcakes and dipping a hand into the bowl of sprinkles. "How's the decorating going?" Beatrice asked in English.

"Depends on who you ask," Zanna said. "Did you know that proper decorations are one of the top-five critical elements for successful parties?" She turned to Pops. "You're not going to recognize your house when Nora gets through with it."

"Bah," he said, shaking his head. "This old place could do with a bit of color, I think."

"It's more than 'a bit,' " Zanna said. "You should take a look."

"In time," Pops said, putting a finished cupcake on a nearby plate and picking up a new one. He glanced at the clock. "Which we've got plenty of. No need to rush things."

Zanna looked up at the clock, as well. Her father's plane was supposed to touch down at noon, and it would be another hour or so until he was out of the airport. They still had two, maybe two and a half hours.

Nora came into the kitchen and headed for the sink. "I believe we can say the hallway is finished," she said. She scrubbed her hands thoroughly, with far more soap and water than Zanna would have thought necessary. "Decorations are on schedule. How are you all doing in here?"

"Good," Beatrice said. She set a perfect cupcake on the plate, and a pang of jealousy shot through Zanna. Beatrice had somehow carved the icing into smooth waves and dollops, with sprinkles evenly distributed all around. Zanna's looked like she had loaded the sprinkles into a shotgun.

Nora finished her ritualistic handwashing and grabbed a towel. "Keep it up. Proper refreshments are the most critical element to a successful party."

"Quite the taskmaster, that one," Pops said after Nora had gone back to the living room.

"She means well," Beatrice said, spreading a fresh smear of icing on a cupcake.

"Oh, I have no doubt. It's a wonderful idea you all have come up with." Pops paused to focus on picking up a gumdrop, then added it to his cupcake. "Whatever happened to that nice young man with the shield?" he asked Zanna. "Did he find the woman who gave you all that trouble?"

"Owin, Pops. His name is Owin." Zanna scowled as her knife dug into the cupcake, spreading crumbs through her icing.

"And no, the Primers haven't found her. I don't think they're looking anymore."

"They're still looking," Beatrice said. "You just—"

The doorbell rang.

"That can't be him!" Nora shrieked as she dashed into the kitchen, eyes wide with a scrambling fright. "It's only eleven! He's not supposed to be here until one! That was the plan!"

Something warm and gooey crept over Zanna's hand. She looked down and saw she had squeezed her cupcake to bits. Icing globbed over her thumb and onto the table.

"It's going to be all right," Beatrice said, half to Zanna and half to Nora. She took Zanna's hands and wiped off the icing with a towel. "They're just cupcakes. Go on. We're right here."

"Don't forget this," Pops said, pressing the frying pan into her hands as she got up from the table. He winked at her, and Zanna just stared at the piece of cast iron for a moment until her brain got around to working again. *Owin's wall of air pressure.* She had to unlock it to let her father in.

"But the decorations!" Nora pleaded. "Libby's still decorating—"

"It's going to be all right," Beatrice repeated, holding Nora and making her slow her breathing down a little. "Promise." She flicked her head toward the front door. "Zanna, don't keep him waiting."

Pops got up from the table. "Come on." He held out his arm for Zanna to take. "Let's go take a walk."

They started down the hallway. "Welcome back," she muttered to herself, the frying pan clutched to her chest. "Hi. Hello. You're back. You're here."

She decided on "hello" and tried it a couple more times, just to make sure she still remembered how it worked. But when she opened the door, what came out of her mouth was an unintelligent half-squeak, a bottleneck of indignation and excitement all smashed together. It wasn't her father on the doorstep. It was Owin and Cedwick.

"Hello!" Owin said. He wore a navy coat that looked thick enough to brave the Arctic and a knitted brown-and-gold scarf. "Terribly sorry about intruding like this. But I did bring biscuits!" In his hands was a platter crammed with a colorful variety of cookies. "Though I suppose you call them *cookies*. May we come in? It's a bit cold out here."

Zanna just stared.

"Well look who it is!" she heard Pops say. "Zanna didn't tell me she had invited you. Come in and stop heating the entire neighborhood."

Cedwick hadn't moved from his spot off on the side of the porch, hands jammed deep in the pockets of his tailored pea-coat. Owin coughed politely. "The barrier, if you don't mind."

Pops chuckled. "Oh, right. I'm too old for these new tricks." He nudged Zanna playfully, but there was a stern tone to his voice. Visitors were sacred in the Mayfield house. "Let them in, Zanna."

The scene was a car wreck, and Zanna could only stand on the sidewalk and watch it happen. She unlocked the barrier of air pressure, and the boys came inside, Owin stamping his feet and handing Pops the platter of cookies. They all shuffled around in the foyer, shedding coats and laughing, and Zanna just kept backing up until the wall was behind her and she couldn't back up any more.

"Zanna, why don't you run and see if we have any tea in the pantry?" Pops said in a slight reproach. She had been quiet for almost a minute, and they were looking at her. Everyone except Cedwick. "And start some water boiling. Our guests are freezing."

Her grandfather's words triggered something, a subroutine

of good manners that had been drilled into her since childhood, and she nodded. But before she could take a step toward the kitchen, Libby grabbed her by the arm, hard. "Zanna, you've got frosting all over you!" she said, spinning her around so the boys couldn't see if it was true or not. "Just a minute, boys? We'll be right back."

The other girls fell in at once. Between Nora, Libby, and Beatrice, Zanna was nearly carried upstairs to the guest bathroom. Neither she nor her grandfather used it, and its pristine square towels always smelled a bit like wilted flowers—and made her feel like she was disturbing the tomb of a long-dead Egyptian prince.

Libby sat Zanna down on the lid of the toilet, and Beatrice shut the door with a decisive *click*.

"You said he wasn't coming," Nora hissed, anxiety plain on her face. "I didn't plan for this!"

"He wasn't supposed to!" Zanna said. Libby twisted the faucet on full blast, covering their voices with the sound of running water. "He told me he'd rather Splutter his ear again."

Libby crossed her arms, looking more like a grizzled cop at an interrogation than a fourteen-year-old girl. "What happened when you went to see him in the nurse's cottage?" she said. "Tell us everything."

Zanna squirmed. "I told you, I went to invite him to my party, and he said no." The girls were silent, and she collapsed under their quiet weight. "And he said that I've been out to get him since the beginning of school."

Libby smirked. "He really doesn't know you, does he?"

"He also called you a barbaric American."

"That's probably accurate," Libby conceded. "Doesn't explain what he's doing here, though."

"Owin brought him," Beatrice said, as if it was obvious.

Zanna groaned. "He was there at the nurse's cottage. He probably thinks Cedwick and I are dating." She ran her fingers through her short hair. "Or that we should."

Libby's eyebrows waggled suggestively, but she kept her mouth shut. Everyone was silent for a long moment. "So what do you want us to do?" Beatrice finally asked. "Should we throw him out?"

"I don't . . ." There was something at the end of that sentence, something monstrous dredged up from inside her—a function she was looking at head-on for the first time. "I don't want him. But I don't want him to be alone, either. I just want us to get along."

The water was still splashing and gurgling in the porcelain sink, and when no one spoke, Libby reached over and turned it off. It drained away, leaving only a small quartz clock on the counter to tick away in the silence.

"Okay. New plan," Nora said sharply. With brisk movements, she pointed at each of them in turn, assigning roles. "Zanna, you explain that this party is for your father. Beatrice can help. Libby, you go finish up the decorations. Get Owin to help you with that. Nobody talks about Self class or real manipulations or the Hemmington family. And *nobody* talks about Zanna and Cedwick together." She counted off the forbidden topics on her fingers, her gaze lingering an extra second on Libby. "We are going to have a nice and pleasant party if it kills me."

"Yes, ma'am," Libby said with a sardonic grin, hopping down from the counter. Zanna looked over at Beatrice, who had been quietly leaning against the door throughout everything, as if it were her job to make sure no one left until the matter had been settled. The small girl had a fierce look to her eyes and just nodded to Zanna, making a little wordless promise between them before she opened the bathroom door.

As the girls entered the kitchen, Owin and Cedwick looked up from the table. They each held a mug of hot tea, but only Owin's had been touched. Cedwick just looked glumly into his swirls of milk, ceaselessly stirring. Pops was nowhere to be seen.

"Ah, hello again," Owin said. The girls held up in the doorway for a moment until Beatrice took the lead and sat down at the table. Then the others followed, surrounding Zanna like a squad of Secret Service. "I'm quite sorry about this. Cedwick told me it was a holiday party. I don't want to impose—"

"No!" Zanna said. Pops would never forgive her if she chased Owin and Cedwick away. But her voice came out high and squeaky. In an instant, her cheeks were blushing.

"It's a welcome-home party," Beatrice said without missing a beat. "Zanna's father is a pilot overseas, and he's coming home today."

"Ah," Owin said. "I suppose that explains the banner in the hallway. Sorry. Had I known, I would have brought a more appropriate gift."

"Well then," Libby said, taking the opportunity. "Come help me finish decorating the living room."

"Pressed into service!" Owin laughed. "I suppose that's only fair. Can I bring my tea?"

"I don't see why not," Libby said as they got up and went into the living room.

A tense silence fell over the kitchen. Nora had covered the topics to avoid—but not really any to use. Zanna racked her brain for conversation, focusing intently on the cupcake she was decorating. Everything she thought of fell into one of Nora's forbidden categories.

"Well, aren't you a cheery bunch!"

Pops entered the kitchen toting an armful of old plastic bags, and Zanna could have thrown her arms around him. He took in the table at a glance. "So quiet! Make some room. That's it, now. Took a while to find, but I've got a surprise for you all!"

They moved the cupcakes down to the end as Pops took up a position at the head of the table. He opened the first bag and poured out a collection of pennies, battered instruction cards, golf tees, interlocked rings, and matchsticks, shushing any questions as he began organizing the junk into piles.

"Now you already know this, so no cheating," he said, wagging his finger at Zanna. With practiced hands, he laid out the nine matchsticks. "The question is—can you turn these nine matches into ten?"

Silence returned, but this time it felt different. Almost comfortable. Zanna wiped the sweat from her forehead as nonchalantly as possible, hoping her cheeks had returned to their natural color by now.

"No one?" Pops said after the minutes had ticked by and the matchsticks were still lying on the table, unchanged. He jangled a handful of wooden nickels. "Come on now, put those brains to work! What about you, young man?"

He pointed at Cedwick, who was still contemplating his untouched tea, and the bottom fell out of Zanna's stomach. In a flash, she saw Cedwick willing the graphite cube to move, refusing to admit that he had failed. Beside her, Nora took a silent and anxious breath.

"I'm completely stumped," Beatrice said, a little too loudly. "What's the answer?" But Pops didn't give it. He just kept watching Cedwick, and the seconds stretched on. Until Cedwick reached out to the matchsticks. Without a word, he rearranged them to spell out *TEN*.

"We have a winner!" Pops said, picking out a wooden nickel and sliding it across to Cedwick. "And there's your prize!"

Cedwick didn't say anything, but he turned the wooden

nickel over, feeling its rough edge. "I've seen that one before," he mumbled.

"Oh?" Pops said. Those were magic words to him. "Well then, let's try something different."

Relief washed over Zanna like blissfully cool water. The next hour passed effortlessly as Pops pulled out puzzle after puzzle. Everyone acquired a little pool of wooden nickels, though the girls made sure Cedwick's remained the biggest. Owin and Libby finished with the decorations, and everyone moved to the living room to ooh and aah over their handiwork. The cupcakes never got finished, but Pops declared they had more than enough, and besides, there were puzzles to do! When Zanna looked up at the clock the next time, it was because someone was ringing the doorbell.

"I think that's for you," Pops said in the quiet pause after the doorbell stopped. Suddenly, Zanna remembered why she had thrown this party in the first place, and her smile faded. *Right.* Her father.

But then she caught sight of Cedwick, who was now on his second cup of tea, and it spurred her on. If he could have a good time, then there was hope for her. The plan the girls had made in the bathroom seemed less impossible now. Everyone could get along.

The frying pan had a good solid weight to it as she picked it up from the counter and took it to the front door. This time she didn't rehearse what she was going to say. There was too much going on inside her head. Instead, she just took a deep breath, felt the comforting heft of the frying pan and its story in her hands, and opened the front door.

A man with a dark-brown traveling bag stood on the front porch. He had a shiny, sunburnt face and a pair of sunglasses tucked into the breast pocket of his pilot's uniform. The shirt he wore was loose at the collar and rumpled, as if he had tugged and pulled at the stiff tie the minute he was free. In his hands was a present wrapped in exotic paper.

"Hey!" her father shouted. "There's my girl!"

He reached out to give her the present, but he stopped at the threshold, held back by the wall of air pressure. A frown creased his reddened face, and he tried again, with no success. "What is this?" he asked after the third time. The joy in his voice disappeared, replaced by a familiar anger. "What's going on? Zanna? Is this some kind of joke?"

"I'm going to explain it," Zanna said. She felt her face beginning to twist into a scowl and fought to keep it level. "I'm going to explain everything. But you have to listen and not interrupt. A lot has happened while you've been gone. A whole lot."

But he was not listening. He was testing the wall of air pressure, seeing if he could break through it with his shoulder. "This isn't funny," he growled. He had put the present down on the porch to shove at the barrier with both hands. "What is this? What did you do?"

"I told you, I'm going to explain it! You never listen to me!"

Her voice was too loud, she realized as the last words escaped her lips. Too loud and too shrill. No doubt everyone had heard her back in the kitchen. They had probably heard her across the street. But it worked, and her father lowered his hands. "Okay," he said, though his eyes said it was anything but okay. "I'm listening."

It was like a ball of steel wool in her stomach. Zanna felt every knot of her father's function jabbing at her soft insides. Her hands squeezed the frying pan, considering for a second, and then gave it a twist.

"Come in," she said quietly. "We need to talk."

Her father put his hand out, trying to feel for where the

barrier of air pressure had been. When he didn't find it, he stepped up into the house and looked around, still breathing hard. Zanna didn't realize how she had backed up when he entered, and now they stood at opposite ends of the foyer, looking at one another.

She had never made it this far in her scenarios. She had imagined the initial meeting a hundred different ways, but she had never managed to push past it—to when they would stand across from each other, to when she would have to explain everything that had happened since last spring.

Her father crossed his muscular arms over his chest expectantly. "Well?"

It felt like swallowing a pill the size of a cannonball. She could spend the next month trying to feel out all the different functions that made him so difficult. What she needed now was something to act on, and on that, everything pointed together.

She crossed the foyer and buried her face in his chest. "I've missed you."

Her father didn't seem to know how to hold her. He tried, first putting his hands on her shoulders and then gingerly embracing her, as if she were a delicate crystal he might smash into pieces. So she wrapped her arms around his waist and buried her face in his unkempt uniform and his musk of diesel and tarmac and flower-scented body wash.

Women's body wash.

She opened her eyes. "Wait—"

Coils of black iron poured out of her father's uniform, like he had been hiding a basket of snakes under his shirt, and they were all coming out at once. The metal caught Zanna around the arms and waist and legs and bound her to him, tighter than a spider wrapping its prey in silk, and her mind clutched the truth, a few seconds too late.

An illusion, hiding the strange woman underneath.

Then Zanna's world exploded in shouts and footsteps. Everyone had left the kitchen to meet her father, and now they were running, charging at the man who wasn't her father, who wasn't even a man but that mysterious woman.

As it turns out, Zanna thought grimly, *the Primers were right about her being a kidnapper after all.*

Libby and Beatrice tackled the woman to the ground in a disorganized, ungraceful scrum, with Nora throwing herself on top after a moment of panicked deliberation. Bound as she was to the woman by bands and bands of iron, Zanna couldn't even brace herself as the girls piled on, and she gasped as the weight squeezed the wind out of her. For a second it seemed like the fight was over, the woman pinned beneath three angry girls. Then there was a great *whumph* and a clap of thunder. Zanna felt the air around her and her captor suddenly shove back, exploding in all directions, and the girls flew like rag dolls. Glass shattered as Beatrice cracked an overhead light with her back. Nora splintered the closet door, and Libby tumbled down the hallway, her knees skidding on the hardwood.

"Get behind me!" A silver whip that must have been Owin's shield darted forward and wrapped around the waist of Zanna's attacker. The boy stood with his legs spread wide, as if bracing against a gale wind. One hand held the other end of his shield-whip as tight-fisted as if he had just lassoed a mad bull. The other pointed toward the ceiling, where he had caught Beatrice on a pillow of air after she'd slammed into the ceiling. He was now lowering her safely to the ground. "Don't!"

This last remark had been aimed at Libby. But the girl ignored him as she got back to her feet, charging in again like a linebacker. She made it two steps before snapping up into the air as if she had stepped into a jungle trap that left her dangling by her feet. Except there was no rope—there was just air around her. Blood oozed out of where she had cracked her head.

"You put my granddaughter down."

Pops stood at the end of the hallway. In his hands was the first weapon he had laid hands on—the frying pan. The sight made Zanna shiver—it *was* her grandfather, but at the same time, it wasn't. There was no twinkle in his eyes, no mischievous boyish grin tugging at his lips. His face was cold and merciless.

"Don't!" Owin shouted again, not taking his eyes off the intruder. "I've got this!"

Zanna's kidnapper finally turned toward Owin. She had not dropped her illusionary disguise the whole time, her mocking voice coming from the mouth of Zanna's father. "With what? That laughing gas you've been trying to stuff into my lungs?" She let out a single, heartless laugh. "Here's a tip for later: Keep it away from your target's nose. Or else she'll smell it coming a mile away."

A subtle disturbance rippled through the air. In a split second, Owin's face contorted, grimacing as he tried to fight off whatever Zanna's attacker was manipulating in the air. His eyes fluttered, rolling madly in a sluggish, dizzy spin, face bright red with exertion.

"I said—" Pops growled, and then he stopped, cut off in mid-sentence. A sound like heartbreak tore out of Zanna, and she thrashed around in her bindings, twisting to see what the woman had done. Pops was frozen in mid-step, the frying pan raised in a swing that would never come down. His mouth hung open in mid-threat. Nothing besides his eyes moved, like a statue with a man trapped inside.

Owin was down to a knee but still holding the whip of his shield. The woman looked down at him, faintly impressed. "Well then," she said, "let's test your electromagnetism."

Electrical current coursed through the black iron enveloping Zanna, and it made her stomach go scrambling, like she had brushed against a live electric fence. But whatever it did to her, it must have been ten times worse for Owin. He shrieked and collapsed, and the silver rope shattered like it was made out of glass. Then there was only silence.

The front hall was ruined. Shards of broken shield littered the floor and stuck in the drywall. The light Beatrice had broken hung from its wires. Nora lay halfway out of the coat closet, her breathing faint. Libby was still hanging upside down. One unpopped yellow balloon bobbed among the tangles of fallen streamers.

An arm of black iron stretched out from inside the woman's sleeve and plucked the frying pan from her grandfather's frozen hand. "Why hello," the woman said, like it was an old friend. She gave it a twist and unlocked the outer barrier of air pressure.

Zanna closed her eyes. They were going to fly soon. She could feel it swelling inside of her. But instead, the strange woman remained in the front hall for just a moment. She looked back into the living room. "Cedwick!"

Zanna had completely forgotten about him. She looked over the wreckage of the foyer again, wondering if he had been thrown somewhere in the chaos, but he wasn't there. All she saw was Nora in the closet, with Owin and Beatrice not that far away.

"Come out, Cedwick. I'm not going to hurt you!"

A spark of hope. He had gotten away. He must have hidden when the fighting had started, and Zanna squeezed her eyes shut, telling him to stay where he was, to stay hidden—

"My father knows," she heard Cedwick say with a touch of arrogance.

The strange woman whipped around toward the couch where the sound had come from, and with a flick of her finger, she skittered the furniture out of the way. Cedwick sat with his back to the dusty wall. He wasn't exactly smiling, but his eyes glittered. "Do what you want with me. I've already told him. He's on his way here now. You won't make it one mile before the Primers get you."

"The Primers couldn't get me before. I doubt they've improved." Zanna's kidnapper gestured around the room. "Look around you, Cedwick. Look at your brother."

Cedwick didn't look.

"He tried to fight me, and he lost." The woman's voice dropped as she kept talking, dropped and dropped until it was nothing more than a frigid whisper. "I would have done the same to you if you had tried. You're the only smart one here. Remember that."

Zanna closed her eyes—partially because she was sure they were going to fly now, but mostly because she couldn't bear looking at Cedwick. He just sat there against the living room wall, not moving and holding nothing.

Her kidnapper stepped over the wrecked closet door to Pops, who stared back with cold vengeance. But she didn't say anything. Instead, the woman just put her forehead to the cage of air pressure he was trapped in, letting a private moment pass in the ruined hall.

"I am sorry," the woman said in a strange, soft voice. "You'll understand. Maybe. Hopefully. Don't hate me too much."

Then she straightened, wiped at something in her eyes, and let the iron carry her and Zanna out the door and into the sky.

CHAPTER TWELVE

ZANNA TRIED NOT to pass out. It wasn't the g-forces, because her kidnapper handled those with ease and made the ride as smooth as a baby in a cradle. It wasn't the wind either, because the woman handled that, as well. No, it was the *height*.

They skipped up in a vertical climb, Zanna's captor deftly parting the shockwave like it was a pair of curtains. No sonic boom announced their ascent. In a silent instant, Zanna's house had disappeared into the jumble of suburbia. It would have been better with the noise. You could tell which way you were falling by the way the wind howled. Without it, there was only the calm heartbeat of Zanna's kidnapper and her own frightened one.

"Breathe."

Zanna smelled something sweet and nitrous-like. It loosened her jaw just a little, though she kept her eyes closed. Brisk, thin air nipped at her nose, but the iron that bound her to her kidnapper warmed slightly, as if she had wrapped her entire body around a freshly poured cup of coffee.

"You really should open your eyes," her captor said. "It's such a lovely view."

Zanna shook her head stubbornly.

"All the Earth laid out beneath us," her captor continued. "All its storms and sunny days. The cities and forests. The great blue ocean. It's astounding. You're not going to get another chance to see it like this."

But Zanna still refused. "What are you going to do to me?"

The woman clucked her tongue. "Don't spoil this moment, you dear, silly child. We can have a nice long sit-down back at the house. I'll make some hot cider. That's still your favorite, right?"

"How do you know that?"

"Are you going to open your eyes?"

Zanna shook her head. It felt good to do something in rebellion, even if the rest of her body was encased in immovable iron. The woman sighed, and the sweet smell of laughing gas returned, this time much stronger than before. Zanna inhaled deep and drifted into blackness.

When she awoke, the sound of the world was back. Snow crunched under her kidnapper's shoes. They were in a forest, near a brook that ran and fell over smooth rocks. Everything smelled of cold pine trees.

They stood at the edge of a picturesque wild-grass meadow deep with snow. The night was black and crisp, the stars sharp as silver needles. Zanna twisted her head around, trying to find anything to get her bearings, but it was just wilderness and shadow.

"Now to see if that was worth it," her kidnapper muttered. Now that they were alone, all the violence in her voice had faded away. She sounded less like a vicious intruder and more like a weary traveler who still had quite a long distance to go. Were it anyone else, Zanna might have felt sorry for the tired, exhausted woman, but the image of Pops in that cage of air pressure was still too fresh in her mind. They hopped over the rushing brook, and the world rippled.

When things realigned, the field was not empty. Standing where the snow and wild grass had been was an old Victorian mansion that looked like it had been ripped right out of a classic horror movie. Its siding was a perfectly faded gray, its gables crumbled just enough to set Zanna's imagination aflutter. As her kidnapper walked up the path that had appeared beneath her feet, the curtains in the front room pulled back to fill the windows with soft yellow light. The front door opened with an atmospheric creak as the house welcomed its owner back.

"Marvelous, isn't she?" her kidnapper said, pausing at the foot of the porch steps to look proudly over the house. "Did quite a lot of work on her. Who'd have thought I'd turn into such a handyman?"

There was a certain charm to the house, Zanna had to admit. A dreamlike, fantasy quality that made her want to explore it, even as her skin prickled with danger. "This is your house?"

"*Our* house now," her kidnapper said. "You're going to be staying with me for a while."

Candles flickered to life as they entered the front hall, filling the house with far more light than Zanna suspected they would have naturally given off. There was still a fair bit of work that needed to be done, namely the peeling wallpaper and the cobwebs in the corners, but some comforts had been included. The hallway rug looked clean, if a little shabby, and the wood banisters and candle fixtures shone with polish. It wasn't as musty as Zanna would have expected, either. Cheery spices wafted from deeper in the house—pumpkin and cloves and cinnamon and chocolate. And a rich, papery scent that comforted Zanna deep in her bones. *Books.* Thousands and thousands of books.

The iron around Zanna loosened and gently set her down on the thick rug of the entrance hall. At her first taste of freedom, Zanna made a mad dash for the front door, but the house slammed it shut, and she just banged her shoulder into it. As if to drive its point home, the door locked with an absurdly loud *click.*

"In here," the woman said, not even surprised at Zanna's attempted escape. "You won't make it to the back door," she said as Zanna looked down the hallway into the depths of the mansion. "Come on now. Don't be dreadful."

Zanna scowled, considering taking a chance, but eventually, she heeded her captor's words and grumpily followed her into the sitting room. Two couches sat in the corner, and a table was covered with ornate silverware. One couch looked like it had come with the house, its seat bumpy with loose springs and the velvet all worn down to moth silk. The other was new and modern, and even though it was a pleasant soft purple, it looked completely out of place in the wheezing mansion.

"It was the best I could do," the woman said, her nose wrinkling at the sight of the new sofa. "Antique Victorian sofas aren't exactly common these days. Eventually, though, I'll find the right one." She sat on the old sofa, leaving the new one for Zanna. A nearby door opened, and a large silver serving tray floated through. Balanced atop it were two steaming mugs of hot spiced cider. The tray offered one to Zanna, and she took it gingerly, wrapping her hands around it and breathing in the sweet scent. Then she remembered where she was, and the smell turned sickly and rotten.

"What?" the woman said when Zanna didn't drink her cider. "I promised you cider, didn't I?"

Zanna stared at her kidnapper through the clouds of steam, wondering if she could make the woman's head explode if she concentrated hard enough. "You won't get away with this."

"Do you think it's poisoned or something?" her captor asked, gliding effortlessly past Zanna's threats. "Please. If I wanted to poison you, I wouldn't offer you a drink. I'd just *do* it."

Zanna lifted the mug to her lips, but at the last possible minute, she threw it right at her kidnapper's face. Jumping to her feet, she scrambled over the purple couch toward the front window, planning to dive headlong through it, but she only made it halfway before the air around her pressurized. The woman pulled her back and sat her down on the sofa again. Between them, the cider had been paused mid-throw. Not a drop had made it to the woman.

"You'll hurt the kitchen's feelings, throwing away its hard work like that," her kidnapper said, making the cider reverse its trajectory back into Zanna's mug. "Try it. I think you'll be surprised."

The air pressure around Zanna relaxed, letting her move again and bringing back the aroma of cider. It was rich with nutmeg and allspice, just as Pops had always made for her. Pops, who had fought to protect her, even though he didn't have a bit of Scientist ability in him.

She poured the woman's cider on the floor.

For a second, her captor looked genuinely hurt. "I'm trying to be nice, Zanna."

"You should have thought of that before you attacked my friends." she said. Somewhere, she felt Libby cheering her on, making her bolder. "Before you attacked my grandfather."

"And *you* should have listened to me and never gone to St. Pommeroy's in the first place. You ungrateful child, I could have just thrown you into a bare iron room and sealed it forever, but did I? I built this house for *you*." The woman met Zanna's anger quickly, before she got control of herself once again and softened her tone. "I want you to be comfortable here. There's a wonderful library full of puzzle books. The kitchen can make almost anything you want—I've already put in the functions for hot cider and French onion soup and a lasagna like Pops used to make. And it's dead simple to add more. Just ask."

Zanna shrank back as far as the sofa would let her. The woman grinned all wrong—too full of teeth, too much white in her eyes. It didn't help that she was still wearing the illusion of Zanna's father over her face. Zanna wished Beatrice were there to put a reassuring hand on her shoulder to steady her. But Beatrice was back in Virginia, in the rubble of Pops's foyer, and Zanna had only herself.

"Who are you?" she asked, her mouth dry.

The woman tried to smile warmly. "Someone who cares for you, Zanna. Someone who knows better than you. There's a dark time coming for the world. For the universe. If you're here, with me, I can save you. I can prevent so many terrible things. If I'm lucky, I can stop it completely." There was almost a note of pleading in her voice. "No one but us will ever know that things were so dangerously close to falling apart. No one will die, and no one will go mad, and things will be wonderful. Isn't that what you want?"

"No." Reserves of spite and anger flooded Zanna's gut, keeping her going as her physical strength began to fade. "I *want* to go home. I *want* to be with my friends and my grandfather, and I *want* you to stuff your doomsday nonsense and leave me alone."

For a moment her kidnapper seemed like she might cry. Then she drew her mouth back into a firm line and rubbed at her temples. "I can't." It was almost genuinely apologetic. "I did take great pains not to hurt your friends more than I had to. Do you know how fragile the human body is? How many chemicals and physics and functions have to be perfect just to keep your heart beating? Your friends are fine. Bruised, perhaps. A little warier about trying to tackle a genuine Scientist with just their bare hands. But alive and well. I can promise you that."

"I don't care what you promise," Zanna said. "You're a monster. How come you're still hiding behind that illusion?"

The woman bristled and then touched her face, as if she had forgotten what it looked like. "Would this be better?" she asked. Her features reshaped like wet clay. The skin lost its sunburnt glow and became pale and rosy. The nose sharpened to an elegant tip. The masculine coarse black hair turned silky and slightly wavy, growing down past her shoulders, though it remained just as thick. The woman brushed her hand through it and yawned, smoothing out her new complexion with her fingertips.

"That's not your real face, either," Zanna snapped. There was something eerie and vampiric about the woman's complexion. Something unsettling about how her eyes didn't quite match the rest.

"And how do you know that?" the woman asked. "Because you think you saw my real face with your little Weierstrass key? Come here. Touch. There's no illusion here. No metallurgy. I'm just flesh. Same as you."

Zanna kept her hands fastened around the empty mug, not accepting the invitation. She might as well have been invited to touch a vat of crackling radioactive waste.

The woman leaned back and spread her arms over the back of the old Victorian sofa. "You know, you shouldn't make things more difficult than necessary. I've tried to be as accommodating as possible, but you must also do *your* share. Don't be so sullen."

"I think I'll be whatever I want," Zanna said. "I don't owe you anything."

"Oh, you owe me more than you know," the woman spat viciously. "More than you could ever know." Then her anger disappeared again as she summoned the little flying serving tray. "I'm sorry. Are you hungry? I didn't realize how late it was—travel never agrees with me. But we can have something quick. Sandwiches, perhaps? A nice meatball sub?"

"No." All Zanna had eaten today was a cupcake, but she wouldn't show her kidnapper that. The reserve of anger she had been propping herself up with was running dry, so she spoke quickly and directly. "I want you to show me to the room you're going to lock me in."

The woman frowned. "Fine."

She led Zanna back into the main hallway. A set of stairs on the left led up to the second floor, but they continued past it toward the back of the house. A small, curved door stood at the end of the hallway, and beyond it was a tall, circular tower pitted with holes in the floor and stray nails jabbing out of the walls, as if something tall and graceful had been torn out, leaving only the splinters behind. *It had been a staircase*, Zanna realized as she looked up the empty tower and saw the remains of a landing thirty feet above her. A spiral staircase pulled right out of its tower like a sapling yanked out of the ground.

Iron ribboned out of the woman's sleeves and wrapped around Zanna before she could fight it. But it didn't bind her as tightly as before, when they were flying and the iron was the only thing keeping Zanna from escaping. Now that they were in her house, her kidnapper held Zanna like a gentle parent.

"Does everyone hate stairs around here?" she muttered as they glided upward.

"No," the woman said. "We just hate redundancy. Stairs are nice for making entrances and filling out atriums, but as for getting from one level to the next, Ironflight is so much easier."

At the landing there was a door of golden metal, like the ones in front of Dr. Mumble's office and the entrance to the Laboratory, but the woman didn't have to put her hand to it or say her name. Instead, it opened on its own. The tower room was soft and painted sky-blue and smelled faintly of fresh cotton, as if it were a sundress hung out to dry on a warm summer day. A bed that looked just like the one Zanna had back home stood in the center, and her entire body ached to crawl in and curl up and perhaps cry a little before she fell asleep. But Zanna forced herself to keep looking around, at least until the woman left her alone. Part of the room was sectioned off by a privacy curtain, and when Zanna peeked behind it, she saw a shower, toilet, and sink, along with a cabinet stocked with the necessary toiletries. The woman had even included a desk in front of the large, singular window that looked out over the mansion's rooftops.

"I hope you like it," she said as Zanna moved around the prison.

Zanna's feet throbbed with each step, and she did her best not to let it show on her face.

"I made it with you in mind. The books are a selection that I think you'll find quite interesting. And when you're done with those, I have an extensive library downstairs. I can show you it tomorrow."

Zanna ran a hand over the desk and crouched at the bookshelf to read the spines. She didn't recognize any of the titles. Again, the bed called out to her, but her captor was still in the room, watching Zanna's every move with appraising eyes.

"I do want you to be happy," the woman said after a while. Her voice sounded like she was far older than the alien beauty of her face indicated. "I'm not cruel, Zanna. I would have been content letting you live as you please, free to do whatever you wanted, if you had just signed that contract as I asked you to in the first place and stayed away from St. Pommeroy's. This is your choice. This is what you forced me to do. But that doesn't mean it has to be unpleasant. It doesn't mean we can't make the best of it."

Her hand made a cautious movement, a little turn from her side, up to offer it to Zanna. As if Zanna would grip it and pump it enthusiastically and say, "Thanks for imprisoning me. I really appreciate it."

Zanna just scowled, and the woman sighed, raising her

hand to brush a stray wisp of hair out of her eyes. "Very well. I will see you in the morning. Good night."

The door snapped shut behind her.

Zanna knew the first thing she should do was scour the entire room for cracks and weaknesses—anything that would help her escape. But too much had happened that day. She pressed her face to the window and looked out toward the forest, searching for anything that would tell her where she had been taken. The pine forest went on for miles and miles. There was nothing else around her. Only trees and snow and a dance of aurora borealis on the horizon. Zanna bit her tongue and cursed herself for not having been able to keep her eyes open on the flight. Nora would have been watching coastlines and geographic formations, gathering as much information as she could. Perhaps that was why Zanna's kidnapper had flown so high in the first place. She knew Zanna wouldn't be able to look down.

There would be time for all this and more, Zanna thought as she began undressing for bed. She wouldn't be making a break for it tonight, but eventually, her captor would make a mistake. The woman would overlook something or accidentally leave a door open, and Zanna would pounce on it. It was a puzzle, and if Zanna was good at anything, it was figuring out puzzles.

Repeating that thought to herself, she curled up beneath the blankets and didn't cry at all.

In the morning she awoke to a bell ringing somewhere nearby, though she couldn't figure out from where. Half an hour later, after she had showered and found fresh clothes in her wardrobe, the woman appeared at the door to bring Zanna down to breakfast.

"Scrambled, with ketchup and toast?" the woman asked as the silver serving tray floated around the table and presented

Zanna with a steaming plate of eggs. "Or have your tastes changed?"

Zanna wanted to knock the tray over, but skipping dinner last night had left her stomach growling. The food was hot, and though she wouldn't admit it, her kidnapper was right. Scrambled eggs with ketchup and toast were one of Zanna's favorites.

A pitcher floated over and filled her glass with orange juice. They ate in a long dining hall filled with torn and faded portraits that the woman had waved a hand dismissively at when they had first come in. "Art was never really my forte. One of these days, I'll find something to replace them with."

Zanna watched the pitcher refill the woman's glass and then duck back into the kitchen. She could hear the clatter of metal and running water behind the door, but she hadn't seen anyone else in the house besides her solitary captor. Either the chef was exceptionally good at hiding, or the entire kitchen had been automated.

"Did you build the kitchen yourself?" Zanna asked.

The woman laughed. She was having the same thing as Zanna—scrambled eggs covered in ketchup with toast on the side—and dabbed away a stray bit at the corner of her mouth. "You've noticed! It was quite a bit of work, but in the end, I think it was worth it. No more chopping onions and scrubbing dishes here. Just ask, and *poof*! It's marvelous."

Zanna finished her breakfast, quietly scoping out the dining room and looking for avenues of possible escape, and the silver serving tray returned to take away the dirty dishes. As it passed her, she tried to nonchalantly peer into its functions, hoping the woman would think she was just admiring the craftsmanship. But when she did, all she could see were numbers. Enormous, senseless numbers. As if someone had given a calculator to a monkey and told it to pound away to its heart's content. They moved and scrolled like the functions Zanna knew, but whether they were coordinates or gravity or something else entirely, she couldn't say.

The woman finished her last bite of toast, a smile on her face. "And what are you doing?"

"Just looking." Zanna pulled herself out of the unreadable functions and touched the tray's decorated edge. "It's very nice. Antique?"

"It's primelocked," the woman said, apparently not fooled at all by Zanna's charade. "The entire house is."

Zanna tipped her head a little to the side.

"But of course you don't know what that is," her captor said. "So let me tell you. I have primelocked this house from the tip of its weathervane down to its subterranean plumbing. It's a tricky little business, relying on the fact that two large primes can be easily multiplied together, but undoing that—factoring that product—is exceedingly difficult. To those with the original two prime keys, manipulation is easy." As if to demonstrate, the tray of dirty dishes folded up into an origami crane on a bed of lotus blossoms. "But to everyone else, it is impossible. If you had a supercomputer tucked away, you might be able to factor it out in six or seven hundred years. Since I very much doubt you do, there is only one way out of here." She laid a hand on her chest and grinned. "Through me. And you will not get the keys from me. You are not nearly clever enough for that."

The silver serving tray scuttled around the table, back to its original form, and the woman laid her dishes on it. "But really, why would you want to leave? Everything you could want is here. Come. I'll show you the library. Perhaps that will change your mind."

They went out of the dining room and down the hallway to

a set of doors upholstered in rich brown leather with polished brass buttons and tacks around the edges. Somewhere out there, a law firm was missing its front doors. Her kidnapper gestured grandly, and the doors threw themselves open.

A delicious, musty scent rolled out, carrying a mixture of spiderwebs and yellowed parchment and leather bindings and gold lettering. Dim light filled the library, even though the only source Zanna saw was a beam of red sunlight streaming through a high circular window in the back. It fell directly onto a comfortable nook of plump chairs and sofas. On the wall behind the sofas, a brittle, yellowing map of the world had been framed, the unexplored waters labeled simply *HERE BE DRAGONS*. Books overflowed the shelves and piled up in the corners, on the tables—anywhere there was space. Its lack of organization would have thrown any librarian into a fit, but for Zanna, it was lovely.

"What do you think?" the woman asked in a hushed tone as Zanna experimentally sunk her hand into one of the pillows. "I've got fiction books, encyclopedias, puzzle books—whatever you like. And if it's not here, I'll go find it for you. Just say the word."

Zanna gave the antique globe on the desk a spin, wondering which of the continents she was on now. Europe? North America? Asia? "This is an illusion."

The woman laughed. "Why would you think that? Is it that hard to believe?"

"Nobody has libraries like this," Zanna said. "Not unless you're some English lord. It's too . . ." She almost said *perfect* but stopped in time. "Too much."

"It's not too much for *you*," the woman said, trying that friendly smile again. "And yes, I admit there have been a few touches here and there. I had to pretty up the sunlight a little—seasonal changes, you understand. Shorter days and less light. And a few controls to keep the temperature and humidity in check. But the books are real. The room is real. It is my gift to you. Because I do want us to get along. We don't have to be enemies."

She held her hand out to Zanna, indicating both the library and her peaceful intentions in one compound gesture, and Zanna's own hand twitched a little, acting on reflex. But then she remembered what had happened at the party—the unconscious bodies of her friends and Pops in his cage—and she made her hands into fists.

"If you want us to get along, then leave me alone."

The woman dropped her hand. "I can't do that," she said. For a second it looked as if she was going to launch into an explanation, but instead, she just rubbed at her eyes. "It's complicated. Everything is complicated."

"Then try me," Zanna said. "I'm not stupid."

That made the woman laugh—not wickedly, but with a good nature. "I know," she said. "Believe me, I know. But I can't. Half of me hopes that one day you might understand and perhaps reconsider your hatred . . . and the other half hopes that day will never come. Just know that this is important. I have my reasons, and they are good. They are so very good."

She held out her hand again, but when Zanna still refused, the woman lowered it, her face hardening into its mask of unblemished and unearthly skin. "As you wish. I have business to attend to. I'm going to lock you in here. Prove that you're a good girl and don't make too much trouble, and I might let you wander around the house eventually. Until then"—she gestured to the books—"enjoy."

The woman backed out of the library, and the doors shut with a *click*. Silence wrapped around Zanna. With nothing else to do, she wandered through the shelves and clutter, taking her time to read every title. Her kidnapper had been telling the truth when she had said there was quite the selection to choose from. But one topic was absent: Science. It was a hole in the otherwise comprehensive library, and Zanna guessed that its omission was not an accident. The woman had been trying to prevent Zanna from attending St. Pommeroy's the first day they had met. This was just the next logical step.

Her captor had been thorough, but she hadn't thought of everything. Zanna went to the shelf with the encyclopedias and took down *Poland–Python*, intending to see what the entry on prime numbers said about factoring their products. But all those thoughts flew out of her head as soon as she opened the inner cover of the book. Someone had owned the book before her, and they had written their claim at the top of the page in a familiar unkempt handwriting.

Mine!

CHAPTER THIRTEEN

IN THE DAYS after her kidnapping, Zanna jumped at every stray sound in the house, expecting the Primers to come bursting through the door to rescue her at any moment. But as days became weeks, her hopes dwindled. After all, the Primers had been looking for her kidnapper since Zanna's first day at St. Pommeroy's, and look how well that had turned out. And if the Primers couldn't help her, there didn't seem to be much hope that her friends and grandfather would fare any better. *No,* Zanna realized as she read through every book in the cluttered library, looking for anything that might help her plans for freedom. Her best hope—her *only* hope—was to escape on her own.

So she played along with her kidnapper's hospitality. After a few weeks of good behavior, Zanna was allowed out of the library during the day while the woman went off to attend to some mysterious business she wouldn't talk about, and Zanna wandered through the corridors with pen and paper in hand, looking for weaknesses and mapping out her prison. Besides the sitting room, dining room, kitchen, and library, there was a dusty office; a couple of spare bedrooms and bathrooms down a narrow hallway that might have once housed servants; a laundry room; a greenhouse full of broken clay pots; and a second, darker sitting room. Zanna didn't care much for the last room because it had a stuffed moose head with creepy glass eyes mounted on the wall. She tried climbing through its fireplace and up the chimney to freedom, but half an hour later, she was just ashy and sweaty and had discovered that the top of the chimney had been welded shut.

She tried all the doors and windows. In fact, on the first day she had been left alone in the library, she had climbed up to the high circular window that the illusionary sunlight came through and had bashed on the glass with her shoe. But none of the windows could be broken. Either the woman had done something to the functions of the glass so it was as strong as steel, or it was some other material entirely, made transparent by illusions or chemical manipulation or a combination of both. Zanna didn't know—the primelock hid everything beneath its impenetrable wall of numbers. All she knew was that the windows wouldn't break, and the doors couldn't be forced. Even when she vented her frustration with one of the heavy wood side tables from the sitting room and swung it with all her strength, the windows didn't budge.

There was another mystery Zanna discovered after a few days, while she was alone, reading about prime numbers, and the rest of the house was dead silent. Softly, through the floorboards, she could hear a *whuff-whuff* sound, like someone working a furnace bellows. After she was allowed to wander the house, she went around to all the rooms, putting her ear to the floor. Whatever the sound was, it came from the basement.

One day, she tried the basement door, even though she had tried it a hundred times before. Locked. But then, as she looked up and down the hallway, she had an idea and headed off to the kitchen. The woman had arranged it so that if Zanna was hungry, all she had to do was pull one of the bell ropes scattered around the mansion, and the serving tray would appear in a few moments to take her order before whisking off to the kitchen. But the real excitement was watching the kitchen in action. So, oftentimes, Zanna just stole a chair from the dining room, plopped herself down next to the cutting board, and shouted commands to the knives and pots and plates that buzzed around like worker bees, watching as they made her meal.

On this particular day when she entered, the kitchen was still. Her captor had a collection of knives so extensive it would put a restaurant to shame. They ranged from long to short, serrated to blunt, and graceful to brutish. It was the brutish one Zanna wanted today. A meat cleaver with a heavy square blade of steel. A knife made for ruthlessly chopping through things like bone and gristle. And floorboards.

The best spot would be in the abandoned office, Zanna reasoned. There was a dusty rug in the middle of the room that she could use to hide the mess she made. The floor was old and creaking. And there was the bonus of not having a creepy moose head looking over her shoulder. The only downside was that the door to the office opened right into the front entrance hall. Her kidnapper might have left her alone for the day, but if the woman returned early, the first thing she would see upon entering would be Zanna attacking the floorboards. Zanna could always close the door, but that would save one, maybe two seconds. She remembered how quickly the house had slammed the front door shut when she tried to make a break for it that first night.

There was no other option than to be quick. Zanna knelt down behind the large desk in the center of the abandoned office and threw back the rug, coughing as a cloud of dust billowed out around her. She had tried hacking at the walls after throwing furniture at the windows, with the same amount of success. But she hadn't tried the floor. It was possible that the woman had treated the floorboards with the same reinforcing functions she used on the walls—but it was just as possible that they had been overlooked. If they hadn't, Zanna was out of ideas. *Only one way to find out*, she thought and then swung the meat cleaver.

It made a satisfying, splitting *crack*, and Zanna grinned. *Overlooked.*

A few more swings, and she had a hole big enough to put her fingers through. With the flat of the cleaver, she levered up floorboards until the hole was wide enough for her body to fit through. Beneath the floorboards was a gap for the cross-beams to run and then the ceiling of the cellar. Zanna reached down into the cool, dank space and felt around. It was brick and crumbled a little at her touch. She put the meat cleaver to the side and stood up, lowering her foot into the hole. With a hasty check out the window to see if the coast was still clear, Zanna kicked, and the old mortar begin to crack and shift under her heel. Zanna held tightly to the desk to make sure she wouldn't lose her balance, and then she kicked again. It broke through with an explosion of dust. For a moment, she held very still with her foot dangling in the black of the cellar, wincing at the sound of loose bricks falling while expecting the woman to appear, demanding to know what all the noise was about. But there was nothing except that mysterious *whuff-whuff*, slightly louder than before.

Zanna looked around for something to lower herself down with. The curtains might work, but she knew that once she tore them down, she wouldn't be able to put them back up properly. Her eyes fell on the bell rope in the corner, but then she nixed the idea. That was so old, it would probably snap as soon as she put any weight on it.

"Stairs," she muttered, peering into the inky depths of the cellar. "Why must you be so difficult?"

Setting the meat cleaver off to the side, she hurried back into the dining room. The curtains had given her an idea. In a small closet off to the side that housed the table settings, Zanna found a stack of spare tablecloths. She took one. She also took a candlestick, but there were no matches in the small closet. No doubt the woman had rounded them up and stashed them somewhere safe, as if Zanna was a toddler in danger of setting the house on fire.

"Hey, you!" she barked at the silver serving tray. "Make me a grilled-cheese sandwich."

The tray roused at the command, almost a little gruff at the tone Zanna had taken. As her request spread, the kitchen whipped into action. An oven mitt detached itself and went to the refrigerator, pulling out bread, cheese, and butter. It carried the ingredients to the cutting board, where a knife and frying pan were waiting. The knife put half the butter in the frying pan and scraped the other half over the bread. Meanwhile, the frying pan went to the stove, which had turned itself on, and began to melt the butter.

This was what Zanna had been waiting for. There were locks on the stove—whether to prevent children from burning themselves or to keep her from blowing the house apart—that Zanna had tried to get around but failed. Everything was controlled with functions inside the stove, and Zanna couldn't get in there, not while it was primelocked. But she could tell it to cook something for her.

As the oven mitt brought her sandwich over to the sizzling pan, Zanna reached up with her candle and poked it into the burner. It melted a good bit of the wax, which splattered over the stove, but the wick was lit. With her light and makeshift rope, Zanna headed back to the office.

The descent wasn't quite as easy as she had imagined. Tablecloths didn't make good ropes on the best of days, and this was further complicated by having to juggle a lit candle. But at least it was a short drop, and after a few minutes of trouble and kicking more bricks out of the way, she was down.

The candle barely distinguished the brick arches five feet in front of her, and Zanna wished she knew how to manipulate light. If only she knew that, she could make the light from the candle fill the entire room with a golden glow like midday. Instead, she picked her way carefully over the fallen bricks, shuffling through the dark and dust with one hand out.

"Stairs," she muttered to herself. "Stairs and lights. I'm never taking you for granted again."

A grid of brick columns with arches stretching between them supported the ceiling, making Zanna feel as if she had wandered into a catacomb. The spiders didn't help much, either. A few odds and ends were stashed down here—shovels and spades and barrels and an empty wine rack. Zanna made a note of the earthmoving equipment. The brick wall didn't look as solid as it used to be, and she might be able to tunnel through it and out of the primelock. It would take a while, but she had all the time in the world.

The *whuff-whuff* sound was close. She stepped around a brick column and saw a massive iron furnace set in the wall beside a dusty pile of coal. Pipes twisted and grew out of the top, disappearing into the ceiling. Zanna knelt down at the open grill and stuck her candle in. Only dust and ash and spiders. Then she noticed how her candle flame flickered back and forth. So that explained the *whuff-whuff*. The furnace was pumping air around. She circled until she found a rusted valve on the side that looked like it had been used to drain water. Propping the candle against the wall and gritting her teeth, Zanna wrenched on the valve until the rust and corrosion broke and it opened.

Cold mountain air flowed out, its scent of pine forests fresh and unmistakable in the dank squalor of the cellar. Zanna nearly let out a cry of delight. Air from the outside! But then she got a better look at its functions, and her heart sank. The air that blew over her hands and tickled at her face had been primelocked. It was just as useless as everything else in here.

Above her, the cellar door unlocked.

Zanna froze, her hands still cupped beneath the open valve. The woman was back already. How had Zanna not heard the front door? She had been so focused on exploring the cellar and figuring out the furnace that she had forgotten how precarious a situation she was in. The office was a wreck. There were splintered boards and dust and a meat cleaver and a tablecloth tied around the desk that led down into the cellar. Zanna stood very still, listening for the woman's footsteps.

Something touched her in the dark.

Zanna screamed. She flailed, and her knuckles connected with something metal and rang with a burst of pain, sending whatever had snuck up behind her skittering back into the dark. Then her ankle twisted on a piece of loose coal, and she fell back against the furnace with a single, echoing *clang*.

Silence returned to the cellar. Zanna had kicked the candle in her panic, but it was still lit, the flame faintly illuminating the side of a bucket. She picked it up. If that had been her kidnapper, the woman wasn't making any sound now. Perhaps she had knocked her head. If so, Zanna wouldn't get another chance to get the primelock keys from her.

Carefully, her heart thundering, Zanna crept through the dark until she stepped on something that was soft and yielding and squished under her shoe.

It was her grilled-cheese sandwich.

The silver serving tray floated out of the shadows, evidently having collected itself from where Zanna had knocked it. It made a small bow, pleased at having delivered Zanna's meal.

"Just you wait," Zanna muttered to the fleeing serving tray. She scraped the ruined sandwich off her shoe and kicked it into the corner. "This isn't over yet, tray."

The incident had rattled her, though, and she brushed herself off, having seen all there was to see in the cellar. But at the stairs, she paused and rubbed her chin, smearing her face with coal ash. The door at the top of the stairs was open. Had it opened for the serving tray? It must have, for as the tray bobbled through the open door, it began to close, and Zanna hurried to slip through. It shut and locked itself behind her, tight as before.

There was a lot to think about. After Zanna had cleaned up her mess in the office by pushing everything down the hole and covering it with the rug, she went to the library. On a fresh piece of paper, she drew a crude floor plan of the house—she had the entire place memorized by now. The serving tray resided in the kitchen, so she marked that. How did it know where she was in the house? She had ordered food before and then wandered off, and each time the tray had managed to track her down and complete its delivery.

Her Self function. That's what the tray had to be looking for. The house had her Self catalogued. It had noticed she was down in the basement and told the tray to take the sandwich straight to her. Which would have meant opening a door that should have stayed locked. Zanna puzzled over this bit of newfound knowledge until she heard the front door. A little while later, the door to the library opened, and her kidnapper walked in.

"Have a good day?" the woman asked. An odor of diesel and dirty smoke hung around her, as if she had doused herself in exhaust before coming back. Zanna barely lifted her eyes from the book she had picked up at random, pretending to be deeply engrossed in it.

"Suppose," she grumbled. She turned a page and stared at

the words, not reading them at all. The woman was still standing by the library door, waiting.

"Come have a snack with me," she said at last. "I want to talk to you."

Fear tightened in Zanna's gut, and she looked up sharply, trying her best to hide the guilt in her stomach. "About what?" she asked, as innocently as possible.

But the woman didn't answer. She just walked out, leaving Zanna to put down her book and follow. They went to the dining room and sat down, the woman calling for lemonade and pretzel sticks. When the tray came out, almost gloating in the way it bobbed around the table, Zanna gave it a glare. "Don't you dare," she mouthed, snatching her lemonade from it.

Her captor took a long drink, taking in the old and ripped portraits before speaking. "Zanna, I'm not your mother. I let you have free rein of my house while I am away because I want you to be comfortable. I want you to enjoy your time here." She pinched the bridge of her nose, as if the conversation had given her a headache, and let out a disappointed sigh. Zanna braced.

"But," the woman said, flicking an invisible speck from her fingertips, "it seems that I have been too lenient. You have been taking advantage of my hospitality."

Zanna shoved the resurgence of guilt down with a handful of pretzel sticks, keeping her gaze level. "I don't call keeping me prisoner very *hospitable*," she said. Snark kept the fear from creeping into her voice.

"What? You thought I would let you run about unsupervised?" The woman laughed. "I'm not that foolish. My house has been watching."

An illusion snapped into existence on the table between them. It was like looking into a dollhouse room that was decorated just like the empty office. A small Zanna, no taller than a pen, hacked away at the floorboards with a meat cleaver. Her kidnapper flipped through the action, impatient to get to the good part where Zanna broke through and kicked at the bricks of the cellar. Then it cut to her tying the tablecloth around the desk and descending into the hole.

One of the woman's eyebrows arched imperiously, daring Zanna to say anything.

"I'm supposed to be escaping," she said, surprising herself with how haughty she sounded. Not that the situation could get much worse. "That's what people do when you lock them up for no good reason."

The woman smiled, but it quickly disappeared. "Well then, by that line of reasoning, I'm supposed to be upset about property damage. I have been overlooking your attempts on my windows and doors, but this—" She gestured to the dollhouse illusion. "I can't overlook this one. You will be locked in your room tomorrow and in the days to come, until you can prove to me that you're not going to tear up my floorboards. This is a historic house, you know. It deserves some respect."

"You and your stupid house can rot, for all I care," Zanna spat.

The woman froze with a strange, stricken look on her face, like someone had shoved a needle in her heart.

Instinctively, Zanna opened her mouth to apologize, but then she remembered who it was she was talking to and shut her mouth again, almost pleased that she had managed to land a hit.

"Very well," the woman said, a little quieter than before. "If you're done, I'll take you up to your room now. The tray will bring you dinner."

Zanna nodded and pushed away her lemonade and the bowl of pretzel sticks. "Fine. I'm done anyways."

The woman's Iron took Zanna by the wrist. She led Zanna to

the tower, with its missing staircase, and deposited her gently but unceremoniously on the landing. Then, without a word of parting, the woman dropped out of sight.

In her room, Zanna crawled up on top of her desk so she could better see out of the large, solitary window. It wasn't even as if she had discovered anything worthwhile in the basement. Running a hand over the nearby radiator, she felt the air seeping out and circulating. Was the woman upset because Zanna had discovered the furnace? It didn't seem like any sort of great earthshaking secret. So the air circulation was handled by an old coal furnace stuffed full of functions. No, it had to be the possibility of Zanna tunneling through the basement walls and out of the primelock. The woman was probably down there right now, getting rid of the shovels and reinforcing the crumbling brick walls.

The lights went out without a word of warning and left Zanna in the starlight. She climbed into bed and pulled the covers around her, but there was too much going through her mind to fall asleep. It didn't sit right. Digging out of the basement would have taken forever. Even with the shovels down there, they were so far north the ground would be frozen solid. There was some other reason her kidnapper was worried. Something Zanna was overlooking.

Where did the tray get my Self function from? The thought was so sudden and unexpected, Zanna's eyes shot open. If the tray had used her Self function to find and deliver her sandwich, it had to have gotten the function from somewhere. But Zanna had never given the woman a drop of blood. She had only done that twice—once for St. Pommeroy's registration and once for the I-beam down in her basement.

There was another way, though. It made too much sense to ignore. Her captor knew a lot about Zanna. She knew that

Zanna was supposed to be attending St. Pommeroy's on the first day of school. She knew where Zanna lived. She knew that Zanna's father was a pilot, that he sent letters with foreign money in them, that his handwriting was messy and sad, and that he always signed with just his name. She knew Zanna liked hot cider and scrambled eggs covered in ketchup and warmly lit libraries. She signed her books just like Zanna did.

The tray hadn't needed to get Zanna's Self function from anywhere. The woman had given it herself.

"No," Zanna whispered to the dark bedroom. Her fists knotted up the bedsheets so tightly the fabric ripped. "You can't be. You can't be . . . *me.*"

CHAPTER FOURTEEN

BEING LOCKED UP in her room was torture. If Zanna let her mind wander for any length of time, it always went back to the idea that she and her kidnapper were the same person. When she tried to distract herself by thinking about Pops and how he was dealing with her absence, she heard his voice telling her to follow where the evidence led, no matter how impossible. When she thought of her friends, she saw them in the wreckage of her hallway, bloodied and unconscious and trapped in cages of air pressure that *she* had made. Zanna couldn't even read any of the books on the shelves without seeing *Mine!* written in her own handwriting on the inside covers.

So she made paper airplanes and origami cranes and created sock puppets to distract herself. But even then, the boredom gnawed off parts of her brain. Every day she looked out at the snowy landscape, the urge to claw at the windows got stronger. What saved her, oddly enough, was Dr. Trout. Zanna couldn't do any of her schoolwork for Mathematics, Chemistry, or Physics without the proper books and notes, but she didn't need any of that to work on Self. And while thoughts about Irons and specializations or meditation exercises made a beeline to painful questions about who she really was, there was one assignment for Dr. Trout that had nothing to do with whether or not the strange woman keeping Zanna prisoner was just a version of herself from the future. The paper on Cedwick.

Zanna wrote and rewrote that paper until her pen was out

of ink and she had to request a new one. In a way, she was thankful for the opportunity to focus on nothing else but getting the words right. The more she worked on it, the more she wanted it to be perfect. The plan that Nora had given all of them in Pops's guest bathroom hadn't stopped just because the party was over. Zanna had a second chance to fix everything.

It was all her fault. With the distance and time to look back on it, Zanna realized she had never even given Cedwick a chance. Everything that she had thought was just him being an arrogant English twerp—him always correcting her, showing off in class—had been his way of trying to get out from under the shadow of Owin and Lord Hemmington. And Zanna had been trying to put him back in his proper place with every chance she got. No wonder he had lashed out in the nurse's cottage that day after the Laboratory.

Eventually, though, even her report on Cedwick came back to the Variable, as Zanna decided to call the woman. Zanna certainly wasn't going to call her by *her* name. It was the Variable who had told Cedwick that he was the only one at her father's party who had made the right decision. Everyone else—including Owin—had lost. The more Zanna rewrote her report, the more she heard that voice creeping in, reassuring Cedwick that he was not useless. She crumpled up the graph paper with a frustrated growl and threw it into the far corner.

She then resorted to drawing the floor plan of the mansion over and over. It was mindless work, but it gave her hands something to do that wasn't tearing out her hair. The Variable had primelocked the entire house, which meant that she had gone through and hidden every single function behind an impenetrable wall of numbers, like translating every book in a library into unbreakable code. She had been thorough, even primelocking the grounds around the mansion. There were keys, but Zanna doubted they were tangible things that could be stolen—

Zanna stopped, her pen pressed against the page. She had drawn sketches of the first floor and the air-pressure barrier around it many times before, but something was wrong. What had Owin said when he had set up the air-pressure barrier at her house? It needed to breathe. Air had to come in somehow. Otherwise, everyone inside would suffocate.

Hesitantly, controlling her excitement, she drew an arrow that crossed the border and labeled it *Air.* But the air coming in wasn't primelocked. That's what the furnace was for. To primelock the incoming air before pumping it into the rest of the house. It was a gatekeeper.

It was never about Zanna digging out of the basement. It was about the *furnace*, the weak point in the Variable's otherwise solid barrier. That's why Zanna had been locked up in her room—so the Variable could put some new defenses on the basement and make sure that Zanna couldn't poke around in it again.

Escape had been in her hands, and she had botched it. Zanna slumped heavily over her desk, letting out a deep sigh that made her papers flutter and skitter away. If only she had figured this out faster, she could have been on her way to freedom right now. She could have dismantled the furnace, undone the primelock, and disappeared into the woods. Instead, she had wasted her opportunity. And there wouldn't be another one.

Unless . . .

Her unfocused eyes snapped back to the papers her breathy sigh had sent scattering across the desk. She pursed her lips and blew again. The furnace wasn't the only way to get air into the house. A breath, a single breath, could be carried in from outside. If her guess was correct about the furnace serving as a gateway, then the first few breaths the Variable exhaled when she came back into the house wouldn't be primelocked.

Zanna scrambled for a new piece of paper. An exhale was not that different from an inhale. Most of the gases were the same. Nitrogen, oxygen, carbon dioxide, and trace amounts of argon and water vapor. She listed all the elements and their atomic compositions, as she had in her early Chemistry classes. Nitrogen was atomic number 7, oxygen 8, argon 18. Both nitrogen and oxygen paired off in diatomic molecules. Argon was a noble gas and didn't pair off at all.

Then the rush stopped, and Zanna came up short, staring down at the page. The words slipped out of her mouth. "What are you doing?"

It was an absurd idea. She couldn't even manipulate the cube of graphite in the Laboratory that had been precisely engineered to be the most basic object in the universe. Her plan was ten times more complicated. Gases moved and bounced and were invisible to the naked eye. They would be subject to the pressure of the room and the air currents. Their coordinates would be all but impossible to pin down. And she would have to be close to the Variable. Very close.

"That's what you get for not figuring it out sooner," she muttered. She had forgone the sock puppets a while ago and was just talking to herself now. "Always making things more difficult than they should be."

Her door opened, and Zanna jumped, fearing the Variable knew exactly what she was up to and had come to nip it in the bud. But it was just the serving tray with lunch. Zanna narrowed her eyes.

"Trying to scare me again?" she said. "Nice try, tray. But that doesn't count."

The tray didn't make any indication whether it cared if that counted or not. It just bobbed beside her, offering its bowl of minestrone with sourdough bread and a mug of hot cider. Zanna watched the curls of steam rise from the bowl of soup and tried to anticipate how they would twist. After all, steam was a gas and would move very similarly to an exhale from the Variable. She got up from her desk and began to circle the room, the tray dutifully tagging along behind her, still offering up her lunch. The steam made a ribbon in the air that Zanna watched as long as she could before it dissipated, paying close attention to how it was torn apart by the currents in the tower room. She moved to the left, and the tray followed. She moved to the right, and the tray changed direction at once, not spilling a drop of soup. With a devious grin, Zanna scampered over her bed and into her makeshift bathroom, the research breaking into a game as she ducked under the tray and ran back to her bed, climbing her wardrobe up into the rafters of the room.

The tray barely paused. It ascended smoothly up next to her, and she had to admit defeat, leaning back against one of the roof beams with a grin. "I suppose I've tormented you enough for one day," Zanna said, wrapping her hands around the bowl of minestrone. But as she spooned up her lunch, an idea came to her, and she put the soup back. "Sorry," she said, swinging down from the rafters. "I lied. Come on!"

The tray followed her like a puppy as she led it over to the privacy curtain—one of those old multi-paneled ones made out of lacquered wood that aristocratic ladies were always ducking behind to throw undergarments around dramatically in black-and-white period movies. Zanna grabbed the end panel and rearranged the privacy curtain so it made a six-sided enclosure around the tray. Then she stepped back and watched.

It took a few seconds, but her hypothesis was confirmed. The tray floated up over the privacy curtain. She patted the tray and put it back in the enclosure, rearranging the privacy curtain into a crude maze. Again, it took the direct path, up and over. Zanna frowned and reset the test, this time throwing her blanket over the top so it couldn't just fly out. For a moment she thought she had it stumped, but then the tray appeared at the exit of her maze and bobbled over to her, seeming slightly annoyed that she still had yet to eat her lunch.

"Okay, that's enough," Zanna said, taking her soup back. "And I mean it this time." The tray bowed, apparently thankful to be free of her demands, and headed back down to the kitchen. She plopped down on her bed and pulled her legs up to her chest, gnawing at the sourdough as her mind worked.

Pathfinding. The tray must be using a pathfinding function. It asked the house where Zanna's Self function was and then made its way toward her. The function seemed fairly robust too. The tray wasn't afraid to backtrack a little, if that's what it took to get to its destination.

Zanna put her spoon down and drew a theoretical line with her finger, sketching the different mazes she had built and how the tray had solved each one. How big an area did it search? She had been clear across the house before, and it had still never failed to find her—that had been obvious from her encounter in the basement.

Did it ever search outside?

Zanna stopped mid-chew. Wasn't the mansion just a maze on a larger scale? All she had to do was get somewhere so distant that the tray had to go outside to reach her. Somewhere where the shortest route to her would make the serving tray unlock the front door.

The chimney.

It came to her so suddenly that she jumped and spilled the minestrone all over her sheets. But she didn't have time to pay attention to the mess. Her mind raced. If she closed the fireplace grate behind her and climbed all the way to the top of the chimney, what would the tray do? It might bump against the fireplace grate. It might spin uselessly in the upper corner of a second-floor room. But it might—just might—think she was on the roof and wander outside to reach her. It just might be her ticket out of here.

The rest of the afternoon stretched on and on. Zanna called the tray back up to her on the pretense of wanting a glass of water; then she made it go through a whole obstacle course made out of bedsheets and privacy curtains. Everything seemed to point to her theory being sound—the tray always found a way out of the maze, no matter how complicated she made it. But every time she felt giddiness at the thought of freedom, she had to remind herself that these were just small-scale tests. The real thing was an entirely different animal.

Far below her, the front door opened.

Panic gripped her tight and fast. She had spent her entire afternoon tormenting the serving tray and had completely forgotten about studying airflow. Quickly, with the desperation of a student cramming at the last minute, Zanna refreshed her memory. She decided to focus on nitrogen, as that was the most abundant element in air. The molecule was diatomic—two nitrogen atoms in a triple bond. Its gravitational function would be slight, its mass minuscule. Coordinates were the tricky part. Gas molecules weren't arranged in nice structural lattices like graphite. Instead, they bounced off one another, the coordinates changing by the millisecond as they collided and scattered. But there was a method to it—as long as she could do the calculations fast enough. Terror thumped in her heart, but she didn't have the time to study any further. If she put this off for one more day, she would go insane.

She slammed a fist on her door. "Hey!" she shouted as loudly as she could. "Hey! Let me out!"

Agonizing silence followed, and Zanna's palms began to sweat. Every moment was another exhale gone, another handful of nitrogen lost somewhere in the house. She raised a fist to pound on the door again, but then it snapped open, and the Variable was on the other side, smirking.

"Well, good evening to you, too," she said.

Zanna did her best to scowl back and hide the trembling that had started in her fingertips. She tried to sift through the air between them, pushing through the primelocked molecules, but the effort of concentration made her eyelids drop, and she stopped. If she closed her eyes, the Variable would know she was up to something, and the plan would be ruined. Zanna had to distract her.

"Let me out," she said. As distractions went, it wasn't her best effort, but the Variable's mouth quirked slightly, amused.

"Had enough of being cooped up in your room?" She let out a breath, and there it was. Air, free air from the outside. Carbon dioxide and nitrogen and water vapor and oxygen, just as Zanna had remembered from school. She snatched at the nitrogen, but the coordinates were wrong, her calculations of its bouncing molecules too slow. It danced out of her grasp, and her face twisted into an even harder scowl.

The Variable still wore that bemused expression on her face, and Zanna remembered that she was supposed to say something in return. But with all her brainpower going toward manipulating the nitrogen, Zanna had completely forgotten the question she had been asked a second ago.

"Let me out."

The Variable frowned. "Not if you're going to be like that. I've told you before, there's no reason why we can't get along.

It will make things so much—" She stopped in mid-sentence, eyes suddenly alert.

Zanna stopped trying to grab the nitrogen at once, but the woman had already caught the scent of trouble. It was going to be the basement all over again—another avenue of escape wasted for nothing—unless Zanna distracted her, and quickly.

She blurted out the first thing that came to mind.

"I know who you are."

As distractions went, it was perfect. The Variable still held Zanna with that intense stare, but its focus had shifted, and the feeling was like a weight off Zanna's chest.

"Do you now?"

"I do," Zanna said, and the conviction in her voice almost surprised her. "There's only one person you could be."

"And who is that?"

The Variable exhaled again, and there was very little free nitrogen left. Zanna would not get another chance after this. So she squared her shoulders and planted her feet and swung for the fences, no matter how it tore up inside her.

"Me."

And there was her chance. When the woman blinked, unable to control the ripple that went through her, Zanna made a bold attempt for the nitrogen. Everything else cleared out from her mind, as if she had swiped her arm over a cluttered table. She forgot she was locked in a tower room in a stolen Victorian mansion somewhere in the far north. She forgot about the madwoman who had imprisoned her here. She forgot about St. Pommeroy's. She forgot about her friends and Pops. There was only nitrogen. Zanna held every shred of knowledge she had, all the calculations to pin down the coordinates of the molecules as they ricocheted off each other, and made them into one complete function.

Everything snapped together like that first day in Dr. Fitzie's classroom when Zanna had learned how to draw theoretical lines, only this was exponentially better. One moment, she had been juggling chemical, gravity, and coordinate functions, and the next, all that was gone, replaced by one grand function of nitrogen. She could dive into it and see the parts that made it tick, but she could also pull back and observe it from a distance. This was nitrogen, this was everything that made it exist, and it was in her head.

Zanna swallowed to hide the grin threatening to spread over her entire face. But she needn't have worried. The Variable had not noticed.

"I am you," the woman said, drawing it out so Zanna could hear the absurdity in the statement. "And how exactly does that work?"

Zanna shrugged. The rush of holding nitrogen—even if it was just half a breath's worth—surged through her, and she wanted to dance around with it, make it stretch and compact and bounce off the walls like a child playing with a ribbon. The sooner she could bring the conversation to a close, the sooner she could be alone again. "No, you're right, it doesn't," she said. "Are you going to let me out?"

The Variable sighed and shook her head. "Not until you've calmed down and proven to me that you're not going to tear up my floors again," she said. "I put a lot of effort into this house, you know."

Responses danced through Zanna's head—quips about the real reason to keep her out of the basement and how she didn't need to tear up the floors to escape—but Zanna held her tongue. She just shifted her weight from foot to foot and her scowl from side to side.

"I see," the woman said after Zanna had been quiet for half

a minute. She backed out of the room. "Tell me when you're ready to be mature about this."

The door snapped shut behind her. Zanna slowly counted to fifty and then beckoned to her nitrogen. It trickled down through the air and came to rest on her palm. She felt nothing change, but she knew it was there, like an invisible extension of her hand. Her mind churned with the effort of keeping its function together, since it began to slip free at the slightest distraction. But it was hers and free of the primelock, and a maniacal, triumphant laugh burst up out of her belly.

"Laughing alone in a tower room, Zanna?" she said when the impulse had passed. "You're right on your way to becoming a mad Scientist."

She pulled her nitrogen out into a long string and went into her bathroom, feeding it into the half-filled bottle of shampoo and then turning the bottle upside down so the gas bubbled to the top.

"Be good," she whispered, like a mother tucking her child into bed. "I have big plans for you."

CHAPTER FIFTEEN

IT WAS DEEP in the heart of night when Zanna threw back the covers of her bed and put her feet to the floor. She had been going back and forth on whether it was better to escape tonight or tomorrow during the day while the Variable was out. Doing it now meant Zanna would have to be absolutely silent. But doing it tomorrow risked the Variable coming home early. As the episode with the basement had proven, the house was watching her. If it could send some kind of alert, the woman would be home before Zanna was down from her tower, and everything would be ruined. It had to be in the night. *This* night.

She glanced out the window as she layered on clothes and wrapped her blanket around her. It didn't seem nearly enough to brave the bitter cold outside, but Zanna had nothing warmer. She spread one of her two bedsheets on the floor, filling it with an extra pair of shoes, a stack of blank paper and pens, and a book of puzzles she hadn't gotten around to cracking open. On impulse, she added the crumpled report on Cedwick she had thrown in the corner. Everything else, she would have to pick up along the way. Knotting the makeshift rucksack together and slinging it over her shoulder made her feel a bit like a homeless Santa, and when she caught sight of herself in the mirror, wrapped up in her blanket and a lumpy sack on her back, she had to stifle a giggle. It felt good to laugh, because the rest of her was scared to death.

She pulled the bell cord to summon the serving tray, holding her second bedsheet and the shampoo bottle with the nitrogen inside. When the door slid open, Zanna slipped out onto the landing. She didn't have to look over the edge to know how treacherous the drop was down to the first floor of the mansion. Her stomach already knew.

"Bring me five roast-beef sandwiches with Swiss cheese, five apples, and a mug of hot cider," she whispered to the serving tray. "And a dinner roll with butter on the side."

The tray disappeared into the shadows below her. Zanna flipped open the cap of her shampoo bottle and let the nitrogen bubble up, catching it as it escaped. The clock had started, and there was no time to dawdle. She had to be down the tower and back up the chimney by the time the serving tray returned with her meal. She tied the four corners of her second bedsheet under her shoulders to make a parachute and then filled it with her small ball of nitrogen, ignoring the part of her brain pointing out just how fragile a contraption she was trusting with her life.

When it was complete, she stood at the edge of the landing, her mind reeling at the black stairless tower below. "But seriously," she muttered to herself, gathering her courage even as her knees threatened to give out from underneath her. "Seriously," she said again, her hands clenched around the bedsheet and her mind clenched around the nitrogen. "Stairs."

Then she jumped.

It went to pieces immediately. A retching, sickening *thud* walloped her in the stomach, and she lost control of her nitrogen. She snatched at it, but its function had changed. Zanna was falling, and her mind blacked out in absolute terror.

Gravity is just a function.

Owin's voice cut through her panic. Of course! She had forgotten to account for the downward acceleration of her body on the nitrogen in the parachute. That was why it had twisted out of her grip as soon as she'd jumped.

Her galloping pulse pounded in her ears, but Zanna focused. Ignoring the part of her mind yelling that she had approximately 1.4 seconds before splattering over the floor, she hurriedly recalculated, hoping she hadn't overlooked anything else. There wouldn't be time for a second chance.

It held.

She came to a stop with a jerk and a muffled grunt. And not a second too soon. The ground was only a couple of inches underneath her, enough that she could tap it with her foot. For a moment she hovered there, waiting for her heart to slow down and her stomach to quiet before she called the nitrogen back into her hand. The bedsheet deflated, and she gathered it up in her arms, hurrying as fast as her shaking legs would carry her.

In order to reach the sitting room with the fireplace, she had to go to the other side of the mansion, which meant passing by the main staircase. In the weird shadows of the northern night, the mansion took on a different face that made Zanna's flesh prickle. She idled at the bottom of the stairs for a moment, looking up at the locked door of the Variable's chambers on the second floor. Their conversation that evening echoed in her head, and Zanna told herself it didn't matter who the woman was. With any luck, Zanna wouldn't see her again after tonight. Then she shivered once and hurried on.

The sitting room smelled of charcoal and mothballs and that stupid stuffed moose head. Zanna waited in the doorway until her eyes adjusted, since there weren't any windows here to let the moonlight in. When at last she could see the fireplace at the far end, she made her way to it—and the lever in the wall that opened and closed the ash grate. It heaved open with a complaint of old metal, and Zanna winced at how the sound split open the quiet night.

She poked her head into the fireplace and suddenly reconsidered her plan. The inside of the chimney was even darker than the sitting room and scratched with the promise of spiders and centipedes and other crawly things that lived in old, shadowy brickwork. Zanna told herself that she had climbed up there before and had been just fine, but the other half of her brain said that the climb had been during the day and that she hadn't been toting a lumpy sack of bedsheets with her. But time was running out—the kitchen had to be finishing her order by now, and the tray would begin looking for her soon. With a grimace, she tied one end of her parachute bedsheet to the lever of the ash grate and climbed into the fireplace.

It was a far tighter fit than before. Zanna pushed the rucksack with her clothes up first, then braced her legs on either side of the chimney, shimmying her way up. The blanket caught on everything and rubbed the soot off the walls, making her eyes water and her nose tickle. When she had climbed up a couple of feet, she gave her parachute a tug. It pulled the ash grate closed with a screech of rusty pieces, and the chimney plunged into complete darkness.

Claustrophobia rose instantly in her throat, and Zanna forced herself to take a long and calming breath, even though it brought more ash than air. She had to climb up. That was enough to focus on. It distracted her from the dark and the spiders and the tight space. Just as she had done when manipulating the nitrogen, she wiped everything else from her mind except moving her arms and legs. One foot and then one hand, slowly inching higher and higher.

It took ages, but eventually, she felt her rucksack bump against something solid and refuse to go any higher. She locked her knees and leaned back against the chimney wall as best she could. Even though the air was freezing, she was out of breath from the exertion of her strange acrobatics. Zanna waited for her heart to stop thumping so wildly, and then she put her ear to the chimney wall.

But there was only the *scritch* of her shoes knocking bits of brick free and the echoing *ping* as they hit the closed ash grate below. Zanna did a rough calculation of how long it would take the kitchen to make five sandwiches and a mug of hot cider. If she was too hasty in climbing back down, the tray would still be inside the house, and she would have wasted her chance. She strained her ears, listening for anything like a door opening or the tray knocking on the other side of the chimney, but the mansion was silent.

Claustrophobia crept back. Without anything else to occupy her mind, Zanna felt every quiver in her legs. Every slip of her shoes. Invisible things with many legs scurrying down her neck. Her knees and elbows yearning for open space. She couldn't stay like this. But she had to give the tray more time.

So she took a deep breath and dove into her Self function.

Her claustrophobia ebbed away when she felt the enormity of the function that made her who she was, but it also brought fresh, new fears she had been trying to forget about. There was no pushing away uncomfortable thoughts in here, not when it was all spelled out in unflinching mathematics.

She and the Variable were the same person.

Now that she had put it into words, the evidence was piling up. Who else would know how to forge a letter from her father? Who else would know how to build a mansion and a library that were the manifestation of Zanna's dreams? Who else wrote *Mine!* on the inside cover of their books in Zanna's handwriting? The more she turned it over, the better it fit. The very first day of school, Dr. Mumble had promised her mastery over space and time. Zanna had seen every other law of the universe manipulated at St. Pommeroy's—was it that impossible to believe in time travel? It would explain how there had come to be a young Zanna and an old Zanna. It would explain the speech the Variable had given the first night about the "dark times coming." It would explain everything.

Zanna twisted away from the thought. The Variable had attacked her friends, had attacked Pops. That alone was enough to convince Zanna they weren't the same person.

But the woman had also asked Pops to not hate her too much.

Zanna scrubbed that last thought from her mind. They weren't the same person, and that was that. Anything telling her otherwise got squeezed until it shut up. She had killed enough time. Her legs quivered with exertion, and she felt as if she was going to be cleaning soot out of her skin for years. As carefully and quietly as she could manage, she began climbing back down the chimney.

"I'm never making fun of Santa Claus again," she muttered, tugging her blanket free of a bit of rough brick. The bedsheet she had used for a parachute was still down at the bottom of the chimney, one end fed through the closed ash grate and tied around the handle. She found the nitrogen she had put back in her shampoo bottle and fed it through the ash grate in a wispy tendril, telling it to pool in the slack bedsheet. Then she pushed it away from her, moving the bedsheet and the handle with it.

A shriek of rusty hinges, and Zanna was free. She wallowed around in the fireplace for a moment, her legs refusing to work properly. Soot billowed around her, and she sucked in a lungful, spitting out a loud, riotous cough before she could clap her hands over her mouth.

It echoed all the way down the hallway. Zanna froze. Something thumped dully around her, like footsteps hurrying toward the sound, and Zanna braced for the Variable to come flying into the room. But it was only her heart in her ears. The house turned over and went back to sleep.

Time was of the essence now. Zanna saw no serving tray in the sitting room and imagined it up on the roof, its pathfinding function noticing that she had appeared back inside the house. It would make a beeline for the door and Zanna had to meet it there. Her legs still cramped and shaking, she forced herself to hurry. In the morning there would be a trail of chimney soot and grime as obvious as a blundering elephant, but Zanna would be gone by then. She had to be.

Every step forced blood into her stiff legs and sent showers of needles up through her knees. Scratches she had suffered while climbing the chimney complained one by one, stinging with the soot and dust rubbed into the wounds. Her breaths were raspy, and her mouth, parched. But step by agonizing step, she made it to the front door.

Everything was silent. There was just Zanna's panting and pounding heart. She stared at the front door and that impossible lock: the one that looked so simple, yet which she had failed to break open after spending days upon days trying. *There are other doors to the outside*, she thought with a sudden fear. The back door in the greenhouse. The servants' entrance. The tray could come in from one of those. Or a window. Or it could never have made it outside in the first place. Zanna had heard no doors open or close, but then again, she had been stuffed inside a chimney for probably the last half hour.

"Come on," she muttered. The words tasted like ash. "Come on, tray."

The door remained closed.

"Come on," she tried again. "Just this once, and you'll be free of me. I promise. Come on."

It was still closed.

Zanna wavered. She calculated how long it should take the tray to make it from the roof to the front door, and she didn't like the number she came up with. "Come on," she whispered. Tears came to her eyes, and it wasn't because of the fireplace soot. It had been such a good plan too. "Please. Let me out."

A *click*, then sharp, bitter air blew in from the mountains. Snow on pine trees and frozen streams. The outside.

It was so immediate and stunning that she nearly missed her opportunity. The tray was almost next to her when Zanna snapped back to life. She ducked underneath the tray, pulling her sack after her. With another *click*, the front door locked, sealing the Variable's terrible mansion again, but this time Zanna was quicker than it. This time, she got out.

The tray spun around and presented itself, pleased that it was finally delivering its meal, and Zanna gave it an affectionate pat. "I knew we'd get along eventually," she said before kneeling to unknot her sack. She stuffed the sandwiches and apples into it and took the butter knife from beside the dinner roll and tucked it up one of her sleeves so she could access it easily. Braving the wilderness with a dull butter knife wasn't exactly her ideal scenario, but it was better than having no weapon at all. She took a few bites of the roll, not wanting to waste it, and washed it down with the cider. It was ice-cold from being outside for so long, but as Zanna stood on the porch of the mansion and looked out at the forest, it was the best thing she had ever tasted.

She drained the cider and put the mug back on the tray. "Take care of yourself now," she said, picking up her rucksack and tying it around her shoulders. "Don't take this the wrong way, but I hope I never see you again."

The serving tray didn't seem insulted by Zanna's remark. It just gave a little bow, as it always did, and headed back into the house, the door snapping open and shut with a final locking *click*.

And with that, Zanna was free.

It was time to get moving. She had to be as far away from the mansion as possible by the time the Variable woke up and realized she was gone. But for a moment, Zanna was content just standing there on the porch, looking up at the stars.

"Okay, Zanna," she said after indulging herself long enough. "Let's get moving." She adjusted the sack on her back. "And you're going to have to stop talking to yourself when you make it back to civilization."

The air out on the porch was still primelocked, but as she headed away from the house and crossed the little stream at the edge of the meadow, it all changed. This was more than a simple barrier of air pressure. A step one way, and there was a shambling, displaced Victorian mansion in the middle of a meadow. A step the other way, and there was just snow and wild grass and the open forest. No wonder the Primers had been useless in finding her. The entire mansion and its grounds were hidden behind an illusion barrier.

This last fact stopped her dead in her tracks. Living in the house for so long, she had almost forgotten what air—real and free air—felt like. She closed her eyes and pulled a handful of nitrogen right down to her, laughing at the ease of it. Then another, just like that. She threw them up into the sky like a magician releasing doves. There was so much around her— snow and stones and trees and air—that her head buzzed with possibilities. All of it could be manipulated. All of it was hers.

~~But only if she got away from the Variable first.~~

This part of her plan had been less rigorously thought out, but she was buoyed by her success so far. The crisp, cold air gave her a second wind, her legs no longer complaining about their cramped time in the chimney, her scratches easier to ignore. She looked up into the sky and found the North Star. She had been taken somewhere much farther north than Virginia—that much was obvious. Therefore, her best bet was to travel south, and fast.

Zanna gathered up more nitrogen, far more than the stolen breath she had been working with, and pumped it into her parachute. It was an awkward system of travel to say the least, but it was faster than traveling by foot. With her teeth gritted, she told the nitrogen to rise, and after a bit of a rocky start that dragged her feet over the snow, she rose up over the pines in a perilous and janky flight.

At first she went slowly, afraid to force her nitrogen any faster than what would be a brisk jog if she were on the ground. But as the night went on and she grew more confident in her abilities, she slowly ramped it up until she was cruising at a decent sprint. Beneath her, the land rolled and rippled. Pine valleys with lakes covered in sheets of snow and ice spread out in all directions, endless and untouched, and as the sky began to go rosy with sunrise, Zanna wondered if she was ever going to see another human. The Variable had brought her here from Virginia in the space of a few hours—how could she have traveled for the better part of a night and still not be out of the wilderness?

Her focus started slipping. Elation and adrenaline only carried her so far, and soaring through the night air of the northern wilderness was a bone-numbing experience, even with all her extra clothes and the blanket wrapped around her. She spotted a bare patch of granite on the side of a mountain and landed to consider her options.

There was perhaps another hour or so until the Variable would wake up and realize that Zanna was gone. An hour to either continue on or find a place to hide. There was no guarantee that she would find civilization soon, but there was also no guarantee she would be safe if she tried to hide. What functions the woman had at her disposal Zanna could only guess at, but she was sure one of them could easily track down a girl in the forest. If she was going to be found, it wouldn't be cowering in a cave somewhere. She looked to the horizon again. If only she could see beyond this ridge of mountains. If only she were higher.

She took a long breath and gripped the knots of her bedsheet parachute. Her stomach clawed and churned against the idea, but deep down she knew it was the only way, even though her sense of self-preservation disagreed vehemently. One last ascent to see if she could spot any sign of civilization. She gathered up the nitrogen, which felt like an old friend now, and filled her parachute, climbing up into the crisp and bright air of morning.

Twenty, fifty, a hundred feet up. Calculations of gravity and terminal velocity and impact forces splattered across her mind, and she did her best to sweep them away. But the higher she went, the less she could ignore, until the clamor in her mind threatened to paralyze her entirely with fear. Strange howling winds twisted around her, tearing out wisps of nitrogen from her parachute. She sucked in breath after breath, the air getting thinner the higher she rose.

This was a terrible idea. Her eyes screwed up tight, desperately clinging to the nitrogen function that was keeping her aloft. Even with the northern chill, cold sweat beaded on her forehead and upper lip, and she felt the sweet black softness of a faint tugging at her brain. At this height, she would smash over the mountain like a water balloon.

"Just one look," she whispered to herself. "And then you can go back down."

Summoning every ounce of willpower left in her tired body, Zanna cracked her eyes open. In all honesty, she was not that high up—a few hundred feet, perhaps—but to Zanna, it felt as if she was on the wing of a plane. Beneath her, the wilderness had no end. It just rolled on and on—but there! A flash like light bouncing off a polished mirror caught her eye, somewhere down over a long mountain back. Zanna rubbed her eyes and focused on the spot far to the south, but there was nothing else. Just smudges of forest and snow hidden with the haze of distance.

It was certainly more than an hour's travel. *If* anything was there at all. It could be a city. It could be an abandoned radio dish. It could be a patch of still water. But it was all she had to go on. The Variable would be awake soon, and she would catch up with Zanna quickly.

"Don't do it," she muttered as her vision began to fade. It was like diving into icy water. Every piece of her fought and howled and told her this was a terrible idea. Every piece wanted to feel stone beneath her feet. Every piece wanted to sleep for a week. Zanna ignored all of that. She gathered her nitrogen in a solid punch, braced herself, and told it to go as fast as it could. With a yank in her armpits like she had been caught up by a passing bullet train, her parachute filled with hurricane wind and sped off.

Wind screamed and ripped around her. It rattled the parachute like she was a doll and it was trying to snap her head off. She bobbled, nearly lost control, got it back by the skin of her teeth, and had almost found equilibrium when everything gave in a horrific instant. Her rucksack came open, and the air was full of fluttering clothes and papers and reports and roast-beef sandwiches. A sound of wordless dismay tore out of Zanna's throat as she saw her provisions scatter into the forest, and her concentration went with them. The nitrogen snapped back into its natural function, and she fell in a tumbling, plummeting trajectory.

This wasn't like when she had fallen down the tower. This time she was end over end, unable to even figure out what was sky and what was earth. The wind was too fast and too loud. She couldn't even make calculations in her head. Terror gripped her so firmly and completely that there was no space for anything but an endless scream. A flash of pines and pink sky, and the ground was close now. It had to be close. She glimpsed treetops and branches and a bird's nest with a very concerned eagle screeching at the incoming girl. Three final words raced through her mind. *Told you so.*

Then she hit and broke. Zanna instinctively brought her arms up to protect her face as she smashed through the nest and the pine trees. Needles whipped against the blanket, and her parachute caught the branches in a knot, suddenly yanking her around like a wrecking ball at the end of its chain. There was not even time to think about deceleration and momentum before she smashed brutally into the trunk of the pine tree with a sickening crunching sound.

Her first thought was that she was still alive. She lowered her arms, opened her eyes, and saw that she dangled a good twenty feet above the ground, her parachute having snared a fistful of branches. The blanket had done a decent job of protecting her as she crashed through the tree—but not decent enough. Nasty new cuts crisscrossed her knuckles and forearms and legs. High above her, the eagle cried to the open sky about its ruined nest.

Then the pain came. It was dark and swallowing and worse

with every breath. Something had cracked in her chest, and blood sponged through her lungs. The pressure felt like someone was trying to squeeze her to death.

"Ow—" she started, but the exertion of speaking doubled the pain of her splintered ribs. Instead, she focused on untying herself from the tangled bedsheet. With grimy and blood-soaked fingers, she undid the knots that tied the parachute around her shoulders and slowly extricated herself, every movement filled with fresh pain. She was still high up in the tree, and just looking at the climb down made her chest ache.

Her first thought was to make a cushion of nitrogen she could lower herself down on, but as she tried to pack the nitrogen together, the functions twisted into something she didn't recognize. Fluid dynamics. Gas pressure. Zanna made a sound that was half-whimper and half-curse at her lack of schooling. She would have to try something else.

If she made a wind strong enough, it could counteract her gravity. Like those indoor skydiving places that used a huge fan in the floor to simulate flight. But it would take a lot of nitrogen moving at high speed, and Zanna's focus kept slipping back to her ribs that she was now sure had been broken in the crash.

There wasn't any other way down, though. Better to fall now, on purpose, than later, by accident, while trying to climb down the pine tree. Zanna swallowed and began to manipulate the nitrogen beneath her. As she willed it to go faster and faster, it picked up snow and fallen needles, making a whirlwind of forest debris. Her head spun with frantic math. She couldn't keep this tornado together for much longer, not in her condition. Zanna stared down into the center, into the flying pinecones and rocks and branches, cursed her luck, and fell without a word.

For a moment her stomach was weightless, a feeling she was becoming far more familiar with than she ever wanted.

But her math was solid. The fountain of nitrogen buoyed her up, countering her downward acceleration perfectly. She took a breath of accomplishment, and her lungs burst in suffocation. At once, the function died, and she fell to the snow, gulping for air. *Of course*, she thought as she writhed with fresh agony. It was just nitrogen, after all. Of course she wouldn't have been able to breathe inside it.

Hot, blinding pain filled her chest. She had only fallen a foot or so, but Zanna laid there for a long time, trying to make her eyes work again as debris rained down all around her. Her ribs were in too much pain to sit up, so Zanna summoned another handful of nitrogen, making it sneak underneath her body and push her up onto her feet. Her balance was terrible, and she had to stabilize herself with a few more gusts. The entire forest swam drunkenly, but at least she was up on her feet. Slowly, relentlessly, Zanna put one foot in front of the other.

It was a long march through the forest, and Zanna tottered with every step. The snow made things treacherous, so she kept a wind of nitrogen ahead of her to expose rocks and tree stumps in the way. Her course was roughly southward, thanks to the rising sun in the east. She tried not to think of the possibility that what she had spotted from the sky was not a city. That she was walking toward an ice-covered lake or some other stray bit of reflective surface that had happened to catch the sunlight.

Her ribs were broken. There was no denying it now. She needed a hospital or at least someone with medical knowledge and supplies, and fast. Or else she would pass out and then . . . Zanna didn't want to consider it. She used the grinding pain in her chest to block it out.

At last she stumbled down a gradual slope and found herself on a rough logging road. The sliver of civilization—the first bit of hope she had gotten in a long while—hit her hard, and she collapsed against a nearby tree while her body shook with maniacal, animal sobs. How glad she was that no one else was there to see her at that moment—a torn and bloody girl beside a muddy road, crying and laughing and nearly vomiting all at the same time. Roads had to lead somewhere. It was the last push she needed. All the other possibilities of what that glint of light had been were swept aside as she started with renewed energy. She had a road to follow now. She would make it through this.

There was light in the distance.

It trickled through the back of her hazy senses. A feeling of early sun that told her that the pines had been cleared out ahead. The logging road came around, and there was civilization.

It was small and still a fair distance off, but it was a city. Roofs peeked over rolling hills, and trucks made their way up and down the streets. There were even a few modest office buildings near the town center, their windows pink and gold with dawn. And at a curve in the logging road, she spotted people.

Zanna had come to a workmen's lot, with a couple of idle trucks and machines and people in blaze-orange milling around with cups of coffee in their hands. Her hand lifted to call out to them, but before she could open her mouth, a thought stopped her in her tracks. *What will happen if I call out to the workers?*

They would gasp and shout and pick her up from the ground and take her to a hospital. They would rub their heads and ask where she had come from and how she had gotten so injured. The doctors would give her anesthetics and make her sleep, and when she woke, there would be hundreds of questions and police and too much to explain. That all sounded fine to Zanna. But what they wouldn't do is defend her from the Variable. What they wouldn't do is alert the Scientists that she was alive.

She needed Lord Hemmington and the Primers. *No*, Zanna corrected herself. The Primers had been no help so far. What she needed was her grandfather, and for that, she had to keep going. So, with a longing sigh, she lowered her hand and skirted around the lot, keeping far away so none of the workers would spot her. The road swayed and dipped, all the buildings and houses along it swaying to a beat that matched Zanna's bobbing head. Her chest was getting worse. An audible *crunch* of grinding bone sounded with every other step.

Then she saw exactly what she needed. A grungy gas station stood at the intersection, its lights still burning away the morning dark, an ancient pay phone on the wall. It was so old it even had one of those yellow books of phone numbers hanging beneath it. Other than an old woman at the pumps and her dog sticking its nose out the window of her pickup truck, the place was empty. Zanna hugged the slat fence that ran around the edge of the lot, only glancing over at the old woman once to check out her license plate. *Canada.* She was in Canada.

The phone hummed a dial tone when she picked it up, and Zanna thanked her lucky stars for that. But making a call required money. Nothing came out when she jiggled the coin return, and nothing was on the pavement, either, save a candy wrapper and a few errantly tossed cigarette butts.

Breathing was nearly impossible now. All the walking since her crash had torn farther into her chest. Zanna steadied herself as a wave of dizziness washed over her. She had made it this far. Only a little farther to go.

Her focus was a trembling string, but she grasped it and reached out for the nitrogen around her. It didn't want to co-operate, and Zanna really couldn't blame it. Pain made it nearly impossible, even though she knew the nitrogen function backward and forward by now. She bit down on her tongue, hoping it would distract her a little from the enveloping pain of her chest, and grabbed a fistful of nitrogen. Carefully, with the precision of a safecracker, she fed it into the coin slot of the pay phone.

It was a bit like fumbling around to find something that has rolled too far under the bed. The nitrogen felt around the levers and scales and internal movements of the phone, and then, without warning, the phone sprang into life, just as if she had fed it a coin, the dial tone changing as a connection was made.

Zanna dialed, but the machine did nothing. *Long distance*, she thought. *Of course.* She tried to repeat what she had done the first time, but the exact movements had already slipped from memory. The nitrogen kept dissipating, and she had to gather it back up again and again. Her eyes closed—not in concentration but out of exhaustion—and the dial tone had still not changed. She bit her tongue hard enough to draw blood, if she had had any blood left in her.

A click, and the phone began to ring. Five times and no answer. Ten . . .

"Hello?"

The sweet, sandpapery voice of Pops crackled over the phone line. It broke Zanna, but she was out of tears, so she just choked and rasped into the receiver. "Pops?"

"Hello? Who is this?"

Zanna swallowed the blood in her mouth. Speaking made her ribs feel as if they were being snapped like a bunch of twigs, but she raised her voice as loud as she could. "Pops, it's me. It's Zanna."

Silence. And then her grandfather whispered in a broken voice, "Oh, my sweet gracious."

"Pops, listen," Zanna said. The world spun. It wasn't a question now of *if* she would collapse, only a question of *when.* "I . . . I'm hurt. I don't have much time. Tell them . . ." She glanced down at the yellow book and the address on its cover, using the last of her strength to read the printed letters. "Canada. Yellowknife, Canada. It's north." Her vision went black, but she kept talking, not even sure if her words made sense. "Yellowknife, Canada. I'm here. Hospital. Tell . . . Cedwick. All of them. Yellow . . ."

She didn't hear what Pops said in reply. The phone slipped out of her fingers, and she went down.

CHAPTER SIXTEEN

ZANNA WANTED TO sleep. She was comfortable and warm, and the air smelled of clean linen. But she also wasn't really safe yet, and so, with a grueling, complaining strength, she opened her eyes.

Her predictions had been correct. Someone had spotted the bloody, ratty girl who had collapsed outside a gas station, and brought her to the hospital. They had taken her shabby blanket and grimy clothes and had given her a thin hospital gown, cleaning and wrapping her wounds in gauze. An IV drip had been inserted into the crook of her elbow, the solution in the bag too molecularly complex for Zanna to figure out. Whatever it was, it did wonders for her broken ribs. The clock on the wall across from her bed told Zanna it was four o'clock in the afternoon.

She lifted the sheets, dreading but unable to stop herself from taking a peek. The doctors had wrapped her chest in a constrictive bandage to keep her ribs from moving around, but a bruise the color of an overripe plum had spread out from underneath the bandage, reaching all the way up to her collarbone. Her skin was tight and shiny, and Zanna dropped the sheet, thoroughly unsettled.

The room was small but comfortable, with a window that looked out at the sunset. Fake flowers stood in a little vase by her side table, along with a tear-away calendar that said it was Thursday, March 24, and a small intercom speaker to let her call the nurses' station. The proper thing to do would be to let them know she had woken up. No doubt there was a pile of questions they wanted to ask her, like how a girl from Virginia had come to end up in the Canadian wilderness with just a couple of bedsheets and several broken ribs. But she held off on that for just a moment, collecting her thoughts out of the haze of sleep and painkillers.

The last thing she remembered was the phone call. Seeing as she was in the hospital, the Primers had not found her yet. But neither had the Variable. The hunt was presumably still on—and with the tattered bedsheet she had left in the pines and the blood she had smeared all over the forest, Zanna had made it exceptionally easy.

"Happy now, Dr. Trout?" Zanna muttered to herself as her fists bunched up the blankets of her hospital cot. "There. It feels terrible to be a failure."

She had been doing so well, and then she screwed everything up in the final stretch. *Typical.* It was just her style to finally figure out an escape route and then ruin it with her own ineptitude. Like the furnace and the mansion basement all over again. A lump of graphite could track her down now. For the Variable, it would be simple.

Zanna's mind was foggy, but it still worked well enough. If the Primers couldn't find her in time—she was sure that Pops had passed her message on, but there was no way of knowing— Zanna would have to fend for herself. What she needed was a weapon. She looked around again, and her eyes settled on the set of cabinets across the room from her. Linens and spare towels were stacked atop it, along with a few glass jars filled with cotton swabs and tongue depressors. With a glance at the door to make sure it was closed, she gathered up some nitrogen and opened the upper-left cabinet with a strong gust. Bandages of all shapes and sizes spilled out. The next one had boxes of tissues. The next, face masks and latex gloves. Frustrated, she went through all the cabinets, but she found nothing to defend herself with. No scalpels or spare hypodermic needles or razors. It was all just bandages and papers and pencils and a jar of old, crusty lollipops.

She frowned. It always worked in the movies. But apparently, hospitals didn't actually keep dangerous objects like scalpels freely accessible to their patients. With a fair bit of effort and some careful gusts of nitrogen, Zanna managed to pick up a box of pencils and carry it over to her, only to see that they were all unsharpened. She threw it against the wall with a muffled curse. No, if she wanted a weapon, she would have to build it herself.

She returned to the cabinet of medical supplies, going over its contents more carefully than before. One by one she inspected each spilled box and open cabinet until she found an old bundle of thermometers hiding under a pile of smocks. With her eyes closed, she cast her mind back to Chemistry and all the memorization Dr. Piccowitz had forced upon them. Mercury was a heavy metal with an atomic number of 80. It would be liquid at room temperature, meaning that its atoms were still bouncing off each other but not as quickly and violently as a gas like nitrogen. Zanna calculated the gravity and forces, slight as they were, and combined everything into a grand function. It took a couple of tries, since mercury was a far more complicated atom than nitrogen, but she persisted until she felt it click. The thermometers rustled, and then one slipped from the bundle, dragged across the room by its bulb. Zanna reached out and snatched it from the air with a grin.

Unfortunately, that was the easy part. She knew she could manipulate the nitrogen around her into a storm that would push away any would-be attackers. But that required a lot of focus. What she needed was a way to do that without relying on her brainpower, which was woozy and exhausted. That meant writing out a function—and Zanna had never done that before.

Her teachers had made the distinction clear multiple times. It was the difference between just knowing the answer and writing out the pages and pages of work needed to arrive at it. Rough spots could be smoothed over in a hands-on manipulation, but a written function did exactly what it said and nothing more. It was that quality, Zanna remembered dryly, that let her escape from the mansion in the first place.

To make nitrogen move meant manipulating its derivative—the function that described how something changed. This was Beatrice's specialty, not hers, but Zanna did her best to remember what the quiet Italian girl had said. She picked out four corners in the air, like she was placing down stakes to mark out a garden plot, and added in all the chemical and physical functions until she held the square of nitrogen in her mind.

She could have manipulated it directly then, but instead, she turned the whole thing over and peeled off the derivative, just as she had seen Beatrice do with theoretical cubes. It seemed like such a fragile, intangible thing, but when Zanna moved her square of nitrogen around, she saw the derivative flicker into life, describing every change she made.

"I owe you, Beatrice," Zanna said, imagining her little friend standing beside her, smiling at the mathematics.

It was tempting to crank up the derivative as high as it would go, but then Zanna imagined a hurricane-force square of nitrogen erupting in her hospital room, flattening the wall and whatever else was behind it, and common sense prevailed. After all, this was a last resort. Hopefully, she wouldn't even have to use it. Hopefully, the Primers would get here first. *Hopefully*.

She summoned up the mercury function, picked up the inert

derivative, and slipped it in among the liquid coordinates and heavy-metal atoms. Then she let go of everything.

Nothing happened. No roar of nitrogen shook the room. No Splutter split her head in two. Zanna peeked out of one eye and saw the thermometer still on her lap, reading a pleasant 24 degrees Celsius. When she reached her mind out to it, she found the derivative at once, hidden among the other functions, just waiting for Zanna to trigger it. She smiled and tucked the thermometer under her pillow. It made her feel a bit safer—but only a bit.

There was one more thing she could do, and it involved the heavy blue curtain beside her bed. Zanna couldn't build a wall of air pressure, but she could make another kind of barrier. With a little bit of work and clever nitrogen manipulation, she managed to close the curtain around her, shutting out the last rays of sunset that were filtering through her window. It was less a formidable barrier and more an early warning system, but Zanna would take everything she could get. In the calm darkness, Zanna sank back into her pillows, the pain in her ribs beginning to lessen for the first time since she had woken up.

Sleep was the best thing she could do right now—a light and wary sleep to get back lost energy and be ready in case the Variable found her first. But Zanna's brain refused to shut down, even though her body ached and wanted nothing more than to lie still for about the next decade. How long she lay there among her troubling thoughts, she had no way of knowing. It seemed like hours. Then the sound of metal rings slipping over the bar cut through her wandering thoughts and brought her back to the hospital room in an instant. Cautiously, she put her hand underneath her pillow and pulled out the thermometer, keeping it hidden among the sheets as she sat up as best her ribs would allow. *It may not be the Variable*, she told herself, even as her skin prickled at the nearby danger. The Primers were looking for her. It might even just be the nurse making his rounds.

"Well, this is rather familiar."

The Variable stood at the foot of Zanna's bed. A luminescence that came from nowhere filled the room, bright enough for her to see that the Variable didn't have a scratch on her. Her hair was a little windswept, and her cheeks were flushed red with the cold of a Canadian winter, but other than that, she was immaculate, her outfit perfectly composed, as if she had just finished fixing herself up in the bathroom.

Every muscle in Zanna's body tensed, and a blinding flash of pain burned across her chest. The thermometer seemed like a twig in her hand, a twig she was waving at an approaching tank. The woman tried not to let it show in her voice, but Zanna could tell by her eyes and the way she breathed. She was furious.

"How'd you find me?" Zanna asked. The Variable hadn't snatched her up at once—she hadn't even brought out her Iron. That meant she wanted to talk first, and Zanna obliged. Every second she could give the Primers counted.

"I had my pick of ways," the Variable replied. "Things don't lose their primelock just because you take them out of my house. That bedsheet stuck out like a sore thumb." Her eyes drifted down to Zanna's chest, and Zanna felt the need to draw the covers up a little higher. "I see you've made quite a mess of yourself. How fast did you hit that tree?"

"Pretty fast," Zanna said. The woman shuffled a little bit, adjusting her stance, and Zanna hurried to think of another question, one that would draw out the encounter and give the Primers even more time to come to her rescue. She wouldn't stop to consider that she was on her own. That her hurriedly constructed derivative was all she had. "Don't you want to know how I escaped?"

A smile crept across the woman's face that almost *might* have been pride. Pride in a daughter who had done something rather clever. Pride in her younger self. "By exploiting the pathfinding functions of my serving tray. Nicely done, I admit. I'll have to fix that when we get back to the mansion."

"*If* we get back."

A laugh slipped from the Variable's lips. "I still mean what I told you before. There's no reason why we have to be enemies. If you want to be difficult, I'll take you back by force, but I'd really rather you came back of your own free will."

Zanna settled back in her pillow and tried to look like she was seriously considering the woman's offer, hiding the goosebumps breaking out over her arms. "Maybe if you told me why. I don't like agreeing to things I don't understand."

"No, you don't," the Variable murmured, with an air of remembrance that made Zanna's skin crawl. The woman chewed on her tongue as her pretty alien face screwed up in thought.

Zanna's guts heaved. She recognized the look far too well. Then the Variable was back, her eyes that blue genius again, her face composed. When she spoke, it was serious and deathly cold, each word considered. "We want the same thing, Zanna. For everyone to get along. For everyone to live. But the only way that happens is if you're with me. Otherwise—Nora, Beatrice, Libby, Owin, Cedwick, even Pops. They are going to die."

It wasn't a threat—it didn't have the right malevolence for that. No, the woman's statement was something else. It was a prediction, but not the fluffy, hand-waving kind doled out by fortune cookies. It was a fact. She had seen it happen.

No, Zanna told herself, the Variable was a liar who would say anything to get her back into that tower room. The Variable knew nothing of what might happen in the future. So Zanna moved, as if action could wipe the woman's dire words from her mind, and grabbed the thermometer. In the mercury, she thumbed the derivative hard, spinning it up into some enormous number and hoping that she hadn't messed up the units of measurement or something else silly. But it worked beautifully. A roar shook the hospital room, a singular upheaval of air as a five-foot square of nitrogen in front of Zanna rammed forward like an angry bull, knocking the curtains and the cabinets and the Variable back in a torrential gale. Bandages swirled and kicked around. A tissue box struck the wall and burst open, spilling a thousand fluttering pink squares into the wind. The fire alarm kicked on.

But Zanna had no time to congratulate herself. Even before she had released the derivative, she was moving, rolling out of bed with one hand clamped over her mouth so she didn't asphyxiate herself on the nitrogen. The IV drip was still in her arm, and with a silent thanks for painkillers, she grabbed the wheeled stand as she headed toward the door. From out of the mess of curtains and nitrogen and bandages at the other end of the room, a streak of the woman's Iron lanced out. Zanna swung the IV pole in a blind and furious panic, miraculously not tearing the needle out of her arm *and* connecting in a solid parry. The lance deflected off to the left, the grasping hand of tendrils meant for her wrapping themselves around an innocent chair instead.

Zanna skidded out into the hallway, accompanied by a whipping of air and scented tissues. Her ribs screamed in pain—medication only went so far—but at least she had the strength in her legs back. Nurses and orderlies were running down the hall toward her, and Zanna took off in the other direction, her bare feet scrambling on the tile floor. She saw a sign pointing toward the stairs and took the corner at speed, slamming the door to the stairwell open with an impact that made her vision dance. Her IV rattled its wheels as she took the steps two at a time.

As she came out of the stairwell, she spotted another sign pointing toward the atrium and the exit, but more hospital staff were heading toward her, with no way around them. With an apology, she gathered a block of nitrogen ahead of her as she ran and rammed it right through, knocking them over like pins. She could still hear the roar of her thermometer above her, like someone had left the window open in the middle of a tornado, and she hoped it was still holding the Variable at bay.

The atrium was empty when she reached it, save for a couple of fake tropical plants. She paused to catch her breath, put a hand to her aching ribs, and looked over her shoulder to see if anyone was following her.

Then the ceiling split apart.

It reminded Zanna of those times when Pops got whole fish from the wharf, and she would watch him clean and fillet them in the kitchen. First, there was a single clean stroke through the yellowed tiles and fluorescent lights, then a few drips of white sparks, and then it widened and peeled back, and she could see all the struts and pipes and the electrical guts of the building.

And the Variable dropped down through the opening.

Zanna took off at once, but she smashed into something invisible before she made it to the door. A wall of air pressure blocked her only exit, and she turned back, taking up her IV in both hands like a polearm. The woman had stepped over the nurses, doing something with the air to keep them on the ground, and stood at the other end of the atrium. She gestured, and the front desk slid back several feet, flattening like a frightened passerby against the wall. Another gesture, and the rest of the furniture and fake plants slid back, as well, so there was nothing between her and Zanna except for a few stray tissues, still floating on the various winds.

The Variable's gaze fell on the IV pole Zanna brandished. "Being difficult, then. You're not seriously going to fight me with that, are you?"

"I don't see why not," Zanna replied. She had to hunch over due to the pain in her ribs, which was back with a vengeance. At least her voice had come out fairly defiant, instead of the cracked and wounded voice she felt inside her chest.

The Variable sighed, and suddenly, Zanna's IV pole slipped from her fingers like a bunch of wet noodles, wriggling snake-like across the atrium to the woman's outstretched hand. Unsupported, the plastic medicine drip-bag fell and split over the tile floor of the atrium. Zanna let out a squeal of gut-clenching pain as the IV needle moved inside her arm.

"That's why," the Variable said, as if she had already explained this a hundred times. "You haven't even learned basic metals yet." From her sleeves, the tendrils of her Iron began to emerge. It didn't reach for Zanna just yet, but the way it bobbed like a raised cobra said it just needed the word. "Now. Come back with me."

"Not until you tell me why." If the Primers were nearby, they must have noticed the commotion in the hospital. She needed more time. If only she had drawn out their conversation upstairs longer. Zanna ground her teeth in frustration. She had played her ace too soon.

"I've told you enough." The Iron crept out another inch. "Are you going to be difficult about this?"

Zanna stuck out her jaw. "Always."

The woman's Iron shot out, and the entire hospital stuttered.

It was the exact same stutter Zanna had felt before in her bedroom. A Weierstrass transformation that chopped reality and the manipulations of the Variable into disconnected points. The furniture the woman had pushed out of the way hurried back to its natural places. The snakelike IV pole clattered to the floor, back in its solid form. The air-pressure barrier she had built around the atrium broke. It took only a second, and then the hospital returned to its smooth operation, the strobe effect gone. Only now there was an imposing man with dark skin, a broad-rimmed hat, and a silver cane standing in front of Zanna, and he crackled with a function of speed and momentum.

The next moment, a sheet of silver metal scooped Zanna up, and she realized that the man had wrapped his cane around her as if she was a newborn chick in its egg. Fingertips of iron glanced harmlessly off the shell, and Zanna heard a terrifying baritone roar out, "Your fight is with *me*!" Glass shattered as her egg broke through the front windows of the hospital and went skidding across the parking lot, smashing through cars and trucks and lampposts. Then, just as quickly as it had wrapped around her, the silver cane let her go, flying back across the road and through the broken hospital wall to rejoin its owner in battle.

Zanna gasped at the contact with the air—it was freezing, and she was still barefoot. There was an obvious trail of destruction across the parking lot—she had smashed right through a box truck—and she wondered for a moment how they were going to explain all of this to the CGs.

"Got her."

Another man, younger than the one who was fighting the Variable but still old enough to be her father, appeared beside her. He knelt and put a heavy mariner's coat around Zanna's shoulders, instantly shutting out the cold and wrapping her in the scent of the sea. Something glimmered on the inside of his left arm—a polished letter opener strapped against his dark sweater.

"Are you all right?" he asked.

Zanna struggled to talk. The IV bag had been ripped from her arm in the commotion, and she felt the absence of pain-killers acutely. "My ribs—"

He squinted at her chest and frowned. "Yup, that's never a good thing. Hang on."

The letter opener stretched and rolled until it was a thin, flat sheet. It slipped under Zanna and lifted her up, cradling her so gently it felt as if she was floating.

"Don't go too high," Zanna muttered, the exhaustion she had been staving off all day beginning to finally catch up with her. "I . . . don't like heights."

"As you wish," the man said, though his attention was directed across the parking lot to where the fight was still going on.

Zanna couldn't see anything, but she heard plenty. Metal on metal, booms of air pressure, and the occasional sizzle of loose electricity. Then she saw what the man had been looking for—his reinforcements. Six more figures had appeared in the night sky and swooped in toward the hospital.

"I'll take her, Henry."

She knew that voice. Lord Hemmington touched down next to them, his badge glinting lamplight as it trickled out of his hand and reformed on his chest. Henry chuckled gruffly and made a casual salute.

"She's broken five ribs, sir. Mighty banged up, to boot."

Lord Hemmington took a glance down at Zanna. "So I see."

He turned his badge into a makeshift stretcher, and Henry transferred Zanna over to him, taking care not to aggravate her ribs any more. "Do not come back to headquarters until that criminal is in custody," Lord Hemmington said with a nod toward the hospital. A solitary figure rocketed up from the building, pursued by seven others, and Lord Hemmington's frown deepened as he looked over the broken walls and parked cars Zanna had smashed through. "I assume this is Xavier's doing?"

Henry said nothing, but that was enough for Lord Hemmington.

"I will have a word with him," the Head Primer said. "See to this mess, Henry. You have the command."

"Sir," Henry nodded. He looked to the parking lot and began repairing the cars Zanna had smashed through, all the scattered parts quickly flying back to their proper places. It was so effortless that Zanna could only stare open-mouthed, even as her body drifted toward sleep. And then she and Lord Hemmington were in the air, flying in the opposite direction toward safety and, she hoped, home.

CHAPTER SEVENTEEN

SHE SLEPT AS she never had before. Her dreams doubled back in mathematical oddities, counting and miscounting her time in captivity. They spilled over a vast landscape and dribbled around the edges to the underside, where silver trays talked, nitrogen shaped itself like all her friends, and functions gushed out of her chest like a fountainhead.

When she opened her eyes, she was in a familiar hospital room. Not the one in Canada but a warm and cozy place, with the smell of fresh flowers and cedar and playful cats in the air. It was one of the rooms in the nurse's cottage at St. Pommeroy's, and it was like something out of a nursery tale.

Lazy sunlight streamed through the blinds, falling over a large cushioned chair with books stacked on either side. Her bedsheets were lilac and patterned with cartoon kittens, with a crocheted blanket over her legs that was just warm enough but not so hot that she started sweating. Zanna half-expected a trio of field mice to come in at any moment, carrying a plate of scones and clotted cream between them. She didn't see any mice as she looked around, but there was a cat with enormous blue eyes on the table beside her bed. It stared unblinkingly at her, and Zanna stared back. There was something odd about it, but Zanna couldn't quite put her finger on it until the cat yawned and began to talk.

"You're awake!" The cat's voice was quaint and countryside English, which only added to the fairytale. "Your grandfather will be so pleased to hear that. He just popped off to the cafeteria for lunch. He's been at your side for days, you know."

"Days?" Zanna asked, rubbing her eyes.

"Four. It's Tuesday, my dear."

Zanna looked at the armchair again, and this time she recognized some of the books stacked around it. Pops must have brought along his collection of puzzle books to pass the time. Guilt flooded through her at the thought of him sitting there day after day, waiting for her to wake up, and her lips quivered. "Four days?"

The cat nodded. "Yes, you were quite out of it. But you're awake now, and that's all that matters!" Suddenly, the cat froze, its speech cut short by something on the other end. Zanna squinted at it, as if it was a phone gone dead, and was about to tap it to see if that would bring it back when she heard footsteps coming down the hall—the short, hurried footsteps of an old man who really shouldn't be running. The door flew open, and Pops was there, cheeks beet-red and mouth smiling so wide that Zanna thought his face would break.

"My darling!" he said, rushing to scoop her up and hold her tight. "I thought I would never see you again."

Zanna put her arms around him, not minding his scratchy whiskers for once. "I'm sorry, Pops," she muttered. She buried her face in his shoulder, wordlessly promising to never leave him again. Pops just kept stroking her hair and crying. "I'm so sorry," Zanna whispered.

"No, no, you don't apologize for anything," he whispered back through his sobbing. "You brilliant girl, you don't apologize for anything."

Zanna wanted to hold him forever. Eventually, though, she had to let go. Pops went to his armchair and pulled an old handkerchief out of his back pocket, blowing his nose with a blast like an ill-tuned trumpet. He used it to gesture at her ribs. "Did Cecelia give you a rundown of everything you busted?"

Zanna shook her head. "I'm guessing it's pretty extensive."

"Not anything I can't manage," the cat said, making Zanna start a little. She had completely forgotten it was still there. "The ribs will take the longest—I'm afraid you will have to stay in bed for at least the next month."

"A *month*?" Zanna repeated incredulously. "Can't you manipulate them back together or something? I thought that's what you did."

The cat smiled softly, and the eerie human expression on its animal face made Zanna's neck prickle. "If only it were that simple. But your bones are under the protection of your Self function. I'd have better luck trying to mend your Iron!"

"My Iron," Zanna muttered. She hadn't thought about picking her Iron in months, but now that she was back at St. Pommeroy's, it came flooding back to her. A long, tired exhale escaped her lips.

"Don't worry," the cat said. "Rest and recuperation are better healers than any science. You'll be up and about in no time."

But rest and recuperation were nowhere to be found those first few days after Zanna woke up. It seemed like everyone at St. Pommeroy's wanted to come down to visit her, and the small cottage room turned into a parade of teachers, reporters, and general well-wishers. Some of them were simple and pleasant, like Mr. Gunney, who surprised Zanna by embracing her grandfather like they were old companions. "Dennis was my eyes and ears," Pops explained when he saw the confused expression on Zanna's face. "Let me borrow his copy of *The Constant* so I could check for any news about you. Clever little thingamajiggy, that newspaper."

Others were a bit more bittersweet. Dr. Fitzie bubbled and

gushed with excitement, but she also brought with her a stack of missed work and dumped it rather unceremoniously on the table. "I thought you'd like something to occupy your time while you rest up," she said, not mentioning the two other stacks of papers and lecture notes that Dr. Cheever and Dr. Piccowitz had already left.

The worst, however, was when the Primer Lieutenant Henry dropped in for a debriefing. Their actual conversation wasn't that bad—Zanna went slowly through everything that had happened since December, with the omission of her suspicion of the Variable being a version of herself from the future. The friendly Primer who had given Zanna his coat in Yellowknife took her story down with a serious expression.

But then Pops confronted him. "Thought you folks were supposed to be protecting her," he said in a voice that Zanna had never heard him use before. She didn't like it one bit. "Thought that's what your air-pressure barrier was for. What do you call this, then? You knew that madwoman was after her—"

"Pops, please," Zanna said, reaching for him.

"Zanna," he said, and it shut her mouth up tight. He jabbed a bony finger at Henry, his whole frame shaking with anger. "Twice now I've been told that my granddaughter has gone missing. Twice now I've had to wonder if I was ever going to see her again. I can't take a third."

Henry nodded solemnly. "The Primers agree completely, sir," he said when no one else spoke. "We failed in December, but it won't happen again. The safety of your granddaughter is our number-one priority. We've arranged with St. Pommeroy's for her to stay here, on campus, until this woman can be caught. It's the safest place for Zanna."

Pops looked around the cozy room, as if appraising its defensive fortifications. "I want to keep an eye on her too."

"Pops," Zanna grumbled.

"Of course," Henry said without hesitation. "You're free to come and go as you please for as long as Zanna remains here. They tell me you've been catching a ride with Dennis Gunney? We can keep that arrangement."

She could tell her grandfather wasn't completely sold on the plan, but he shook Henry's hand anyway. "Hope you're not paying them," he grumbled to her after Henry had left. "Bit of a mess, aren't they?"

"Pops," she groaned.

"I'm just worried about my granddaughter, that's all," he said—and didn't bring it up again.

Her friends came to visit her during lunch and every other spare moment they had, surrounding her bed and catching her up on everything that had happened since December. They were the same girls Zanna remembered from her father's welcome-home party, but at the same time, she couldn't help but notice how each of them had grown while she was gone. In Nora's case, the growth was quite literal. She had gained at least two inches, though her uniform still fit perfectly. Libby was experimenting with dark purple lipstick and eyeshadow and was back to dating Amir, but what really stood out was that she had chosen her Iron—a blackened fire poker that left ash on her hands. Beatrice hadn't found an Iron yet, but she had found a boyfriend. "His name is Tomas and he's a sophomore from Barcelona," Libby said while the small girl blushed and pushed her fingers together. Zanna smiled as they prattled on about the end of the school year and possible specializations, doing her best to hide her unease. Her friends were blooming, and she was still the awkward and unsure runt of a weed she had been at the beginning of the school year.

It didn't help that in the first few days of getting back, Mrs.

Turnbuckle's silver cat slipped into the room and hopped up onto the table. "Zanna," it said, as it always did when she had a visitor, "Dr. Trout is here to see you."

What perfect timing. Zanna groaned. "Fine," she said, setting aside the table of electronegativity Dr. Piccowitz wanted her to memorize. "Let her in."

Moments later, there was a knock on her door. Dr. Trout entered with the solemnity she always carried with her, wearing a blue-patterned robe with a dusty twilight-colored scarf around her head. She glanced over the piles of work the other teachers had brought, her face creased deeply in that permanent frown. With barely a flick of her hand, her baseball bat reshaped itself into a gnarled farmhouse chair, and she sat down, adjusting her robe and spreading her palms over her bony knees.

"You owe Mr. Hemmington a paper."

Zanna apparently did not even merit a "Welcome back."

"I lost it," Zanna said after recovering from the unorthodox greeting. "Somewhere out there in the Canadian wilderness. When I was escaping. From a madwoman. In case you missed it."

"I figured you would have an excuse for not doing it," Dr. Trout said with a bit of melancholy to her voice. "He had one too."

"I *did* write it," Zanna said stubbornly. "It's not an excuse. I really did lose it."

Dr. Trout rocked ever so slightly in her chair, which set off a choir of squeaks and groans from the old wood. The fact that Zanna actually had written the paper didn't seem to impress her one bit. "Ms. Mayfield, you are on the verge of failing my class."

This time, Zanna's words worked—fast. "*Failing*? In case you haven't heard, I've been a little busy recently. You know, getting kidnapped and trying to escape. It doesn't leave a lot of time for schoolwork. So I'm sorry that I haven't had a lot of time to dedicate to your stupid class because I was busy trying to survive. I almost died out there, I almost—"

Her voice cut off abruptly, her brain finally catching up with her mouth and telling it to shut up. She had never yelled at a teacher before. Back-talked a little, maybe, but never outright yelled. Especially when that teacher was Dr. Trout. Now Zanna was certainly going to fail the class.

But Dr. Trout just listened, her face a smooth brown stone. When Zanna didn't say anything more, she gestured to the work Dr. Piccowitz had left on the table. One of the hard acrylic cubes with a small elemental sample trapped inside the transparent polymer floated up from the pile. This one was fluorine, and Dr. Trout contemplated the pale-yellow gas for a moment. "I do not deny that these last few months have been difficult for you," she said. "The trials you have faced are more than any of your peers. But the study of Self is not schoolwork. Not in the sense that it may be left behind or forgotten in your bedroom or lost somewhere in the bottom of your backpack. All your other professors brought you work that you have missed, but for me, you never left my classroom. The study of Self continues for as long as you live."

Zanna didn't feel like trying to sit upright any longer. Dr. Trout's words made her sink lower and lower, each one like a weight on her shoulders. "Doesn't mean that I'm failing," she said glumly, her bottom lip stuck out in a pout.

Dr. Trout set the acrylic cube on a small wooden surface that grew out of her chair, the *click* as she put it down sharply pronounced. "You have been given an opportunity that very few at this school ever receive—an ordeal. Your friends have not had such a luxury. They have had to do their searching and contemplation through study and reading and quiet reflection. They have had no fire-forged moments. No crucibles.

No magnificent crises. But even then, they have made great progress. What have you done with that same time? I look at you, and I see the same girl who came to my class in September. I see that nothing has changed inside you."

"I changed *plenty*," Zanna snapped before she could stop herself.

Dr. Trout raised one of her bushy eyebrows in response. "Tell me, then," she said dryly. It was the tone of someone who knew full well what the answer was going to be. "Who is Zanna Mayfield, and what is her Iron?"

She was a time traveler. She was a Variable. She was a woman with unerring beauty and silky black hair and a Victorian mansion she had stolen right out of the ground. She was cruel and vicious and completely mad . . .

The words nearly made it out. Zanna felt them burble like an upset stomach and rise all the way to her tongue. But when she opened her mouth, what came out was something else entirely.

"I don't know."

To her credit, Dr. Trout didn't smile at having her point proven so neatly. Instead, she made the smallest *tut* in her throat and then waved away the fluorine sample, which floated back across the room and put itself away.

"You have been given a great gift, as odd as that may sound," she said, only after the cube was back and her gaze was once again upon Zanna. "Many of us do not ever find ourselves tested as you have been. Those of us who do, we are too old for it. We break under the strain. Our functions and our bodies have become brittle and stiff with the years. We have built a life upon its foundation, and when crisis hits, it cracks the very stones. It collapses us. We emerge believing we are stronger, but that is a lie. A pile of rubble is stronger than a house, only because it cannot collapse again. One cannot be destroyed if she never rebuilds."

She paused to lick her lips, and the sound was audible in the cottage room. When she spoke again, there was almost a flicker of emotion to it. "You are young and have only just begun to build. What might have broken in an older woman will merely reshape. Take that. Build upon that. You have seen the truest Zanna Mayfield there is—the one that exists when the world around you does not."

Zanna looked down at her feet beneath the blankets and wiggled her toes. The sickening urge to tell Dr. Trout everything had receded, but it had left something rotten in her stomach.

The professor rose, her chair returning to its baseball-bat form, and she swung it over her shoulder. "I do not take pleasure in failing my students," the steely-eyed woman said, "but I will if need be. Convince me that you have thought about what we have talked about."

"Dr. Trout—"

Zanna clamped her mouth shut before the rest of her sentence escaped—but not before the professor turned back from the door, eyebrows raised in question. "Yes?"

There was nothing to say. Or, rather, there was too much. The professor's challenge bored deep in Zanna's mind: "Convince me." Zanna could do that and more. She could open the floodgates and drown Dr. Trout and her unwavering gaze with exactly how well she knew herself.

Instead, she looked down at the bandages wrapped around her ribcage and pushed her fingertips together. "Time . . . time travel," she squeaked out. "Is it possible?"

A strange look flitted through Dr. Trout's eyes. It might have been the memory of another girl who had asked a similar question. Or she was just trying to decrypt Zanna's question. "That is a strange thing for you to be concerned about."

"It's just—we were talking about it earlier," Zanna said. Something about Dr. Trout and the presence she carried with her made it so difficult to lie—but it wasn't really that much of a lie. Zanna *had* been talking about time travel earlier. As long as Dr. Trout didn't ask whom Zanna had been talking about it with. "And I was curious," Zanna added.

"Curious about what?"

Zanna gulped. "Whether it was possible. I mean, time's just a function, right? Probably really complicated but still a function. It has to be; it exists."

Her professor turned from the door, and with each step she took Zanna shrank a little more. At the foot of her bed, Dr. Trout leaned in, and there was no space left for Zanna to shrink into. "So what is your question, then? You seem to have answered it already."

"But—" Dr. Trout's ability to cut right through her made Zanna squirm like a worm on the dissecting table. She tried to make it sound like she was stating a fact, but it still came out a question. "But no one's done it?"

"Correct." The professor leaned back, and Zanna gulped. She had been breathing shallowly—and not because of her broken ribs. "To manipulate time, one must manipulate the universe. All its stars and planets and heavenly bodies and the space in between. And those are the simple elements."

She then prompted Zanna to finish her implied question with a raised eyebrow.

"Humanity," Zanna filled in after a moment of thought.

"Precisely," Dr. Trout said. "Stars may be taken apart like the machines they are, and planets can be held in your grasp, but understanding the Self of someone else—just one other person, let alone all of humanity—is impossible. That is why we carry Irons. That is why we study our own function and no one else's. It is impossible."

Of course the professor would bring the conversation back to her class.

Zanna hung her head. "I see," she muttered.

"I hope you do," Dr. Trout said. "I truly do." She headed toward the exit again, but at the door she paused, as if a thought had suddenly come to her. Whatever it was that had crossed her mind, she apparently didn't think it important enough to put into words, and with a soft shush of linen, she left.

Those last words, however, lingered long after in Zanna's mind. After the school day was over and Pops had taken the bus back home, she still couldn't focus on anything but Dr. Trout's visit. Not about Zanna failing Self—that was hardly a surprise to her. Rather, she thought about what Dr. Trout had said about time travel.

"To manipulate time, one must manipulate the universe."

Zanna knew that the Variable was powerful, but she had always thought there was some upper bound, some limit to what the Variable could do. But as Zanna mulled over Dr. Trout's words, that small comfort faded away. To come back in time, the Variable had taken apart the universe and put it back together in a younger configuration.

At that thought, a shiver ran through Zanna, even though she was curled up under Mrs. Turnbuckle's ever-warm crocheted blanket. Because if the Variable could do that, then there was no limit to her abilities.

And she was still out there.

CHAPTER EIGHTEEN

ZANNA'S RECOVERY FLEW by, just as Mrs. Turnbuckle had predicted. The days filled with springtime, and the trees outside the cottage bloomed with large white flowers. Soon, Zanna was well enough to leave her room and sit out in the backyard, with its wrought-iron tea table and matching chairs. She took to doing her classwork there, sketching out derivatives for Dr. Fitzie or vector calculations for Dr. Cheever with the endless Atlantic for a backdrop. Occasionally, Mrs. Turnbuckle's cat—whose name Zanna had learned was Ferry, short for Fahrenheit—wandered out to paw at the acrylic chemical cubes and ignore the studying girl.

It was on one such outside morning, while Zanna was scooping up the last of her scrambled eggs and ketchup and skimming over friction coefficients, that the Particle arrived. Particles came and went from the cottage all the time, and Zanna paid most of the small silver marbles no mind, accepting them as just another fact of life as a Scientist. But this one was different. It moved faster than any Particle she had seen before. And it was large—almost the size of a bowling ball—and glossy black. Zanna's head whipped around as it passed, but by the time she turned, it had already found the letter opening in the cottage's back door, reshaped itself into a long and flat snake, and slipped through.

Her legs were still a little weak, but Zanna pushed herself up with the help of the tea table, unable to stop her curiosity.

She hobbled through the back door and poked her head into the waiting room to ask Mrs. Turnbuckle if she, too, had seen the strange message. But in the doorway, she froze. Behind the desk sat the black sphere, now large enough to swallow a person whole, and her nurse was nowhere in sight.

A strangled cry slipped out of Zanna. Instantly, she gathered a handful of nitrogen and spun around, expecting to see the Variable swooping in at any second while Mrs. Turnbuckle was restrained. But there was nothing out in the yard except her homework and Ferry.

Uneasy and unbalanced, she scrambled over to the black sphere. Perhaps the Variable had mistimed her assault, in which case Zanna had to act quickly. The sphere was some kind of alloy, but a complex function not unlike a primelock kept her from peering any deeper. Zanna knocked on it and heard nothing echo inside. She tried pounding on it with the heel of her hand, and when that didn't work, she grabbed a particularly thick book. She had just raised it over her head when the sphere sprang into action. As Zanna jumped back, knocking papers and little cat figurines from Mrs. Turnbuckle's desk, the sphere split open and shrank back to its original size, revealing her nurse once again, who looked entirely unharmed.

"Heavens!" she cried, a hand over her heart at the sight of Zanna standing over her with a raised book of anatomy. "What on earth are you doing?"

"I thought you were in danger," Zanna said, feeling thoroughly foolish. The adrenaline sloshed around inside her, not sure where to go now. She handed the book back. "Sorry."

"Well, bless you for worrying, but as you can see, I'm perfectly fine," Mrs. Turnbuckle said, fluffing up her curly brown hair in demonstration.

"I saw that—" Zanna tried to point to the black globe, but it had already left the cottage. "What was it?"

The nurse's mouth wavered a bit, the corners unsure what they were supposed to be doing. Mrs. Turnbuckle had to decide for them, and she smiled. "Nothing you need to worry about. A special message from the Head Primer. The boys do like their security protocols, you know. Anyhoo, I think you've gotten quite enough fresh air. Back to bed with you."

Zanna didn't move. "Was it about me?"

Mrs. Turnbuckle only shooed Zanna back toward her room, already shuffling things around on her desk and cleaning up the mess Zanna had made. "It's nothing to worry about, my dear. Just a regular checkup. Now move along. Your grandfather should be here very soon."

"My homework's all outside—"

"I'll bring it in," Mrs. Turnbuckle snapped, a little too quickly. "You just tuck yourself back in bed, that's a good girl."

Zanna's nerves screamed that things weren't right and there was a whole lot to worry about, but she turned anyway and went back to her room, climbing into bed and batting around an acrylic cube of beryllium as she thought. The Primers did not send top-secret messenger Particles just to chat.

Zanna balanced the cube on her index finger and made it spin like a top, staring blankly at the brittle steel-grey element inside. It had to be an update on the Variable. Maybe Lord Hemmington had managed to corner her somewhere, and the message was just that soon, Zanna would have nothing to worry about ever again. She chuckled humorlessly at her optimism. If the Variable was powerful enough to go back in time, the Primers were out of their league. Plus, there was still the look on Mrs. Turnbuckle's face to consider—the brave smile trying to hide what seemed like fear. Something had happened with the Variable, but it wasn't good news.

A brief knock on the door, and Pops walked in, Ferry following at his heels and meowing. Zanna waved and beckoned to the silver-and-orange cat, inviting it to hop up on her bed, but Ferry ignored her, preferring to stay by Pops and head-butt him in the ankles.

"How are you doing today?" Pops asked as he settled into an armchair with a groan and picked up the book he had been working on yesterday.

"Fine," Zanna said. She glanced over at the cat in the corner—not Ferry, but the metal one that Mrs. Turnbuckle talked through. Right now it was silent, holding its head upright with its blue eyes fixed on the opposite wall, but Zanna knew it was listening.

"Is that Mr. Gunney's *Constant*?" she asked, nodding toward the newspaper her grandfather had come in with. He said it was, and she flipped through it, her eyes skimming for any strange occurrences or hidden clues as to what might have prompted Lord Hemmington's message. But the headline of the day was about a new sorting function a Scientist in Antarctica had written. Zanna found nothing suspicious on any of the other pages, and finally, she handed the paper back, dismayed.

The rest of the day followed in much the same way. Zanna tackled the mystery of the messenger sphere in every way possible, but all her attempts came up short. When the girls came to visit her over lunch, as they always did, Zanna asked Nora if she or her parents had heard any recent rumors in the Scientist community, but the girl just shrugged. Zanna told the group about the high-security Particle—but not about her suspicions, always keeping Mrs. Turnbuckle's ever-present cat in mind. Nothing appeared in *The Constant* that afternoon, either, except for more bickering over sorting functions. Zanna stared down at the page of mineral crystallography she was supposed to be memorizing, not absorbing any of it. There was another way for her to figure out what was going on. A question she hadn't yet asked.

What would she do if she were in the Variable's place?

Zanna picked up *The Constant* and turned to the archive. At her touch a selection of back issues appeared. She flipped through them, the illusionary text changing with a sophisticated and elegant function. The last real news of the Variable had been several weeks before, when she'd given the Primers the slip somewhere around Greenland. Zanna read the story intently now, taking in every detail. Then she closed her eyes.

She imagined she stood on a glacial plain dotted with craggy, lichen-covered rocks. Snow-covered mountains rose in the distance. Her hair was long—longer than it had ever been—and the bellowing wind whipped it out behind her. Beneath her slim black dress, Zanna felt iron wrapped around her like a warm embrace, keeping her from freezing in the Greenland wild. She breathed in the pure air. The Primers had finally given up, and she could show herself once again.

Now Zanna imagined she was back at the mansion, but she wouldn't stay there. The Primers would sweep the forest, and while she had faith in her cloaking functions, it was better not to take the chance. So she uprooted the mansion and took it . . .

Zanna stopped, suddenly back in her bed at St. Pommeroy's. With the Variable's powers, the woman could have gone anywhere in the world. It would have been child's play to hide somewhere out in Siberia, or the middle of the Sahara, or the Mariana Trench. She might not even be on Earth any longer.

But Zanna wouldn't have hidden. Zanna would have made a plan.

She let her mind sink into the Variable's world once more.

It would be easy to deduce that the Primers were keeping Zanna at St. Pommeroy's. It was all over *The Constant*. The school was heavily fortified, so a full-out attack like the one at her father's party would be out of the question. But if the Variable could get Zanna to step outside the school, it would be much easier. If the Variable had something Zanna wanted, perhaps.

Zanna came back gasping for breath, a hand to her chest, her head scrambled. The Variable's world had been so real. She felt as if she had been there on the purple sofa in the mansion just moments ago, fixing the exploits in the tray's pathfinding functions. Now she was younger again, with short hair and broken ribs. Now she was Zanna once more, but she knew what the Variable had done.

A hostage.

Sickness twisted around in her stomach. The Variable had gone after her friends and was holding them prisoner until Zanna gave herself up. No doubt the message from Lord Hemmington was the instruction to keep Zanna safe and inside the nurse's cottage at all costs. That was why she had been confined to her bed all day—because the Primers knew exactly what Zanna would do if she found out.

Sweat crept down her neck. She couldn't sit here while her friends were being held by that woman. The Primers didn't have a clue about the Variable. And if they couldn't rescue Zanna before, what use would they be in rescuing her friends now? Zanna eyed the motionless cat in the corner of the room, her mind working on an escape plan. How quickly could it raise an alarm? How quickly would Mrs. Appernathy's candelabra be on her?

And what about her grandfather? He was still here, sitting in his armchair and steadfastly ignoring Ferry, who had taken a particular interest in him today. Zanna couldn't just jump up and run out without a word of explanation. But she didn't have the time to fill him in, either. Maybe if she wrote a note. It wouldn't explain everything, but at least he wouldn't be so worried.

"Do you have any scratch paper . . ." she started, pointing to the pile of books and papers on the table beside her grandfather's chair, but her voice trailed off before she could finish the question. Something about the situation tickled at the back of her mind, something like a loose pebble in her brain, and she tilted her head to free it.

Her grandfather was working on the same puzzle book from that morning.

It had to be the same one. There was an unmistakable picture on the cover, an awful computer graphic of some scatterbrained guy falling into a pink vortex of question marks. Her grandfather hadn't turned a single page. He had been staring at it all day.

Gears shifted. Names rearranged themselves, and she could have almost smacked herself for her sloppy reasoning. How could the Variable kidnap her friends when the classified message had arrived that morning and she had seen them at lunch? But Pops was different. The house in Virginia only had Owin's barrier of air pressure for protection, and the Variable had already gotten through that once. And there was no question whether Zanna would come to rescue her grandfather.

"Hey, Pops?" she said slowly.

He looked up. "Yes?"

A mix of fury and apprehension rose within her, and she had to control the shaking in her hand as she pointed at a jar of tongue depressors on a nearby shelf. "Can you hand me those popsicle sticks?"

"What for?" he asked, setting his puzzle book aside. He kept his place with a pencil instead of a slip of paper, she noticed.

"You'll see." She shifted a bit and put her Mathematics book on her lap so she had a surface to work on. When he stood up and fetched the jar, it was a little too fast for his age. Zanna held her tongue. She had to be sure.

He handed the jar over, watching as she laid out nine popsicle sticks in neat parallel rows. Another anomaly. He should know what she was up to by now. He should have known when she asked for the jar. "Now," she asked when she was finished, "can you turn these nine popsicle sticks into ten?"

He froze. Beneath the bandages, her heart slammed, but she kept still and kept her mouth shut. The evidence grew with each tick of silence.

"I told them you'd figure it out," her grandfather said at last, and it did not sound like him at all. The voice was cold and roaring like a river tearing down through the mountains. In the blink of an eye, her grandfather was gone. Where he had been sat the man with the silver cane from the Yellowknife hospital. Even though she had only seen him for a moment, Zanna had never forgotten his face. His skin was darker than even Nora's and well cared for, with only a few faint wrinkles around his eyes. A manicured goatee of hair the same bright silver as his walking cane outlined his mouth. A black, flat-brimmed hat shaded his incongruously green eyes.

"You—"

"Xavier Morrow," the man said with a touch to the brim of his hat, like they were passing each other on the street. "We have met before, Ms. Mayfield."

She lunged, scattering the popsicle sticks across the floor as she grabbed him by the lapels of his black suit. "What have you done with my grandfather?"

"*I* have done nothing," Xavier said.

His cane came between them and pushed her back in a gentle but firm manner. It was surprisingly strong for such a slender instrument—or perhaps Xavier subtly manipulated its inertia so Zanna had no choice but to release his suit and sit back on the bed. He lowered his cane, and Zanna's body wanted nothing more than to jump at him again and wrestle out an answer, but she thought better of it. Instead, she gathered up her bedsheets and the crocheted blanket in her fists and growled down in her throat. "She took him, didn't she?"

Xavier nodded again, his eyes brightening at her logic. "They told me you were clever. Yes, he is being held hostage at the moment. But the situation is under control. I expect it to be resolved by morning, and then you and your grandfather will be reunited."

Zanna's fists tightened. "You don't understand," she said, trying to make it sound more like a fact and less like the whine of a bratty girl. "She's after me. That's all she's been after. That's the only way to get my grandfather back."

Xavier let go of his cane, which remained upright despite nothing supporting it, and took off his hat, inspecting the brim and brushing off a few spots of dust. "We are well aware of her demands. Do not think of us as idiots." He replaced his hat, and beneath the shadow of its brim, his eyes gleamed like a wild cat. "This is our job."

"Whatever you're planning, it's not going to work. She's thought of everything." Desperately, Zanna thought for a moment about explaining everything to Xavier, but her body decided for her. The words got lodged somewhere around her stomach. "She's more powerful than you can imagine," Zanna heard herself saying, disgusted by how weak her voice sounded. "I have to go. It's the only way—"

"You are going nowhere," Xavier said. His cane pushed Zanna back into her pillows.

It would have to be a fight. This time, when her body asked to lash back at Xavier, she didn't stop it. With a flash of manipulation, she grabbed all the nitrogen under her sheets and threw it at Xavier, hoping that he would get tangled up in the blankets long enough for her to make a run for the door. But before she could even think about her next step, the air set all around her, as solid as concrete. The blankets had barely moved an inch.

"Don't," Xavier said, not even blinking at her attempted escape. He held the air for a moment longer to nail his point home and then released it. Zanna slumped back like a rag doll, her skin tingling as if she had just peeled off a thick layer of dry glue. Not even the Variable's manipulations of air pressure were that solid. Zanna gulped greedily for oxygen.

"You don't understand," she said when she got her voice back, a hand massaging her throat. "You've been wrong about her this whole time. She's not . . ."

Xavier, however, just looked down his nose with the glare of a man stuck babysitting a spoiled child. He had stopped listening to her a long time ago.

That was when the door opened.

Xavier had his back to it, but from the bed, Zanna could see it clearly. It swung open an inch, barely wide enough for someone to peek through—for *three* someones to peek through. A tall dark-skinned girl, a pale strawberry-blonde, and an Italian.

There was no time to explain the situation. No time to tell them that her grandfather was being held hostage and she was the only one who could rescue him—and that the man at her bedside was trying to prevent that. No time to explain *how* she knew all of that. She could only move and hope they kept up.

Zanna grabbed the first chemical sample she laid eyes

on—lithium. And just as she expected, Xavier snatched it from her, his knowledge of its functions so comprehensive that Zanna felt it slip from her fingers in an instant, just like before. But that was what she was counting on.

"Help me!" she shouted, before Xavier could freeze the air around her. The cube of lithium had momentarily distracted him, an opening of a few seconds, and Zanna hoped it was enough.

A heavy, wet *crunch* smacked through the room, and Xavier went limp. He pitched forward with a grunt, hat knocked off, as something black and round and the size of a grapefruit bounced off his skull and rolled across the room—a *cannonball*. It was so unexpected that Zanna just stared at it as the dark trickles of blood worked through Xavier's cropped silver hair. Then the girls were around her.

"What did you *do*?" Nora shrieked, but it wasn't at Zanna. It was at Beatrice, who was retrieving the cannonball from the floor.

"He's fine," she said, hoisting the heavy ball of iron up like a shot put.

Libby pulled Zanna from the bed and hugged her tight, away from the fallen Primer.

"That's Xavier Morrow," Nora said, still frantic. "You just knocked out a lieutenant Primer." Her eyes couldn't decide where to look—at the man with blood oozing from his head, at Beatrice and her cannonball, or at Zanna and Libby in the opposite corner. She at last decided on Zanna. "What's he do-ing here?"

Zanna's head felt light as a feather, and she pinched her eyes shut for a moment. Things were firing off left and right. She had to hold it together, like an unknown function. She could figure this out. "We—"

"Oh Zanna," the cat behind her said, suddenly springing into animation. "Your friends are here—"

It stopped, and with it, the room went cold. The cat's electric-blue eyes did not move in their sockets, but Zanna felt Mrs. Turnbuckle looking through them on the other side, darting from Zanna to her friends to Xavier on the ground, who was trying to get up to his hands and knees. The cat saw everything that had happened, and then from its mouth screamed an air-raid siren that no living animal had ever made.

"Run!"

No one argued. Tumbling and crashing into one another, the girls pounded down the hallway. Alarms were going off all around them, and when Zanna looked back over her shoulder, she saw heavy blast doors of golden alloy snap out of the walls. They sealed each of the cottage rooms, and when they closed, the sound went with them, cut off swiftly and completely.

"What's going on?" Nora screamed from behind her.

The girls burst through the hallway door and into the waiting room, where Mrs. Turnbuckle looked up from her desk with her mouth in a perfect pink circle of shock. One of her hands was on a gold ingot, the other clutching a half-finished tea cozy she had been knitting. As Zanna skidded in behind Libby and Beatrice, the needles wriggled and slipped out of the loops of yarn, and all the cat figurines rose from the desk, intent on ushering Zanna back to her room.

Zanna said every apology she knew and then bowled her poor nurse over with a gale of wind. Lace tore from the curtains. A shelf of collector's plates smashed to the floor. Mrs. Turnbuckle toppled off her chair with a soprano cry, one of her floral-print slippers coming loose and flying off in the havoc. The figurines crashed back onto the desk in disarray.

"Keep going!" Zanna said as Beatrice looked back at what

had become of the waiting room. Suddenly, there was a crash of metal on metal, and Libby lunged forward, fire poker out. A door slid out to seal the front entrance, but Libby had gotten there first and wedged her fire poker into the gap. One second later, and the girls would have been trapped in the cottage.

"So are you going to explain what's going on?" Libby said between clenched teeth.

"Not really the time for it," Zanna answered as she slipped through the gap. Beatrice followed closely behind her. "But I will, I promise. We just have to get out of here first."

"I'm going to hold you to that," Libby grunted. Her fire poker began to bend under the tremendous strength of the door. "Nora, a little leverage would help."

"But—" the girl started. She pulled out the stainless steel ruler that she had claimed as her Iron on the first day and looked from it to the door that was slowly crushing Libby's fire poker, eyes white with fear. "My Iron—"

"*Nora*." Libby's voice shook with the effort of keeping the door open. Fire blazed in her eyes as she grabbed the air in the narrow door gap and told it to stay right where it was. "That ruler ain't your Iron, and you know it."

The door slipped an inch, and then Nora moved, her mind apparently made up. She jammed the ruler into the gap, reinforcing Libby's failing fire poker and wedging the doors open enough that she could dart through.

"You three go on. Not going to make it," Libby said between her teeth. Another inch slipped, and Nora's ruler buckled under the stress. The manipulation holding the air in place teetered on a Splutter. Zanna could taste the tipping point of paradox in the air.

"Shut up!" Beatrice snapped. She squeezed the cannonball between both her hands. Zanna caught on to her plan at once and copied her, though she didn't have an Iron to help her focus. Together, they grabbed the air in the doorway, reinforcing Libby's manipulation. The threat of a Splutter made Zanna's head split like firewood to halfway down her spine, but she closed her eyes, shutting out the alarm and the fear for her grandfather and the storm of her own emotions. She focused on the air.

A sound from Libby like she had been punched in the throat, a final massive slam of metal, and then everything went silent. The air was gone, pushed out of the way as the door closed, and with it, the cottage had been sealed. Nothing was coming out until it was unlocked. A limit had been reached.

Libby lay wheezing on the stone path. Apparently, Nora had pulled her through—and rather violently at that. The girls crowded around her, and she waved them back with her bent fire poker, getting up under her own strength. Blood smeared around her nose, and she wiped it with the back of her hand. In the doorway, an inch of Nora's once-perfect ruler stuck out like the remains of a squashed fly.

Beatrice rounded on Zanna at once, the small girl ablaze with righteous anger. She jabbed with a finger, completely ignoring Zanna's bandages. "Okay," she said. "You better start explaining. Right now."

But Zanna looked past her into the afternoon of St. Pommeroy's. The alarm in the cottage that had been cut off by the limiting door had gotten picked up by the other buildings. Lights flashed, and Mrs. Appernathy squawked out of what seemed like every corner, ushering students to the cafeteria. Giant shadows passed overhead. The islands were coming in like birds to roost. And then, with a quake that she felt all the way down in her bones, an enormous function was thrown in the belly of the school and the iron bowl began to close up.

"Fine," Zanna said. "Keep up. I'll explain on the way."

CHAPTER NINETEEN

ZANNA DIDN'T HAVE a direction in mind, so she took off back toward the Candela. As she ran, she did her best to fill the girls in on everything that had happened since the message from Lord Hemmington had arrived that morning. "She's got Pops," Zanna said as they hurried through the plaza with the statue of Hippocrates. She could have sworn that the stone eyes of the kind-looking man followed her and her friends as they passed by. "I've got to get out of here. I've got to find him."

The path turned around an ivy-covered building, and she pulled up short. In the lockdown, the administration tower had come to life, its tranquil English garden now full of Particles, as if someone had kicked a beehive. Teachers shot across the empty space, somehow not colliding with the millions of silver spheres whizzing around. The tower at the center of the garden had opened like a wardrobe, its many shelves of offices open to the outside. At the top, its bright candle flame burned an angry martial-red.

"Man, that seems like overkill," Libby said as the girls piled up one after another behind Zanna, who had skidded to a stop.

"Oh, we are going to be in so much trouble," Nora whispered.

"I have to get out of here," Zanna said, as if the mere act of repeating it over and over would make it come true. The iron shell sealing the school was visible above the buildings. It had been waiting for all the orbiting islands to come in, but now that they were docked, the shell resumed its lockdown faster than before.

"The Primers are walking into a trap," Zanna continued, ducking back a little into the safety of the stone archway. "They've been wrong about the Variable all year. I don't know what their plan is to rescue my grandfather, but I do know it's not going to work. They still think she's just trying to kidnap me, when it's nothing like that."

"The *who*?" Libby asked.

Zanna smacked herself on the head. "The Variable. The woman who kidnapped me."

"Ah, because she's an unknown. Gotcha." Libby snuck another peek out at the administrative courtyard. "So . . . what? Were you planning on just rescuing him by yourself?"

"There's no one else to do it," Zanna said. She struggled to get the words right. "The Primers don't know her like I do. They don't know what she's capable of. But I do. I know how she thinks, how she plans things out . . ." Her throat tightened as the words "I know her Self" almost slipped past her lips. Instead, she said, "I know her."

A particularly angry horde of Particles came buzzing through, and the girls flattened against the wall. Nora pinched her lips together and shook her head, eyes transfixed on the Candela in lockdown mode. Zanna couldn't blame her. They were already in a heap of trouble for attacking Xavier and poor Mrs. Turnbuckle. No reason to make it any worse.

A cold, firm object slipped into her hands, and for a moment, Zanna wondered if it was a piece of iron. But it was Beatrice, hefting that cannonball up to her shoulder with one hand as she squeezed Zanna's with the other.

"Nobody kidnaps Pops and gets away with it," the small girl said. "I'm with you."

"Girls!" a voice behind them shouted. They all jumped and spun around, recognizing Mrs. Appernathy at once. The statue of Hippocrates was pointing at them, directing an approaching squad of lampposts. "All of the students are to report to the cafeteria at once. Stop standing around!"

"What's the plan, then, fearless leader?" Libby muttered. Arms emerged from the lamppost poles—long, spindly green things with open palms to escort them off to the cafeteria.

"I don't know," Zanna whispered. The lampposts herded them away from the Candela. "I can't . . ." She had been expecting a plan to come to her, but there was nothing in her head except thoughts of her grandfather being locked up in the Variable's mansion. "I can't think—"

"Oh, for the love of science, *here's* the plan," Nora said, and she raised her hand. Pinpoint lances of pure oxygen coalesced out of the air and hit the lampposts square in the joints, where the metal was as bright as a new penny. In the blink of an eye, a heavy patina like crusty green barnacles sprouted from the surface, and the lampposts stuttered to a halt like old, arthritic men. "Run!"

The word revitalized them, and they took off into the chaos of the Candela's garden. Mrs. Appernathy shouted for them to stop, her lampposts pulling the patina back into the metal so the posts could move again, but that took time, and the girls were already halfway into the garden, running with their heads low to avoid all the overhead Particles. Libby threw a dust storm back over her shoulder, ripping the rose petals and topsoil from the nearby flowerbeds to conceal them.

"Head toward the parking lot!" Nora shouted as she slammed a door open with more ferocity than Zanna had previously thought the well-composed girl could muster. "Hurry! Before he makes it to the cafeteria!"

"He?" Zanna asked. "Mr. Gunney?"

"What?" Nora said. They were inside the castle wing now, and she shot a few preemptive blasts of oxygen at the sconces, rusting them to the wall. "No, you dummy!" she shouted as she knocked over a candelabra. "*Cedwick!*"

The name almost made Zanna trip, and she had to stick her arms out like a toddler to regain her balance. "Cedwick?" she asked.

"Yes," Nora said, as if it were the most obvious thing. "He's got a car. And he's the only one crazy enough to let you borrow it. Now hurry! Before he gets locked up in the cafeteria!"

As they crossed into the ancient Greek part of the school, Zanna looked up through the columns, and her stomach dropped. The iron shell was almost completely closed. Only a small circle at the very top still let the afternoon light through, and that was shrinking rapidly. They burst into the entrance hall with the reflecting pool and olive trees, and Zanna spotted a familiar figure down at the far end, slowly moping his way toward the cafeteria with his chauffeur, Sophie, in tow.

"Cedwick!"

There was no time to explain. Cedwick and Sophie had barely turned their heads before the girls were on top of them. Had Sophie known what was coming, she might have put up a better fight, but the girls had surprise on their side. Four uncoordinated bursts of nitrogen hit the woman at once, and she nearly lifted out of her shoes, crashing back into an olive tree.

"Come on!" Libby shouted as she grabbed Cedwick by his tie. The olive trees were swaying and groaning in a way that Zanna didn't like at all. She surged forward, overtaking Nora in the lead as she dashed through the main archway and out into the parking lot.

Dr. Trout stood before her.

How Zanna stopped, she had no idea. One moment her legs were pounding away like maniacs, and then she was perfectly still, staring at the woman in her way. Her professor looked as she always did, baseball bat held lightly in one weathered hand and a stack of books tucked under the other. Like the entire school was not screaming and flashing and running wild around her.

Then she was gone, as quickly as an illusion vanishing. Zanna hadn't even had the time to swallow and explain why she was here and not in the cafeteria.

"*Oof!*" Nora exclaimed as she ran smack into Zanna. "Why'd you stop?"

"I don't know," Zanna whispered. There was nothing in front of her except the courtyard.

"What in the world is going on?!" Cedwick shouted, trying and failing to twist out of Libby's iron grip. "What did you do to Sophie? We're supposed to be—"

"Your limousine," Nora demanded. "Where is it?"

"There!" Beatrice answered for Cedwick, pointing beyond the row of buses to the visitor parking.

Mrs. Appernathy shouted from the lampposts for them to turn around, condemning them to years of detention. In the silver-gushing fountain at the center of the courtyard, something like a monstrous hand rippled up angrily. They ran without looking back.

"My grandfather's in danger," Zanna said by way of explanation. "And the Primers, they're walking into something they don't understand. We're their only hope."

Cedwick squirmed. "You can't be serious," he said, piecing together why they needed his limousine at once. "My father—"

"Is in danger," Zanna finished. They made it to the limousine, but the doors were locked. "I can explain everything, but we have to go." She checked the shell. Almost shut. "We have to go *now*."

Cedwick didn't move. Libby tried to pry one of the doors open with the tip of her fire poker. It didn't budge. "Come on!" she said through gritted teeth.

"Please," Zanna said, as calmly as her heart would let her. "Please, Cedwick. I need your help."

For a second, she didn't think he was going to do it. Then he let out a sharp exhale and touched the limousine, disengaging the lock. The door popped open at once and the girls piled into the back as fast as they could.

"You do know how to drive this, right?" Nora asked as Cedwick climbed into the driver's seat. The boy's fingers flew over the dashboard.

"Of course," Cedwick scoffed, which made Zanna grin a little. It reminded her of the cocky boy she had met—and loathed—on the first day. The limousine jerked as he twisted his hand around, pulling back on a polished chrome lever that ran deep into the function engine of the automobile. With a little bump, it rose from the ground.

"Faster," Nora said. The girls all crowded up to the front to peer out the windshield, fighting for space. St. Pommeroy's iron shell was nearly closed, and they were going too slowly. "*Faster*," Nora said again, and Cedwick grumbled something in response, making adjustments as quickly as he could. They were still too slow, and the gap was only ten feet across.

"Faster!"

Cedwick punched something, and they flew. An instant of weightless terror shot through the limousine, and then Zanna slammed against the backseat with the other girls, speed holding her in place. It let go as quickly as it had grabbed them, and Cedwick cooled the engines, safe outside the iron shell.

"*Ow*," the pile of girls moaned in unison as they disentangled themselves. Beatrice's cannonball had apparently socked Libby right in the nose, and she handed it back with a few choice words about what reasonable people should choose for their Iron. Zanna winced at the pain in her ribs as she sat up, but a few cursory pokes with her finger told her that at least they hadn't broken again.

Cedwick looked back at them, the limousine evidently running on autopilot. "Okay," he said, a little flustered but wide-eyed at the thrill of their narrow escape. "Start talking."

The girls were silent, and then Zanna realized all of them were looking at her. At once, her face went bright-red, and she looked down at her empty hands. If she had an Iron right now, she would hold it tightly and draw strength from it, but the best she could do was a bit of nitrogen gas, and that gave her no comfort. "My grandfather was kidnapped sometime this morning," she said. "That's why Xavier was in my room. He was part of the cover-up. The Primers are trying to rescue Pops, but it's not going to work. Your dad has been wrong about the Variable—the woman who attacked you at my house—since the very first day. He thinks she's just some kidnapper, but she's not. She's more powerful than any Scientist I've ever seen. They're walking into a death trap."

It was cold in the limousine, cold and bitter like a barren mountaintop. Now that Zanna had a few moments to sit still, the impact of what she had been telling herself had time to permeate. The words *death trap* were especially heavy.

"So . . . what? You're going to warn my father?" Cedwick asked. The pessimism in his voice cut quick. "Because he won't listen to you. Trust me, I know."

"I know," Zanna said, her chin raised. "He didn't listen to me earlier. No, we're going to rescue my grandfather."

"Just like that?" Cedwick said dryly. "Do you have any sort of plan?"

"I do," she said, though that wasn't quite accurate. She had known what the plan would have to be ever since she had properly understood the situation, but like so many other things, she had been steadfastly ignoring it. It was stupid and reckless—and the only possible thing that had a chance of working. "This whole time, the Variable's only been after one thing. She wants me to live with her. So I will."

Zanna might well have told everyone she was going to walk into a meat grinder. They recoiled at once, Libby letting out a "What?!" through the wad of napkins she was holding to her nose to stanch the bleeding.

"There's no other way," Zanna said, trying to shout over the other girls, who were all talking at once and telling her it was the worst idea she'd ever had. "I'm trying, I really am, but I can't—"

"I did *not* just brain a Primer so we could hand you back over," Beatrice said with a scowl.

"Or break every rule of St. Pommeroy's emergency protocol," Nora added.

"Or steal my father's limousine," Cedwick said.

"Or smash my nose!"

"Please, listen," Zanna said, trying to calm the ruckus in the limousine. "*Listen!*"

That managed to silence the group, though Zanna could still see the disagreement plain on their faces. She let out a long breath. "The Variable's been trying to keep me out of St. Pommeroy's this whole time. Don't ask me why"—and she stuttered a bit at that part—"but that's what's going on. Everything with the illusion at the beginning of the year, at the party, all of this—it's one attempt after another. She wants to do a trade. Me for my grandfather. So I bet you that the Primers are putting together some sort of metallurgical illusion of me and are hoping to trade that off instead of the real thing. But no matter how complex they make it, it's not going to be enough to fool her. She—" The words caught again, and Zanna had to work around them. "She'll see right through it. And I don't know what she might do to the Primers if she gets angry."

When Zanna stopped talking, none of the girls seemed convinced, but at least they didn't all start talking at once. "That's still not a plan," Beatrice said. "That's just you getting captured."

"No, it's me being a decoy," Zanna said. "She's going to expect the Primers to send a metallurgical illusion. Lord Hemmington would never willingly turn me over to her."

Cedwick grumbled something that no one could make out, but Zanna pressed on. "That's our opening. The Variable's not expecting the real me to show up. She's going to be confused. Her guard will be down. *That's* when the Primers have to rush in. Not before. While she's looking for the illusion that doesn't exist."

"You'll never get my father to go along with that," Cedwick said.

"I'm not asking permission from your father," Zanna replied, eyes flicking up to the boy. "He's just going to have to keep up with us."

"He'll just as soon arrest you for interfering with a Primer operation," Cedwick said.

"Along with attacking several teachers, setting off a school lockdown, and stealing a limousine," Zanna recounted. "Trust me, what your father thinks of me is the least of my worries right now."

"Well, I don't like it one bit," Nora said bluntly. "I don't even need to run the probabilities to tell you they are *not* good."

"Then give me a better plan," Zanna said. "Because the way I see it, it's either this, or I never see my grandfather again."

Nora didn't back down entirely, but she didn't have a good reply either. None of the girls did. Libby let out a hock of dried blood and threw away her stained napkins, her eyes catching Beatrice's for just a moment. The limousine balanced delicately.

"It'll work," Beatrice said at last, nodding back at Libby. She turned her head toward Nora. "We'll make it work."

Nora sighed. "This is an *exceptionally* disorganized plan."

"I'll assume that's a yes. Cedwick?" Zanna asked.

He drew his hands down over his face. "Can't really go back, can we?" he muttered. "All right. Buckle up."

He dropped back down into the driver's seat, and the limousine shuddered with a rough start. Apparently, Cedwick had yet to figure out the proper finesse for operating the machine, but he seemed to know enough. With another acceleration that the girls were better prepared for this time, the car leapt forward.

As they traveled, Zanna rested with her head back on the fine upholstered seats, preparing herself as best she could. Truth be told, she didn't like the plan any more than the other girls did. They were right, as always. It was foolish and dangerous and would put her face-to-face with the Variable again, with only the vaguest hope of backup. But there was no other way to get her grandfather back. Of that, she was sure.

"*Psst.*" Zanna opened her eyes and saw Libby wiggling her eyebrows at her, the whisper sneaking out between her barely pursed lips. The girl shot a meaningful look at the front of the limousine.

"What?" Zanna mouthed. But Libby just shot another look, and then Zanna understood. Cedwick. Go and talk to Cedwick.

Zanna shook her head, but Libby was insistent. A little begrudgingly, Zanna slid all the way down the sofa to the front. Cedwick looked up from the controls with a little jump of surprise.

"Hey," she started, fumbling for a topic. "So where are we going?"

Cedwick pointed to a screen. It was a map of the United States with three blips of light on it. Two were nearly on top of each other, with the third on an interception course. "In case we ever got lost," he said to explain the tracking system.

"So the Variable's out in Kentucky?" Zanna asked, peering at the two blips of light that represented Lord Hemmington and Owin. "Why?"

Cedwick shrugged. "You're the one with the answers."

"Hardly." She looked back at Libby for help, but the girl shook her head and pointed back toward Cedwick. Zanna twisted her mouth around, thinking. "And I guess . . . I wanted to say thanks?"

He just grunted. "I didn't really have much of a choice about it, did I? Kind of got dragged along."

"You could have left us back at school," Zanna said. "You didn't have to come along. So thanks."

"Like I said," he muttered as he reached for something on the dashboard that changed nothing about how the limousine flew, "I didn't really have a choice."

Zanna tried to find a good place to rest her eyes, but everything made her stomach squirm. She couldn't look back at Libby, who just scowled back at her. She couldn't look out the windshield at the colorful clouds passing by, or else she'd remember how high up in the air they were. She couldn't look at her hands, since they looked more like the Variable's with each passing minute. So she looked at Cedwick. It was the first time she had seen Cedwick since the party. He had never visited her in the nurse's cottage. He had missed a lot of school over the winter, the girls had told her when she mentioned his absence—something about battling a nasty case of pneumonia. It certainly looked like it. His features were a little sharper than she remembered, his cheeks a shade more hollow, his eyes darker and more sunken. Or perhaps that was the effect of the lighting in the limousine.

"I wrote that paper for Dr. Trout," Zanna said quietly. "But I kind of lost it when I was escaping. It's probably part of some eagle's nest now."

Cedwick shrugged. "It's fine. I'm better now. I figured some things out." As if to prove it, he held up something she had missed in the chaos of their flight from St. Pommeroy's. Draped over his shoulders like a clunky scarf was a length of heavy iron chain—the kind she would expect to find in a medieval dungeon.

"You found your Iron!" she said.

"Yeah. Did you?"

"No." She didn't feel like burdening him with the story of Dr. Trout's visit and the threat of flunking out of Self. Somehow, in the quiet travel of the limousine, it felt inappropriate, and Cedwick was carrying enough on his shoulders already.

"It was strange," he said suddenly, as if answering a question she hadn't asked. "Finding it. Because some part of me always knew. Scientists say they 'found' their Iron—like it's some kind of major discovery. But in the end, I always knew what my Iron would be. I always knew I wasn't going to join the Primers like dad and Owin. The hard part was admitting it. Admitting who I was."

He had said the entire thing without looking back at her, but something about his tone made her sure that the words had been only for her. Zanna dropped her head a little closer and whispered, as if they were the only two in the limousine at that moment, "I guess I have a lot to admit about myself."

"Yeah, that's the way it works," he muttered, suddenly looking ashamed of the conversation. She could hear the note of closure in his voice and see it in the way he jabbed something on the dashboard, this time slowing the limousine with a slight bump of deceleration.

Zanna huffed in frustration—not with him but with herself. *One day*, she thought, *I will actually say something helpful instead of making everything worse.*

"Go wake your friends," Cedwick said briskly, clicking a few more functions in the limousine as it came to a stop. "We're here."

Dusk covered the ground below them. Cedwick had parked the car several hundred feet in the air over rolling farmland that was divided into plots by a crisscross of scruffy trees and sagging barbed wire. At the top of a hill in the largest field sat the mansion, commanding the view in all directions. Harsh white light picked it out of the twilight. Two Primer camps had been established a fair distance off, each with its own giant spotlight. The entire scene made Zanna breathe carefully, as if she had just stepped into a very strict library and had become aware of how loudly her heart was thudding in her chest.

"There's a Weierstrass down there," Beatrice said as the girls looked out the limousine's windows. "An enormous one. Radius at least two hundred meters."

"I don't see anything," Libby said.

"That's hardly a surprise," Nora muttered. "How'd she manage to write a Weierstrass that big? I've never seen one used like that."

"She's expecting the Primers to use an illusion, remember?" Zanna said. "That's why she's got a Weierstrass."

"But that size!" Nora said, her voice filled with awe. "It circles the entire house."

The tips of Zanna's ears tingled with a strange elation, as if she had just overheard someone talking about her. "I told you, the Primers have underestimated her. There's a bubble of air pressure underneath that Weierstrass. And inside that is completely primelocked. That mansion is a fortress."

"If that's so," Nora said, her eyes still glued to the scene below them, "then you can forget about smashing and grabbing. The minute we drive this limousine into that Weierstrass, all of the manipulated functions are going to fail. Unless we rewrite everything in discrete calculus."

They looked at their Mathematics expert, but Beatrice shook her head. "Not a chance," she said sadly. "I wouldn't even know where to begin."

"We don't have to *drive* it through the Weierstrass," Libby said, gesturing with her hands to sketch out her idea. "We can drop in. Let gravity do the work for us. As for the barrier, just hit it with enough force, and it'll burst like a balloon. Air pressure's only useful across a wide surface area. Concentrate enough force in one spot, and the function won't hold."

Nora didn't share the girl's enthusiasm. She fixed Libby with a death stare. "So, you want to crash us into the ground."

"Into the barrier of air pressure," Libby corrected her. "It's basically a giant pillow, y'know."

"And how are we going to get out?"

Libby shrugged. "The Primers will cover us. I mean, this thing's got reinforcements on it, right? Lord Hemmington wouldn't send his sons off to school in a limousine made out of just metal." She looked over to Cedwick, and he nodded in confirmation.

"It's an alloy," he said, looking over the metal parts of the limousine. "Not really inherited, but it means something to Sophie. Should be strong enough."

"So we jump out, grab Zanna and Pops, and jump back in," Libby said with a smile. As if to prove her point, she rapped the tip of her fire poker none-too-gently on the limousine's window.

The glass made a dull and thick sound, far from the fragile tinkling Zanna might have expected. "Perfect."

It wasn't enough to wipe the frown from Nora's face. "I just want to say again that this is a terrible plan."

"Consider it noted," Libby said haughtily, glancing out the window at the Primer camps. Her Southern accent grew more pronounced the longer they waited. "They ain't going to stand around forever."

Zanna looked down with her at the scene below. The face of the stolen mansion was impassive and bleached, like a collection of bones left to burn in the sunlight. It had no deliciously creepy shadows, no atmospheric cobwebs. Only pale, unpainted shutters closed up tight and a tower without a staircase, waiting for Zanna's return.

"Set me down at the edge of the Weierstrass," she whispered. "And get ready."

CHAPTER TWENTY

ON THE FIELD, the wind was strong and cold. Only the most daring of flowers were beginning to lift their heads. Zanna put a hand to her chest, checking that her ribs were still holding together, and took a quick look around. She had lost sight of the limousine as soon as she had stepped out of it, but whether it was hovering behind her or Cedwick had already taken it up into the sky, Zanna had no way of knowing. At the thought of the car spinning in free fall, a wave of sickness washed over her, and she was thankful that her role involved staying on the ground. Even if it was more dangerous down there.

Her hands wished for something to hold on to, something iron to reassure her and keep her steady, but there was nothing. As if she needed another reminder of how much of a failure at Self she was. Instead, she just opened and closed her fists, pumping blood through them, and looked back over her shoulder. The limousine had complicated illusions to keep it cloaked, but she had nothing, and the Primers were sure to notice a girl suddenly appearing in the no-man's-land between their camps and the mansion. She had to get moving quickly.

Zanna took a deep breath and stepped into the Weierstrass.

It wasn't her first time inside the transforming function, but this time something about it was different. When she had brandished the key given to her by Dr. Fitzie and chased the Variable out of her bedroom, the way the Weierstrass broke the functions around her into a slideshow almost seemed ticklish, like someone was gently massaging her head. Now, with almost a year of Scientist schooling behind her, it was sickening. Zanna glanced at the nitrogen and oxygen that swirled around her, and it was like staring wide-eyed into a strobe light. Even though she knew these functions backward and forward, there was nothing to grab. Everything blinked like stop-motion and threatened to split her head apart.

She stopped trying to pin down anything in the Weierstrass, and the ache in her temples dulled a little. It wouldn't help to go into this with a sledgehammer pounding away at her brain. There was already one working on her heart. Voices shouted from behind her, pushing through the wind and Weierstrass. The Primers had finally spotted her. One of the spotlights swiveled a bit, sweeping down from the mansion to catch her and her lonely walk up the field. There wasn't any hiding now. A tiny voice had been telling her that she could still back out if she just turned and ran, but now the Variable had certainly noticed her. So Zanna kept walking.

This was the far edge of the Weierstrass, and it felt like the edge of a canyon. The silence ahead of her was palpable, and she reached out a hand to the barrier of air pressure to test whether she could still pass through it. But of course, she met with no resistance. After all, it had been constructed with the Variable's Self function as its key. With *Zanna's* Self function.

One of the Primers had found a megaphone and was shouting into it, telling her to turn around and return to camp. Zanna ignored him and pushed her hand through the barrier until she felt the primelock on the other side, like the icy water beneath a frozen lake. There was no obvious marking, no visual difference to the patchy Kentucky farmland, but Zanna knew the next step would take her into the woman's domain. Outside in the Weierstrass, there was still a chance she would manage to escape, if it came down to it, but inside the bubble of air pressure, there would be no backup until Cedwick and the rest came down with the limousine. If that even worked.

Pops wouldn't have thought twice about it.

She crossed.

There was no wind inside. No sound of the Primers shouting at her to turn around. No sound at all from the outside. She cupped her hands around her mouth and exhaled, balling up the nitrogen and tucking it behind her back. It wasn't much, but it felt good in her hands as she looked up at the crumbling mansion. Without an Iron, it was the best she could do.

"Hey!"

The mansion was silent.

"Hey! Give me back my grandfather!"

Zanna tossed the nitrogen from one hand to the other as the mansion remained unmoved by her shouting. Everything that had to go right in order for her to make it back out of here seemed like a list of impossibilities. But then, before fear got the better of her and she turned back down the hill, the front door opened, and the Variable stepped out onto the porch. She put a hand up to shield herself from the harsh light of the spotlights and then made a gesture, causing the light to dim considerably. Not so much that Zanna couldn't see, but enough to give them a little privacy.

"Welcome back," the woman said. If the Primers had been trying to wear her down by drawing out the situation, it obviously hadn't worked. The Variable was immaculate. She had even shaped her long black hair into a cascade of loose curls that any movie star would have killed for, and Zanna felt something ruffle her own hack-cut mop of black hair, even though there was no wind inside the bubble.

There really was no going back now, and Zanna dug for the

courage that had been leaking out of her with every step up the hill. "Where's my grandfather?" she said as fiercely as she could manage. On the word *my* she stumbled a little, her tongue first trying and then discarding *our*. "If you've hurt him—"

"Relax," the Variable said, and she triggered a function in the house. The tower room that had been Zanna's prison separated as easily as someone removing the lid from a jar, and it drifted over the rooftop and down into the front yard, settling gently with a creak of timber. Light from the single circular window spilled across the farmland. Another bit of function from the Variable rolled the wall up like a window shade, and there was Pops.

He sat at the writing desk with a book in his hands, peering around at his new surroundings. "Pops!" Zanna shouted. Every inch of her wanted to run across the yard and wrap her arms around him, but she held her ground. There was no sign of the limousine, and she couldn't glance up in the sky to check, fearing the woman would notice and the element of surprise would be ruined. Zanna had to stall. "Are you okay?" she shouted.

"Zanna?" Pops squinted over the desk. Another surge of emotion tore through her and nearly swept her from her spot and into his arms. There was something in Pops's voice that she had never heard before—fear. Fear that Zanna was doing exactly what it looked like she was doing. "What are you doing here?"

"It's going to be all right, Pops," she said, turning away because she couldn't blatantly lie to his face. She faced the Variable instead. "Release him. You have me. Let him go."

The woman nodded, and the tower room began to reshape. Floorboards split and stacked up on top of each other. The desk slid off to a side, and the chair Pops sat on lowered until its four legs rested on the bare earth. A pillow of air brought over the puzzle book he had been working on and deposited it in his lap. Then the room reassembled itself, unrolled the wall, and flew back up to its spot atop the tower, reattaching without so much as a crack in the shingles.

"He's free," the Variable said.

Pops turned his head one direction and then the other, taking in the mansion and the spotlights and tasting the primelocked air with a dubious expression. He got up from the chair clutching his puzzle book, and for the first time, Zanna was thankful at how slow he could sometimes move.

"Zanna?" he asked again, with that same sound of uncharacteristic fear.

"It's fine, Pops," she said, still unable to look at him. Fractures cracked across her heart, and she knew if she turned her head—if she let herself look at him—everything would break. She swallowed and thrust an arm back toward where she had come, back toward the Primer camps.

"He walks," she said. The only hostage exchanges she had ever seen were in movies, and Zanna wasn't sure what the protocol was supposed to be in the real world. *But then again*, she figured wryly, *neither does the Variable*.

"And you come here," the woman said, pointing to a spot next to her on the porch. "Quickly now."

More time. Zanna walked as slowly as she could without being obvious about it. As if she were savoring the last few steps of freedom. Where was Cedwick and his limousine? Calculations of falling bodies clicked through her head. How high up had they gone? Zanna touched the nitrogen that she had slipped up her sleeve, reassuring herself it was still there and under her control. If the limousine didn't arrive in the next few seconds, it was all she had left.

Her shoes stopped at the base of the porch steps, not daring to climb. Something like a live rabbit twitched in her chest.

"Don't you want to confirm my function?" Zanna said, remembering the plan they had decided on and shifting her feet to stand a little wider. *That will buy Cedwick time*, she thought. It would also occupy the Variable's attention. "I could be an illusion."

But the woman barely glanced over Zanna. "My dear, I confirmed it when you stepped in here," she said. As easy as identifying herself in a mirror. She brushed her hair back over her shoulder and beckoned again. "Up here," she coaxed. "Next to me."

No time left, and the limousine was not coming. Zanna still had the nitrogen, but that was of little use. If she were closer, she could clamp it over the Variable's mouth like a rag, but that would mean climbing the steps onto the porch. And every scrap of her said that if she set foot in the mansion, that would be it. To anyone else, it may have been only four steps of battered gray wood, but to Zanna, it was a prison entrance.

She had no choice, though. She had given Cedwick and the girls all the time she could manage. She had tried to keep the woman distracted—and had failed. Her foot rose in its muddy shoe to take the last steps of freedom she would ever have.

Then, with a twist of sky and night, the limousine appeared. It was nose-first and true, and Zanna saw at once why they had been late. Libby's fire poker was jammed in the front grill, its hardened tip pointed like a lance. It hit with a crunch of metal and glass, and the entire barrier warped, punched down like a heavy weight on a trampoline. The whole thing must have taken only a fraction of a second, but to Zanna, it was forever. The barrier stretched all the way until Libby's fire poker touched a particularly tall tuft of grass, like a girl bending over to touch her nose to the scent of a blooming flower.

And then it popped.

Wind rushed around Zanna, whirls of dust and debris as the air pressure exploded out of the hole Libby's fire poker had made. It took only an instant, a horrific and deafening instant. Zanna saw the limousine fall the last foot to the ground, its body battered from its reckless plunge, and then everything roared in a terrific backdraft as the function broke.

She was thrown sideways, crashing into the scraggly flower-beds beside the mansion's porch, but she found her feet quickly. In the dust cloud, she could just make out the limousine, its doors open as Libby and Nora ran out to collect Pops and get him back inside the vehicle. Beatrice stood guard, her cannon-ball ready and hoisted over her head.

The Variable. Zanna's head whipped around to the porch, but the woman was gone. There was only the limousine and Zanna's friends helping her grandfather along as fast as he could make it.

"Zanna!" Beatrice stole the nitrogen out of the interior of the limousine and wiped away the dust cloud so she could see better. They spotted each other, and the girl held out a hand. "Come on!"

Zanna stumbled the few feet to Beatrice and clung to her, thankful for the small girl's steadiness. "She's gone!"

"Get in!" Beatrice said, shoving her toward the limousine. Libby and Nora were already inside with her grandfather. Upon seeing him, the last bits holding Zanna's heart together shattered, and she dove into his arms, blubbering. Everyone was shouting at once—Libby was shouting at Cedwick to cloak, and he was shouting something back about primelock, and Beatrice wanted to know where the Primers were. But it was Nora's voice that caught Zanna's attention.

"The house!"

Zanna raised her tear-filled eyes to the limousine's window

and gasped. It was like watching a tree getting pulled right out of the ground, roots and all. The field buckled in vicious cracks as the mansion's foundation began to emerge. Just like the flying islands of St. Pommeroy's, the house was supported by a bowl of iron, with clods of soil and rock clinging to the tarnished metal. It lifted out of the ground with the gravity of a sleeping monster come to life, rising just enough to look down imperiously at the limousine. The girls clutched each other as if they had awoken a dragon.

Beatrice came to her wits first. "Cedwick! Move!"

"It's the primelock—" he started, and then a horrifying crunching sound filled the limousine. The entire car tipped up on its front wheels, and the girls slid with a tumble of muddy shoes and screams into a pile. Iron tendrils wrapped around the limousine, picking it up like a toy. Cedwick sprawled awkwardly over the console, hitting buttons left and right, but nothing could stop the house from reeling them in.

"We're okay," Nora managed to get out, though it sounded more like she was reassuring herself than anyone else. She had caught Pops when the car had been grabbed, protecting him as best she could. "The protective alloys of the limousine—"

A bright point appeared in the limousine's roof and un-zipped it, peeling back the metal like a tin of sardines to reveal the Variable. She hovered a few inches above the porch, arms open and fingers spread. Her perfect hair whipped in the wind of the burst air-pressure barrier, as wild as the angry, monstrous functions of her mansion. Every metal object on her house had come to life—every gutter and weathervane and balcony railing—and stood ready, like a hand of five hundred fingers about to close into a fist.

"*You*," she cawed. Iron shot from her sleeve and grabbed Zanna around the waist. Seeing an opportunity, Beatrice threw her cannonball, but a shield of black iron bloomed from the woman's other sleeve, and the ball glanced off with a *clang*.

"Stay," the woman growled as Nora and Libby tried to jump from the limousine. Bright copper wire sizzled past Zanna's ear and tangled around the girls, pinning them down like animals in a net. The limousine crunched as the house tightened its grip.

Zanna fought at the iron around her waist, but it was useless. The cold, unstoppable lash of it dragged her from the car and across the yard. As the girls screamed for her, Zanna let the nitrogen leak out of her sleeve and tried not to think about the implications of the words *last resort*. She waited as the Variable brought her closer, close enough that Zanna could see how the woman's face twisted with the strain of her manipulations. Her tongue stuck out a little between her teeth, the smooth mask of her face broken as she screwed up her mouth and half-closed her eyes in concentration.

A voice cut through all the mansion iron and wind and boomed deep in Zanna's bones. "This is Lord Baxter Hemmington," it said. "We have your house surrounded. Release the children and surrender at once."

At least twelve men and women appeared inside the perimeter of the Weierstrass, all bundled in long coats and scarves that flapped in the wind. They carried polished wooden boxes on their backs, each no bigger than a picnic basket and made up of at least fifty minuscule drawers. Henry, the one who had debriefed Zanna after her escape, stood to the far right, his letter opener in his hand. Lord Hemmington took point, though Zanna almost didn't recognize him at first, since he had traded his customary gray suit for full-plate armor, complete with helmet and visor. The thing that gave him away was the sheriff's badge, still somehow pinned to the medieval breastplate. Beside him and a little behind was Owin, shield drawn and ready. Together, they made a picture of ancient chivalry, of knight and squire, and Zanna swelled with renewed hope.

But then she made the mistake of catching a glimpse of the Variable, and the bravado shortly deserted her. The woman wore the little smirk Zanna knew all too well. It was the one for when she already knew the answer and was just waiting for someone else to catch up with her.

"Baxter," the woman said with a thick, patronizing tone. The house's gutters lifted the limousine a couple of feet higher, displaying it to everyone gathered around the yard. "Don't you recognize your own machine? Don't you wonder how it found its way from your garage all the way out here?"

A sudden knife of iron from her sleeve cut into the shred of limousine and yanked Cedwick out of the driver's seat, dangling him like a trophy. "Your boy," she said. Froth spewed from Cedwick's lips as he grabbed at the iron around his neck, fighting to breathe. The Variable squeezed a bit tighter. "One step from any of you, and I'll snap his feeble little neck."

His feet made a horrific suspended dance, twitching and kicking at nothing, and Zanna moved without thinking about it. As the Variable looked over the Primers, holding them to their positions, Zanna shoved every scrap of nitrogen she had down the woman's throat. All she needed was a few seconds of weakness while the woman coughed and sucked for air. A few seconds, and the Primers would rush in, and Cedwick would be saved.

But her nitrogen did nothing. She felt it there under her control, clapped like a hand over the woman's nose and mouth, but the Variable didn't falter for an instant. Instead, she just turned her head, and Zanna gulped, feeling like a wild predator had caught her scent. There was no perfection left in that face. Awakening her mansion had twisted out ugly features. It made her eyes bulge and her cheeks sink down and her hair go tangled and thick and knotted.

"Don't," she growled, and the nitrogen was gone in a flash of primelock.

Zanna gasped at how easily it had gone. At least when Xavier had yanked the gas out of her control, there had been a moment of struggle. A struggle she had quickly lost, but one she had seen how to win if her abilities had been better. The Variable, however, simply took, as if the nitrogen had always belonged to her.

"Release the children and surrender," Lord Hemmington repeated. "You are surrounded. You have no escape."

The Variable snapped back at once to the Primers, laughter crackling out of her like discharged electricity. It wasn't the laughter of a madwoman. Zanna knew that now because the Variable had dropped her perfect pretty face for one with eyes too big for it, a sideways mouth, and a choppy mess of untamable black hair. A face Zanna knew so well.

"I have no escape?" The Variable laughed because she finally got to show off. "I have a *mansion*."

Her hands closed into fists, and the mansion unraveled. Glass pulled out of its window panes and reshaped into needles a foot long. Floorboards pried themselves out of beams. Only the porch remained intact—the only proof that the hulking, angry swarm of wood and furniture and knives and books and glass and bricks rising behind them had ever been a house.

It struck without a word.

Zanna had never seen real Scientists fight before, having missed her chance in Yellowknife. In her mind, there was some unwritten honor code to it, like gentlemen at a duel standing thirty paces away and valiantly throwing functions at each other. All that vanished when she saw how the Variable wielded the howling storm of what had been her mansion. It washed over the Primers and beat them down without mercy. Sparks flew as nails and butcher knives stabbed at the protective shells a few Primers had managed to get up in time. It found cracks and pried them apart and tackled the Scientist inside. The air whipped back and forth in thunderclaps that liquefied Zanna's bones and broke the defenses of the last few stubborn holdouts. The mansion swarmed over the fallen Primers like hungry rats.

Zanna had been right about one thing. The Primers never stood a chance.

The storm pulled up, as fast as it had pounced. Tables and floorboards and library shelves and overstuffed armchairs all hovered in a field of debris ten feet above the grass, looking down at the subjugated Primers. Some were wrapped up in conglomerates of pewter and brick, others were caught by air pressure. Lord Hemmington was being restrained by a mass of polished wood and cushioning that Zanna recognized after a moment as the purple sofa from the sitting room, now squashed and squeezed around him. At his throat was her old friend the serving tray, sharpened to a razor's edge. Then she saw Owin, and her heart strangled out a cry. He was facedown on the ground, arms and legs pinned by a wrestle of fire-scorched metal that must have once been the fireplace ash grate, and there was blood leaking through his coat. A needle of window glass stuck out of his shoulder at a crude angle.

"Stop it!" Zanna said, even though the storm of mansion had all but frozen in place. Her arms were bound tight against her body, but she still managed to make little rebellious fists, useless as they were. "You can't—you *can't*!"

The first one had been a plea, but the second one surprised her. It was a fact, and the Variable must have heard the difference. She looked down at the girl coiled in iron and tipped her head to the side, as if she had never seen Zanna before and was curious about how she worked. Then the woman grinned, her teeth bloody from biting her tongue too hard.

"Yes," she whispered, "I can."

Another constriction of the gutters around the limousine to prove her point, and the girls inside yelped. Cedwick's feet had stopped kicking. He was still breathing, but barely. Something dangled from his limp form, long and knotted and swaying. His iron length of chain, still held even in unconsciousness.

I always knew what my Iron would be, Cedwick had said. *The hard part was admitting it. Admitting who I was.*

But hadn't Zanna already admitted it? First in the tower room while snatching the Variable's breath and then in the hospital? It was the reason she had asked Dr. Trout about time travel. The mere fact that she was here, having figured out what the Variable's plan was for her grandfather, meant that she had admitted it. The fact that she and the Variable were the same person.

No, the function inside her whispered back. She never really had. It was at best a curiosity, and at worst a tactic she had employed to try and catch the woman off guard. It had been used and then set aside, not carried with her always like a real Iron should be. Even now, she couldn't call the Variable by her true name. Zanna took in the scene again, forcing herself to look at it with new eyes. The Primers were helpless, pinned down by morphed furniture and dining room paintings and that horrifying stuffed moose head. Owin was bleeding. Cedwick dangled by his neck. The limousine with the other girls in it was a scrap of its former self, so wrapped up in gutters and copper wire that it looked more like a spider's prey than an automobile.

All of this was her future. *She* would do this. Not the woman. Not the Variable. *Her*.

Beneath her, the porch began to rise, lifting the orbiting

cloud of mansion debris that was still menacing the Primers beneath it. She and the woman were leaving, and if she didn't do something now, there would be no coming back. Zanna took one last look at the Variable—at her future self—and closed her eyes.

The answer had always been there in her function. It was obvious now, jumping out from the other inscrutable complications. Her mind touched the iron that bound her. This was *her* Iron, this had always been hers, and she knew its name now. Something handed down from generation to generation, something imbued with family and time, something stubborn and clunky and dangerous and endlessly useful. The frying pan Pops had given her. That was her Iron. It always would be.

When she opened her eyes, nothing had changed. The Primers were still at the mercy of the mansion. Her friends were still captive and choking. But Zanna looked at it anew. Maybe that was what caught her future self's attention. The difference between looking at a stranger and at a reflection.

"I know your name," Zanna whispered, and it struck louder than anything her future self had bellowed that night. Her voice had changed, as well—from the meek, guessing girl to one who knew, firmly and finally.

Her future self heard it, and her eyes widened just a fraction. Zanna gritted her teeth. She knew exactly what her perfect, clean, and powerful future self would call herself. Something so she would always be first. "Your name is Anna."

Her mind reached for the Iron that was her grandfather's frying pan. A heavy, protective function of Self surrounded the metal, stronger and denser than the primelock could ever hope to be, but Zanna knew what she was looking for. The twisting functions of Self were not so alien to her now. And there in its coils, she found what she needed. The story of her frying pan being passed down from generation to generation and everything it had meant to them. Everything it had meant to her grandfather. What it meant when he had given it to her. She understood.

Zanna squeezed her eyes and thought about her friends. About the Primers. About Pops. She didn't have enough of a grip on the frying pan to control it in any meaningful way, but she understood enough of its story to sink her fingers in. Enough to put all her mental weight behind and scream and pull away.

Enough to Splutter it.

CHAPTER TWENTY-ONE

DEATH SMELLED LIKE flowers and metal polish. Zanna was wrapped in an endless void without a single point of reference anywhere to be seen. She couldn't even see her limbs or her body. Just a consciousness out in absolute blackness that smelled like a garden crossed with a machine shop.

She frowned. Or, at least, she did something close to it, for she wasn't sure she still had a mouth to frown with. But if she could smell, that meant she had a nose, and sure enough, when she crossed her eyes, the familiar blurry shape of her nose appeared, rescued from somewhere out in the void. Next, she took a breath and felt the air course into her. Lungs and a chest. Shoulders with two arms and two hands. Hips, two legs, two feet. Like someone searching in a darkened room, she went slowly and felt around, rediscovering all the parts of her body. Everything fit back together, and everything hurt like the dickens.

When she opened her eyes, she was in her bed, in her bedroom, in Virginia. Every inch of her body felt like it had been torn apart and put back together, which seemed only fitting, considering the magnitude of the Splutter she had ripped open. Painfully, she turned her head toward the window and saw her grandfather sitting at her bedside, a pencil tapping against his lips and a puzzle book open on his lap.

"Pops" is what she tried to say, but it came out as something closer to a wounded pig's squeal. It got his attention, though, and when he lifted his eyes, his face lit up in joy.

"Ha! I knew it!" He clapped his hands together, knocking the pencil from his grasp and sending it skittering off into a corner. " 'She might never wake up,' bah! Bah, I say!"

Zanna tried to say something again, but Pops apparently didn't catch it, having gotten up from his chair to ramble and fumble through the books and scrap paper on the nearby desk. "Ah, yes," he said, finding a small shoebox with a piece of floral paper on a ribbon attached to it. Inside was a miniature windup kitten made out of burnished brass. Pops adjusted his glasses to read the instructions. "Place kitten beside open window. Insert key and make one full turn. Stand back."

The window was already open, bringing in the scent of flowering dogwoods and spring breezes, and he put the kitten down on the sill. "Insert key," he said, his fingers fiddling with the fine construction. "And make one full turn." A few seconds later, the kitten purred to life. Its head turned around to take a panoramic shot of Zanna's bedroom, and then it jumped up from the sill and zoomed into the sky.

Pops whistled. "Can't just use the phone like normal people," he said, turning from the window back to Zanna. "Sometimes, I just don't know what this world is coming to." He shook his head playfully, a boyish grin spreading across his face. "Well? Do you have anything to say for yourself?"

Her tongue felt like it had been stretched out and smashed with a hammer. "*Ow*," she croaked.

"Ah!" He turned back to the clutter on the desk. "Cecelia also gave me some instructions for when you wake up. Just have to find the little scoundrel . . ." He rummaged around until he found a matching floral envelope that had apparently come with the kitten messenger. "Here you are." He cleared his throat dramatically. " 'Touch your thumb to each of your fingers. Touch your tongue to each of your teeth. Wiggle your toes.' "

"Pops," she tried again, and this time her croak was close enough to actual words to get his attention. He stopped reading the list of therapeutic exercises and adopted a more serious tone, sitting down in his chair to answer all the questions she was too weak to ask.

"It's May," he said, reaching over to take her hand. "You've been asleep for nearly a month, I reckon. Cecelia told me you did something right foolish out there. Some madcap 'paradox' thing that darn near killed you."

Zanna dredged up her voice. "Splutter."

"Scamper, I'm going to have to take your word for it," Pops said. "You know I'm no good with that Scientist stuff. All I saw was this crack like a strike of lightning, and then everyone around me was on the ground and howling in pain. Thought we'd been bombed or something."

Zanna's throat clenched. Of course the other Scientists would have been caught in her Splutter. "I'm sorry." Her voice fell apart, and she had to rebuild it. "The others . . . ?"

He patted her hand. "Just fine. That one in the armor got us all out. Can't remember his name for the life of me."

She didn't have the strength to remind him it was Lord Hemmington. "Am I in trouble?"

That made Pops laugh, big and boisterous and nearly deafening. "Not with me! Can't speak for the others, though. I heard about what happened at school. I did tell you not to make too much trouble."

Zanna sighed. It would have been ridiculous to imagine she was going to get away completely scot-free. Mrs. Appernathy was surely going to be less forgiving than her grandfather. But at least it didn't sound like Lord Hemmington was arresting her for stealing his limousine and interfering with a Primer operation, and she could live with that.

There was one more question she had to ask, and she worked up to it. "Did—" It was like a boulder she had to move but couldn't find a decent grip on. "What about *her*?" She willed herself to say it. "What about Anna? Did we get her?"

Pops nodded, and it told her everything. "You got her, scamper. She's not going to bother you ever again."

The next week made the days after Yellowknife seem like monastic sanctuary. Apparently, while she had been asleep, the story had gone around St. Pommeroy's several times, each retelling growing more and more ridiculous. The girls visited, and Nora brought Zanna her own copy of *The Constant* so she could page back through its archive and read all the coverage for herself. And there was a lot of it. Everyone from Nora, Beatrice, and Libby to Xavier and Mrs. Turnbuckle had been interviewed multiple times for their role in "bringing down one of the most dangerous criminals known to Science," as one young hotshot reporter described it. There were hundreds of pictures and articles, a special report of the high-security vault the Learned Society was constructing under the Brazilian rainforest just to hold Anna, and even an animated scene that Zanna could pull out of *The Constant* like a children's pop-up book. It depicted the mansion and the limousine and the Primer camps, with big arrows and timelines breaking down the events of that night to the second.

Of course, as soon as the news had leaked that she was awake, it was Zanna's turn to sit for pictures and talk to reporters and recount the entire story, starting with her first day of school. But for the most part, everyone from the big *Constant* reporters down to the fashionable Japanese girl who ran the

St. Pommeroy's school paper, *The Candlefoot*, asked the same questions.

"Why did you do it?"

I had to.

"Were you afraid?"

Absolutely.

"Would you do it again?"

Yes.

Eventually, the fervor died down, and Zanna was able to get a little peace and quiet. She knew things would never go back to the way they had been, but she managed to find a little bit of normalcy. The girls visited and gossiped about Libby breaking up with Amir yet again. Nora revealed that she had chosen her Iron—not a ruler but a crowbar with spots of chipped paint. "In case I need to hold any doors open again in the future," she said, a giggle slipping out. Pops brought them lemon bars that were so sticky they had to stop and go wash their hands afterward. Her schoolwork had piled up while she was comatose, and on top of it all, St. Pommeroy's wanted her to write an essay on the importance of heeding to authority in times of crisis—and do some other remedial tasks as her punishment. When she offhandedly mentioned to Nora that she had been prepared for something far worse, the girl's face grew dark. "Don't push it," she said coldly. "A lot of people wanted it to be more severe. There was talk of expulsion. I think even the Learned Society got involved." But she wouldn't say any more.

When exam week rolled around, Zanna was still too weak to get out of bed, so her professors came to her, instead. One by one, they ran her through an exhausting battery of tests, covering everything she had learned over the last year. The written portion was simple enough, but the practical portion was grueling. For an entire afternoon, Zanna juggled physics and chemicals and wrote functions while her professors watched in uncharacteristic solemnity, only speaking to direct her to use a different element or manipulate a different function. The whole experience made her feel like a performing monkey.

At last, hours after her brain had been reduced to jelly and her bedroom window had gone dim with sunset, her teachers leaned back in their chairs and shared a wordless exchange. "Well then, I think we've seen enough," Dr. Cheever said for all three of them, scribbling away on a piece of graph paper held by his horseshoe Iron. "Unless I'm forgetting something?"

Zanna's gaze flipped between Dr. Fitzie and Dr. Piccowitz, silently urging them both to keep their mouths shut and not re-member any more tests for her to do. Her disheveled Chemistry professor fruitlessly tried to organize his papers and checked his pocket watch.

"No, I think that's everything," Dr. Fitzie said brightly.

"Finally," Zanna said, not even trying to keep the exhaustion from her voice. She shoved all the chemical samples away from her and sank back into the pillows. "How'd I do?"

"We'll send out results in a few days," Dr. Piccowitz said diplomatically. But when he looked away to consult his pocket watch again, Dr. Fitzie grinned and gave her a thumbs-up.

True enough, a couple of days later her report card arrived—with a catch. Pops knocked on her bedroom door, but when he came in, he wasn't alone. Dr. Trout was with him, a single piece of folded graph paper in her hands.

"Do you have a few moments?" her professor asked, in that tone that said she already knew the answer. She set her baseball bat down at Zanna's bedside, and it reshaped into a gnarled stool, complete with a side table for her to put Zanna's report card on.

"I guess," Zanna mumbled, her brain trying to find its feet.

Pops ducked back out into the hallway, closing the door behind him.

"There is something I would like to ask you," Dr. Trout said. "It shouldn't take long. Understand?"

Zanna gave herself a swift mental kick and nodded. "I'm ready."

"Good." Dr. Trout laced her fingers together. "Here is my question. Have you found your Iron?"

All Zanna had to do was lean over to her nightstand and grab the handle of the frying pan that was waiting for her there. But something about Dr. Trout's presence made Zanna move carefully and deliberately, as if she was showing off a museum artifact. She picked up her frying pan and felt the muscles in her arm work to lift its heavy cast iron. It was here in this room, in this very bed, that she had first met it. Sharpened to a threatening point and held against her throat by Anna. Now it was in her hands, and it felt good.

"Yes," she said, looking into Dr. Trout's eyes and not wavering. "This is mine."

A moment of silence passed. The professor seemed to be doing a calculation in her head, the hard corners of her mouth twitching a little. Then she reached a conclusion and produced a silver pen from somewhere. With a scratch of nib against paper, she wrote a note on the report card, fanned it briefly to dry the ink, and handed it over.

Three perfect scores marked off Mathematics, Chemistry, and Physics, with encouraging notes from her professors in the margin. But at the bottom, in the uneasy dark-red ink of a bloodsucking pen, Dr. Trout had given her a solid *D*. In the margin beside it, she had simply written *Needs considerable improvement*. But it was a passing grade. Barely.

The stool creaked as Dr. Trout rose and turned it back into

the baseball bat. It seemed as if she would slip away without another word, but Zanna looked up from her report card and caught her at the door. "Dr. Trout?"

The professor turned back. "Is there something else?"

There was, but Zanna couldn't put it into words just yet. One finger flicked at the corner of her report card, bending it back and forth nervously. Her other hand reached down to her lap and rested on the handle of her frying pan. "Why didn't you stop me at St. Pommeroy's?"

Dr. Trout's face never changed. She just kept her stare, with its thick, lowered eyebrows.

Zanna squeezed her frying pan and stared back. It hadn't been an illusion or some other trick of optics. She knew what she had seen on her way out to the parking lot. Dr. Trout had let them pass without a word.

Her teacher drew a breath through her nose. "Mistakes," she said. And then she turned sharply for the door before Zanna could ask her anything else.

By the time graduation day rolled around, Zanna was well enough to walk, though Mrs. Turnbuckle didn't approve and said she should have at least another three weeks of rest. But Zanna insisted, forcing herself up on legs that still wobbled uneasily with Splutter pains. It took her a long time to put on her school uniform. Her fingers trembled involuntarily and made buttoning up the blouse especially difficult, but at last she looked at herself in the mirror and smiled. *Time to go catch the bus.*

Her grandfather let out a low whistle as she came into the kitchen. "Look at you, my little scamper."

Zanna's cheeks flushed red. "They're supposed to arrange transportation for the parents. That's what Nora said."

He pointed at a letter from St. Pommeroy's over on the counter that had apparently been addressed to him for once.

"I know. Don't you worry, now. Wouldn't dream of missing it." With his whiskery chin, he indicated the frying pan she clutched tight to her chest. "You take care of that, now."

She hadn't even remembered picking it up from her nightstand. "I will."

"It's yours," Pops said. "It always was."

Zanna took a breath. Her body still felt wiggly and haphazardly sewn back together, but holding the frying pan in her arms gave her enough strength to continue. "Pops," she said, "they're putting bets on what I'm going to decide today." Ever since she had admitted to one of the reporters that she didn't have any particular specialization in mind, *The Constant* had been abuzz with speculation. Even her teachers had not been immune to it—during her final exam each one had confided in her, when the other two weren't in the room, that she would be a perfect fit in Mathematics, or Chemistry, or Physics. It was supposed to be cheeky and friendly, but to Zanna, it had felt more like getting pulled apart all over again. "And I don't know. I don't—"

"Zanna," Pops said. He stopped wiping down the counter and looked right at her. "Forget about all of them. This is *yours*. Do what you have to. I will be proud of you for that, and that alone."

She swallowed the rest of her worry. "Okay."

He grinned and shooed her away with his dishcloth. "Go on, then. Buses don't wait for the likes of you and me. See you in a little bit."

The morning was warm with springtime and sun, but Zanna couldn't shake off her shivers. She clutched her frying pan all through the bus ride, as if one of the laughing, excited students around her was going to steal it and run away. The girls were ecstatic to see her up and about, and she tried to share in their excitement, but the inevitable specialization decision soured everything, no matter how bright and loud the day was.

St. Pommeroy's was a riot of color. An illusion of robin's-egg blue had been painted over the ancient marble, and the leaves of the olive trees in the entrance hall were a startling white. Metallic streamers decorated every archway and column, fluttering valiantly in a stiff wind that wasn't there, and fireworks burst in the sky, somehow visible despite the bright sun. The girls waited with the other freshmen in the entrance hall, milling around aimlessly, recounting horror stories from exam week, snapping pictures, and showing off their Irons. Tomas, the sophomore Beatrice was dating, snuck in to congratulate them all. Then he and Beatrice disappeared, and Libby said to not look for them.

Benito had brought a roll of aluminum foil, and he blew it into a shiny silver ball that he then tossed over the crowd. It floated over to Zanna's group, and Libby swatted it away so fiercely that it nearly sailed out of the courtyard.

"Hey," Nora nudged Zanna playfully. "You okay?"

Zanna snapped back to reality, realizing that she had been staring blankly at the reflecting pool for some time. "Yeah," she muttered. "Just thinking, that's all."

Tyson and Amir broke into their little circle with uproarious prankster laughter. Both of the boys had gone with musical instruments for their Irons—Tyson's was a trumpet, and Amir carried an alto saxophone. As more students gathered around, the two boys broke into a jam-band melody, climbing up onto the lip of the reflecting pool to better show off their antics. Nora and Zanna exchanged a knowing glance and could only shake their heads.

"Zanna?"

Even without raising his voice one bit, Zanna heard Cedwick

clearly through the noise of the impromptu concert. He had shouldered through the mass of clapping students and stood with his hands shoved into his pockets, the heavy chain laid over his shoulders. Zanna was alone. Somehow, Nora had disappeared completely and silently.

"Hey," she said. "Fancy running into you here."

"I'm glad to see you out of bed," he said. In the ruckus, he had to take another half-step forward, and Zanna frowned when she saw that he, too, had gone through a growth spurt. Not as pronounced as Nora's, but Zanna definitely had to look up a bit in order to meet his eyes, when she was sure they had been on the same level at the beginning of the school year.

"Yeah, I'm glad to be out." She rolled her shoulders around and had to stifle a wince as some lingering Splutter pain shot through her. "Did you have to write that silly paper about heeding authority too?"

He nodded. "We got off easy."

"I know."

"You know which specialization you're going to pick?"

Heat rushed to her face, so bright and obvious that she didn't need to put her answer into words. "It really doesn't matter," he said quickly as she tried to hide her burning face. "Don't let Nora tell you otherwise. All it means is one of your classes will be different next year."

The genuine apology in his voice brought a small smile to Zanna's face. "I seem to remember someone telling me that if I wanted to be a Primer, I needed to specialize in Physics."

Now it was Cedwick's turn to look away. "I don't think either of us is getting into the Primers now. My father wouldn't even read my application."

Tyson and Amir jumped down from the lip of the reflecting pool, taking the crowd with them as they marched around the entrance hall. But Zanna stood where she was and so did Cedwick.

"Here." He pulled a piece of graph paper out of his pocket. "I know it's late. And Dr. Trout's probably forgotten about it by now. But I still wanted you to have this."

Zanna's stomach clenched up. "Is this what I think it is?"

"It's my report," Cedwick said, taking her by the wrist. "I just thought—"

"Attention!" The voice of Mrs. Appernathy filled the courtyard, silencing the screaming freshmen and the parade of musical instruments. "We will be entering the auditorium soon. Form a line in alphabetical order!"

She sounded more snappish than Zanna remembered. Her torches were out in full force today. When Zanna looked back, Cedwick was gone. In her hand was his report.

"Hurry up!" Mrs. Appernathy shouted from all around them. The students assembled into something that might have been a line, if Zanna squinted and used a very theoretical definition. She tightened her grip on the crumpled report Cedwick had handed her and trundled all the way to the back of line.

"Doors are opening!"

It wasn't a long walk from the entrance hall to the auditorium, but the line moved slowly, and Zanna was at the very end. She had never been in the auditorium before, though she had heard all about it from Nora. And she had spotted the white dome from the air many times—it stood out like a sore thumb among the school's tangle of mismatched rooftops. But she had never set foot in it until now.

It felt as if she had just set foot in the Colosseum. A gently sloping aisle led from the entrance down to the circular stage in the center. Floating chairs filled with parents, older students, and staff ringed the massive room. The same trick of light as in the classrooms flooded the auditorium—bright as noonday sunlight but not hot at all. Twelve enormous pillars stood around the arena like notches of a clock, decorated in silver and brass and quartz and carbon.

The applause filled her lungs like a thick, intoxicating aroma. She stumbled and blinked on the threshold, too awed by the sight and sound to enter. Only Mrs. Appernathy's candelabra bringing up the rear broke the spell. "Keep moving, Mayfield," she said gruffly. "Don't think I'm not watching you." So maybe the woman was still a bit sore . . .

The first couple of rows had been reserved for the freshmen. Something reminiscent of ripples across a pond shivered through the arena as Zanna walked down the aisle, people adjusting functions in their chairs to float a little higher and get a better look. High above the center stage, a screen broadcast a live feed of the proceedings, even though she didn't see any cameras around the arena. At the moment, it was panning across Dr. Fitzie, Dr. Cheever, and Dr. Piccowitz, who were up onstage and wearing proper academic robes of voluminous black silk with soft velvet bonnets. Behind them were dozens of empty chairs on risers, waiting for students to come up and populate them. Then, suddenly, the screen cut to her. Her, walking down the aisle with a dumb amazement plastered across her face and the frying pan clutched to her chest, and the entire auditorium rose and applauded and cheered until she couldn't even hear her pounding heartbeat.

Somehow, she made it all the way down the aisle. Somehow, she found her chair. The screen cut away from her to sweep over all the freshmen and then up to Dr. Mumble on the stage, who greeted everybody and launched into a short welcome speech with the passion of a wet cardboard box.

"I will now hand the program off to Dr. Trout for the

announcing of specializations," Dr. Mumble said, stepping aside. The Self professor rose and took the podium with a domineering expression. A golden book rose from a case that Zanna hadn't noticed before and floated over to Dr. Trout, who opened it to a page and licked her lips.

"Adam Reughel."

He had chosen a shovel for his Iron, an old and well-worked one. Dr. Trout shook his hand, whispered an instruction in his ear, and gestured out to the crowd.

Adam cleared his throat. "Physics," he said, and a third of the crowd burst into applause. Dr. Trout pointed him to Dr. Cheever, who beamed and held out a large book—a paper one, not gold. Adam signed his name and took a seat behind the professor.

Dread began to creep over Zanna, and her fingers tightened around the handle of her frying pan. It was all so public. Not that your specialization was a secret, but she hadn't thought the actual moment of decision would be anything like this. *Of course*, she thought, *for everyone else there isn't a decision.* They had figured out their specialization weeks ago. In Nora's case, it had been more like months. They hadn't been putting it off until the last minute . . .

"Beatrice Scotti."

Zanna craned her neck. Her friend looked so small as she climbed up on the stage. Dr. Trout had to bend over a little to shake her hand. But then Beatrice turned to face the crowd, and her face went up on the screen, and there wasn't an ounce of fear in it.

A cannonball, indeed.

"Mathematics," she said, loudly and clearly. Dr. Fitzie let out a "Whoop!" and embraced her before Beatrice was allowed to sign the book and take her seat.

Dr. Trout went through a couple more names of students

that Zanna had only exchanged a few brief words with. Then came one she recognized.

"Cedwick Hemmington."

There was a strange silence in the crowd as Cedwick took the stage. It was like the silence that had preceded Beatrice but even more reserved. After all, this wasn't just one of the five freshmen who had helped to bring down a madwoman. He was the son of Lord Hemmington. Had the past year gone differently, Zanna might have been just another student, but Cedwick would always have been watched closely by the Scientist community. The thought made her chest squeeze, as if she had momentarily forgotten how to breathe. No wonder he had gone with such a heavy Iron on his shoulders.

"Go, Cedwick!" someone shouted. *Owin.* Zanna recognized the voice at once. The crowd broke into laughter, its tension loosened, and Cedwick glared up at his brother. He twisted the length of chain around his fist.

"Chemistry," he said, almost spitting the word out.

Zanna wished that she could see Lord Hemmington's reaction at that moment, but instead, the screen showed Dr. Piccowitz grinning as Cedwick signed the book and took a seat. The crowd applauded politely.

"Liberty Wilder."

The name caught Zanna off guard, for she didn't remember anyone in her class named Liberty, but then she saw Libby get up from her chair and take the stage, her face twisted in a frown. When she shook hands with Dr. Trout, it was a cold and violent movement. She threw her shoulders back and stared down at the crowd, as if daring them to call her by her real name again.

"Physics," she said.

One by one the students took the stage, and with each one, Zanna's dread grew a bit more. Everyone seemed so confident—even the quiet boys who huddled together and never glanced over at Zanna in class managed to stand up straight and tell everyone that they were specializing in Mathematics. Zanna put a hand to her stomach. Her paradox pains were turning bad. She should have heeded Mrs. Turnbuckle's advice and stayed in bed today.

"Nora Elmsley."

Nora rose with a smile, her crowbar swung easily over a shoulder. It fit her so perfectly, Zanna couldn't imagine her with any other Iron. Especially not some fancy ruler.

Nora took the steps in perfect time, stopping dead center on the screen. Her voice rang out without hesitation. "Chemistry!"

Now came the waiting. Endless waiting as students Zanna barely knew crossed the stage and gave their specialization, each one walking a bit more slowly and taking a bit longer than the last. *This is what waiting for the gallows must feel like*, Zanna thought as she sank lower in her seat and tried to calm her wriggling stomach. After a while, she just wanted to get it over with.

She had never let go of Cedwick's report. The paper was crumpled from her anxious wringing, and she smoothed it out on the back of her frying pan. His handwriting was only marginally better than hers, so she had to read it slowly. Then she read it again, even slower. And then a third time.

"Zanna Mayfield."

Her head jerked up. All the freshmen seats were empty, all except for hers. Carefully, she tucked Cedwick's report into a pocket and walked down the aisle, trying to be as steady as all the other students had been, but she knew it was obvious. Her knees trembled, and her stomach felt like one big bruise. This was a dead-man's walk, but she faced it with every scrap of strength she could muster. If she could stagger out of the

Canadian wilderness with just a handful of nitrogen, she could make it up onstage.

"Congratulations," Dr. Trout said as Zanna got closer. Everyone was still applauding, and bile bubbled up in her throat. Sweat beaded on her forehead, in her armpits, and behind her knees, even though there were no hot stage lights here. No one here knew her. Not the teachers and parents and students out in the crowd. Not her friends onstage. Not Cedwick—or his report. Not even Pops. To them all, she was a girl who had escaped single-handedly from the clutches of a maniac and had then gone back to rescue her grandfather in a daring sacrifice. If they knew that the criminal the Primers had hauled off was the same person standing before them, what would they do? Not applaud her, that's for certain.

There's a dark time coming for the world, Anna had said. *I can prevent it. I can prevent so many things if you're here with me.*

"Zanna," Dr. Trout prompted.

She had frozen up completely. All three of her professors leaned forward, their faces hungry.

Otherwise, Nora, Beatrice, Libby, Owin, Cedwick, and even Pops, Anna had continued, *they are going to die.*

Zanna stared at the hands wrapped around the handle of her frying pan. How the tendons tightened beneath her skin and the veins made faint blue lines. How her knuckles bulged. How different they looked from those perfect killing hands of her future self . . .

And then she had her decision.

"I choose Self!"

The room went absolutely silent. Her teachers stared with expectant expressions still glued to their faces, as if Zanna was just joking and her real choice was still to come. But that was her choice, and the moment dragged on. No one spoke.

"Well done."

Zanna looked up, and her mouth fell open. Dr. Trout was smiling.

"Well done, indeed," the professor said, and it was louder and grander than any applause possible.

ACKNOWLEDGMENTS

SCIENCE IS BUILT upon the shoulders of giants, and so too was this book. Thank you first and foremost to my family for encouraging me every step of this journey. Thank you to my brother Russell for putting up with my endless questions about calculus, and to my sister Leanne for being my very first teacher. And a special thanks to my Mom and Dad for being at my side throughout it all and being my first and biggest fans. I love you all more than I can say.

I owe an enormous debt of gratitude to Jen Fulmer for many, many writing chats, editing discussions, and frantic text messages. Thanks also to Kenton Fulmer for always being the perfect host to two talkative writers and never minding if we monopolized the conversation for hours. Thank you to Laura Steward for reading through the manuscript in one night and calling me up to demand answers, as well as being an excellent book-hunting companion. Many thanks to Steph O'Neil, Joanna Meyer, Rose Marie Green, Devan Soyka, Alice Chiang, Susan Roberts, and Colleen Brenner for donating some of their time to read through the manuscript and offer their ideas.

A great many thanks to my fearless agent Laura Zats at Red Sofa Literary for picking Zanna up and dusting her off. I would be lost and suffering from a lack of cat pictures without you. Thank you also to Mari Kesselring, Reece Hanzon, Ashley Wyrick, and Megan Naidl at Jolly Fish Press for their guidance and advice. I'm eternally grateful to have you on my team.

And thank you, for reading.